THRONE OF VANRIS

THE WARDEN'S SON
BOOK FOUR

NIKKI McCORMACK

ISBN: 979-8-9903922-5-0
First Edition 2024

Published by
Elysium Books
Bellevue, WA

Written by Nikki McCormack (https://nikkimccormack.com/)
Cover Design by Robert Crescenzio (https://robertcrescenzio.artstation.com/)
Map Design by Melissa Nash
Typesetting and Design by Brian C. Short
Editing by Alexander Lockwood

•

Here it is. The final book in Kasiel's tale. If you have stuck with me this long, then I thank you, and Kasiel thanks you. This book is for you.

•

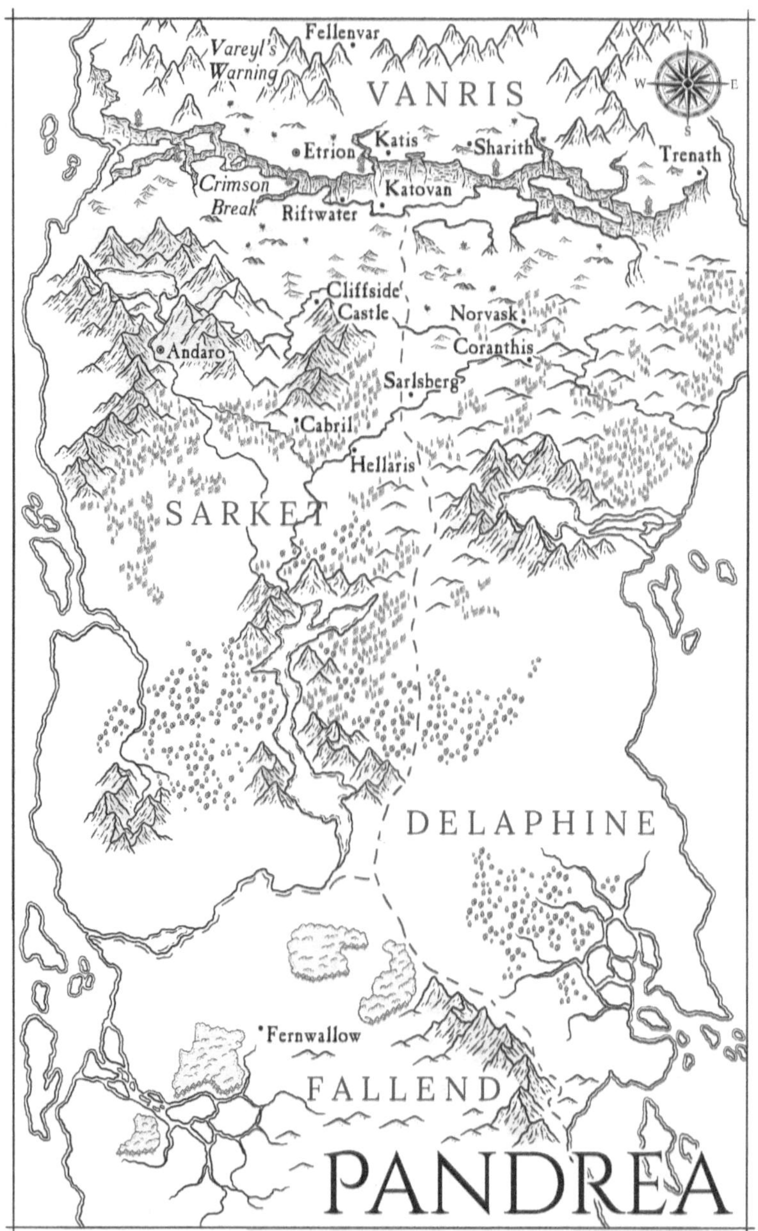

Vareyl's Warning
Fellenvar
VANRIS
N
W
E
S
Etrion
Katis
Sharith
Trenath
Crimson Break
Katovan
Riftwater
Cliffside Castle
Norvask
Coranthis
Andaro
Sarlsberg
Cabril
Hellaris
SARKET
DELAPHINE
Fernwallow
FALLEND
PANDREA

Kasiel soared high over the Crimson Break, using his Feral ability to look out through the eyes of a sandhawk. It was one of two raptors he had started working with consistently over the last couple of months. He finished investigating Sarket's military company from above. They had gathered on the far side of a plateau south of an enormous black Vanrian watchtower, preparing for an attack. The same watchtower the company Kasiel had arrived with was now camped alongside. With the sandhawk's superior distance vision, he could scout out the Sarketi force's numbers and armaments while keeping the raptor out of range of their arrows. The enemy knew he could use birds this way now, which made the blameless creatures popular targets for their archers.

With the scouting run complete, he turned the raptor out over the plateau, coasting on wind currents. The war-torn desert landscape glowed with rich reds and golds in the late afternoon sunshine. This place, an area typically associated with conflict and death, became beautiful in that light.

"We need to talk about my cousin." Jethan's voice startled him from his musing.

Falling back behind his own eyes, Kasiel encouraged the raptor to return to him and glanced over at his tehnaak. "Is now really the time for this conversation?"

"Why not? You weren't scouting anymore. I could tell by that contented smile you always get when you're just flying along for fun. And we're well away from Etrion and the source of the problem. Seems like the perfect time."

Kasiel held up his arm, giving the returning raptor a perch upon which to land. He frowned at Jethan as the bird's talons dug into the leather gauntlet he wore for that purpose. "Velara isn't a problem."

"Isn't she? If my aunt finds out that you two are sleeping together on a somewhat regular basis, she might just have you beheaded." He gave a meaningful glance toward Kasiel's groin. "Or be-something-elsed."

Kasiel chuckled. "You always have a way with words, tehnaak."

He launched the raptor again, sending it toward camp while he walked to where his kanodrak, Niskenya, waited near Jethan's carefully controlled mount. The horse was getting used to the massive, vaguely feline predator, given how often they rode together, but it was easy enough to keep a light mental leash on the animal as a precaution.

Jethan walked with him. "Kas, I don't want to see either of you hurt."

Kasiel blew out a heavy exhale, his elation from the flight fading. "Does it matter that we love each other?"

Jethan swung up into the saddle, the unwanted sympathy of his gaze falling on Kasiel once he settled in the seat. "Not to the khevarin or any of the suitors lining up to try for Vel's hand."

"We can talk about this later."

Jethan frowned at him. "A succinct way of saying you're going to ignore my concerns and keep doing what you're doing."

Kasiel swung up on Niskenya, her silver-gray scaled

hide smooth under the hand he placed on her shoulder. The kanodrak's view on the subject was simple. She was an alpha of her species. As the Feral bonded to her, he should have similar privileges, at least as far as she was concerned. That meant his choice of mates and the freedom to pursue whatever he wanted to do, among other things. The finer details of human social structure were inconsequential to her. The more time he spent connected to her, the harder it was to remember what rules he was supposed to be following and why.

"We'll talk about it later," he restated.

"Sure, we will." The roll of Jethan's eyes said he didn't believe that. "What are your thoughts on our new friends from Sarket hiding behind that plateau?"

Kasiel gave his tehnaak an appreciative glance before answering. "I think I have an idea of how to welcome them."

*

As dusk started sinking over the Break, Darro woke Kasiel and Jethan from a quick nap. They grabbed some food before heading out again. The entire unit came with them this time, setting up a small camp with no fire on the plateau. Niskenya settled on ground that still radiated warmth from the day, curling around Kasiel to give him something to lean against. Jethan sat cross-legged close by in case he needed anything. The rest of the unit took shifts standing watch, most in their spirit sibling pairings; Kince and Darro, Merrin and Avris, and newly bonded Tath and Nerith. Wedro and Etris remained unpaired and Kasiel wasn't sure if they ever would be, at least with one another. They had their similarities, but those were all things they somehow seemed to find annoying in each other. Their differences, like Etris's Speaker ability, also led to friction between them.

In truth, Merrin seemed to be the only one Wedro really connected with since his tehnaak's death, though there didn't appear to be a romantic element there, as with Darro and Tath.

Kasiel's gaze drifted to Nerith, recalling in vivid detail the intimate moments they had shared. How often did romance blossom within units like this one? Given all the time they spent together and how stressful missions could be, he suspected it happened with some regularity.

Nerith met his eyes, and Kasiel realized he had been staring at her for at least a minute, noticing how light from the sliver of moon gave a soft glow to her silvery hair. He pulled his gaze away. He had made his choice. It wasn't fair to Nerith or Velara to let his mind wander.

Closing his eyes, Kasiel turned his focus to his beasts and the creatures of the desert, where it belonged. He started by moving a few small songbirds into the Sarketi camp near the command tent while there was still enough light for them to be seen. Then he waited, watching and listening. As expected, it wasn't long before someone came asking after the general.

Once summoned, the general, a stern-looking man with chestnut hair and a well-trimmed beard that showed hints of gray, emerged and scanned the area. The soldier who asked for him had barely started speaking when the general's dark eyes lit upon the songbird perched on a rack of weapons, demonstrating that he at least had perceptiveness worthy of his rank. He snapped a hand up to silence the other man.

"How long has that bird been there?"

"What bird, General?" The soldier and the two guards standing outside the tent followed the direction of the general's gaze.

"You thrice-cursed idiots! I told you to keep this place clear of wildlife. That includes the avian variety."

The general produced a dagger from somewhere, throwing it with shocking speed, but the bird was faster, flitting quickly up out of the way.

Kasiel grinned.

Next to his physical self, Jethan asked, "How's it going?"

"Just saying hello," Kasiel answered.

While continuing to watch through the eyes of the bird, he reached out to a pack of desert dogs, drawing them toward the Sarketi camp. When the dogs were close enough, he set them to howling. The general fell silent, him and the men he had been reprimanding turning to stare out into the deepening darkness. Throughout the camp, conversations faltered.

"Look at the horses," a soldier next to the general whispered.

Kasiel had reached out to their horses, making them all turn and stare at the central tent, rather than out toward the noise of the predators as they normally would.

"Shit," the general muttered under his breath.

"It's him, isn't it?" one guard asked. "The Warden's son is here."

The general turned on the men with him. "Are you soldiers or children?" he shouted. "If you're soldiers, I expect you to get back to your duties or get some sleep. We march on the tower at dawn."

Kasiel moved the wild dogs to the southern edge of the enemy camp to continue their chorus. Then he brought some of his tethdraks out as full dark fell over the landscape, guiding them to different points around the enemy camp and encouraging them to call out to each other periodically with their distinctive shrieks and clicks. Soon the Sarketi soldiers were all staring out at the darkness, meals and conversations forgotten, many of them flinching whenever a shriek broke through the night. They whispered to each other. Some kept their volumes up, trying to sound brave, but he could hear the tremor in their voices through the ears of his beasts.

Kasiel smiled and settled in for a long night of tormenting their enemies. Laying her naturally armored head on her paws next to him, Niskenya purred.

After a few hours of strategically moving beasts around the camp, getting them to make noise whenever the enemy soldiers started to relax again, Kasiel felt Niskenya perk up. His cliff cat Irith did as well, letting out a low growl where he lay stretched at Kasiel's feet, one front paw draped possessively over Jethan's leg. Kasiel drew back some of his ability, investing in Irith to hear what had gotten his and Niskenya's attention. A few seconds later, he caught the faint sound of something moving at the edge of the cliff near where they were sitting.

At his prompting, Irith extended his claws, getting Jethan's attention with a slight prick of those sharp points against his leg. Jethan opened his eyes, looking into the cliff cat's bright blue ones. He sat silent for a few seconds until the faint sound of something shifting caught his attention, then gave a slight nod.

Irith stood, padding silently into the stunted, thorny brush nearby. Jethan, his movements careful and quiet, took his sword and went around in the opposite direction. He gave a subtle gesture toward the cliff with one finger by his leg to Merrin, who stood watch a short distance away. Kasiel lost track of them after that, turning his efforts back to managing his psychological assault on the company from Sarket. It wasn't until a few minutes later, when he heard the soft creak of a bow being drawn, that he pulled his attention back to his current location again.

Someone cried out. An arrow whizzed past a few feet in front of Kasiel, making his heart jump in his chest. He glanced toward the bushes at the cliff's edge.

Jethan and Merrin emerged after a few seconds, alternately leading and dragging a Sarketi scout between them. The young man had blood running from a split lip and a minor cut above one eye. Jethan was holding a Sarketi shortbow in his free hand. Irith came out of the brush behind them, ears perked and looking quite pleased.

Niskenya raised her head, snarling as they shoved the scout to his knees in front of Kasiel. The youth cringed away from the big predator, his breath coming in quick, panicked gasps.

Jethan gestured to their captive. "What would you like done with him?"

Kasiel struggled to maintain his awareness of the many beasts he was controlling while dealing with the current situation, but he succeeded at faking a reasonable level of composure. "You were after me?"

"Who else would I be after? Mind-crafter freak," the man hissed, showing some courage until Niskenya growled again, at which point he almost fell into Merrin trying to shy away from the kanodrak.

"Kill him?" Jethan asked, his tone deceptively casual.

"Oh, can we please?" Merrin infused convincing enthusiasm into her voice.

The Sarketi scout twisted away from her now, then from Jethan, looking every bit like a cornered animal about to panic. Irith stepped close behind him and growled. The youth tried to lunge to his feet, catching himself on his hands inches from Niskenya's face when Jethan swept his legs out from under him. He froze, trembling as the kanodrak stood and snarled, her nose nearly touching his head.

"Tie him up and keep him quiet for now. We'll decide what to do with him in the morning. Maybe Niske can eat him." Kasiel closed his eyes, returning to the collection of beasts he had gathered almost before he finished speaking. Some part of him was distantly aware of the protests of the frightened youth as they took him away.

When the first hints of dawn crept over the desert, Kasiel watched several groups of Sarketi soldiers sneak away toward the south. He let them leave, struggling to hold on to his focus through a rapidly worsening headache. When there was adequate light for them to be seen, he urged his tethdraks and the other beasts back from the camp, silencing the noise that had plagued the enemy soldiers through the night.

A few other units in the Vanrian company joined them on the plateau. Darro and the rest of Kasiel's unit mounted up and rode back down with them, heading out around the plateau. They took the Sarketi scout, throwing a cloak over him to keep his presence hidden in their ranks. Irith and Niskenya stayed with Kasiel. As the others departed, he and the two beasts moved closer to the southern edge of the plateau. Using only a raptor now, he watched the slightly reduced Sarketi company pull together to make their march north. They had barely gotten into formation when a warning blared from a horn one of the Sarketi scouts carried.

The Vanrian force, with Darro and Kince in the lead, came into view along the side of the plateau. Sarket's general, his mouth set in a grim line, led his company out to meet them. The two sides stopped about ten yards apart. Sarket still had a greater number of soldiers, even after some defections, but that only gave them the advantage if they didn't count the combat ability of the tethdraks now emerging from the surrounding landscape, their reddish-brown scales allowing them to remain hidden until Kasiel was ready for them to be seen. As he guided them out around the enemy company, he had the raptor shriek a warning to Kince, then landed on the arm the man held out. The perch gave him a nice vantage through which to watch the rising fear in the eyes of the Sarketi soldiers as the tethdraks made their presence known.

"It looks as if your company shrank in the night, General," Darro called out.

The man's eyes narrowed. "Where's your captain?"

"Our ahninveth?" Darro corrected with a bitter smile. "He is exactly where he needs to be. Out of your reach, but close enough to manage these beasts."

Kasiel drew two packs of wild dogs out into the open on the flanks of the Sarketi company. As he did so, he moved through the enemy horses, making them stand statue still, heads lifting to look toward the top of the plateau. Then he urged Niskenya to the cliff's edge, having her stand where they could see the kanodrak with him on her back, well out of range of their arrows. Several enemy soldiers started trying to pull their horse's heads down, but the animals wouldn't respond.

Through the raptor, Kasiel could see fear in the general's hazel eyes as he stared up at the distant figure on the plateau. Now to see if his plan worked and all that effort throughout the night was worth it.

"I have orders to allow you and your soldiers to leave here unharmed if you agree to ride directly south out of the Break," Darro said, a cutting edge in his tone. "An extremely generous offer, considering our tethdraks alone could decimate your company."

"There are other fronts we can attack on." The general glowered up at Kasiel when he couldn't get his horse to lower its head. "The Warden's son can't be everywhere at once."

From the raptor's vantage on Kince's arm, Kasiel could see the wicked smirk that curved Darro's lips. "Is that your final answer?"

Was this the right thing to do? The Vanrian company was primed to fight. The tethdraks wanted it too, bloodlust resonating through them. But just because combat was what they were all trained for – what they expected – didn't make it the best option. How would more killing bring them any closer to ending the war? His unit was his family. He would rather see them struggling to find their place in a peaceful Vanris than lying dead on a battlefield.

The Sarketi general's hand moved toward his blade. Kasiel's answering rise in tension sent a ripple of growls through the tethdraks and desert dogs. He felt Niskenya's muscles tighten as she prepared to move. The man's gaze swept over the snarling beasts partially surrounding his company. His hand sank away from the weapon.

"Tell your ahninveth we accept his offer... this time."

Kince smirked at the raptor. "He already knows."

Proving the point, Kasiel urged the tethdraks and desert dogs to back away, giving the Sarketi company room to retreat. Then he relinquished control of their horses.

"Until next time." Darro inclined his head to the general.

"Oh, General," Avris called out, reaching down to cut the bonds off the youth she and Merrin had kept obscured with their horses. "I think this is yours." The Sarketi scout wove his way quickly through the Vanrian force back to his company. "Gutsy little calloch. You might want to promote him."

The general only scowled at them while one of his soldiers gave the scout a hand up on the back of his mount.

Kasiel gripped Niskenya's saddle. Pain speared through his head now, making his stomach turn. When the Sarketi general ordered his company to retreat, Kasiel moved the desert dogs out and set them free. He held the tethdraks in place until after the enemy soldiers were on their way and the Vanrian company began pulling back. Then he called the reptilian beasts to him and urged Niskenya away from the cliff face to where he could dismount and throw up in privacy.

The pain got worse, continuing to spike out of control. By the time his unit reached him, he was kneeling in the dirt next to his own vomit, clinging to the stirrup of his distressed kanodrak's saddle to keep from falling over. Nerith and Tath rushed to his side, helping him to his feet and moving him away from the rejected contents of his stomach.

"You overdid it, didn't you?" Tath asked, going to dig through her packs after Jethan took her place, helping Nerith guide him to a seat on a nearby rock.

Kasiel closed his eyes to the pain, straining to maintain a visual link with the raptor he had watching the enemy company to be sure they departed as expected. "I didn't know that was possible."

"It depends on how strong your ability is." Nerith rested a hand on his arm as she reached out to accept the flask Tath brought over. She opened it and held it up to his lips. "Drink this. It should take the edge off and ease some of the nausea."

When he squinted his eyes open, Tath was scowling at him, her hands on her hips. "You've been running a substantial number of beasts for over twenty-four hours without a break. You need to rest, Kas. You aren't invincible."

Irith pushed between Nerith and Jethan, coming up to headbutt Kasiel affectionately in the face hard enough that it almost knocked him down. He wrapped an arm over the big cliff cat's shoulders to steady himself.

"Thanks, Break-blasted brute," he muttered, grimacing at the persistent ache in his head.

Niskenya came up behind Tath, one of her elongated upper canines almost touching the healer's shoulder. She made a distressed grumble deep in her throat.

Tath startled and stepped to the side. She gestured to the massive predator. "See, Niske agrees with me. Kenna's at the watchtower. She can manage the tethdraks while they're idle and give you a chance for some proper sleep."

He shook his head, keeping the motion slow and small to avoid aggravating the pounding in his skull. "That isn't necessary."

Nerith's lavender eyes flashed. "Do you want to keep this headache?"

Kasiel considered her. She was always the most beautiful when her fierce side came out.

Nerith averted her gaze, and he cringed inwardly. They weren't a couple anymore. He couldn't keep looking at her that way. This was what he had been afraid might happen when he agreed to have her stay in the unit as Tath's tehnaak, but she was someone he trusted and an excellent healer. He was going to have to adjust to the idea that their relationship was different now. Preferably before he drove her out of his unit with his inappropriate glances.

His head throbbed. Turning away from Nerith, he found Jethan staring at him with a look that would accept no more arguments. "All right. Let's go find Kenna."

Jethan nodded approval and came to help Kasiel to his feet.

asiel woke sometime later to the sound of people talking in the adjacent room. The inveth of the watchtower guards had offered him her private quarters as a place to rest in appreciation for his unusual routing of the enemy force. The individual he could hear speaking now was another tower guard whose voice he vaguely recognized, though he didn't know the man's name.

"I don't understand why Dhomen Nevias put him in charge of this. All he did was drive them off. Now another Vanrian company will end up fighting them somewhere else."

"Watch your tone, friend. You're talking about my ahninveth." It was Darro who responded, a dark edge of warning deepening his voice. "Besides, we don't yet know how this will play out in..." Darro trailed off as footsteps entered the room. "Dhomen Nevias," he greeted.

"Inveth Darro," she greeted in turn. "If anyone wishes to question why I put Ahninveth Kasiel in charge, you can tell them it is because his goals currently align with Khevarin Seylin's. That's all you really need to know. If you must have more, I can say that, like many of us, he wants to bring an end to this war to protect the people he cares about. By intimidating the Sarket company into retreating, he reminded them we have the power to inflict catastrophic losses on their troops, but also put forth a clear message that we are open to solving our issues peacefully. Should their leadership answer that with more aggression, then we may have to respond in kind. From this point forward, however, any time they suffer substantial losses at our hands, they'll have to reconsider what happened here, in conjunction with the loss of their Delaphinian allies, and perhaps wonder if it might be time to consider other options. I could not be more pleased with today's outcome had I orchestrated it myself."

The guard was silent.

"What of Fallend?" Darro asked, leaving Kasiel no time to bask in her approval. "Any sign of them following in Delaphine's footsteps?"

"That information is privileged, Inveth."

Though her reply was unhelpful, Kasiel caught a hint of lift in her tone that suggested things on that front might be progressing favorably. Odd as it was, the idea of Fallend joining their alliance was immensely comforting. Though most everyone he had been close to in Fernwallow was dead now, a couple of them thankfully so, a nostalgic connection to the village where he had grown up lingered deep within him. Knowing that Professor Edmund Danovan – the man who raised him in isolation while keeping secret his role in the death of Kasiel's mother and the cutting of his ears – was dead helped erase some of the bitterness that colored memories of his childhood in the far southern kingdom. Now he could look back at the happier ones and appreciate them for what they were. He could remember Danica the way she deserved to be remembered, rather than as he last saw her, standing defeated at her execution.

Someone knocked on the door. "Are you awake, Ahninveth Kasiel?"

"I am now," he answered, trying to sound groggy. "Come in, Dhomen Nevias." He sat up as she opened the door.

"I apologize for waking…" Her eyes narrowed when she looked at him. The scar running from above her eyebrow, through the curved line of symbols tattooed under that eye, and down to her jawline, added severity to her appearance. A look enhanced by the braids of red hair worked tight against her scalp above her pointed ears. "You were already awake, weren't you?"

Kasiel chuckled. He had worked with Nevias enough to respect her as a military leader, and knowing she was his ahndhomen Adnar's tehnaak was gradually leading to an almost familial fondness for her. "Only just."

Warmth infused the smile that broke across her lips, making it apparent that developing affection wasn't one-sided. "How is your head?"

"Better."

"Good." She shut the door behind her. "Our scouts confirmed that Sarket's company retreated across their border. Their forces further west along Vanris's border are pulling back as well after some decisive victories on our side. Whether they intend to regroup and try again or reconsider their assault is unclear, but I'm encouraged. A few of the other Vanrian companies will stay along the border to keep an eye on things. Our company is heading out for Etrion within the hour. There are concerns that Sarket's withdrawal here could herald an attack on a different front."

"Delaphine?"

She nodded. "The khevarin wants some of our best units available in case we need to assist our new allies. That means we need to get your unit back there."

It was still disconcerting to be a prized military asset. It often felt as if he were experiencing the world through someone else's eyes. This wasn't who Edmund raised him to be. In fact, Edmund raised him to be exactly the opposite. Docile. Quiet. Accepting. But here he was, leading one of the most valued units in Vanris's army. Would it ever feel like anything other than a strange dream?

The important thing now was that they had succeeded here and were returning to Etrion. Back to the city he called home and the woman he loved. A place where the people he cared about would be safe for a time, as fleeting as that time might be.

He got up and started pulling on his jacket. "How many others are upset with how I handled things?"

"There will always be people who object to how you do things or who think they could have done better. Casting judgment on the decisions of others is easy. Leading is not. The best advice I can give you is to accept criticism when it is due to you and always be confident in your choices." She reached for the door, pausing with her hand on the lever. "In this instance, for every bloodthirsty soldier who believes fighting was the only answer this morning, there are ten more who are grateful not to be picking up the bodies of friends or lying among the dead right now."

Her words resonating within him, Kasiel gave a solemn nod and followed her out.

She wasn't wrong. After they struck out for the southern capital of Vanris, he got the odd scowl from some members of their company. What he got far more of were expressions of appreciation and admiration that, while often couched in the jocular and irreverent manner of soldiers, carried the weight of sincerity. He even overheard a few soldiers telling some of his companions how fortunate they were to serve in his unit. It was a dramatic change from his former status as the hated and mistrusted earless southerner they saw him as when he first arrived in Vanris. Plenty of people still doubted and disliked him, but if he didn't mess this up, their numbers would continue to dwindle. The best way to do that was to keep trusting and supporting the ones who helped him get to this point. Jethan foremost among them.

It took two days to reach the military city of Etrion with its towering black walls. Upon arrival, Kasiel dropped Niskenya, Irith, and the tethdraks off at their enclosures for some well-earned rest. Then he joined Dhomen Nevias and his unit to go before Khevarin Seylin, ruler of Vanris, and Jethan's aunt. They met in the familiar circular room with its curved dais at the back, upon which stood a long, curved table. For once, Kasiel's father, Dhomvalen Arhk Cavenos, wasn't there. In his absence, a larger number of the khevarin's personal guards stood watch around the room next to the black stone walls. Ahndhomen Adnar, Kasiel's commanding officer and Nevias's tehnaak, sat at one end of the table, his tethdrak alongside him. Dhomen Branith, head of the city guard, also occupied a seat along with the Evoker, Ahndhomen Setera.

His father's absence wasn't the only anomaly in this council. Khesran Velara, now first in line for the throne, sat behind the table, the faintest glimmer of pleasure lighting her silver eyes when he walked in. Kasiel did his best not to react to her presence or even look at her for longer than might be considered appropriate.

She had two braids worked into her dark, blood-red hair along one side of her head, exposing a pointed ear adorned with two jeweled, black metal ear cuffs and one of the claw-shaped earrings her younger brother had gifted her, with a blood-red gemstone dangling from the point of the claw. The faint white tattooed symbols of her ke'hanoath, bordered in a thin line of silver, formed a permanent tiara upon her brow. The scars that made a sideways V on her cheek, the longest reaching across the bridge of her nose, were partially obscured by her hair, left loose on that side. Those on her neck, from that same attack in Norvask, were visible where they reached partway across her throat.

Kasiel and his unit knelt before the khevarin. She wore a draping, pearlescent gown, the flickering light from sconces around the room and the crystalline chandelier overhead dancing orange and gold over the shimmering surface. Her long white-blond hair was woven through with thin silver strands that connected to a silver and dark metal tiara resting on her head. With her pale blue eyes gazing down at them, the delicate silver lines of her ke'hanoath curving beneath them on her cheekbones, she was the perfect image of icy refinement.

"Dhomen Nevias, you return to us much sooner than expected." Her soft voice cut through the room like a blade.

"Yes, Majesty." Nevias bowed her head in a gesture of respect.

"Report to us the outcome of your mission."

Nevias proceeded to describe the events at the watchtower. Partway through her telling, Kasiel was aware of the khevarin's gaze shifting to him, picking him apart. When Nevias finished, Seylin gestured for them to rise, her long silver nails gleaming like tiny daggers in the light.

"Ahninveth Kasiel," she began once they were all standing, "it seems you have earned our favor yet again with your actions. It is rare for such an encounter to end with no bloodshed. Why did you choose this approach for dealing with Sarket's force?"

"I saw no need to risk Vanrian soldiers when I could undermine the confidence of our enemies and route them without fighting, Majesty."

"And your unit supported you in this?"

"In full," Jethan answered.

She was silent for a moment as she scanned the others. Her head moved in the slightest of nods when her gaze finally returned to him. "This defeat will linger in their minds as they struggle to hold ground against us. It is well done, Ahninveth. You and your unit may rest and recover from your travels. Vanris will have need of you again soon."

"Majesty."

Kasiel sank into a partial bow, his gaze meeting Velara's as he straightened, her faint smile sending a shock of unexpected vitality through him.

The unit departed together, their military formation and decorum dissolving the minute they stepped out into the hall.

Avris grinned at Kasiel. "You know, I'm relatively certain the khevarin didn't know who most of us were before we saved you, country boy. Now she sees us regularly."

"Isn't that the truth." Jethan sounded put upon. "I could get away with a lot more before you made us so popular."

Kasiel laughed and shoulder-bumped his tehnaak. "Don't pretend you don't like it. Besides, we all got here together."

"Is this where it gets emotional?" Wedro asked. "Because I think that's my cue to leave."

"Horse shit." Merrin threw an arm around his shoulders. "You're going to clean up and meet us at The Twisted Vine, where we'll all get drunk and profess our undying love for each other."

"Hmm. I can drown myself in mead, but I'll have to put up with you callochs..."

Kince barked a laugh. "Like you wouldn't spend an hour with your worst enemy for a few mugs of Vanrian Black Mead."

"Well, if that's what we're drinking..." Wedro smirked, the expression exaggerating the divot in his upper lip from the scar that ran down his face. A disfigurement acquired on the mission his tehnaak, Chander, was killed on. Kasiel suspected the emotional wounds from that experience were a lot more severe than the visible ones, though they were showing signs of healing.

"Come on, you callochs." Darro slid an arm over Tath's shoulders. "Let's get going. The sooner we rinse off this grime, the sooner we can crack a stone and celebrate coming home with the same number of scars we left with, thanks to our clever Feral leader."

"That's something worth celebrating," Tath added, casting a quick smile at Nerith before she nestled in the crook of Darro's arm.

Once they agreed upon a time, they parted ways, going to clean up in their own homes, or rooms in the palace in his and Jethan's case. It felt good to scrub the grit of travel from his hair and body and put on fresh clothes from the well-stocked wardrobe. Once dressed, he stopped in front of the mirror and considered the man looking back at him. His red hair had gotten even longer, two braids against his scalp revealing the tattoo on his cheek and the ear on that side with its pointed top cut off.

A little over a year ago, he was still hiding his cut ears from the people of Fernwallow, so they wouldn't know he was Vanrian. He continued to keep them covered here until the khevarin gifted him a set of decorative dark metal ear cuffs designed to symbolically replace the missing portion of his ears. Since he started wearing those in battle and at formal occasions, he also stopped objecting to having his hair braided back in the Vanrian style. Somewhere in the last few months, he had grown accustomed to having one, or both ears exposed, even when he wasn't wearing the cuffs.

Yes, his ears ended in scars. Many people here had scars. Velara, Wedro, and Nevias all had scars they couldn't conceal. He and Nerith even had similar ones on the same cheek. He was through hiding his scars. They weren't his shame. They were Edmund's and Garrick's, and those two were dead now.

Slipping the dark metal dagger his father had given him in the sheath at his belt, Kasiel left the palace to join his unit.

A few hours later, he and Jethan made their way back, stumbling only a little. It was still early evening, but weariness from days of travel and the fact that Jethan was expecting to meet up with Velara's tehnaak, Keyla, kept them from staying out as late as they might have.

"Don't have too much fun," Kasiel called after Jethan as his tehnaak turned off down the hallway to his rooms.

Jethan turned around, walking backwards for a few strides. "Is that really possible?"

Recalling the time he had found Jethan thrown in the deeps after an evening with a young lady, he could only smile and shake his head. "For you, Jeth, I'm pretty sure it is."

"I disagree." Jethan laughed and turned around, raising a hand to wave back at Kasiel. "Goodnight, tehnaak."

Kasiel was already taking off the belt and dagger when he walked through the door into his sitting room. He stopped immediately, catching the scent of spicy sweetness in the air before he noticed the figure standing near the fireplace, dimly lit by a single burning candle. Her silver eyes gleaming with pleasure at surprising him.

Kasiel smiled, tossing his belt onto a chair, and crossed the room with a few long strides, lifting her into his arms and claiming her lips in an ardent kiss.

Velara matched his passion, sliding her hands under his shirt when he set her down and breaking the kiss long enough to pull it off. Within minutes, a trail of their clothing led to the bed and Kasiel eased her onto the covers, slowing the pace as he kissed his way down her neck.

"I'm not this patient," she breathed, letting out a soft moan when he brushed his fingers along the curve of her waist and inward.

He moved up for a moment to meet her eyes and grinned. "You will be." Then he resumed trailing kisses down her torso.

Later, when they had burned through their initial passion, she lay pressed against him, her head resting on his shoulder as she traced a finger across the long scar over his heart where Edmund had almost ended him.

"Vel."

Her hand stopped moving. "Oh dear."

He shifted to look at her when she rolled onto her back. "What?"

"You're thinking something, and I feel a lecture brewing." She glanced up at him, lips pursing in the start of a pout.

"How are you here? You should be in your room with guards standing watch."

"I Charmed them to think their shift was over and they wanted to get some sleep."

He pushed up on his elbow. "And went wandering around the palace alone?"

She frowned at him. "Yes. I live here now. I should be able to walk the halls by myself."

He reached out, moving her hair from her face, intentionally brushing his fingers over the scars on her cheek. She flinched away. "You've barely survived two assassination attempts already. Please don't make an easy target of yourself."

She sat up, and he struggled for a moment to focus on her words and not the shape of her naked body. "In Trenath and Norvask, not here. Besides, I'm no longer being married off to a foreign prince."

"True, but you shouldn't be sending your guards away. You could have sent me a message like you usually do."

"I wanted to surprise you."

The genuine disappointment in her eyes twisted something in his chest. "The fact that you love me always surprises me." Her expression softened in response to his words, and he leaned in to kiss her.

She looked him over when he drew away to sit beside her. "No new injures this time?"

"Not this time. Any good suitors?" He tried to sound teasing, though the prospect of her being married off was something he didn't find even a little humorous.

"Oh, a few that were tolerable." She ran one finger along his collarbone to the chain of his ke'hanoath, then followed that down to the symbol over his breastbone. "None that hold a candle to my Feral soldier."

He caught her hand and kissed it before settling it on the sheets between them, clasped in his. "What happens when your mother loses patience and picks one for you?"

She pulled her hand free and crawled over to straddle him. The position alone was unfairly distracting. "We run away together." Her tone was playful, but something in her expression hinted at poorly concealed sorrow.

He rested his hands on her waist and met her eyes. "What's wrong?"

Her gaze sank to his chest. "Nothing."

"Too late. I can see it in your face." He caught the glimmer of tears threatening in the corners of her eyes and moved her off to sit beside him again.

She rested her head against his shoulder. "They all stare, Kas."

"At the scars?"

"Mm-hmm."

"Are you sure they aren't just staring because you're beautiful?"

"Don't patronize me. I can tell the difference."

He slid his arm around her, pulling her closer, and pressed his lips to her head. "Anyone who sees only your scars may as well be blind. You were beautiful before, and you are even more beautiful now."

"Don't lie to me," she snapped, pulling away.

"I'm not, Vel. The more I get to know you, the more beautiful you are. Your scars are such a small part of you, and the honest truth is that I barely see them."

She turned sideways, placing her legs across his. "Is it any wonder that I can't find a suitor? No one will ever be as perfect for me as you are."

He met her eyes. Jethan was right, this couldn't continue much longer. They were living a dream, one they would both have to wake up from soon. If her brother hadn't removed himself as heir by trying to have her assassinated, they might have had a chance, slim though it was even then. Now she was heir to the Vanrian throne. This relationship was never going to end the way they both wanted it to, but maybe, for a little longer…

Velara leaned toward him, sliding her fingers into his hair, and he met her kiss. His hands settled at her waist, and he pulled her against him. Opening her mouth to his questing tongue, she deepened the kiss, moving to straddle him again, and this time, his body was ready for her. As she sank onto him, his worries faded from his mind.

Velara snuck back to her rooms after that second coupling. Kasiel had followed her far enough to watch and make sure she made it there safely, then returned to his bed and drifted to sleep amidst the scent of their lovemaking.

Pounding on the door woke him with a start early the next morning.

He snatched up the black robe draped over a chair beside his bed and went to see who was there. Three guards stood outside. They wore dark metal armor like all the palace guards, with a stylized kanodrak engraved on the sides of their helms, but something in the exquisite make of the black and purple gambesons they wore underneath made his gut coil into knots. These were Seylin's personal guards.

"Your presence is required," the woman on the far right said.

"May I take a minute to put on some clothes?"

She responded with a curt nod.

"Has something happened?" he asked, raising his voice as he went to his wardrobe and pulled out clothes suitable for an impromptu audience with the khevarin.

The silence that met his question did nothing to ease the dancing of his nerves. He slipped into the bathing room, using a sponge at the basin to wash away any lingering aroma of his nocturnal activities with Velara. When he came out, an attendant was setting a covered platter of food on his table. She offered him a silent bow before hurrying back out between the guards.

Kasiel grabbed his belt with the dagger on it and the woman lowered her spear point in threat.

"You will bring no weapons, Ahninveth Kasiel."

Nerves now screaming, he set the belt down and walked out. The woman took the lead. The other two, unnervingly, fell in behind him, as if intending to ensure he didn't try to run. They escorted him down a hall he had never taken within the depths of the private quarters. Guards stood at attention at intervals along the polished black stone walls. The swirling black and light gray marble floor had subtle lines of silver and purple woven through it, illuminated by sconces every eight feet.

A set of dark-stained double doors at the end had an elaborate depiction of a roaring kanodrak carved across them. The image made him think of Niskenya, and he almost reached out to her. She was ever-present in his mind, but the intensity of their connection varied. Right now, it felt as if she were still asleep or perhaps just resting after a kill. Whatever was happening here, it might be better not to draw her in. Upsetting her would gain neither of them anything, since she couldn't help him when he was deep in the heart of the palace.

The guards outside the doors opened them to admit Kasiel, revealing an elegant sitting area with several white chairs and couches arranged before a stone fireplace nearly large enough for him to slide his bed into. A long painting above it depicted a field of yellow, purple, and pink wildflowers with an enormous mountain looming in the distance beyond a thick forest. A scene from the Vanrian homeland before a chain of volcanic eruptions rendered it uninhabitable.

The khevarin stood with her back to him alongside a long, elegant side table upon which a set of crystalline goblets and matching carafe were arranged. She wore a full-length black and silver dress with a simpler cut than those he usually saw her in. Her silver nails tapped the side of the carafe, making a soft chiming sound.

When the door closed behind Kasiel and the guards, the sudden prick of two spear points against his neck forced his chin up, and he froze. The taste of metal filled his mouth, and he barely stopped the instinctive call to Niskenya and Irith. The third guard came to stand to one side in front of him, staring at him with a cold intensity.

Seylin turned to face him, deadly fury lighting her eyes. "How far have you taken things with my daughter?"

His chest constricted, a chill sweeping down from the spear points pricking his neck and out through his arms. Lying would make it worse. There were ways they could find the truth, and one of her guards was almost certainly an Evoker, most likely the man currently staring death at him.

Seylin glanced at the guard in front of him. When the man nodded, her eyes narrowed. That definitively answered the question of whether he was an Evoker, at least. She approached and pushed the point of one long, tapered fingernail under Kasiel's chin, forcing his head up a little more. The spears pressed forward enough that the tips punctured the surface of his skin. He forced himself not to react, knowing the smallest movement could lead to greater injury.

"I should have you put to death for this," she hissed.

It was the first time Kasiel had seen so significant a break in her careful composure. It wasn't something he ever wanted to see again. "I'd rather you didn't," he said, forced to speak through clenched teeth with those three points digging in beneath his jaw.

Her fingernail pressed in harder, and the spears did the same, as if they all shared one mind. He sucked in a breath with the sudden sharp pain, feeling a trickle of warm blood run down both sides of his neck from the points of the spears. Next time, he was going to listen to his tehnaak. Assuming there was a next time.

"Is this a game to you?" Seylin demanded.

"No," he swallowed. "I love your daughter, Majesty. I would love her regardless of who she was."

"You are a fool if you think love is relevant here, Ahninveth." She took her fingernail away and wandered to the side table, setting her hands on the edge. The spears eased back a fraction. "Unfortunately, I cannot have you executed. You have become a hero to my people, and we need you in our army now more than ever. Not to mention, Dhomvalen Arhk seems to have actually grown fond of you."

"There is another option," Kasiel ventured.

Her sharp gaze snapped back to him and Kasiel caught his breath when the spears pressed in again.

"You may be a hero in this country and the dhomvalen's son, but you are still an earless boy raised by our enemies. There is no circumstance under which you could ever be an appropriate suitor for my daughter."

Kasiel immediately focused his thoughts on his night with Velara. The taste of her lips, the feel of their bodies joined, moving together, sweating, moaning, anything to avoid wondering why his father had lied to him about Seylin considering him a match for Velara. The Evoker, suddenly bombarded with images of the khevarin's daughter naked and locked in a passionate embrace, cleared his throat uncomfortably, his cheeks coloring.

Seylin glanced at the man and scowled. "Get out of his head," she snapped. "We have the information we were looking for." At a brisk wave of her hand, the spears also moved away.

Kasiel let out a shaky breath.

Seylin straightened, her regal composure returning. "We are sending your unit to Delaphine with Dhomen Nevias's company. Your father and Dhomen Aleren are there now, meeting with representatives from Fallend. You will report to them first. Afterwards, you will be deployed along Delaphine's western border, where you will help defend our allies against attacks from Sarket. You depart tomorrow morning. Until you are gone, Khesran Velara will remain confined to her quarters. You are to make no attempt to reach out to her. By the time you have returned from Delaphine, assuming you survive the fighting, she will be engaged and perhaps wed to a proper suitor. If we find that you have spoken to anyone else about your illicit relationship with our daughter, not even your father will be able to save you from execution. Do you understand?"

If only he could believe he had done nothing wrong, he might argue with her, but he couldn't. He was what she said, an earless boy raised in the south. A past he had no control over. One that no amount of heroics would erase. He had no right to Velara's hand, and certainly no right to her body, even if she had chosen to give it to him. As the heir to the Vanrian throne, that had never really been her choice to make.

His throat tightened, and he lowered his gaze. "Yes, Majesty."

"Excellent. If you perform well, you may eventually find your way back into our favor. Now, get out of our sight."

The guards stepped aside, clearing his path to the door, so Kasiel spun on the ball of one foot and strode from the room. When he turned down the hall his personal chambers were in, he found Jethan walking away from his door. For an instant, his tehnaak smiled, then the expression faltered.

His gaze sank to Kasiel's neck, and his brow furrowed. "What happened?"

Kasiel wiped his neck, not surprised when his fingers came away smeared with red. He grimaced at the blood, then gestured silently toward his rooms. Jethan led the way. As soon as they were inside, Kasiel threw the bolt on the door and told his tehnaak what had happened with the khevarin while he cleaned the blood off his neck at the basin in the bathing room. Once he was done, he eyed the small wounds. On the one side, at least, his hair would cover it.

"You should have stuck with Nerith," Jethan muttered as they walked back out to his sitting room.

Kasiel gave him a hard look.

"Sorry. Not helpful."

"Not even a little." He picked up a stoneglass bottle sitting on the table and poured some Vanrian Black Mead for himself and his tehnaak. As he passed the mug to Jethan, he met his eyes. "Something else bothers me about all of this."

"Something other than my aunt threatening to have you executed?"

Kasiel breathed a humorless laugh. "Yes. On our way back from Doran the first time, when we were bringing Velara here, my father told me Seylin had considered matching me with her daughter prior to the alliance proposal with Delaphine. I'm not sure I would have ever considered crossing the line with her if it hadn't been for him putting that thought in my head. But my encounter with your aunt just now made it abundantly clear that she has never considered me an acceptable match for her daughter."

Jethan leaned forward in his seat. "You think your father wanted you to get involved with her?"

"I don't know, but he said something else that made me wonder the night she was made Seylin's official heir. He told me I had become the symbol of Vanris's might, and that, with very little effort, I could win the heart of this country. I can't help wondering if he's manipulating me to some end, though I don't have a clue what that end might be."

Jethan sat back and took a long drink of his mead before responding. "I feel like there's something to this, but right now, regardless of your father's intentions, my aunt is taking matters into her own hands, and there isn't much we can do about it."

Kasiel glanced at Jethan over the top of his mug. "I appreciate you not saying I told you so, but I'm pretty sure you don't mind her ending my relationship with Vel."

"Let's be honest, you sleeping with my cousin has been awkward for me, but mostly I was worried about what was going to happen when my aunt found out. It actually went better than I expected." He leaned forward again, setting his mug on the table. "I know you love her, and I know she feels the same about you. This won't be easy for either of you. All I can say is that I am here for you, tehnaak. I will continue to be here for you no matter how I feel about your choices, but when the khevarin decides your relationship is over, it's over."

The urge to scream out his rage welled up inside him, but it wasn't just him. It was Niskenya and Irith reacting to the distress he was struggling to keep hidden. Jethan was right, again. The khevarin got the last word. Her daughter. Her country. Opposing that would bring his life to an abrupt end, and yet, he still wanted to fight it. Niskenya encouraged him to fight it.

"Do you think Merrin's busy?"

A smirk curved Jethan's lips. "Feel like sparring, do you?"

"You have no idea."

Jethan finished his mead, then stood. "Well, if we can't find her, I'm happy to stand in as long as you don't let Niskenya help."

Kasiel forced a smile. "We'll see."

A short time later, Merrin stood at the edge of the sparring ring, leaning on the railing along with Jethan, Wedro, and Avris. Irith lay inside the rail at their feet. Kasiel faced off against Dhomen Farren. The combat instructor, who had been there when they arrived, had immediately challenged him to a match. The fire burning in his eyes went well with the aggressive, sharp red lines of the ke'hanoath climbing up his neck. That expression made Kasiel wary, because it felt like a reflection of the anger he was barely keeping contained. If they were both trying to burn off their tempers, it could get out of hand quickly.

"So, south into Pandrean Alliance territory again?" Avris was asking.

"The Pandrean Alliance is dead," Wedro corrected.

"It's wounded and limping," Farren countered, his gaze never wavering from Kasiel.

Kasiel adjusted his grip on the practice sword. "You don't think Delaphine will withdraw from the alliance with Vanris, do you?"

"I think they fear us more than they fear Sarket right now, but I'm willing to bet Sarket will try to tip that balance. One thing we have in our favor is that Delaphine and Sarket worked together long enough that many Sarketi soldiers have friends and family across those lines and may hesitate at being ordered to attack their own." He stared at Kasiel, eyes narrowing. "What do you think, Cavenos?"

"I think negotiations with Fallend, even though their military isn't as strong, will play a significant role in how stable our alliance with Delaphine is. We lost the advantage of a political marriage with Prince Elijah's death, but Fallend's support could boost Delaphine's confidence."

He lunged when he finished speaking, attempting to catch Farren by surprise. The dhomen deflected his strike as if he had been waiting for it and barely missed a blow to Kasiel's arm as he darted back out of reach.

"You've developed more of a head for political strategy, but your combat skills could still use some work," Farren said, a savage hunger in his grin.

Too bad that made no difference in his standing with the khevarin. Then again, it wasn't his abilities Seylin objected to; it was his past and his disfigurement. Things he couldn't fix.

Anger swelled in him, and he felt Niskenya stirring in his mind. He attempted to push back against her – he wanted to win this fight alone – but she patiently and effortlessly moved past his resistance. Then she settled, passing a sense of calm and focus through to him, smothering his anger.

Kasiel took a deep breath. The kanodrak knew what she was doing. Attacking with his rage was going to get him hurt. What she didn't understand was that he wanted to feel pain. Physical pain. The kind of pain he knew would heal in time. Velara hung in the back of his mind, the woman he loved who he was now being ordered to abandon. He had been forced to do that to Nerith once, leaving her to face her father alone in Doran. An incident that opened the door to several arguably poor decisions. His life didn't belong to him. Vanris owned him. The people, the khevarin, and his father.

Fury burst through Niskenya's comforting, and he lunged at Farren. Their eyes met, and the dhomen smiled as he swapped his sword to his left hand. Kasiel came in fast and strong. Niskenya withdrew. They exchanged a flurry of attacks, blocking and dodging each other's strikes. Then Kasiel hit the ground hard enough to knock the wind out of him. He wasn't even sure where the blow that downed him had come from, but his sword lay several feet away and pain radiated through his chest.

Farren held a hand down to him. "That's what I was waiting for."

Kasiel drew a strained breath and accepted the offered assistance, letting the other man pull him up. A slow clap behind him drew his attention, and he turned to see the Feral kanodrak rider, Jhanik, leaning on the rail with his tehnaak, Keryk, and his tethdrak flanking him. The man's light blond hair was freshly shaved on both sides, showing off the symbols of his ke'hanoath tattooed on his scalp. His strong jaw lifted slightly, so he looked down his nose at them.

Kasiel drew in another breath, his diaphragm slowly relaxing, then faced the man. "When did you get in?"

"About an hour ago. Apparently, we'll be riding back out tomorrow with Dhomen Nevias. As much as I would love to watch Dhomen Farren beat the horse shit out of you some more, I have another reason for seeking you out."

Something in his tone sent a ripple of unease through Kasiel. Reaching out with his ability, he tried to reconnect with Niskenya and met up with a wall of silence. It didn't surprise him she was angry. He had cast her aside for the sake of his temper. That would need to be addressed right away. He strode over to Jhanik, aware of his companions and Irith heading around the outside to join them.

"What is it?"

"I've been told Khevarin Seylin wants the kanodraks to remain here this time. I was hoping the son of the dhomvalen might have enough influence to change her mind."

Kasiel's gut clenched, twisting like a nest of snakes. Seylin was punishing him. Of that, he had no doubt. Trying to take away his greatest strength and foundation as a Feral, and one of his most valued companions. He couldn't imagine not feeling Niskenya's presence in his mind for months on end. Not to mention that he was a far more effective fighter with her instincts guiding him.

The wall of silence in his mind shattered and Niskenya surged in, protective fury flowing out from her. Kasiel smirked to himself. So, she had still been there, lurking. Leave it to the kanodrak to find a way to hide herself in his own head.

"The khevarin may not be as inclined to listen to me with my father out of the city," he said, seeing no need to mention that she would rather watch him lose his head right now than give him anything he wanted. "We might have better luck if we start with someone who understands why this is a bad idea."

"Ahndhomen Adnar."

Kasiel nodded. A hand came to rest on his shoulder, and he turned to see Avris standing there.

"You don't need us for this, but we'll see you at The Twisted Vine later, right?"

He met her pale green eyes for a moment, trying to get past her guarded look, but she was always one to keep her inner thoughts to herself. "We'll be there. We only get one more night in the city. Might as well enjoy it."

"Good." She turned to Wedro and Merrin. "Come on, kids, let's go cause trouble elsewhere."

Merrin shook her head, a crooked smile touching her lips as she glanced at Farren. The combat instructor nodded and beckoned her over with an ominous curl of his fingers.

"Or maybe we'll stay here a while longer." Avris

shook her head at her tehnaak, though a fond smile curved her lips.

Kasiel almost wanted to stay and watch. Merrin was the best fighter in his unit. If anyone could give Farren a real challenge, she was the one. But he and Jhanik had a problem to deal with.

"Good luck, Dhomen Farren," he called, ducking out of the practice ring. Then, with Jethan and Irith by his side, he joined Jhanik's trio to go speak to Adnar.

They were entering the building that overlooked the tethdrak enclosure when an earsplitting series of roars shook everything in the structure. Kasiel could feel the surge of rage that flowed through Niskenya as she put her powerful lungs behind voicing her opinion on the khevarin's decision. She wasn't the only one causing a scene. Jhanik's kanodrak, Arkos, and some of the others lent their awesome voices to her protest, making a racket that the entire city would hear.

A guard hurrying out almost ran into them on their way through the door. She made as if to dart past, then stopped as she registered who they were.

"Ahninveth Kasiel. Ahninveth Jhanik. Ahndhomen Adnar needs you both in the kanodrak enclosure immediately."

Kasiel smiled. "Does he now? Whatever for?"

Jhanik smirked and Jethan pressed his lips together to suppress a grin.

The guard scowled at him as another chorus of roars rang out and gestured firmly toward the source of the racket. Jhanik's tethdrak shifted his feet, uneasy with the uproar from predators even more deadly than it. Irith's hackles went up and the cliff cat sank into a defensive posture.

Kasiel set a hand on the cat's shoulders, sending a

sense of comfort across to him. "Oh, that. We'll head down now."

"Thank you." She gave a sour smirk and stepped out of their way, apparently not amused by his flippancy.

When they arrived at the base of the lift in front of the tethdrak canyon habitat, several of the beasts were running around, expressing distress at the commotion in the next canyon with a barrage of nervous clicks and shrieks. Jhanik and Kasiel left their tehnaaks and companions there and continued through the tunnel to the kanodrak habitat.

Kasiel rarely saw more than one kanodrak in the front at a time. They were solitary creatures outside of mating, rarely interacting unless their bonded companions brought them together on missions, as had happened more than once with Niskenya and Arkos. Today, their two kanodraks were both up near the bars with all six of the other vaguely feline beasts within sight, stalking about and growling in response to the irritation Niskenya and Arkos were feeding into them.

When he entered the front area, Niskenya made a chuffing noise in her chest and padded to the bars. Arkos approached as well, his attention on Jhanik, though the big male lurked off to one side, leaving Niskenya plenty of space. Like his kanodrak, Jhanik remained a few steps behind, deferring to the whims of the matriarch of the group. Kasiel walked directly to the gate, aware of Adnar emerging from a door in the canyon wall and striding out in a swift interception course.

"Ahninveth Kasiel, what is the meaning of the unrest your kanodrak is provoking?"

Kasiel inclined his head to the ahndhomen, then he closed the last couple of feet to the bars and held a hand through to Niskenya. She stilled, pressing her forehead to his palm, her sides heaving with the effort of her raging. After a few seconds, he backed away and faced Adnar. "I believe Niske and Arkos are expressing their displeasure with the khevarin's plan to send us to Delaphine without them, sir."

Backing his words, Niskenya reared up, slamming her front paws into two of the bars. Dust rose from a growing crack in the stone at the base of one bar. A new fracture in the rock overhang was also spreading between the tops of the bars. This was clearly not the first time she had struck them today.

Adnar's gaze took in those same concerning developments, his expression darkening. "I understand Khevarin Seylin's concerns..." He trailed off at the furrowing of Kasiel's brow, eyes narrowing a fraction. "Or perhaps I don't. Either way, I am not sure it's wise to send you both into the field without them."

"I agree. We could be gone for some time, sir. We will almost certainly be in combat situations. What sense is there in sending Feral kanodrak riders out on a possibly extended campaign without their strongest assets?" He glanced at Niskenya. "Assuming those assets will even agree to stay behind."

"I get the feeling there is more to this than I am aware of, but sending kanodrak riders to support our allies without their kanodraks not only makes no sense but is also an unnecessary risk of valuable resources." For once, Kasiel didn't mind being reduced to a valuable resource, so long as the Feral ahndhomen was on their side. "Let's speak with her. I am sure the khevarin will see reason." Adnar started walking toward the exit tunnel, Jhanik quickly falling into step behind him. They stopped and turned back when Kasiel didn't follow. Adnar's brows pinched. "What are you not telling me, Ahninveth?"

"Apologies, Ahndhomen. Khevarin Seylin is upset with me right now. You're apt to have more success without me there, but you might wish to point out that

Niskenya has no intention of letting me leave without her." He glanced up at the crack in the overhang for emphasis.

Jhanik breathed a laugh. "You're something else, Cavenos."

"Don't encourage him." Adnar gave the other Feral a sharp look. "Does your kanodrak feel the same?"

Jhanik met Kasiel's eyes. They both knew his connection with Arkos wasn't nearly as strong. They both also knew that he had no interest in deploying without the beast. He faced Adnar. "Yes, sir. I'm afraid Arkos stands with Niske on this."

Adnar eyed the two kanodraks for a moment, his jaw clenched. Then he nodded, his gaze locking with Kasiel's. He was aware of which bonded pair was at the heart of this disturbance. Niskenya was the alpha in the enclosure. She almost always got her way. "I will fight to see that you are not separated from them for this campaign. Ahninveth Jhanik, you come with me. Ahninveth Kasiel, until we return, I expect you to keep them from tearing down the bars."

"Yes, Ahndhomen." As the two departed through the tunnel, he turned to Niskenya and put his hands between the bars again. The kanodrak rubbed her face against it. "I can't stop her from taking Velara away, but I won't be parted from you."

The rumble of a deep purr in her chest accompanied a wave of affection and devotion across their connection. That protective, almost maternal presence broke through the barriers he was hiding his pain behind. Velara, the woman he loved, was out of his reach now. In truth, she always had been, but holding her in his arms and being wanted by her made their relationship seem plausible. Like something that was meant to be, regardless of the obstacles standing between them. An inevitability rather than a violation.

He pulled out his key to the enclosure and walked in. The other kanodraks watched him, ever resentful of another creature in their territory, but they wouldn't bother him. He belonged to Niskenya. As she walked up to him, the other beasts slowly dispersed out into the habitat. She sank beside him, and he accepted the offer, climbing up on her back. The first time he had ridden her without the saddle had been after he escaped the prison cell in Edmund's stronghold. They had won that battle. They would win this one too.

*

Kasiel watched Coranthis growing larger on the horizon, its square buildings like a vast collection of boxes piled haphazardly on the steep hillsides leading down to the river. He didn't like this city, and not just because he found the construction style unattractive. It reminded him of Danica's execution and the attack that gave Velara her scars and killed several other Vanrians. Unwelcome memories on top of the more recent incidents that made him loathe to think about Velara, but at least the khevarin hadn't gotten her way with everything.

He placed a hand on Niskenya's shoulder, welcoming the affection the kanodrak offered in return.

According to Jhanik, Adnar hadn't needed to put up much of a fight to get Khevarin Seylin to change her mind. Like everyone else in the city, she had heard Niskenya and the other kanodraks expressing their outrage. Once the Feral ahndhomen told her about the cracks in the stone at the front of the habitat from Niskenya's assault on the bars, she relented, though she apparently pointed out that she was doing so strictly out of respect for the revered beasts.

Coranthis wasn't their final destination. They wouldn't be entering the city itself. A Delaphinian company had joined them when they crossed the border into Delaphine. A second, larger company was to meet them between the city and an equestrian facility a few miles southwest of it where they bred and trained military horses. From there, as he understood it, they would be shown to where the negotiations with Fallend were being held.

Dhomen Nevias had driven the Vanrian company hard from Etrion to this point, promising them a chance to rest once they reached the negotiation site. Kasiel welcomed the aggressive pace. Travel always required a certain amount of focused attention with the need to manage the birds he scouted with and his tethdraks – of which he and Jhanik had ten each this time – and ensuring the calm of the surrounding horses. Irith was also with him, but the cliff cat had formed enough of a bond with Kasiel and the rest of his unit now that there wasn't much need to direct him. With the exhaustion of his beasts piled on top of his own at the end of each day, he quickly fell into a routine that involved little thought. Travel most of the day, eat at the proper intervals, settle his tethdraks at night, sleep, and do it all again the next day.

The company veered slightly right at a branch in the road, heading southwest away from the city, and slowed their pace to a walk. Even with the advantage of Niskenya's greater size, he couldn't see much ahead of him other than rank upon rank of mounted soldiers. Now that he thought about it, he wasn't sure where in Etrion they stored this many horses. Somewhere, in carefully managed canyons, they had crops and livestock, but he had trouble imagining it on this scale. Another Vanrian company from east of Etrion had joined up with theirs before they crossed the Break, so not all the animals here came from the southern capitol, but he still didn't recall seeing that many stables in the city. Maybe there was a horse habitat somewhere he hadn't found yet.

He breathed a laugh at the idea of some vast canyon like what the tethdraks and kanodraks had, only filled with herds of horses. Happy horses, kicking up their heels and racing around like foals between missions.

"He can smile."

Kasiel glanced over, a little surprised to see Nerith now riding beside Jethan. Her thoughtful regard threw him off as much as her light tone.

"It's true. I've seen it happen a few times." Jethan gave him a wink.

"Sometimes you need to get away from home to see things more clearly." Nerith absently patted her mount's neck when the animal tossed its head. The smile she gave Kasiel offered an understanding he didn't think he deserved from her.

The unit knew about his relationship Velara, or at least that they were in one. They were all too close to him not to have noticed the flirtation and affection in their interactions over the last several months, though most didn't know how far it had gone. He had told them before leaving Etrion that the khevarin found out about that relationship and was livid, emphasizing the importance of keeping it all secret to avoid further punishment for him and prevent her fury from falling upon them for not reporting it.

"I'm not a big fan of fighting, but it is nice to run with my beasts now and then." Kasiel swept his awareness through his tethdraks as he spoke, checking that all was well.

"Something only a Feral would ever say," Jethan said with a chuckle.

Nerith breathed a laugh. "Kas, for someone who dislikes conflict, you certainly have a way of finding it." The look she gave him told him she wasn't just referring to the military kind.

He gave her a sideways glance, a wry smile curving his lips. "There may be some truth to that."

"Excuse me, Ahninveth Kasiel." His Speaker, Etris, her long blond hair pulled back into a single braid, moved up on his other side next to Irith. "You're wanted near the front."

Kasiel inclined his head to her. "Thank you."

Reaching his ability out, he moved the horses between him and the side of the column to create a path for Niskenya. Several soldiers glanced at him, knowing full well who had taken away control of their mounts, though none appeared bothered by it. Some even smiled or nodded in greeting, their respectful and occasionally envious gazes following the kanodrak as he rode past.

He chose to exit to the right of the column because the grassy hillside there left more space to travel up the line than the stand of trees now obscuring their view of Coranthis on the left. When he emerged, he immediately spotted a familiar figure watching the column pass.

General Itana Kedran sat on her mount like a regal statue, her long black hair worked into an abundance of tiny braids and bound partly up on her head. Her dark skin and confident posture made him think of Danica as she had been before the events that broke her. They were both courageous people, but Danica never got the chance to show the world how amazing she could be.

Itana grinned when she spotted him. Her grins always made him feel like she was about to introduce him to her mace again and somehow expected the experience to be thoroughly enjoyable for both of them.

"General Kedran," he greeted, soothing her horse as Niskenya paced over to her. The kanodrak stopped beside her, facing the company so that he might speak with Itana and still have an eye on the column. He needed to keep his tethdraks in formation, after all.

"Ahninveth Kasiel." She watched Irith as the big

cliff cat sat beside Niskenya, then met his eyes. "How is your arm?"

"Inexplicably nervous suddenly," he answered, grinning as he glanced at the mace she wore. A shudder of genuine dread moved through him at the memory of that mace smashing down on his forearm, but he suppressed it.

Itana barked a laugh. "You have a good sense of humor, Ahninveth. My mace no longer yearns for the breaking of your bones, but it does look forward to crushing our enemies together."

He gave her an appraising glance. "You're coming to the border with us?"

"Yes. I have no desire to lounge about here listening to talk of alliances when our people are under attack. I will accompany the Vanrian army to the current front with a Delaphinian company of my own."

"It will be good to fight alongside you." He meant that. Itana was a powerful warrior and practical as well. Given his tendency to be driven by emotion, she could provide a valuable balancing influence.

Her gaze drifted to the Delaphinian emblem behind the seat of his saddle on that side and her smile widened. She laughed. "That is not how I remember it, but perhaps it is more appropriate than it first appears."

Kasiel glanced back at the emblem depicting a mace breaking against someone's forearm. The people of Sharith had gifted it to him as an expression of gratitude for his efforts in saving them. "It isn't my design. A smith in Sharith made it."

"As I said, it is a more accurate depiction, in a way. That battle was pivotal in pushing Delaphine toward seeking an alliance with Vanris. I may have shattered your arm, but you shattered the confidence of an entire country. One of these things is an impressive achievement."

Kasiel met her dark eyes, touched by the respect he saw in them and answered with a grateful smile. "I'll have you know my arm was quite impressed by what you achieved there." He habitually flexed the right forearm, feeling the lingering weakness and reduced sensation from muscle and nerve damage.

"I've seen you fight with your left arm, Ahninveth. You will never convince me I did not do you a favor." She smirked and lifted her reins. "Come, let us join the others."

They ended their journey at a sprawling estate with five massive stables near the manor surrounded by hundreds of acres of pastures. The equestrian facility, as it turned out, was actually the location of the negotiations. As working stables went, Kasiel had never seen anything so grand.

A large Vanrian company already had a camp set up in some fields not far from where the Delaphinian troops had their facilities set up. Another company watched their arrival from a field on the opposite side. Their lack of heraldry made it clear they were part of the group from Fallend, not yet ready to declare allegiances publicly.

Kasiel barely had time to settle the tethdraks and meet back up with the rest of his unit before Dhomen Nevias came looking for him. "Ahninveth Kasiel, if you would come with me, please." Jethan walked up beside him and the dhomen shook her head. "Just Kasiel."

He shared a curious look with his tehnaak before nodding. "Yes, Dhomen."

Fortunately, she didn't object to Irith following him as they headed for the east wing of the sprawling manor. Perhaps his father wished to speak with him.

As soon as they were in the halls of the building and out of earshot of anyone, he asked, "What's this about?"

"I was not given that information, Ahninveth. I am

simply following orders." Her stride didn't slow.

"Whose orders?"

Nevias turned at a door with two Vanrian guards standing outside of it. One of them greeted her and opened it. Kasiel followed her into a substantial study, its walls lined with bookshelves and tasteful paintings depicting peaceful coastal scenery. A modest fireplace sat unused in the warmer weather. Dhomen Aleren, the khevarin's tehnaak, sat behind a heavy wooden desk, her shoulder-length blond hair pulled back in a tail with two braids worked into it on each side.

She stood when they entered, offering Nevias a slight bow. "Dhomen Nevias."

Nevias returned the greeting, then pulled a sealed letter out of the satchel she carried. "I received orders to deliver this to you along with Ahninveth Kasiel once we arrived."

Kasiel's gut dropped as Aleren accepted the letter. "Thank you, Dhomen Nevias. You may leave us."

As Nevias walked out, Aleren opened the letter and read it, pausing once to arch a brow at him. Her gaze moved across the page a few times before she held it over a candle and watched it burn, shaking it out when only a small corner remained.

"Not your wisest decision, Ahninveth Kasiel." Her hard gaze drilled into him. "I do feel for you. I have spent more time around Khesran Velara than her mother has, so I know how persistent she can be when she decides she wants something." She blew out a heavy breath. "You must have known you would be the one to suffer when Seylin found out."

"In my defense, I'm still something of an idiot when it comes to the rules of society and rank."

She let out a weary chuckle. "I'm afraid that won't help you."

Kasiel swallowed and forced himself to hold her

gaze. "May I ask how she means to make me suffer?"

"For now, she has ordered me to keep you on the most active fronts until you get killed or she finds another way to put you to use away from her daughter."

"What of my unit?"

Her brows went up. "Naturally, they will suffer your folly with you. Perhaps you should keep that in mind next time you have a substantial choice to make. Assuming you get that chance. I can give you a couple of days to rest then you will head west to help Delaphine fight their former allies. Use the time well. It may be the last opportunity you have to relax with your companions." She began sweeping the ash off the desk. "Good luck, Ahninveth Kasiel."

Upon leaving the study, Kasiel went in search of his father, but the dhomvalen was tied up in a meeting with dignitaries from Fallend and Delaphine. As members of the Vanrian nobility, or royalty in Jethan's case, Kasiel and his tehnaak were provided rooms in the manor and an invitation to join the formal dinner. It was already drifting into evening, which left them little time to clean up from the road before they needed to head to the dining hall.

Kasiel left Irith out with his unit. He didn't know how receptive the people from Fallend and Delaphine would be to the cliff cat's presence, and a formal dinner wasn't the best place to find out.

When they arrived, a steward introduced them as Ahninveth Kasiel Cavenos, son of Dhomvalen Arhk Cavenos, and Lord Jethan Markanis, nephew to Khevarin Seylin Markanis. Kasiel was uncomfortable anyplace where those affiliations were an essential part of their identities. The members of the Delaphinian and Fallenese delegations watched the two of them with interest. It was on the modest end of the formal affairs Kasiel had attended in the last year, but tables laden with rich foods and wine, and soft music played by a small group of musicians warmed the atmosphere. Most wore understated attire, given the lack of higher royalty present and the distance many of them had traveled to be there.

Kasiel focused on watching and listening. Dhomen Aleren and Dhomvalen Arhk, pale Vanrians with their distinct, pointed ears, sat closest to the two delegates from Fallend, a man with brunette hair and brown eyes and a woman with dark caramel hair and hazel eyes, both with olive skin. The dark-skinned representatives from Delaphine sat on the far side of them, creating an interesting visual progression from light to dark. Unexpectedly, General Itana Kedran sat alongside the Delaphinian group. It surprised Kasiel that a former mercenary turned general had a place at the table. Then again, during the events around the attack on the Vanrian contingent at Norvask, he had noticed that the Delaphinian king seemed to hold her in high regard.

Clothing styles were different around the table as well. The Vanrians wore a great deal of black, purple, and silver in keeping with their country's colors, with white or ivory shirts to provide contrast. They used fabrics that had a visual softness to them, often cut in a fitted style with jackets that hung longer in the back. The Fallenese group wore square-cut clothing of a thicker material, oddly in more blue, green, and tan shades rather than their country's black and gray, while the Delaphinians wore bright colors and elaborate patterns that complimented the warmth of their dark skin. The cuts fell a little closer to Fallend's square edges, but more embellishments in ribbons, buttons, or braided cords created a visual interest that held his attention for much of the early part of the meal.

He was putting a bite of roasted pheasant in his mouth and admiring the Delaphinian fashion when Jethan nudged him under the table and glanced meaningfully toward Aleren.

Kasiel shifted his attention to the conversation.

"If Fallend's royal family is interested in arranging a political marriage, there are still possibilities despite the change in Khesran Velara's situation," Aleren was saying. Her gaze drifted to them. "In fact, my understanding is that Lord Jethan and Ahninveth Kasiel might both be eligible for such arrangements."

Kasiel's stomach dropped. He noticed a slight tensing in his father's posture next to him, suggesting that this eventuality may not have been discussed with him. Jethan forced a smile and Kasiel offered an expression that might have qualified as such. On Jethan's other side, Dhomen Nevias looked like she had eaten something rotten.

Marrying him off was another way to keep him away from Velara, though not one that had crossed his mind before this moment.

"It surprises me that Khevarin Seylin would consider tying up a valuable military asset like Ahninveth Kasiel," Itana said, a faintly conspiratorial glint in her eyes when she met his across the tables.

Aleren shifted in her seat and glanced down at her food for a second, the comment apparently hitting a nerve. Perhaps she didn't fully agree with her tehnaak's determination that he needed to be removed from Etrion by whatever means necessary. He wasn't sure if he could use that to his advantage, but he would keep it in mind.

Arhk's icy gaze fell on Aleren. "General Kedran makes a fair point."

The female delegate from Fallend, Lady Katerin De Clare, either missed the tension in the moment, or chose to ignore it. "We shall convey that information to the royal family. As far removed as we are from Vanris, such an arrangement might provide some reassurance." Her hazel eyes focused on Kasiel, and he made himself meet them until she looked away.

Aleren seemed happy to move on to other subjects after that. Kasiel's appetite faded, but he ate well, more to ensure his fitness for the fighting ahead than out of any concern about being impolite. If they could discuss his and Jethan's futures in front of them with so little care for their feelings on the subject, he could quietly despise them all without guilt.

When the dinner ended, Arhk approached Kasiel as he was getting up to leave. "I'd like a moment, Ahninveth."

"As would I, Dhomvalen." He caught Aleren frowning after them as he followed his father out. She must have known Arhk would object to such an offer being made without his leave, assuming that was even what he wanted to talk about. Either way, he hoped their departure together made her uncomfortable.

They didn't speak on their way out to the far corner of the extensive gardens behind the manor. The grounds were lit for the evening with occasional lanterns placed strategically to draw attention to the most attractive decorative plants and sculptures. They stopped next to a drooping ornamental willow and Arhk scanned their surroundings. His eyes darkened at the edges and a mild pulse of pressure swept out from him.

"What was that?" Kasiel asked.

"Anyone nearby just experienced a chill of unease that will compel them to leave the area. I would prefer to keep this conversation private."

Kasiel glanced around, spotting the dark silhouettes of two individuals as they got up from where they had been sitting next to a tree several yards away and headed toward the manor. "A useful trick."

Arhk watched the two go, then faced Kasiel. "Seylin caught you with Velara?"

Kasiel's jaw tightened. He suspected his father knew something was up between them, but to have him admit it this boldly was like having the dagger in his back yanked out just so it could be driven in again from the front. "You knew?"

"Knew? No. Not for certain, but I had hoped my encouragement was not too subtle for you. Although, to be honest, I had not expected you to be quite so successful, nor brazen enough to take her to your room in Norvask and put the alliance and your freedom at risk."

Anger flared bright and hot in Kasiel, pushing him to lash out. Then he felt Niskenya, Irith, and the tethdraks responding to his temper, getting up from their places of rest with a burst of defensive fury. He wrestled his emotions down, pouring reassurance through his connection to them all.

"You really are trying to get me killed, aren't you?"

"Killed?" Arhk's eyes narrowed. "Did Seylin threaten your life?"

"Yes. She threatened to have me executed, and she directed Aleren to keep me and my unit on the most active fronts until I either die in battle or she comes up with something else to do with me. Worse, she tried to send me out here without Niskenya." A flicker of satisfaction swept through Kasiel at the darkening in Arhk's eyes and the rise in pressure around them.

"She should know better than to think I would let her get away with that."

A chill moved through Kasiel then. Would his father really go up against the khevarin for him? While the idea that he might care that much was gratifying, the reality of what such a confrontation could lead to was unsettling. "If you aren't trying to get me killed, what are you doing? You admit to nudging me toward Velara. Why?"

Arhk gazed out into the night, his jaw tensing.

Kasiel drew a deep breath, struggling to keep his temper at bay, and his beasts calm. "Have you ever considered that, if you told me what you're trying to accomplish, I might be willing to help you?"

Arhk glanced at him. "You are young, Kasiel, driven by passion and emotion. You have grown far more since your arrival in Vanris than I ever expected, and I am proud of you, but I am not sure you are ready yet to share my burdens."

Proud.

Kasiel hung on that word for a moment, not wanting to speak and lose the echo of it that lingered in his ears. Arhk was proud of him and admitting it. The latter was almost the more shocking of those things.

"Give me a chance."

Arhk considered him as though taking his measure, the chittering of insects filling in the silence as seconds ticked by. A bat darted through the light of a nearby lantern, taking advantage of the bounty drawn in by the glow. Then the dhomvalen nodded to himself, coming to some decision. His eyes darkened again, another abrupt pulse of pressure sweeping out around them, making sure no one entered the area.

"I have worked closely alongside Seylin for many years," he began. "From the moment we learned you might be alive, a new distance formed between us. A subtle unease that is most pronounced when all three of us are in the same room. When our scouts reported in with rumors about a Vanrian youth in the south, she initially insisted it could not be you, and suggested sending an assassin to resolve the problem, if there even was one. When the majority decided upon a rescue mission, she warned me many times not to get my hopes up, saying that, if it was you, I might not like the young man you had become. Since your return, she has often lamented your humble upbringing to me. Setera is the one who discovered that Seylin was manipulating me. Encouraging me to be disappointed in you using her carefully chosen words and her Enkindler ability."

A foul taste rose in the back of Kasiel's mouth, and his stomach coiled into a knot around his recent meal.

Arhk met his eyes. "You recall the morning after your unit helped save Speaker Therin, when you and Nerith were summoned before the council?"

Kasiel nodded, blocking out the quick surge of remembered hurt and anger at Nerith's betrayal and Seylin's manipulation of him.

"As you may recall, Setera was also there. Seylin brought her in to help verify the accounts of the incident. I asked her to pay attention to Seylin's thoughts and memories while you were in the room, to search for a reason she might want to keep me from growing closer to you. Not the easiest task, with Seylin's attention focused on you, but Setera is a close friend and a very skilled Evoker. She caught a flash of memory in which Seylin was lamenting to someone about how she would never get me to accept the position of dhomvalen while my wife and son were in the way. The potential implications of that did not sit well with me. A few days later, I drew Seylin into a careful conversation about you while my guards, including Evoker Zafyr, were with me to see if I could learn more." He trailed off, eyes narrowing with anger, both current and remembered.

"And?"

"She hastily removed herself from the conversation, but I had caught her unprepared. Ahnvaris Zafyr learned Seylin had your location fed to a southern group that was conducting strike missions across the break to kill mind-crafters. The expectation was that you and your mother would both be killed, which explains why she was so confident you were dead after it happened and insisted searching for you would pointlessly endanger Vanrian troops. She seems to feel that having you in my life now threatens her control of me."

"Which it does." Kasiel swallowed, trying to rid

himself of the sour taste of loathing on the back of his tongue. "Khevarin Seylin arranged for my mother and me to die so she could manipulate you into accepting the role as her dhomvalen?"

"Yes. She needed someone powerful and feared at her side to discourage anyone from attempting to dispute her rule in the early years of the war, when there were many factions that disagreed over how the conflict should be handled."

"What happens now?"

Arhk regarded him thoughtfully. "Why did she not act on her threat, and have you executed for the liberties you took with Velara?"

Kasiel didn't like his choice of phrasing, but this wasn't the time to argue over details. "She wants to avoid a scandal. She also said she still has need of me and that I've gained too much favor among the populace to disappear quietly."

"Yes. And you are my son."

Kasiel nodded. "But that doesn't tell me what we do about this."

A faint, sinister smile curved Arhk's lips. "I would think it was obvious."

"Not to me."

"We take her country from her."

Kasiel reflexively glanced around, all too aware they were speaking treason now. "How?"

"You have done well so far by making heroes of yourself and your unit, and by disrupting her relationship with her heir."

Kasiel felt like someone punched him in the stomach. "You did deliberately nudge Khesran Karith toward interfering with the alliance."

"Trying to assassinate his sister was more than I thought the coward capable of. I might have been more circumspect had I known he would go to that extreme,"

Arhk said, making no effort to deny it. "But we are beyond that now. The time has come for you to end this war."

Kasiel scoffed. "Just like that? At least you're not asking for much." He realized when Arhk's expression didn't change that his father was serious. "How am I supposed to end the war?"

"Last year, I threw you and your unit into the fire to see if you would burn. You seized that fire and burned our enemy to the ground with it. When you returned to Etrion, you brought back your tehnaak, our missing mind-crafters, and the man who abducted them."

"We took down the operation of a single man and his hired mercenaries. For this we would have to subdue an entire kingdom."

A spark lit in Arhk's eyes that Kasiel wished he could dismiss as madness. "Look at the other things you have accomplished, Kasiel. You enabled the rescue of the people in Sharith. You earned the respect of the king and queen of Delaphine when you brought down the traitors in Norvask. You terrified an entire Sarketi company into abandoning their mission in the Break. You cannot do this alone, but if Sarket refuses to bend, then you and your unit are our best weapon with which to break them."

Kasiel watched another bat dart in through the light of a lantern, drawing a few deep breaths to calm his nerves. "Assuming I could accomplish this and not die in the process, what would it gain us?"

"Vanris." There was a malicious edge to Arhk's smile. "You should get some rest. You have a heavy burden on your shoulders. How you choose to carry it could change the course of our history." Arhk started walking away. "Goodnight, Kasiel."

Kasiel watched him go. So many questions danced on the tip of his tongue, but going after his father to try dragging the answers out of him now would only increase the risk of them being overheard speaking of things that could get them both executed.

"Goodnight, Father," he murmured, calling on Irith with his ability.

As he waited for the cliff cat to come to him, he made his way to the opposite corner of the garden, closer to where Irith would enter. His head buzzed with barely controlled panic. If he somehow managed to be instrumental in ending the war, what would happen then? How far would Arhk take this? How far was *he* willing to take this?

Seylin had arranged his mother's murder.

"Deep in thought?"

The feminine voice caught him by surprise, though he managed, somehow, not to startle visibly. He glanced over and spotted the female delegate from Fallend sitting on a bench, the light from the nearest torch barely illuminating her features. It was unnerving to see her sitting out there alone. Did she have no concern for her own safety?

"Lady Katerin De Clare, isn't it?" He leaned into the polite, partial bow he had seen Dhomen Nevias and a few others offer the delegates.

She inclined her head. "It is. And you are Ahninveth Kasiel Cavenos, The Warden's Son. Crimson Claw of Vanris."

Conversing in Pandrean Common was still relatively easy, though not as effortless as it used to be. "I hadn't heard that last one yet. Why crimson?"

"For the blood upon your claws, of course, and it does go nicely with the red hair and tattoos. The name seems to be gaining popularity." She regarded him thoughtfully, then gestured to the far end of the stone bench. "You still speak the common tongue with a hint of a native accent," she said as he sat. "To think, the key to our destruction was under our noses in Fallend for twelve years, and we never knew it."

"Isn't it a bit pessimistic to call it your destruction?" He rested a hand on Irith's shoulders when the cat padded out of the darkness and sat beside him. Katerin eyed the animal, her posture stiffening with a hint of unease. "Perhaps this is the beginning of a better future for all of us, especially if Sarket gives up their offensive."

Her laugh had a bitter edge. "The Sarketi people live for war. Before the Vanrians came along, Delaphine and Fallend were constantly defending our borders against their attempts to expand. Fallend lost hundreds of thousands of acres to their advances, a small percentage of which was returned to us as part of the alliance agreement. I wonder how soon they will come to take it back if we agree to ally with Vanris."

"You will gain our support if we become allies. Our company came down here to help protect Delaphine's borders. We're heading to the front the day after tomorrow. We would do the same for Fallend." He scratched behind Irith's ears and the big cat pressed his head into Kasiel's hand, purring loudly.

Katerin's gaze rested on the cat for a moment, her posture relaxing some, then she looked Kasiel over. "You seem a decent young man for a mind-crafter. The princess might fancy you. She has always had a taste for more exotic things."

Kasiel arched a brow at her, boxing up his anger to keep Irith from lashing out in his defense.

"Apologies. For all of that. It was rude." She made a slight swirling motion with her hand as if to encompass "all of that," then took a drink from her mug.

Kasiel sniffed the air, using Irith's more precise sense of smell, and caught a familiar scent. "Vanrian Black Mead. Good choice."

She smirked. "Yes, your people do make a fine mead."

To his surprise, she offered him the mug. "Would you care for a drink?"

A strange offer, but he accepted it and took a swallow before handing it back to her, curious to see if she would still drink from it after a Vanrian mind-crafter had done so. She glanced into the mug, her shoulders rising in a slight shrug, then took another swallow.

"You don't strike me as someone who wants to be part of all this?" Kasiel ventured.

Her smirk showed more of that bitterness. "A mind reader too, are you?" She took another drink and set the mug on the bench between them. "I got into politics at a young age, when I was foolish enough to think I might make a difference. We do have many women in positions of power in Fallend. I suppose we are not so different from Vanris in that respect."

Kasiel took another drink from the mug. "I have lived in both places. Fallend longer than Vanris. I think the most prevalent shared trait between the two is that both have the temerity to believe we're so different."

She tracked his hand with her gaze as he placed the mug back between them, then her eyes met his. "Hm. You are far more interesting than I expected."

He breathed a soft laugh. "I won't let that go to my head."

"Kas?" Jethan walked up, dropping into a quick partial bow when he spotted Katerin in the shadows. "Apologies. I hope I'm not interrupting."

Katerin stood. "Not at all, Lord Jethan. I was about to head in."

Kasiel got to his feet. "Would you like us to escort you?"

She smiled at that. "No, Ahninveth, though I appreciate the offer. I am not quite as helpless as I might seem. Goodnight to you both."

"Lady De Clare?" Kasiel waited until she turned to

look at him. "You could still make a difference."

She glanced at the mug that she had left sitting on the bench. "Perhaps."

"You end up in the most interesting company sometimes," Jethan said once she was out of earshot. "How did the conversation with your father go? Is he going to save us from being married off by my aunt's temper?"

He glanced at his tehnaak. What would it do to Jethan, to their bond, if he told him what his father said Seylin had done? "I don't know about that, but he would like us to end the war."

"Huh." Jethan stood staring after Katerin until she disappeared in the darkness. Then he faced Kasiel. "I guess we'd best start working on some strategies."

Kasiel chuckled and put a hand on Jethan's shoulder. "If only I had your optimism."

efore sunup the next morning, they assembled the unit in Kasiel's room in the manor to put together something of a plan, or at least get one started, while using Irith's exemplary hearing and sense of smell to ensure no eavesdroppers. They all knew now that the dhomvalen had tasked Kasiel with ending the war and, whether or not they thought it was possible, they were on board to help him try. The darker part of what his father told him he hadn't shared, not even with Jethan. Especially not with Jethan. Ending the war was an admirable goal. One that conveniently aligned with the khevarin's purposes. If his father had plans to turn that into a coup, as Kasiel saw it, the less his unit knew about that, the better.

"We need information," Jethan said, taking another bite of the meat-paste-filled pastry he had claimed from the selection on the table.

"They have a substantial library here," Avris said. "I found it when I was snooping around yesterday. Wedro and I can look in there to see if they have any useful books about Sarket. Maybe volumes from before we came to Pandrea. They might resort to old tactics now that they're operating without their strongest ally."

Kasiel wouldn't have thought of either Avris or Wedro as the literary type. His mistake in making surface judgements, perhaps. A flaw he would need to work on if he ever wanted to be the leader they deserved.

"Excellent idea." He turned to Darro, who sat on one corner of the bed, leaning against the bedpost. "You look like you have something to add."

Darro nodded. "While those two are doing that, the rest of us could go out to the campgrounds and see what we can learn about Sarket from the Delaphinian and Fallenese soldiers. Kince and I have the rank and experience to approach some of their officers. We can let you and Jethan handle the dignitaries and General Itana, since she seems partial to you, Kas."

"We need to be delicate." Kasiel scratched Irith's head as he spoke, soothed by the rumble of the cliff cat's purring. "A lot of these soldiers were – or in Fallend's case, still technically are – allies with Sarket. They don't trust us yet. We need to approach them with respect. If we handle this tactfully, we could help sway Fallend in our favor. Do the opposite, however, and we won't end up in anyone's favor." Given that, maybe it was fortuitous that Avris and Wedro were interested in the book research. Neither was known for their diplomatic skills or patience. Meanwhile, Kince, as caustic as he could be, had a talent for earning the respect of his military peers and Darro had a disarming authenticity to him. "I trust you all. If any unit can pull this off, it's this one."

"Don't worry, Kas." A teasing smirk curled Kince's lips. "Anytime your father puts a target on your back, you can rely on us to help make it bigger."

Kasiel chuckled. "Thanks." He stood, Irith getting up with him. "Let's get this done then. We reconvene here at sunset."

Kasiel and Jethan walked out with the others, then wandered around the back with Irith to give the cliff cat a brief run before they went to work. As they strolled along in the early light, Irith pouncing on the occasional unlucky butterfly or industrious insect, Kasiel gave Jethan a surreptitious glance. Could his tehnaak feel the weight of the secret hanging between them? Jethan and his aunt might not be close, but he couldn't imagine a scenario in which accusing her of arranging to have him and his mother murdered was going to go over well. Particularly if he included the part about his father plotting to take the country from her.

Jethan tucked his hands in his pockets, gazing out over the rear pastures full of well-bred horses. "Are you going to tell me the rest?"

Kasiel's chest tightened. He set Irith loose to run the length of a long, empty field. "I can't, Jeth. It's not the right time."

Jethan glanced over, brows pinched. "I'm your tehnaak."

And the khevarin's nephew.

Kasiel looked away, watching the streak of dark blue-gray that was his companion sprinting across the fenced area, ripping up occasional clods of dirt and grass, then flipping around mid-stride to pounce on them as they flew through the air. Under different circumstances, he might have laughed at the kittenish antics of the big predator, but not today.

"I know."

Jethan faced him. "I know. That's all you have to say. It feels like someone slammed a wedge between us last night."

Someone did.

"We'll talk about it. I just need a little time."

"It's something your father said, isn't it?" Jethan pressed.

Kasiel didn't respond.

"Fine. I trust you, tehnaak. Just make sure you talk to me before this wedge becomes a permanent wall, all right?"

"I will." He drew a breath and let it go. "I'm not going to worry about Itana today. She's riding out with us. I think I have an opening with Lady De Clare. If you're willing to speak with Delaphine's dignitaries, I'll see where I can get with Fallend."

Jethan's lips pressed into a tight line. He didn't appear to like that they were changing subjects, but he nodded after a few seconds. "I can handle them. I am quite Charming."

Kasiel gave him a warning look. "Don't get yourself in trouble."

"I'll keep it subtle if I use it at all."

When Irith had run himself out, they headed for the large patio between the back of the manor and the garden. Many of the representatives from the different countries had gathered there, enjoying a relaxed morning meal at several stone tables arranged around the space. Some had finished eating and wandered away from the food to converse or were lingering near a longer table where the serving staff had arranged some fine pastries and a selection of drinks.

Kasiel and Jethan walked toward the back door with Irith padding beside them, his dirty paws leaving prints along the pale stone of the patio. Kasiel spotted Nevias near the drink table. She caught his eye and arched one brow, calling him over with a jerk of her head. Kasiel changed course, suppressing a smile.

"Ahninveth Kasiel, Lord Jethan." Nevias nodded to each of them.

"Dhomen Nevias," they both greeted.

She stepped close to Kasiel and lowered her voice. "Perhaps you could find a way to clean Irith's feet before you take him back into the manor."

Kasiel glanced down, feigning surprise. "Oh. Thank you for pointing that out. I have a feeling our hosts wouldn't appreciate cliff cat prints through the halls."

He looked around as he spoke, spotting Lady Katerin De Clare standing up from one table. Her long hair hung loose over her shoulders and the simple blue dress she wore served to further elongate her thin frame. There was a fragility to her build that, after speaking with her once, struck him as rather deceptive. He offered her a smile that she returned without hesitation. A promising sign.

"You can avail yourself of some pastries – there are more than enough to go around – and perhaps enjoy a walk along the garden paths before you go inside," Nevias suggested.

Kasiel had eaten enough with his unit, though the selection here smelled even better than the ones the servant had brought to his room that morning. "I'm fine, thank you. I'll just take Irith out. Feel free to partake if you want, Jeth."

Jethan smiled and took a step in that direction, his gaze locking on a Delaphinian representative who was approaching the pastry selection. "Now that you mention it, I'd love one. I'll catch up with you in a bit."

As his tehnaak strolled away, Kasiel turned to find Katerin walking up beside Nevias. She took a fine glass goblet of a sweet wine for herself, then met his eyes and picked up a second, offering it to him. "Care to walk with me, Ahninveth Kasiel?"

He was aware of Nevias's suddenly wary regard as he accepted the glass. He gestured to Irith. "We were heading out for a walk anyhow. We would welcome the company."

As they made their way toward one of several paths leading out into the gardens, Kasiel noticed another pair of eyes watching them shrewdly. His father tracked their departure, his expression carefully neutral. Kasiel offered him a nod, raising his glass slightly before turning his attention to Katerin.

"Does your father disapprove of our speaking?" Katerin asked.

"He doesn't care what I do, so long as it supports Vanris and makes him look good." Kasiel matched her private conversational tone and volume, letting his answer suggest a distance between him and his father that would hopefully encourage her to relax with him.

"He seems a shrewd man. Not one who gives off the demeanor of a loving parent, but an excellent negotiator. Now, his son, on the other hand..." He caught her faint smile out of the corner of his eye, inviting him to take the obvious bait.

"What about his son?"

"I understand you led a relatively quiet life in Fernwallow. A vastly different place from that intimidating colossus you call home now, assuming you call Etrion home."

Kasiel smiled at the leading comment. "I do call it home. Have you ever seen Etrion?"

"No." She took a sip of her mead. "I only know it from tales I have heard. A massive military city with towering black walls. I've heard it described as hostile, threatening, and cold."

"It merely looks that way from the outside. Vanris may seem fierce, but its culture is built on a foundation devoted to family and connection between people. My father may not be the warmest man, but I have built up a family of people I care deeply for there. My tehsheyn."

She looked at him, the faint web of lines at the edges of her eyes becoming more pronounced as her brows pinched down. "What did you call it?"

"Tehsheyn. It's like the tehnaak or spirit sibling concept you may be more familiar with. Tehsheyn is a person's spirit family. Not connected by blood, but by something arguably stronger."

Irith bounded after a butterfly, and Kasiel pulled

him back with a quick thought. The cat turned, tail drooping, and peered up at him. Crouching down in front of him, Kasiel took the big predator's face in his hands, their noses almost touching.

"Sorry, my friend, I think you've killed enough innocent insects today."

A flicker of amusement bubbled along their link, providing inadequate warning before the big cat licked him in the face. Kasiel nearly fell back, catching himself on one hand. He laughed and shook his head as Irith bounded up the path, pouncing on a leaf this time. Standing, he wiped away the moisture with the back of his hand.

Next to him, Katerin brought her hand up, politely covering her soft laugh. "You have a knack for making one forget how dangerous you and your beasts are, Ahninveth Kasiel."

He allowed a hint of genuine sorrow to flash across his features. "I don't want to be dangerous, Lady De Clare. I would much prefer a peaceful life where I don't have to watch the people I care about get killed or kill those others care about."

Her expression sobered. "Unless I am mistaken, your glance earlier said you wished to speak with me. Why?"

"The same reason you were willing to do so. Strategy. To learn about our enemies and our friends, and figure out which we are," Kasiel answered, holding her gaze.

"I thought your father was shrewd, but you also have a knack for this." She started walking again. "Ask me your questions, Ahninveth."

The door was open. "You said that Sarket lives for war, but what makes them good at it? What makes them such a formidable military power?"

"Excellent question. Their soldiers are quite disciplined

and well-trained, though, from what I have heard, yours are no less so, but their greatest asset is their alchemy. All the bombs the Pandrean Alliance used in battle, the very things that always gave us a fighting chance against Vanris, were developed by Sarketi alchemists. Delaphine and Fallend have alchemists of our own, but they trained in Sarket, and the ones who trained them have secrets they have never shared with us. When you face them, expect some surprises in that area. Cruel, deadly surprises."

Kasiel watched as she stopped and cupped the bloom of a yellow and peach rose in her slender fingers and leaned over to sniff it. A sad smile graced her lips for a moment, some sorrowful memory, perhaps drawn forth by the scent.

"Surprises like what?"

She straightened and continued walking, her lips pressing into a bitter line for a moment. "When we fought them long ago, they would bury bombs beneath the soil. Some combination of liquids in separate fragile vials that would explode when the weight of a footstep cracked them, causing the substances to mix. An evil the softer ground along parts of the Delaphine-Sarket border will lend itself nicely to. They never taught our alchemists that trick. Sarket was unwilling to trust us enough to give us all their secrets. That is only one. There may well be others."

The mere thought of such a thing sent a chill through him. To have the ground explode beneath you with no enemy in sight.

She gave a solemn nod. "Good. Such an idea should bring you dread. Be wary of disturbed soil if you enter their territory."

"Why tell me this? You haven't agreed to an alliance with us yet, have you?" He set a hand on Irith's shoulders when the big cat returned to his side.

"I like that you want to end this war for the sake of

the people being hurt by it, Ahninveth," she answered, ignoring his second question. "The people of Sarket are not bad, though their culture does encourage aggression in them. I would still spare them suffering if I could. Sarket's leaders, however, are a pompous bunch of self-aggrandizing bastards who cannot be bothered to learn diplomacy. I find King Lodmund particularly distasteful. He is on his fourth wife. Her predecessors and their babes all died in childbirth. Perhaps if he ceased marrying women who are children themselves, he might have the heir he so desperately craves. I cannot imagine why anyone would be disappointed to see him fall from power."

"You speak as if you expect them to lose."

She gave him a piercing look as he was raising his glass to his lips. "You and your beasts alone are worth more than any one company in their army. In fact, if I wished to gain their favor for Fallend, I would find a way to dispatch you here."

Irith's hackles went up, and he snarled in response to the flush of unease that swept through Kasiel as he lowered the glass without taking a drink. The big cat's bright blue eyes glared a warning at Katerin. Kasiel let the cat carry his anxiety, clinging to his calm, confident facade.

Katerin glanced at the cat. "And regret it," she murmured, taking a drink of her mead. She met his eyes.

"As we proved with Delaphine, nothing discourages a country from war faster than a few overwhelming losses," Kasiel said.

"And you are going to show Sarket this, are you?"

"I plan to."

"What if they end up showing you?"

A flash of sorrow cut into him like a blade through his chest. "I know how to lose, Lady De Clare. I have lost plenty. But what I'm best at is winning when I shouldn't have a chance. I'm done losing."

She smiled at him, though, unexpectedly, tears shone in the corners of her eyes. "Perhaps you are."

*

When the unit gathered in his rooms again that evening, it was with reports of varied success. Jethan had obtained considerable information about current battles between Delaphine and Sarket, as well as some history of their conflicts prior to the arrival of the Vanrians. Kasiel didn't ask if he used his Charmer ability, though he had a feeling it had come into play. Conversations with Delaphinian soldiers and officers resulted in a collection of relevant details about tactics and counter strategies now that they were counting on Vanris for support. Fallend's troops had been less forthcoming. Not a surprise given that their leadership hadn't yet decided on whether to forge an alliance with Vanris.

Wedro and Avris found more history around the prior conflicts between Delaphine and Sarket, including mention of the buried bombs Katerin had told him about. With their departure looming, Jethan and Kasiel skipped the formal dinner that night. They called instead for a meal for the unit to be delivered to his room where they began compiling lists of Sarket's strengths and weaknesses, their favored strategies historically compared to more recent battles, details of the country at the border and beyond. Anything that might prove useful went into their pool of knowledge.

The group eventually split up a little after dark, and Kasiel lay on top of his bed for a time, head buzzing with an overload of information. He was finally drifting to sleep when a knock woke him. Getting up, he threw a shirt on, deciding after a moment that the casual pants he had gone to bed in would be good enough for most anyone likely to visit his room at this hour. When he opened the door, he regretted that choice, but it was too late to do much about it.

"Lady De Clare?"

"Apologies if I woke you, Ahninveth Kasiel." She cast a glance at the guards standing outside his door. "There is one more thing I wished to share regarding our earlier conversation, and I was not confident I would get the chance before your departure in the morning."

Kasiel stepped to the side and held out a hand to welcome her in, offering a nod to the guards to set them at ease. "Please, come inside."

Her gaze took in his attire, and she cleared her throat softly before accepting the invitation. As he shut the door, she turned to face him, gesturing him closer with the curling of one finger.

Kasiel walked over, taking comfort from the fact that Irith remained stretched alongside the bed, watching her quietly. If the cat sensed a threat, he would have made it known by now.

When he stopped, Katerin stepped uncomfortably close. "This may be of no use to you, but King Lodmund's queen is not in Andaro. He has her hidden in the stronghold at Cabril, east of the capital."

"Closer to the front?"

"I suppose he may believe his enemies are less likely to look for her right under their own noses."

"How do you know this?"

Her jaw tightened for an instant. "His new queen is a dear friend to my daughter, Hannah. When the girl found out she was pregnant, she asked Hannah to visit her. If I had known what was coming, I would never have allowed her to go. After Delaphine broke from the alliance, King Lodmund refused to let Hannah come home. An effort to ensure that at least one of us would vote against changing sides, I suspect. I am not supposed to know where they are, but my daughter is a clever girl. She started sending me coded letters once she became a political prisoner."

Kasiel met her eyes, feeling the weight of the words she hadn't yet spoken pressing down on him. "Why are you telling me this?"

"Because it is information you could use to your advantage. I do not want them there. Either of them. I do not want them with him, and I think you are their best chance at getting away from Lodmund and surviving this." She pulled a small ring off one pinky and, taking his hand, placed it in his palm and pushed his fingers closed over it. "This was a gift from Hannah and my husband. Something to show her that you have my trust."

He shook his head, opening his hand to reveal the fine silver band with three green stones set upon it. "I can't promise you anything. Cabril isn't a target right now."

"You cannot promise," she paused, searching his face, the shine of desperate hope in her eyes, "but you will try if the opportunity arises. I can see that much in your eyes." Before he could respond, she hurried to the door. "I should go. Be well, Ahninveth Kasiel."

Then she was gone, and he dropped the small token into the pouch that carried Sylaryth's claw.

The blast of a nearby explosion sent a chain of tension through the mixed Vanrian and Delaphinian military company. A plume of smoke rose into the sky from somewhere beyond the ridge they rode alongside. Niskenya was the only creature in the column near Kasiel that didn't startle at the unexpected noise, almost as if she were expecting it. The kanodrak did let out a low, angry growl that made Jethan's horse next to them flinch a second time. Irith, on their other side, took a step closer to the larger predator, the big cat's hackles and tail fluffing up.

Kasiel placed a hand on Niskenya's shoulder, sweeping a sense of reassurance up and down the column of horses and beasts as he did so. His ability ran briefly up against Jhanik's in the minds of half of the tethdraks and some of the mounts. He expected a push back, but the other Feral only glanced over at him and dipped his head in a slight nod of acknowledgement. Whatever the man thought of him on a personal level, they seemed to have come to a place of respect and acceptance when it came to working together for their country.

With that done, Kasiel glanced up the steep ridge to the right of the roadway. He could get a much better view from up there, and the dense trees up top would keep him out of sight of the enemy if he was careful.

Niskenya followed his gaze, peering up at the steep climb. The footing would be risky for a horse, but not so for a kanodrak.

"Hold up." Jethan lifted a hand, stalling Kasiel as he tightened his grip with his legs in anticipation of the climb.

Kasiel looked at his tehnaak, habitually trying to pass along a sense of expectation before remembering that he couldn't do that with people. Was he getting that accustomed to using his ability with the beasts or did Jethan somehow remind him of an animal?

He smothered a grin. "What's wrong?"

Jethan smirked, tossing his head to get a lock of his light brown hair out of his face. "Nothing specific. I could just see that you were about to be up to something, and I wasn't sure if I should try to stop you or merely wish you luck."

Kasiel grinned in response to a push of encouragement from Niskenya and took full control of Jethan's mount, keeping it steady as the kanodrak moved closer. He held a hand out to his tehnaak.

Jethan stared at the hand as if he had never seen such a thing before. "You're not serious?"

Niskenya huffed with impatience.

Without wasting another second, Jethan grabbed the offered hand and Kasiel helped him across to the kanodrak's back behind him. He held on tight as they turned out of the group and Niskenya lunged up the steep hillside, leaving the column. His tehnaak's sudden death grip around his waist was almost enough to pull Kasiel out of the saddle, but he tightened his hold with his hands and legs as Niskenya shifted her weight to help keep them on board. In seconds, they were at the top, looking down over the army passing below, several of their companions watching them with raised brows.

"You can stop trying to split me in half with your

arms now," Kasiel said with a restricted laugh.

Jethan's grip relaxed. "Sorry, I was just trying not to die."

They began weaving through the trees, Kasiel peering ahead for a vantage point that would give them a view of the conflict.

"I think I see why Velara and Nerith were both so taken with you now." Jethan relaxed a little more, letting go to shake the tension out of his arms.

Twisting in the saddle, Kasiel glanced over his shoulder at him. "Are you saying they like me for my kanodrak?" He regretted asking the moment he saw the grin that split Jethan's face.

"Well, Kas, you do give a good ride. I think I'm feeling a little flush." He waved a hand at his face as if fanning himself.

Kasiel rolled his eyes and faced forward. "You're awful."

Assuming an exaggerated feminine voice, Jethan slid his arms back around Kasiel's waist and pulled in against him. "Oh, Kas, it's so far down. I think I just need to snuggle up closer... for safety."

"I will push you off," Kasiel threatened.

Jethan started laughing and Niskenya growled, bouncing up on her hind feet so that he had to grab on tighter. The kanodrak's threat only made him laugh harder.

"She's as sensitive as you are," he gasped around his laughter.

Another explosion, louder from up here, caught their attention and Jethan sobered.

"Come on, you calloch." Kasiel encouraged Niskenya toward the far side of the rise. "We're up here for a reason."

"About that. I'm pretty confident Dhomen Nevias didn't pass back any orders, so why are we up here risking her wrath?"

Kasiel glanced in the direction the head of the column would be with a slight twinge of regret. "I hadn't really thought through that part, but we're up here now. It's a little late to worry about making her mad, isn't it?"

"Oh, don't get me wrong, tehnaak. I don't mind you stepping out of line. Your unpredictable abandonment of protocol is one of my favorite things about you."

"Protocol." Kasiel sighed. Perhaps if he had grown up in Vanris, he wouldn't keep forgetting that there were proper ways to do things when you were part of a larger military force. "We might as well see what we can learn. Maybe she'll be more forgiving if we return with something useful."

"I think it's the unintentional part that makes it so charming."

Kasiel pushed a branch out of the way, barely resisting the urge to let it hit his tehnaak in the face. They continued through the trees until they found an opening on the far side where the ridge ended in an abrupt drop-off. Niskenya stopped, aware of the need to remain unseen. They both dismounted and crept up near the edge, staying low and not venturing outside the cover of the trees and undergrowth. From their vantage, they could see past the deep forest that obscured their view of Delaphine's camps and the area near the tree line to where active combat took place amidst a chorus of shouts, screams, clashing weapons, and occasional explosions. A substantial chunk of Sarket's army gathered atop a rise in the open plains beyond. They had blocked Delaphine from moving out of the forest. Another company was coming up the road behind Sarket's main camp in the distance, presumably to join the effort. It was smaller than the enormous column Kasiel's unit rode with on Delaphine's side, but that offered little comfort given how big Sarket's force already was.

Jethan pointed to the left and right corners in front of the enemy encampment, where the land sloped down toward the active battlefield. Strategically discarded equipment created a haphazard fence that might not be as noticeable from below. A warning for the soldiers inside the camp. From their vantage, it looked like a deliberate border, the dirt beyond it disturbed in many places.

"What do you want to bet they trapped those areas?"

Kasiel nodded. Pooling the information they had compiled before leaving the negotiation site with Vanris's existing knowledge earned fighting Sarket as part of the Pandrean Alliance provided valuable insights. Now it was time to see how useful that would prove to be in an actual confrontation.

"Delaphine will be actively trying to keep them from setting bombs within the tree line where disturbed ground will be harder to spot. That constant vigilance is going to keep the Delaphinian troops feeling harried and chip away at their morale."

A mental nudge from Niskenya warned Kasiel they had company coming. He reached out with his ability and touched immediately on Arkos as Jhanik rode up to join them. The other Feral dismounted and snuck up beside Jethan.

"Dhomen Nevias was hoping you might consider rejoining the column."

Jethan gave him a wry look. "As in, she's waiting with her sword out, ready to cut our legs off so we don't wander out of line again."

"Something like that," Jhanik answered, his gaze moving to the view.

Jethan did the same, contemplating the scene. "Sarket has very few units actively engaging. They look... settled, like they're waiting for something before they make their move," he observed.

"I suspect they're trying to unsettle Delaphine's troops," Jhanik offered, his attention shifting to the enemy camp. "They may also hope to draw them out into the open, where they've had an opportunity to set traps and can pick them off more easily."

Jethan glanced between Kasiel and Jhanik. "How easy would it be for the tethdraks to smell those buried bombs?"

"They..."

"I think..."

Kasiel and Jhanik started speaking at the same time. Their eyes met and Jhanik inclined his head, deferring to Kasiel. Somehow, Niskenya's dominance over Jhanik's kanodrak was gradually translating into a similar hierarchy for them. He wasn't sure if that was how it always worked, but he preferred it to the previous open hostility.

"They should be able to sniff them out with little difficulty." Kasiel paused briefly, waiting until he got a nod of agreement from Jhanik. "Whether they can move through them safely would also depend on how close together the bombs are positioned."

Jhanik clenched his teeth, tension rippling through the sharp lines of his jaw. "We can't send the tethdraks in there. As effective as they are, they'll get slaughtered fighting that many alone."

"True." Kasiel met Jethan's eyes. "We should assume Sarket knows about our company. They would have scouts watching the roads, correct?"

Jethan nodded.

Kasiel gazed out over the field for a few seconds. "I may have an idea, but let's get back down to Dhomen Nevias before I get you both into more trouble."

Jhanik chuckled. "I don't think either of us needs any help in that area," he said, sneaking back from the cliff.

When they returned to the road, the column had stopped. Dhomen Nevias and General Itana sat their mounts at the base of the ridge. A light breeze rippled Nevias's red hair, reminding Kasiel of flames. The scar down the right side of her face, cutting through part of her ke'hanoath, enhanced the severity of her glower as she watched them descend. Itana, in her usual fashion, looked aloof and distantly amused. At the bottom, Kasiel gave Jethan a hand down, so he could return to his horse before he offered the dhomen a partial bow.

"Dhomen Nevias."

"Ahninveth Kasiel, why do you have a Speaker in your unit?"

Kasiel met her eyes, an uncomfortable twisting sensation in his chest that he stubbornly ignored. "For quick communication between officers."

"Is there a reason that you did not have Omren Etris reach out to my Speaker before you went scouting up that ridge?"

"Not a good one, Dhomen." He bowed his head. "I apologize. It won't happen again."

"If only I could believe that." She blew out a heavy breath. "Did you learn anything useful?"

"Yes, Dhomen." He shifted his gaze to General Itana, meeting the perpetual challenge in her dark eyes. "I have an idea, but we need to ask Delaphine to fall back."

Both women considered him in silence for a tense moment, sharing a brief look between them. Then Nevias nodded. "Come. You and your two accomplices will join us in the main tent at the Delaphinian camp. We can discuss your thoughts there."

*

As the sun began setting on the horizon that evening,

Delaphine sounded the call to draw back their troops. Archers from Delaphine and Vanris provided cover fire to help the engaged soldiers escape the field, though the effort still resulted in some fresh injuries. It wasn't unreasonable to expect that Delaphine might pull back and reconsider their approach now that reinforcements had arrived, especially given that the Vanrians brought new alternatives with them in the form of mind-crafters and beasts.

The Vanrian force's arrival would, hopefully, instill fear in the hearts of Sarket's soldiers, knowing what they could be up against now. Pulling back would leave the enemy troops time to contemplate that altered dynamic. They also hoped Sarket would find the temptation to try planting bombs within the edge of the tree line irresistible during the break in fighting. While that would normally be an unwelcome development for their side, the current plan relied upon Sarket's love affair with their alchemical explosives.

Several archers and soldiers stayed out to keep watch along the outer edges of the camp near the current zone of conflict. They had to risk some people to make it convincing. If Sarket found the area entirely abandoned, they would know something was amiss. Jhanik set a line of tethdraks at the edge of the main camp interspersed with Delaphinian soldiers, providing a border that those keeping watch could retreat behind if they got into trouble.

Kasiel moved his beasts out into the trees beyond where they posted the watches, having them lay amidst the denser underbrush under the cover of darkness. A combination of his unit and some Delaphinian soldiers waited a little farther back, ready to move in after the beasts. Every stage of the plan included representation from both sides. Kasiel had insisted on that almost as vehemently as Itana had. If they were going to be an alliance, they needed to work together like one. Once everyone was in position, they waited.

Sarket held back until about an hour after midnight. Then five teams made up of three people each, their dark, hooded attire designed to help them disappear in the night, snuck across the battlefield. They ventured as deep into the trees as they dared and began setting traps, working their way backwards to avoid stepping on their own bombs. They were barely visible even to the tethdraks in the darkness. Without the beasts, they would have gone unnoticed. Each trio consisted of two soldiers acting as lookouts for the third, an alchemist laden with two thick leather bags full of the supplies needed for setting their traps.

After watching them set a couple through the eyes of his tethdraks lying half-buried in forest detritus, Kasiel got the idea of how it worked. They carried the two substances that would explode when combined in separate bags. The alchemist dug a shallow hole and, with extreme care, placed one fragile vial from each bag together in the depression before brushing dirt cautiously back over them. While they worked, Kasiel had his tethdraks taste the air, discovering what danger smelled like so they could better avoid it.

Seated on Niskenya behind Jhanik's line, Kasiel watched and waited, his nerves on fire. People were going to die after he gave the signal. High among the many things he wouldn't miss if this war ended was the horror of deciding when someone else's life would end. No matter where they were from, he didn't want to be the one making that choice for them.

When each team had one or two bombs down, he opened his eyes and gave a quick gesture with two fingers toward the tree line.

Etris answered with an abrupt nod, her gaze turning inward.

Kasiel closed his eyes and put his full attention back to the tethdraks. At his direction, the beasts lunged up from their hiding places and charged in. Sarketi soldiers placed themselves between the alchemists and the beasts. All five of the men setting the bombs turned as if to flee. Then Vanrian Dampeners hit them, stealing their sense of sight to make them blind in the darkness. Three of the alchemists dropped to their knees, choosing to surrender rather than risk stepping on their own bombs while the tethdraks made quick work of the soldiers. One of the other two dropped his bags and tried to run, tripping and falling in the dark.

The fifth did something unexpected. He took the two flasks he was about to bury and slammed them together. The explosion rang out, a bright flash of fire lighting the darkness. Kasiel reeled as the searing blast hit one of his tethdraks and pieces of the bomb pierced the beast's thick hide. Pain flashed through him, the burning sensation excruciating, but he maintained the connection.

Struggling to focus, he set his other beasts to guarding the four alchemists until their side could secure them. Then he nudged Jhanik, who was maintaining an awareness of his tethdraks as a backup, and passed control of them over. With that done, he and Niskenya sprinted down toward the explosion and the injured creature. He was aware of Nerith and Tath galloping after him.

Who else had been near that position?

When they got there, plenty of others were already helping, dealing with the injured and controlling the fire to keep it from spreading into the camp. The substance from the bomb clung to surfaces, making it difficult to extinguish the flames. They found Wedro among the injured, a Delaphinian doctor helping peel burned armor from his left arm and shoulder. He had burns on his neck on that side as well, and some of his hair had burned away.

"You're an unlucky calloch," Tath said, hopping down to help.

"I'm alive," he answered through gritted teeth.

"True." She touched the doctor's arm. "I can handle him if you need to see to others."

"Thank you." The man turned to a wounded Delaphinian soldier being guided over whose face was a blacked mess of burns.

Niskenya followed Kasiel to where the tethdrak was limping into view. Delaphinian soldiers working to control flames that still licked up the sides of some trees shied away from the injured beast. Their Vanrian counterparts glanced at it, then at Niskenya with Kasiel on her back, and continued their efforts. The tethdrak had burns over most of the front of his body and sharp pieces of shrapnel peppering his chest, his thick hide saving him from any life-threatening wounds. One eye appeared scarred by the flame and Kasiel could feel the poor beast's agony as he turned to him with hope and trust, a sensation that reminded him too much of Sylaryth's last moments.

He leapt down from Niskenya and hurried over to the injured creature, placing a careful hand at the back of his neck where the scales were undamaged, then passed calm and comfort into him while nodding back to Nerith. She dismounted and joined him with a pack slung over one shoulder.

Walking up close, she scanned the burns and pieces of shrapnel sticking out of his hide and shook her head. "You poor creature. Let's see what we can do for you."

"Thank you," Kasiel murmured, his free hand sinking to the belt pouch that still held Sylaryth's claw.

The nocturnal effort was the extent of Kasiel's idea. A way to get their hands on some of Sarket's bombs and take away a few of the other side's alchemists to level the field between the two armies. At the very least, facing the threat of Vanrian troops with their mind-crafters and beasts along with the possibility of having their own weapons turned against them could fracture enemy morale. How else those advantages would get used was up to people with considerably more experience. The strategy they came up with was one he wanted no part of, but in which they had assigned him a pivotal role.

Kasiel struggled under the weight of regret. It was an emotion Niskenya didn't share. The kanodrak vibrated with energy, ever confident and eager to protect him by eliminating their foes. He waited astride her back in the shelter of trees lit by the glow of early morning with his unit around him. Because they were requiring him to do so much with other beasts, Nevias made the call to give all twenty of the tethdraks to Jhanik. Kasiel had resisted passing the wounded one over. It didn't seem right to abandon his responsibility to the creature or to force the other Feral to bear that sustained sensation of pain flowing across the link. Jhanik eventually convinced him by arguing that he would have more than enough fresh pain to deal with by the time the morning was through. It was a reality Kasiel dreaded.

The need for rest already sat heavy on his shoulders. He had gotten two hours of broken sleep after their side finished securing the four surviving alchemists, tended to injuries, and put out the fires. Their nocturnal efforts earned them components to assemble a fair number of bombs along with men who had intimate knowledge of how to use them and create more. One of those men had apparently caved quickly under questioning with the help of a Vanrian Evoker and Frightener.

This was a historic military operation in that it was the first time this many mind-crafters had deployed across the southern border to fight, let alone do so in support of another kingdom. As a child, the idea of becoming one of those timeless figures who helped to shape history had struck him as almost romantic. To-day, they would forge history in blood, as he suspected it often was, but this time, it would be at least partially his doing. His plan provided the components for what came next. The potential violent outcome hadn't sunk in when it was merely a concept trying to pull together in his head.

All the horses in Kasiel's unit were under his con-stant influence to keep them from spooking around his beasts. Many of them had grown more comfortable around the predators, making it so he only needed to keep a passive awareness of them in case intervention became necessary. Kince's gelding was one of those that required almost no attention anymore. The animal flicked its ears toward Niskenya with a hint of curiosity as Kince directed it up alongside them.

"Are you doing all right, Ahninveth?" An edge of hostility sharpened his tone.

Kasiel looked over at him, noting the tightness in the man's jaw and the way he stared hard ahead. "Not really."

Kince gave a curt nod. "Good. You should never be all right with helping slaughter people."

A flush of guilt heated his face. He had played a significant role in making this possible. "You think what we're doing is wrong?"

Kince looked at him then, his expression haunted by things Kasiel had no desire to know. "Of course, it's wrong. It's a sound plan. That doesn't make it a moral one. I'm a little surprised you're so deeply involved in it."

"I'm following orders." His throat constricted around the words. Had he disappointed the man? Was that what this was? "Are you upset with me?" he asked, painfully aware of Jethan's tense silence on his other side.

Kince drew a deep breath. "No. I'm not upset with you. Objectively, I'm impressed with how effective your idea was last night. What I'm upset about is our country putting you in the position of having to be part of something like this. You're a good person, Kas. What you do today will weigh on you for the rest of your life."

It would. He didn't doubt that. The same way some of Kince's past experiences still tormented him. Kasiel faced forward, peering out toward the field where General Itana Kedran and a contingent of Delaphinian soldiers lined up just outside the tree line. A formation of Sarketi officers faced them from near the opposite side of the field, a substantial portion of their force arranged behind them, ready and, judging by the constant shifting, eager to end the waiting.

Kasiel glanced around him at his unit – his family – then turned to Kince again. Darro had moved up on the far side of his tehnaak. He met the other man's eyes for a second, recognizing the quiet determination there that reflected his own. In that moment, he realized that everything Darro did was to protect the people he cared about, his tehnaak foremost among them. When they first met, he never suspected that he would someday feel such a strong kinship with the man.

"That's why we have our tehsheyn," Kasiel said. "So we can guide each other back out of the darkness when this is over."

Darro's head dipped in a nod of approval, his expression unchanging.

A tight smile pulled at Kince's lips, and he gave Kasiel an appraising look. "Maybe we will come out of this all right in the end."

The sound of someone shouting across the battlefield drew their attention.

"General Kedran, it has been a while." The speaker was a man at the center of the front enemy line, dressed in gleaming steel armor. His bay horse tossed its head, pulling against the firm grip he had on the reins.

"Not nearly long enough, General Evanson," Itana called back, her mount relaxed despite the tension in the air. A subtle deception they could thank Jhanik for.

Through the eyes of a raptor seated in a tree behind Itana's line, Kasiel could see the Sarketi general's scowl shadowed by the rim of the steel helm he wore, his thick black beard obscuring the expression some. "We know you arrived with a company of those Vanrian mind-fuckers, General Kedran. We saw you riding in yesterday. I assure you, if you do not send my people back across to us right now, I will set that forest on fire, and you'll find that your new Vanrian bedfellows burn just as well as the rest of your soldiers."

Kasiel used the bird's sharp vision to spot riders in the second row with heavy leather bags slung over their shoulders. He turned to Etris, where she waited on his right flank behind Jethan. "Send word to our officers to have their archers watch for six riders in the second row carrying satchels. They'll need to pick them off first if anything goes wrong. They can't let them reach the tree line at any cost."

Etris nodded, turning her focus to sending his warning out to their officers. Kasiel swept his awareness through six more raptors, currently resting on the arms of some of his companions, getting them ready to move. He couldn't let himself think about what he was asking them to do, or rather, what he was being ordered to do with them.

"Your men," Itana was calling back, her deep voice carrying easily across the distance, "invited themselves over to our camp last night. We are providing them with food and rest, as any reasonable host would. Perhaps you should treat them better if you want them to come back next time."

General Evanson's fingers tapped the hilt of the sword he wore at his waist. A heavier axe rested in a harness on his back. His narrowed eyes and tight jaw betrayed anger, but the way he scanned the tree line suggested a wariness of the troops their side had waiting out of sight. He wanted to attack, but he wasn't about to risk his soldiers recklessly.

Kasiel glanced over at Dhomen Nevias through his own eyes, catching a quick gesture she made with one hand.

It was time.

A voice in his head confirmed that seconds before two Enkindlers moved a few steps closer to the forest's edge. Today, they weren't here to bolster their own troops.

As he felt the inspiring overflow of the Enkindlers' abilities, his stomach clenched. He sent the one raptor up, watching the first several ranks of Sarketi troops start shifting more in their saddles. Moving his awareness out, he touched on the enemy horses in those same ranks, delicately encouraging the animals forward. Where his body waited, he heard sounds of allies moving their mounts through the trees, ready to play their part.

The overflow from the Enkindlers grew stronger, a sign that they were ready for a response from the enemy soldiers, encouraging them forward. Kasiel increased his influence on the Sarketi horses in response, giving them a more forceful nudge. Several broke the line, lunging forward. Some of their riders still had the self-control to pull them back. Others relented to the influence of the Enkindlers, drawing weapons and bellowing war cries as their mounts charged.

All it took was a few soldiers breaking the line, and a flood followed, General Evanson's shout for them to halt drowned out by war cries and the pounding of hooves. The Enkindlers and Kasiel had deliberately excluded him and his small group of officers and heralds from their manipulations. Itana and her line backed their horses into the edge of the trees as a stream of the best Vanrian and Delaphinian riders galloped out around them, splitting wide to go up either side of the column Kasiel forced the oncoming Sarketi horses into.

He sent the raptors up, having them collect carefully tied sets of flasks that each handler held out for them in their talons before sending them out over the approaching soldiers. The allied riders, carrying two similar bundles each, directed their mounts with their legs. They lobbed the bombs out into the charging Sarketi force, then turned out to arc and back around toward the forest as their enemies went down in explosions of shrapnel, fire, and blood.

Flashes of unfathomable pain hit Kasiel, the Sarketi horses suffering the same awful fate as their riders. He released the animals that were struck, freeing himself from the ongoing anguish. Sweat broke out over his body as he maintained his connection with the others. He had to keep them moving, even knowing the horrible death that waited for them. Those were his orders. Each one that went down stabbed a blade of sorrow and guilt through his chest, along with another flash of excruciating physical pain. The horses didn't deserve this. He wasn't sure the soldiers did either, but if he backed out now, it could imperil the lives of his allies.

Struggling to focus through blasts of agony, Kasiel had three of his raptors drop their bombs on ranks of foot soldiers toward the back that hadn't been drawn into the charge. The other three flew over Sarket's camp. Two successfully dropped the alchemical explosives on a couple of larger tents. An arrow hit the third, sending it careening away from its mark. The resulting explosion on impact hit part of the camp toward the right flank, where cooks, smiths, and other supporting civilians were going about their tasks. Kasiel's stomach turned, threatening to empty itself.

The Dampeners advanced then, robbing Sarket's soldiers of sight and sound, depriving them of the sensory guidance necessary to escape the burning horror of their own bombs. Screams of wounded and dying men and their horses filled the air along with the stenches of smoke and seared flesh. Some horses fled the chaos with manes or tails burning, forcing Kasiel to stop them so they didn't set other areas on fire.

It felt like an eternity, though only minutes had passed, before a horn rang out in a wavering hollow note, a desperate call for retreat. When the smoke cleared enough, they could see two men standing alongside General Evanson, holding aloft pale blue banners of surrender. The general sat on his mount with his head bowed, both hands clenched around his reins, his shiny armor spattered with the blood of his own men, gore blanketing the field of slaughter around him. Some of the Sarketi soldiers who hadn't joined the charge or taken damage in Kasiel's raptor attacks rushed out to help the injured, focusing on those they could get close to amidst the fire, looking for anyone who had a chance of surviving their injuries. One of the other Sarketi officers near the general dismounted and threw up alongside his horse.

Kasiel released the raptors, slid from Niskenya's back, and also threw up. He wasn't the only one who did so. Every muscle trembled from the bombardment of secondary pain he had endured and the horror of what he had done. The bombs were Sarket's barbaric invention, but their side had used them in tandem with mind-crafters to create a horrifying level of destruction.

Kasiel leaned against Niskenya and closed his eyes, his head pounding with the effort of controlling so many creatures at once, the carnage of the bombs as seen through his raptors' eyes playing back in his mind.

"It's over, Kas." Jethan placed a hand on his shoulder.

They allowed Sarket's surviving men to search the field for survivors while Delaphine and Vanris sent troops across to take control of the other camp. General Evanson and one of his officers were to be escorted around to the main Delaphinian tent. To Kasiel's distress, Nevias called on him and Jethan to join her and Itana there as well. He brought Irith to his side as they followed her.

"I see now how powerful your abilities can be. Why did you not end this war a long time ago?" Itana asked as they stepped through the front opening.

General Harel, one of the Delaphinian officers, waited inside, his curious and wary gaze tracking them as they entered.

Nevias gave Itana a shrewd look, hesitating a moment as if unsure how much to say. She cast a mysterious glance in Kasiel's direction before answering. "Vanris never wanted to conquer the Pandrean Alliance kingdoms. If we could not peacefully interact with you, we hoped you might at least leave us alone. It is not as if you have anything in your kingdoms that we require to live comfortably on our side of the Break. By rebuking you as gently as we could, we kept you poking around the border looking for weaknesses and focused on minimizing our losses in the hope that you would eventually give up your crusade to destroy our mind-crafters. Had we turned you back more violently from the start, it would have made you feel justified in your hatred and encouraged your efforts to get rid of us. Do you see the problem? By unleashing our full capabilities against the Pandrean Alliance, we would have forced ourselves into a position in which we had no choice but to conquer you completely."

Itana responded with a slow nod. Her gaze also drifted in Kasiel's direction for a moment. "Then why now? Why attack Sarket with such ferocity here and allow Delaphine to see what you are capable of?"

"For a long time, we could minimize casualties on both sides merely by using Frighteners and Dampeners to break enemy morale. After the betrayal in Katovan and the successful abductions of our mind-crafters by the professor to make his elixir that emboldened you all, it became clear we would never dissuade the southern kingdoms with our approach. Now that Delaphine is our ally, letting you see what we are capable of while acting in your defense merely encourages you to remain such. Sarket shows no sign of coming around. It appears as if the Pandrean Alliance may have actually helped to restrain their aggression. They have only gotten more determined and brazen with their attacks since Delaphine changed sides. We cannot sit back and allow them to devastate our allies, particularly if we wish to bring Fallend into the fold."

Some soldiers escorted General Evanson in then, along with another of his captains. With his helmet off, his cropped black hair stuck out in disarray. The mixture of disbelief and rage in his eyes looked ready to explode into something, though whether that would be weeping or shouting remained to be seen. Both men had blood spattered on their armor despite not having engaged in combat. A testament to the extreme violence of what had occurred on the field.

Kasiel couldn't help staring at the captain, his hand seeking Irith's head for the comfort of the contact. There was something unnervingly familiar in the dark-haired man's features.

Itana stepped up, regarding the Sarketi officer with a weary resolve. "Now, perhaps, we can finally have a conversation, General Evanson."

Evanson broke over toward rage. "You miserable bitch! Those were good men! Some of them had families—"

"And you don't think our soldiers that you have killed with your bombs up to now were good people with futures and families?" she countered.

His brows pulled down, and he cast an accusing look around at Nevias, Kasiel, and Jethan. "You turned on us. You invited this."

Itana gave a firm shake of her head. "We tried to reason with you, but Sarket refuses to give up its thirst for battle."

"That wasn't a battle," Evanson roared. "It was cold-blooded slaughter!"

The Sarketi captain placed a hand on the general's arm, but the man shook it off.

Itana took a step back, a hint of sorrow weighing down her features. "Yes, Brand, it was a slaughter. Your men did not deserve to die that way. Do you want to know why they had to? Because a full-scale massacre of your troops was the only way to get your attention."

Kasiel felt sick again. The way she spoke the general's first name reminded him that these people knew each other. They had fought together for years. The reality of that caused a twisting sensation in his chest. General Evanson was trembling, his expression crumbling before the devastation of what had happened. His head hung as though suddenly too heavy to hold up. The captain placed a hand on his shoulder, and he let it stay this time.

"I am sorry this is how we meet again, Captain Danovan," Itana said softly to the other man.

The familiarity struck Kasiel like a hammer then. He took a step forward. "Captain Kassian Danovan?"

The man's eyes narrowed at him. "Do I know you?"

Nevias moved up beside him. "Lord Jethan, perhaps you could use your natural Charm to help Itana with the general and his captain."

"Yes, Dhomen Nevias."

"Ahninveth Kasiel, come with me." She started walking around the soldiers guarding General Evanson and Captain Danovan.

When Kasiel moved to follow her, Danovan stepped forward as if to intercept him. One soldier blocked him with her blade. He glared past it at Kasiel. "You're the boy my brother took in and cared for all those years. The one who betrayed him and dragged him off to be executed in Vanris."

Tension rippled through the air. Irith growled.

"Ahninveth Kasiel Cavenos," Kasiel introduced, anger tightening his voice. "You seem a little misguided regarding the role your brother had in my life. I am the boy your brother kidnapped. He killed my mother and had his companions hold me down screaming in the mud while they cut my ears. I'm the one he experimented on and lied to for twelve years. It's a pleasure to finally meet you." He finished with a sneer.

Kasiel turned to follow Nevias out, then stopped and turned back, aware of the dhomen reaching out as if to discourage him. She seemed to think better of it and withdrew her hand. "Ever wonder why, in twelve years, he never introduced us? Well, there's something else you might like to know about your brother. I once asked him how he chose my name. He said he picked it to honor the memory of his late brother, Kassian, who died in the war. It seems he lied about that, too."

The captain stared at him, his mouth hanging slightly open. Kasiel followed Nevias out. All the way to her tent, his body shook with rage, with the anguish of the beasts and men he had helped force to their deaths, with childhood memories broken anew by Edmund's betrayal.

Nevias stopped inside the privacy of her tent and faced him. "I am sorry, Ahninveth. I would not have taken you in there had I known."

"Why *did* you want me in there?" he snapped, yearning for a place to unleash the tempest of emotion.

Irith pressed close to his leg, confusion passing through their link in response to his hostility aimed at a person the cliff cat thought was part of the group.

Nevias's expression softened, though her scar kept an edge of hardness there. "I wanted to get you away from the field and keep an eye on you until we could talk. You might recall that my tehnaak is also a Feral. I understand a little of the nightmare you must have gone through out there. Is there anything I can do to help?"

His legs felt weak. Before they could give out, he walked over and sat down on her cot, dropping his head into his hands. "Never ask me to do something like that again."

Nevias sat next to him and put an arm around his shoulders, her hard military edge melting away. "I can't promise you that, Kasiel, but Adnar cares deeply for you, and so do I. No matter what happens out here, you will always have people who are willing to help you through it."

When Kasiel rejoined his unit, their mood was unusually somber. The typical dark humor that kept them from sinking too deep into the horror of war appeared to elude them this time. What they did have to offer him was something different. Darro met him as he approached their section of the camp – an area made larger than others by the need to accommodate the ten tethdraks under his control again – and put an arm around his shoulders, walking in with him that way in silence. When they were almost at the center, Darro stepped away so Kince and Merrin could each give Kasiel a brief hug. Neither said anything, merely held him for a moment, then moved aside.

Avris embraced him a little longer and popped up on the balls of her feet to place a light kiss on his forehead. Nerith also held him for several seconds, pressing a soft kiss to his cheek before she let go. She gave his hand a quick squeeze as they stepped up next to the fire. Tath, Etris, and Wedro, the latter's hair now trimmed shorter to even it out and his arm slathered with a burn salve, gave him solemn, sympathetic nods. The meaning in all of it felt the same. We care about you. We are in this together.

"You seem to have lost your tehnaak," Wedro observed, a raw edge of pain in his voice.

"He's Charming our new friends."

"Ethically, this entire campaign is horseshit," Tath muttered, poking at a scrape on her arm that she had gotten while helping with injuries during the night.

"Give him a break, Tath. That carnage wasn't part of Kas's idea," Merrin countered. "Besides, it isn't often Jethan gets to use his ability with the approval of his officers."

"Our actions last night certainly enabled that carnage." Tath swept a hand angrily toward the battlefield.

Kasiel sat cross-legged on the ground, the weight of his actions pressing down on him.

Nerith sat beside him and placed a comforting hand on his shoulder.

"We're not just fighting for Vanris now." Darro sat next to Tath and claimed her hand. His tone encouraged understanding. "We're fighting to protect our allies and to end this war. Sarket doesn't want to negotiate. They only want to punish Delaphine for betraying their alliance and us for pulling them away. What we did out there, awful as it was, may have been necessary. Sarket has seen that we can be reasonable. Kasiel showed them that when he drove their company off near our watchtower with no fatalities on either side. Now they know how dangerous we can be when provoked. It's up to them to decide which they prefer."

"I just wish it didn't have to be so violent." Tath rested her head on Darro's shoulder.

"I'm confident no one wishes that more than Kas," Nerith said softly.

Kasiel shifted out from under her hand and got up.

"That's probably true, tehnaak," he heard Tath agreeing as he walked away.

"I know it is," Nerith replied.

None of them followed him. He still felt sick. Not only in his stomach, but in his heart, too. He walked through the trees into the midst of the tethdraks, seeking the injured one. A surge of welcome pushed through the persistent pain of the beast's injuries when he approached it. Kasiel placed a hand on its scaled head where it lay and crouched next to it. The burns were raw, the wounds from the shrapnel stitched where necessary.

"Don't you understand that your pain is my fault? I made this happen to you?"

A bitter chuckle startled him, drawing his attention to Jhanik leaning against a nearby tree, the other Feral so still until that moment that he could have been part of the forest. Kasiel hadn't noticed him there with his focus on the wounded tethdrak.

"Maybe he wishes you understood that he wants to fight for you."

Kasiel straightened, biting back several bitter, impulsive retorts. "What are you doing out here?"

Jhanik glanced around at the reptilian beasts settled among the trees. "I came out to lure them in some snacks and stuck around to seek clarity. Maybe you haven't noticed, but few people get what it's like to be a Feral. To perpetually hold the lives of other intelligent creatures in your hands. To have them trust you unconditionally while you compel them to risk those lives." He met Kasiel's eyes, his chin lifted in that slightly haughty way that seemed to have become an affectation for him. "Until today, I honestly did envy you the strength of your connection to them and your ability to see through their eyes."

"Until today." Kasiel echoed softly. "Did you ever want to be something other than a soldier?"

Jhanik shrugged. "I don't think I'd have much value anywhere else."

Kasiel looked around at the tethdraks now, half of them currently under Jhanik's influence. His gazed stopped on the two kanodraks resting not far apart on one edge of the group. Like him and Jhanik, they seemed to have learned to at least tolerate each other's company. "I suspect you would."

Jhanik chuckled. "I'm not sure I've earned your backing, Cavenos, but I appreciate it."

Kasiel managed to dredge up a crooked grin. "I'm not sure I've earned yours either."

Jhanik's return smile appeared quite genuine. Then he glanced past Kasiel, his eyes focusing on something else. "Looks like you've got company coming. We'll talk another time." He gripped Kasiel's shoulder briefly before he walked away.

Kasiel turned to see Jethan approaching, his steps slowing as he got close to the edge of the tethdraks. Irith had grown attached to most of their unit and was at this moment curled up among them at the camp. Unlike cliff cats, tethdraks tolerated and sometimes even bonded with the Ferals they worked with, but they had little patience for anyone else. Rather than encourage his tehnaak to wander out among them, he gestured for him to wait and walked to him.

"Did I just see you and Jhanik being companionable?" Jethan asked when Kasiel joined him.

Kasiel gave a slow nod. "Well, we are both Ferals."

"True, but one of you is a calloch?"

Kasiel gave him a sideways look. "Dare I ask which one?"

"A little mystery keeps things more interesting," Jethan answered with a grin.

"Ass," Kasiel muttered, rolling his eyes at his tehnaak before he started walking toward the campfire.

"Wait." Jethan caught his arm, his expression sobering. "Are you all right?"

"I've had better days. How did your visit with Sarket's officers go?" he asked, eager to redirect the conversation.

"General Evanson was a hard one to win over, even with my special skills. Captain Danovan barely spoke a word after you left. I think what you said caught him by surprise. Did Edmund really name you for him and tell you he was dead?"

Kasiel nodded. "The bastard lied like it was as normal as breathing."

"I've gotten that impression."

They strode to the campfire in companionable silence. For the time being, it seemed as if Jethan was willing to ignore that Kasiel was keeping something from him. He suspected his tehnaak was trying to avoid adding to his stress under the circumstances. Many people judged Jethan for his royal lineage and his propensity for mischief. They rarely seemed to notice how patient and giving he could be.

A distant, wistful smile touched Jethan's lips then.

"Thinking of Keyla?" Kasiel ventured.

"Is it that obvious?" He made a show of glancing down at the front of his trousers.

Kasiel chuckled and popped him lightly on the arm. "I know you like her for more than that."

"Guilty as charged. Though, I certainly don't mind that part. I'd probably like her just as much if we weren't sleeping together. She's an amazing person. Smart, clever, talented." The fondness in his smile lent sincerity to his words. "Have you been thinking about Vel much?"

Kasiel glanced at his hand with the khevarin's tattoos on the back of it and heaved a sigh. "I've been trying not to. If your aunt has her way, Velara will be engaged, possibly married, by the next time I see her, assuming I ever do."

Jethan's brow crinkled. "Why wouldn't you?"

Kasiel gestured in the vague direction of the blood-soaked battlefield. "Maybe you missed the whole war part."

"Stay positive, Kas." Jethan's tone was firm, almost angry. "You may not believe it, but your attitude has an enormous impact on your chances of surviving a deployment."

"He's right," Kince said, apparently overhearing them as they rejoined the unit. "Believing you'll succeed is as big a part of winning a fight as your skill with a weapon."

Kasiel took a seat near the fire. "You have the ears of an owl."

"You would know," Kince answered with a faint grin.

When they had settled, Merrin's pale gray eyes focused on Jethan. "Learn anything useful?"

Irith stretched out in front of them. The cliff cat placed a paw on Kasiel's knee, his claws pricking the fabric of his trousers, and began grooming it. Jethan accepted a steaming mug of chak, a bitter drink the Delaphinian troops were fond of, from Darro. They were all trying it, though only Wedro appeared to be finding anything to appreciate in it so far, and Kasiel suspected that was more of an act just to be contrary.

"I know we're riding a further south tomorrow morning to go help on a different front and move away from the mess here. General Evanson and the Sarketi alchemists will be our less than enthusiastic traveling partners. We're also taking charge of any injured who aren't fit to ride or march. General Kedran said we could leave them under guard at a military hospital near tomorrow's destination. They're going to allow the rest of those who survived this morning's encounter to depart with Captain Danovan," he cast a brief look at Kasiel as he said the man's name, "tomorrow to deliver another offer of negotiation to Sarket's leadership."

"What are the odds they'll consider it this time?" Avris asked, glaring at her mug.

"I don't know." Darro tossed a sprig of evergreen needles into the fire, watching as they crackled and let off a spray of sparks. "They'll be furious about what happened here, but unless they're complete idiots, they'll also have to recognize what keeping this up could cost them, especially if Fallend comes to our side."

"I worry more about what it will cost us if they don't." Nerith was looking pointedly at Kasiel as she spoke.

The others followed her gaze, worry furrowing their brows and tightening their lips.

He forced a bitter smile. "They won't fall for the same trick twice, right? We're going to have to try a different tactic next time."

Darro's frown wasn't reassuring. "That may not make it any less awful, Kas."

"Maybe not," Jethan returned, "but if we put our heads together, maybe we can come up with a plan to help preserve the sanity of our ahninveth and the rest of us too by the next engagement."

Determined nods around the campfire gave Kasiel a glimmer of hope.

"There might be another way." The intensity in Kince's tone captured their attention. "We could take this farther." He gestured around at them with a twig he had been chewing on. "Our leadership has shown they are willing to break some people, some units even, to accomplish their goals. It's not an unreasonable sacrifice when you consider what the outcome could be. But, because of Kas's abilities, he is becoming one of those people at risk, and us one of those units. We call each other tehsheyn, but if we were truly tehsheyn, we could balance the burden of this stress between us and gain a deeper awareness of one another on the battlefield. Why don't we make it real?"

A profound silence hung over them for a few seconds

until Avris shook her head. "We'd need a Bondmaker."

"What's a Bondmaker?" Kasiel asked.

Tath shifted to face him, leaning into Darro as she did so. "They're like a Heartsmith, in a sense, but where a Heartsmith can read the threads of a person's life to tease out the story of who they are, a Bondmaker can tie the threads of separate individuals' lives together. That's what happens with tehnaak pairings. It can also be done for larger groups to create true tehsheyn, though it's not common."

Darro slid an arm around her shoulders. "There should be a Bondmaker here. They often send them on high-risk campaigns in case someone loses their tehnaak and can't cope. They can essentially cauterize the broken thread to ease the pain, though it makes it more difficult for that person to bond with another tehnaak later, so also not a process that's done often. Regardless, it's unlikely we could do it now. It's something we would have to request formally and get permission for."

Niskenya touched Kasiel's mind as she came up behind him out of the deepening darkness, inviting him in. He accepted, easing in to look out of her eyes. Now he better understood what he could see through her. The strands of violet light she saw connecting the pairings around the fire were the individual life threads that had been tied together by Bondmakers. The weakest of those, unsurprisingly, was that between Nerith and Tath, but their pairing was new. And yet, though no Bondmaker was involved, he and Niskenya also had such a connection.

Her vision altered then, and suddenly he could see different strands of light. Pale gold in color, these threads flickered around each of them, those between tehnaaks, except in Nerith and Tath's case again, tied together. Interestingly, the one between Tath and Darro also made a connection. Some others came close to doing so, as if a natural bond were joining those individuals on its own. One such near union existed between Wedro and Merrin, and another, to his surprise, almost linked him with Nerith.

A wave of confidence and encouragement flooded through him from Niskenya. Kasiel drew back, falling behind his own eyes. The others had fallen quiet, watching him.

"If you want to make our tehsheyn real, it won't take much."

Etris's brows pinched. "What do you mean?"

"Niske can see the threads. She's shown them to me before."

Jethan gave him a sideways glance. "You never told me that."

He met his tehnaak's eyes. "It was Niske's secret. I might not have mentioned it now if she hadn't brought it up."

Kince took a drink from his mug. His face twisted comically in on itself, and he made a small wheezing sound as he set the offending chak aside. After taking a sip of water from a flask Etris offered him to wash out the taste, he glanced around at them. "I say we try it."

"What happens if it works?" Kasiel asked.

"We gain an increased awareness of one another." Kince pointed to each of them with the twig as he spoke. "Our stress, our sorrow, our joy, some of everything becomes balanced out between us a little more. Not to the degree that it does with a tehnaak pairing, but a small part of the weight of what we face out here would spread across the ten of us, taking some pressure off each individual and our pairings. Maybe we could keep our ahninveth sane in the days to come."

"You're making a big assumption," Jethan teased.

Kasiel bumped him firmly with his shoulder, almost spilling his drink.

"Harder next time, please," Jethan said, frowning at the mug. "Making me dump this would be a huge favor."

"I'll see what I can do." Kasiel smirked at his teh-naak, then turned to the others. "If I'm asked to do anything else like what I did today, this could end up working out better for me than for the rest of you."

Wedro leaned in, his visible burns adding a heaviness to the unnerving intensity in his gaze. "Not if it keeps us from losing you."

Did they care about him that much? Kasiel couldn't come up with anything to say in the several seconds of silence that hung between them.

Avris broke the moment. "We still need the approval of our commanding officers."

"Out here, that would be Dhomen Nevias for all of us," Jethan said.

"You needed me." Nevias emerged from the darkness, her gaze locking on Etris for a moment.

They looked at Etris, and the Speaker's cheeks colored. She clasped her hands before her – hands that could wield a heavy axe like a toy – and lowered her gaze.

"Thank you, Etris," Kasiel said, earning a relieved glance from her.

"What is it your unit requires, Ahninveth Kasiel?" Nevias looked them over, searching for what might be amiss.

He glanced around at them, waiting until each nodded before turning his attention to the dhomen. "Do we have a Bondmaker here?"

"Two for this campaign." Her eyes narrowed, her gaze trying to pluck his intentions from his expression. "Why?"

"We would like to make our tehsheyn official, with your approval, of course."

Nevias's lips pressed into a tight line as she glanced

around at each of them, getting the same response he had. She met his eyes again. "No." She held up a hand to stay their protests. "Before you try to argue, I'm not saying no, never. I'm saying no, not this minute. A true tehsheyn could have a substantial impact on how you fight. If you are doing it for the right reasons, it could make your group much more effective in combat. If not, it could be crippling. It is my job to make decisions that will maintain the efficiency and stability of the soldiers under my command."

"Is it?" Wedro's tone was sharp, accusatory.

Nevias's shoulders sank, a deep apology in the look she gave Kasiel then. "And weigh that against the things I must ask them to do for Vanris." Her resolve seemed to waver when she glanced around at them again, her gaze lingering longest on Wedro and Etris. "Over the next few days, I will try to find time to speak with each of you alone. If I am satisfied afterwards, I will grant your request."

"In the interim, perhaps you could try not to destroy our Ahninveth," Nerith snapped, catching even Kasiel by surprise with the sharpness of her tone.

The dhomen inclined her head slightly. "I will try. For all your sakes. If you are serious about this, you will need to make sure there are no potentially damaging secrets between you." Her gaze lingered the longest on Kasiel, as if she suspected there were things he might not have told them, though she couldn't possibly guess at how substantial the secrets he was keeping really were. "It can undermine the bonding process. For now, get some rest."

A serpent coiled in Kasiel's gut as he watched her go. Secrets like the things his father had revealed to him. How and when was he going to share that with them? Could his relationship with them survive what his father had told him?

They sat around the fire for a while, a contemplative mood subduing their conversation. Kasiel couldn't help wondering if any of the others had secrets that troubled them as they considered the step they were talking about taking together. After a time, they began slipping off to their bedrolls.

"Goodnight, Kas."

He looked up at Nerith as she walked past. What did it mean that a near connection still existed between them after everything? Did it mean anything at all? Did he want it to?

"Goodnight, Nerith," he answered.

She paused for a second, her foot hanging mid-step as if she might stop, drawn perhaps by the weight in his tone. Then she gave herself a small shake and resumed walking, leaving him alone with his thoughts.

The minute he lay down and closed his eyes, the day's events started playing back in his head. The pain, the death, the screams of the innocent animals and somewhat less innocent soldiers he had forced to their violent ends. It was a long time before he slept.

evias was true to her word. Throughout the next day, on the journey south, she called various members of Kasiel's unit up to ride with her. By the time they reached their first stop outside the city of Sarlsberg, where they dropped the injured Sarketi soldiers at a large military medical facility, she had spoken with Avris, Merrin, and Tath. He resisted the temptation to listen through their horses, no matter how compelling it was. If he couldn't respect them enough to give them privacy in this, there was no way he could let them commit to becoming true tehsheyn with him.

It was mid-afternoon when they arrived at the next front. Nevias sent Nerith, her most recent interview subject, back to rejoin his unit as they made their final approach. She fell in on the opposite side of him from Jethan, leaving enough space for Irith between them.

"Did you eavesdrop?"

He frowned at her. "No. What kind of calloch would I have to be to eavesdrop on these conversations?"

She arched a brow at him. "Were you tempted?"

"Are you kidding?" Jethan gave him a teasing grin. "He was fighting the urge so hard he was practically having a seizure in the saddle."

Kasiel didn't deny it. "I am human."

A slight smile curved her lips.

At that moment, a silent signal passed through the ranks, and the army rippled to a halt.

Nevias wants you up front.

His smile vanished as he met Etris's eyes and nodded to indicate he had gotten her message before glancing at Jethan. "Nevias requested me. You can stay back here and chat if you like, tehnaak."

Nerith shook her head at the same time Jethan voiced his objection. "No. After the way they asked you to use your ability at the last confrontation, I think it's more important than ever to show a united front."

"I agree," Nerith added. "We can talk at camp."

Kasiel nodded, grateful to have their support.

Darro and Kince moved to the front of the unit as the senior officers under his command when Kasiel and Jethan broke from the line. They loped up the side of the column, Kasiel subduing the horses they passed to keep them from panicking at a kanodrak coming up on their flanks. He couldn't do the same for the many Delaphinian soldiers who attempted to shift away despite the lack of response from their mounts.

When they reached the front, Nevias watched him approach like a small child might watch some insect they were considering pulling the legs off just to see how many it could still stumble around without. A few other officers from both sides were also there, including Itana, her perpetually ominous grin more welcoming than Nevias's unnerving regard.

"Dhomen Nevias," Kasiel inclined his head, noting the hard edge in Jethan's tone when he greeted her in turn.

Nevias's brows lifted a fraction at that, but she made no comment. "Ahninveth Kasiel, I would like you to scout ahead and see what the situation is on this front."

He cast his ability out in a wide net before she had even finished speaking, quickly jumping into the mind of a raptor nearby. The bird tried to refuse him for a second, giving him the mental equivalent of a snap of its beak. It was the most resistance he had ever gotten from a bird of any kind, and it made him instantly fond of the creature, as misguided as he realized that reaction probably was.

Being as gentle as he could, he urged the raptor south, following the road until he spotted the large Delaphinian camp with a fierce battle in progress in the rolling fields to the west of it. Weapons clashed amidst shouts of rage and the screams of the wounded. A Sarketi soldier wielding a bladed polearm unlike any he had seen before caught his attention. The man swept his weapon around into the spine of a Delaphinian fighting one of his fellows. The Delaphinian arched back, staggering into his opponent's sword, any chance he had of surviving the first injury negated by the second. As the man with the polearm turned to find his next victim, a Delaphinian mace smashed into the front of his helmet, and he crumpled. That was as much fighting as Kasiel cared to see.

Moving beyond that, he soared over the sizeable Sarketi camp stretched across acres of land. The largest tent toward the center would be the command tent. Farther back from the battlefront were the smiths and other civilians who supported the army. Flying high overhead, Kasiel relayed what he saw to the officers.

"Who has the upper hand?" General Harel asked.

"It doesn't look like either is winning at this point," Kasiel answered.

"If we announce our arrival loudly enough, we might convince Sarket to pull back and regroup," Nevias suggested. "Either way, we should move our archers in to give Delaphine's troops cover and have someone sound the retreat. We need to come up with a strategy now that we can put our mind-crafters into play."

The word play used in such a context put Kasiel's hackles up. He was faintly aware of a reactionary growl from Irith as he circled the enemy camp several times with his borrowed wings, drawing attention to the raptor. He let the bird have enough control to avoid getting hit when two archers aimed up at it, but both men lowered their bows after a moment without loosing the arrows they had nocked.

One of them bolted for the command tent, shouting, "General Thrasser!"

A man in steel armor with several stripes of rank on one shoulder came out and looked up at the bird. Kasiel recognized the general with his chestnut hair and well-trimmed, graying beard. This was the same man whose company he had turned back by harrying them with his beasts all night in the Break.

General Thrasser watched the eagle make its deliberate circuit. Kasiel maintained the blatant surveillance long enough to see fury and a hint of fear growing in the man's expression. Then he sent the raptor diving in to tear off a Sarketi banner that hung by the tent entrance.

"Should I shoot it, General?" one of the archers asked.

General Thrasser held up a hand to stay him. "No." He scowled as the raptor made one last circle with the banner in its talons, shaking his head as he spoke. "Delaphine's reinforcements have arrived, and they have the Havaad-cursed son of The Warden with them."

Kasiel smiled as he turned the bird toward where they waited. "I have a feeling they'll want to pull back and regroup."

"Ahninveth, are you intimidating our enemies again?" An unmistakable edge of fondness crept into Nevias's voice.

"Just a little. Their leader is the general I ran off

near our watchtower."

"Well done, Ahninveth," Itana praised. "Should they choose to pull back, there may be an opportunity to speak with them. If we can arrange that, I have an idea for how we might win this battle before it starts, especially if this man has already been routed by you."

"I like the sound of that," Nevias said.

Kasiel did as well. He raised his arm as the raptor swept in with the torn banner. The surrounding officers startled at the abrupt arrival of the massive bird, but their shocked expressions, at least those of the Delaphinians, changed quickly to awe. It was one of the biggest raptors he had worked with yet, its feathers the deep blue-black of a raven's, but with gleaming gold ones sweeping back around its eyes, and along the lower edges of its wings and tail. The creature was magnificent and quite heavy.

"That is a Nightstar Eagle," Itana breathed. "They are very rare. A symbol of great power and fortune in the southern kingdoms. Revered among the followers of Havaad."

"That explains why the archers didn't loose their arrows." Kasiel nodded to the bird. "I suspect he and I may work together again."

He cautiously removed the banner from its talons, earning a smirk and an arched brow from Nevias. With a quick lift of his arm, he helped it launch back into the air, maintaining the link with it. A creature his enemies were reluctant to harm might come in handy in the days ahead.

After watching it fly for a few seconds, he turned and handed the damaged banner to Itana. "What is this idea of yours, General Kedran?"

*

They reached the front a few minutes later, riding up over a hillside north of the Delaphinian camp where Sarket's force would be certain to see their numbers and that they had Vanrian troops and beasts with them. When the horns blared out to announce their arrival, it was only a few minutes before retreat sounded from the opposing side. Sarket had the numbers to fight the Delaphinian force that was already there, but the arriving companies changed the odds, especially given the Vanrian advantages.

Those actively fighting made a chaotic retreat to their separate camps. Kasiel and his unit moved to the off side of the hill, keeping his and Jhanik's tethdraks visible. Itana's plan required his ability, but in a way that might at least allow him to sleep tonight if it worked.

Their force hadn't quite settled before a group rode out from each side to parley upon the abandoned battle-field. Itana was part of that formation once again, and Nevias this time, the two riding to either side of the bound Sarketi General Brand Evanson. Kasiel stayed far back with his unit, observing through the Nightstar Eagle. It was clear by the acting out of their horses before anyone spoke that the sight of the defeated general distressed the officers and men on Sarket's side.

"General Thrasser," Itana called, "before we get distracted by tales of your recent failures, General Evanson would like a chance to tell you how his battle to the north of here went." Itana turned to the man next to her. "Go ahead, General, share your story."

General Evanson stared at his bound hands, his shoulders starting to shake. "They got some of our bombs in the night. Their Feral abominations took control of our horses and... There was blood." He looked at his hands as if they had that blood upon them. "I've never seen so much blood."

Disgust crawled through Kasiel when the general

started sobbing. The man had broken, but it wasn't him that inspired the disgust, it was what they had done to break him. What he had helped them do that left this man stripped of his dignity and spirit.

In the center of the opposing lineup, General Thrasser pulled his reins tight when his horse reacted to the tension by lunging forward and rising in a half-rear, fighting his rider. Kasiel quieted the animal and sent it back into the line, a simple undertaking that drained all color from the man's features.

Now.

At the command from Nevias's Speaker, he reached out to the line of cavalry behind the Sarketi officers, convincing the horses to lie down where they stood. Their startled riders had no choice but to dismount or go down with them. As he influenced the animals, he could feel the overflow of an Enkindler's power encouraging the dread growing in the hearts of their enemies. One of the unhorsed cavalrymen turned and ran back toward his camp. A second followed.

General Thrasser said something then, his words not reaching across the distance.

"I am afraid I missed that, General," Itana called.

"We surrender!" Rage and humiliation restored color to his face, making it a bright, furious shade of red.

"A wise decision," Itana answered.

At General Thrasser's command, his troops began disarming. Delaphinian and Vanrian soldiers hurried out to collect weapons and take control of the enemy camp. Kasiel turned away. His job was done, this time without bloodshed, though, somehow, he didn't feel that much better about it. His unit wouldn't be involved in securing the troops. Nevias warned him that every time they used his abilities like this, word would spread, and he would become a greater target. A progression the khevarin would undoubtedly appreciate, though

Nevias seemed determined to keep him out of reach of their enemies as long as possible.

He drew a plump mouse out into the open and set the eagle after it, then looked around at his unit. "We might as well get our camp set up. This will take a while."

He walked away once they settled in to go check on his tethdraks where the beasts lay at the edge of a large grove, resting after feeding on a couple of deer he had lured in for them. Jethan accompanied him. The dark of evening fell around them as his tehnaak absently peeled the bark off a twig he had picked up.

"My aunt can't really mean to kill you off. You're too valuable."

Kasiel bounced quickly through the nearby beasts, ensuring no one was close enough to overhear their conversation before answering. "If the war ends, she won't have any need of me."

"Peace is a fleeting thing. There's always someone looking to ruin it." A satisfied smile curved Jethan's lips as he peeled a thin strip of bark down the full length of the twig without breaking it. "She's too shrewd not to realize that."

"Maybe she'll consider that after her temper's had time to cool."

Just as Kasiel got a hint of irritation from one of the tethdraks ahead of them, Jethan slowed his stride, pointing with the nearly naked twig in the same direction the beast was staring. Through his own eyes and the tethdrak's, Kasiel spotted a young Delaphinian man sitting against one tree, his head in his hands. It seemed rude to bother him, given that he appeared to have come here for privacy, but Kasiel wasn't comfortable leaving anyone alone this close to his beasts.

"Hello?"

The youth lifted his head, his curly dark hair framing

a face damp and puffy from crying. His eyes narrowed when he looked up at them. "This is your fault." His voice was raw with his obvious grief. "You and your fucking mind-fuckers."

Jethan glanced at Kasiel, who shrugged and gestured toward the soldier with a subtle jerk of his head, setting a calming hand on Irith's shoulders.

"I'm sorry, but what's our fault?" Jethan asked, and Kasiel could feel the soothing rolling off him as he moved closer.

"Fucking Vanrians." The youth dropped his head back into his hands before Jethan could make eye contact. Then suddenly he was sobbing. Deep, heartbreaking sobs.

Kasiel held back, watching as Jethan crept in closer and crouched next to him. He reached out, placing a hand on the soldier's arm.

"Don't touch me!" He jerked his arm away, but he looked at Jethan now, glaring into his eyes, tears streaming from his own.

"Tell me," Jethan whispered, that soothing not so powerful now, as if he had decided a more subtle approach might be in order.

"My best friend is..." he paused, swallowing hard. "He's lying on that field. He was engaged to my sister. We used to fight together, drink together. We did everything together. Until you..." His voice cracked, his face twisting with misery as he wiped his sleeve across his unfortunately damp nose. The sobs started again.

"Easy." Jethan sank to his knees and sat back on his heels, catching the soldier's attention again. "Try to just breathe."

Staring into Jethan's eyes, the soldier tried, his breath hitching.

"You can do it."

Kasiel continued to observe, stuck somewhere between

sorrow for the stranger and fascination with his tehnaak. After a few seconds, the soldier's breathing evened out, the sobs coming under control again.

"How did he die?"

"He was from Sarket. The soldier who fought at my side is now my enemy." The way he said those words made it sound like a common phrase, perhaps recently become so. "Of all the stupid luck, we ended up facing each other on the battlefield. One of the other soldiers in my unit ran him through when I hesitated. I caught him as he fell and watched him choke on his own blood." The youth wiped away fresh tears. "If not for..."

Jethan shook his head. "No."

"If not for..." The youth stared at Jethan, unable to finish the thought.

"If not for what?" Jethan prompted gently. "You know why he died."

The young man sniffled, peering into Jethan's eyes now like he might find his friend hidden somewhere within them. "I do?"

Jethan nodded. "This stupid war."

"This war. You're right. This fucking war." The soldier didn't resist when Jethan pulled him into his arms and held him while he cried more.

"This fucking war," Jethan echoed softly.

Kasiel crouched down next to Irith, burying his hands in the cat's fur. "It has to end."

Jethan looked over the young man's shoulder at him. "We're going to end it."

Kasiel nodded firmly. Decisively. "We are." Not because his father told him to. Not to steal Vanris from the khevarin. They would end it because suffering like this was cruel and senseless, and ending the war would protect the people they all cared about.

When the soldier had cried himself out, Jethan helped him to his feet. Kasiel held back still, unsure how the young man would react to Irith and the fact that he was a somewhat notorious mind-crafter. Not that Jethan wasn't a mind-crafter too, but he didn't know if the soldier had realized that yet.

"That's Kasiel. I'm Jethan. What's your name?" Jethan offered a friendly smile, and Kasiel couldn't tell if he was still using his ability or not. If so, he had scaled it back significantly.

"Emil." He looked from Jethan to Kasiel and back again. "You're one too, aren't you? A mind–"

"Crafter." Jethan's expression grew more serious. "I am."

"Can you... Can you make it hurt less?"

Sorrow tempered Jethan's gaze. "I can make you feel better about this moment, but no, none of us can really do that. I'm sorry."

Emil nodded, his gaze moving to Kasiel and Irith again. A hint of fear flickered in his eyes. "You said you're going to end this war. How?"

Kasiel drew in a breath and stood, leaving a hand on the cliff cat's head. "We would prefer to end it through alliances like what we have with your kingdom now, and possibly Fallend. Sarket isn't listening, so we have to find another way to convince them it's in their best interest to do so. That doesn't always have to mean killing. You saw what happened today."

"I did. Just a few hours ago, I might have said it was impossible to bring Sarket around without bloodshed," he paused to wipe lingering moisture from one cheek, "but I'm starting to believe Vanris could do it."

"Only with the right allies," Jethan countered.

Emil faced Jethan. He rubbed at the back of his neck with one hand, looking distinctly uncomfortable. "You know, I came out here planning to join him."

"You were going to—"

"Kill myself. Yes." He picked up a dagger that lay

half hidden in the dry grass, also grabbing the stripped twig that Jethan had dropped when he crouched next to him. "This is his dagger. I took it off him when I left his body on the battlefield. I thought I could use it to find him again." He tucked the dagger in his belt and twirled the naked twig in his fingers. "I suspect we're all the same when you look beneath the surface." His dark-eyed gaze moved to Kasiel again. "Why? Why do you want so badly to end this?"

"Because we've also lost people we cared about. We want to stop the war for the sake of everyone we can still save." Kasiel hoped Jethan, Niskenya, and the rest of his tehsheyn were among those.

Emil dropped the twig and nodded. "Maybe there's a reason to keep trying then, for now." He turned to Jethan once more, looking him in the eyes with fresh determination. "Could you... just a little?"

Jethan struggled to pull up a smile and placed a hand on Emil's shoulder. The overflow of soothing that poured off him made Kasiel light-headed. "It's going to be all right, my friend. We're going to save so many people now that we're working together."

Emil's sudden smile brightened his features, lighting up his dark eyes. "We are, aren't we?" He gave Jethan a hug before striding off toward his camp.

When he was gone, Kasiel walked over and put an arm around Jethan's shoulders. He couldn't remember a time he had seen his tehnaak look this heartsick. Hugging him close, he said, "You did good, tehnaak."

Another, smaller Vanrian force arrived in the morning, led by Dhomen Aleren. She didn't look pleased when Dhomen Nevias called Kasiel into the command tent along with the higher officers. A state that appeared to worsen when they stood around a planning table brought in on one of the supply wagons and Nevias praised him for his critical contributions to the last two encounters. Nevias, for her part, looked increasingly confused by the woman's response until she finally dismissed the other officers from the tent, keeping only Kasiel and Aleren there.

"What is going on here?" Nevias demanded.

Aleren glanced around at the thin tent walls. "How secure are we?"

Nevias turned to Kasiel. "Ahninveth, if you could check the area."

Kasiel had already called the eagle in to perch on a nearby tree. After he had gifted it with several rodents the previous night and that morning, it was already growing to welcome his intrusions. With a quick survey through its eyes, he ensured no one was lingering close to the tent. He held onto that visual connection with the bird.

"We're secure."

Aleren's jaw clenched. She turned on Nevias. "You've

grown quite reliant on Ahninveth Kasiel's ability."

Nevias regarded him with a hint of pride. "He has proven to be one of our greatest assets in breaking the foundation out from under Sarket."

"Of course he has." Aleren scowled at him as if he had offended her with his usefulness.

Kasiel stubbornly held her gaze, the raptor's fierce nature encouraging his defiance as much as Niskenya's did. Irith nudged his leg, the cliff cat an unexpectedly calming counterbalance.

"What is going on?" Nevias demanded again.

"Ahninveth Kasiel is currently out of favor with Khevarin Seylin."

Kasiel almost laughed at that. Such a delicate way to say the khevarin wanted his head on a pike.

"I don't understand." Nevias looked at each of them. "Kasiel has done great things to protect Vanris. He even served as a personal guard for the khevarin's daughter and risked his life to shield her from a would-be assassin, and he..." Her eyes widened. He could almost see her putting the pieces together in her head. She stared at him. "Tell me you did not..."

He lowered his gaze. Somehow, it was different facing Nevias's disapproval. Aleren and even Seylin he could defy with little guilt. Nevias, he respected and cared for too much. She had become, like Adnar, something of an unconventional parental figure, despite being a commanding officer.

"You see my problem. Seylin wants me to put him at risk. To say that she is angry with him is understating the situation. However, as you pointed out, he is one of our greatest assets. I feel like we would be fools to throw that away." Aleren tilted her head to the side, considering him as if he were nothing more than the weapon Seylin had once told him he was.

"Do I have a say in any of this?"

"Not really," Aleren answered too quickly. "Not after what you have done."

He could feel Niskenya growing irritated in response to his roiling emotions. This wasn't the place for an angry kanodrak. Irith started growling and Kasiel silenced him with a thought, trying hard not to get his own hackles up.

Nevias stiffened, seeming to grow taller as she faced the other Dhomen. "I realize she is the khevarin and your tehnaak, Dhomen Aleren, but we both know Seylin is not approaching this rationally. The harm is done, and the two are separated. We have a war to fight, and we need to use every advantage to keep it from getting messier than it already is. We had our show of power, which Ahninveth Kasiel was an essential part of. But it is our ability to turn the tide without bloodshed that is going to keep us our allies. Something he has also proven quite skilled at."

Allies, plural?

Kasiel perked up at that. "Did Fallend join the alliance?"

Aleren's sharp gaze snapped to him. "That information doesn't leave this tent yet."

"Understood, Dhomen Aleren."

"But you are right, Nevias. Reports of the encounter in the Break, where he turned back General Thrasser's force without a fight, played no small part in helping to win Fallend over to our side." She drew a deep breath then and exhaled frustration. "In fact, I'm not sure what you said to her, Ahninveth, but Lady Katerin De Clare seemed quite impressed with you. She openly admitted that your actions and words helped to pull her to our side."

Kasiel struggled not to smile at the surprised look Nevias gave him.

A slight smirk tugged at her lips before she turned

to Aleren. "We are agreed then."

Aleren shifted back. "Are we?"

"Yes. We both recognize that we need to protect our Feral asset and provide him with the resources he requires to help us defeat Sarket. For the good of Vanris," she added, pointedly not looking at him now.

Kasiel did his best to emulate the expressionless look his father had perfected. Jumping between his beasts to check in on them took away enough of his attention to make that easier. The eagle had settled, turning to scanning the area for rodents when Kasiel wasn't compelling him to watch for eavesdroppers. Niskenya had also relaxed, going back to gnawing absently at the leg bone of a large elk she had chased down just before dawn. The tethdraks were restless. It was nearing time to let them hunt if they didn't get to fight soon to keep them from becoming aggressive with each other. Irith's rough tongue licked the side of his hand, the cat losing interest in the proceedings now.

He pulled his attention back when Aleren finally responded.

"We are a long way from Etrion." She tapped the table with her gloved fingers in a manner that reminded him of the khevarin. "Seylin is not here and was perhaps not at her calmest when she wrote that letter to me. I believe she would want us to make the best decision for Vanris. That means you, Ahninveth, and your unit, will be treated as the heroes of Vanris that you are. It also means we will keep you on the front lines as long as we can do so without compromising you to end this war. Your unit is in this for the duration."

Kasiel inclined his head. "We were planning on it."

Aleren narrowed her eyes, searching his face for something. He scrutinized her in return. Did she know what her tehnaak had done to his family? How could she not? Then again, she and Seylin had lived in separate cities for many years. For tehnaak, they didn't seem especially close.

"The dhomvalen didn't come with you?" he asked.

"Dhomvalen Arhk took a small unit north to report back to Etrion. I am uncertain whether he will choose to join us again."

That didn't surprise him much. Arhk had his agendas, and he typically did as he pleased. Had it always been that way, or had Seylin ever had a stronger hold over him?

"You may go, Ahninveth," Nevias said. "See to your unit. If the other officers are still nearby, tell them we are ready to resume planning."

"Dhomen Nevias. Dhomen Aleren." He inclined his head to each of them before heading for the exit.

"Ahninveth," Aleren stopped him before he could step out. "Lady De Clare was very interested in your potential for a political marriage. Perhaps for her daughter or even the youngest daughter of the Fallenese royal family. That should give you something to hope for. You could end up marrying up after all."

A flash of anger swept through him. The eagle launched into the air with a shriek and Irith growled. A deep, rumbling roar sounded across the camp. Aleren's brows lifted. He said nothing, since his beasts had made his feelings clear enough, and stepped out of the tent.

When he got back to the campsite, the others were taking advantage of the break. Darro and Merrin both sat busily sharpening their blades. Nerith and Tath were arguing with Wedro over the proper care of his burns. Avris and Jethan appeared to be teaching Etris some variation of the dice game he often saw Darro and Kince playing, while Kince leaned against a tree, smirking at them and chewing some dried meat.

For a moment, Kasiel stood by a tree at the edge of the area, watching them unnoticed. Niskenya trotted up to the opposite side of the camp, her sudden arrival drawing the attention of his companions. They looked at her first, then followed her gaze across to him. No one spoke for a second. The eagle swooped in and landed on a branch above Kince.

"If that thing shits on me—"

"You'll have had it coming," Darro interrupted. He set his sword aside and started rubbing at the leg he had broken in Coranthis.

"At least it would be sacred bird shit," Avris added with a laugh.

Kasiel grinned and continued into the camp. Irith trotted over to Jethan, head-butting his hand hard enough that he dropped the dice he was holding.

"That roll counts," Avris declared.

"Only if Irith is playing." His tehnaak scratched the huge cat behind the ears. "We heading out, Kas?"

"Not officially yet, but we'll be heading west soon, I expect," Kasiel answered, encouraging the eagle to move to a different tree.

"Why west?" Darro asked.

Kasiel borrowed the eyes and ears of the eagle for a second before answering, ensuring they had adequate privacy. Given that his tethdraks were on one side of them and Jhanik's were on another, not many people were apt to wander close.

He still lowered his voice as a precaution. "I expect we're going to need to keep Sarket's attention on us."

"We got Fa—" Wedro cut himself off at a sharp glance from Kasiel.

They were all looking at him now, seeking confirmation of what Wedro had almost said.

He answered with a subtle nod. "We should take advantage of the time we have to make sure we're ready for the next confrontation. I doubt we'll get to hang back out of the action every time." He crouched down to dig into his pack. This was an excellent opportunity to check the edge on his weapons. The dark metal blades required a particular type of sharpening stone.

"I thought we followed you so we wouldn't have to fight." Avris rolled her dice across the stump they had made into a table. "We just sit back and watch while you do all the work."

"While my beasts do all the work, you mean?" His tone came across blunter than he intended.

"If it only took beasts to do what you do, Kas," Darro said, digging deep into his thigh muscle with the heel of his hand, "then Jhanik would be the one they keep calling into the command tents and sharing privileged information with. He's more exper—"

Whatever else he was going to say got lost when the eagle dove in front of Kasiel. A loud crack made several of them jump and one of its massive wings hit him as it tried unsuccessfully to arrest its momentum to avoid slamming into the ground. In the instant before impact, Kasiel spotted an arrow clamped in its talons.

Merrin, Wedro, and Jethan caught on immediately to what was happening. They sprang to their feet, scanning the forest and grabbing for weapons. Irith and Niskenya were already running into the trees in pursuit of the hidden archer without direction from Kasiel. Merrin and Jethan sprinted after them. Tath grabbed Wedro's arm, holding him back, likely out of concern for his recent injuries. Kasiel dove in behind the eyes of the nearest tethdrak, joining the pursuit in his own way.

It wasn't necessary. Normally, he would have expected Niskenya to catch the assailant, but Irith, being much smaller than the massive Kanodrak, had a slight advantage weaving through the trees. Kasiel felt the surge of satisfying exhilaration as the cliff cat leapt onto the back of the fleeing archer and brought him to the ground. He stopped the tethdrak and dove in behind the cat's eyes, hoping to catch him before it was too late.

He tasted blood, savage satisfaction coursing through him, muscles trembling with a combination of excitement from the brief chase and fury in response to the attack against his bonded companion. Voices reached his ears as Merrin and Jethan jogged up, though he couldn't understand the words. He looked at the two new arrivals, awaiting their appreciation of his kill. The man lay next to him, spine severed by powerful jaws, empty eyes staring.

"Kas?"

He snapped back to himself, disoriented by how completely he had melded into Irith, all but becoming the cliff cat.

Nerith stood with one hand on his shoulder, her brow furrowed. "Your new companion needs you."

He glanced at the eagle standing by the fire, looking more than a little dazed. The bird was easily over two feet tall. Scanning their camp, he noticed Kince was gone now too. With his help, Merrin and Jethan could handle one dead archer for the moment. Niskenya might not allow them to lay hands on one of her kills, but Irith would. The cliff cat had effectively adopted all of them.

He knelt next to the eagle, getting a burst of pain as he expanded his connection to it. The arrow lay broken near the bird's talons, snapped in two by its powerful beak, but that wasn't the only thing that contributed to the cracking sound they all heard. He could see a minor fracture on one side of its beak. Whether the arrow had struck the raptor's beak, or he had cracked it breaking the shaft wasn't clear, but the damage was done.

"Where's Kenna when you need her?" he muttered.

He had spent time with her and Adnar learning how to care for various wounds, but most of that involved kanodraks, tethdraks, and cliff cats, for obvious reasons. They hadn't had time yet to do more training for his less consistent avian companions beyond the impromptu lesson on imping back when he had Kitrix.

"I can help if you promise to keep him from biting a finger off," Nerith said, starting to turn away. "I just need to grab a few things."

"What do you know about birds?" He winced when he realized how insulting the question sounded.

I'm calling Dhomen Nevias over. Someone just tried to kill you.

He nodded to Etris, and a shudder swept through him. The tethdraks were restless, their clicks and some screeches sounding across the camp. He tried to calm them, but he was far too keyed up to be effective.

He looked at Etris again. "Can you reach out to Jhanik's Speaker and ask him to take the tethdraks for a few minutes?"

"No need." Jhanik came up behind them then, his tehnaak and tethdrak flanking on either side of him. "Pass them over. I'll calm them. What happened?"

"Thank you." Kasiel felt the nudge of the other Feral's presence in the beast's minds and gave him control, ignoring his question.

He heard Etris telling Jhanik that someone had tried to kill him while he reached out to Niskenya. The kanodrak was prowling the wooded area the archer had shot from, searching for additional threats. With the tethdraks on two sides, most other units had set up campsites a little away from theirs. It still surprised him that someone had snuck in that close. Then again, they didn't know yet if the individual was from Sarket. The soldier could have easily been part of the Delaphinian force given how new and fragile that alliance was.

He switched to Irith and saw Merrin and Jethan carrying the body back. Kince wasn't with them. The person dangling between the two was southern. Light of complexion, so not a native of northern Delaphine, though that didn't narrow down the options a great deal. He wore a Delaphinian tabard over his leather armor, but it wouldn't be difficult for a Sarketi soldier to have gotten their hands on one of those.

"Kas?"

He came back. Nerith was there, holding a satchel now. She knelt next to him. "If you care to know, I asked Kenna to teach me some things about working with beasts. It seemed like a reasonable request since my ahninveth is a Feral."

"You did?" He glanced over, stumbling into her captivating lavender eyes. "Thank you. I'm sorry for—"

"It's fine. Someone just tried to kill you. You're allowed to be a little rude."

Jhanik came around and crouched on the other side of the massive bird. "I've got a bit of experience with raptors too, if you don't object to my help."

Kasiel met his eyes. He couldn't keep from wondering if the other Feral was merely trying to earn favor with Nerith, but then, even if he was, it wasn't Kasiel's place to object to that anymore. Right now, he needed to prioritize the eagle either way. It had saved his life.

He forced a nod. "Thank you."

Nevias jogged up then with a group of soldiers in her wake. She stopped a few feet back, her sharp eyes homing in on the broken arrow. She split the soldiers up using a couple of quick gestures. "Search the area. Watch out for the tethdraks."

"I'll keep them calm," Jhanik said, inspecting the injured beak while Kasiel kept the raptor from lashing out.

Nerith caught his attention with a touch on his arm. "Go talk to Dhomen Nevias, Kas. Three sets of hands are too many here. Just keep your eagle relaxed until I can get some sedative into him."

Reluctantly, he nodded and left the bird to them,

standing to face Nevias. "Someone took a shot at me. The eagle intercepted the arrow, and Irith took down the archer. Unfortunately, he killed him before I could stop him, so we won't be asking him questions, but Merrin and..." He trailed off, gesturing to Merrin and Jethan as they arrived with their burden.

"Let's see what we've got." Nevias started toward them.

Kasiel could feel the raptor fading. He glanced down at Nerith, and she nodded.

"He'll be out in a few seconds. Go with her."

He nodded and followed Nevias to where they were setting down the body. Aleren, Itana, and Harel joined them there.

"Havaad have mercy," Harel muttered.

Nevias narrowed her eyes at him. "You know this man?"

"His brother is one of my most promising young officers. This will not go over well."

Kasiel placed a hand on Irith's head when the cat trotted up next to him, drawing comfort from the beast. Things always had to be complicated.

Itana nudged the body indelicately with the toe of one boot. "We will need to question his brother and anyone close to him to see if they share his feelings about our allies."

"I would like at least one of our Evokers involved," Aleren stated.

Harel's gaze shifted to Kasiel, a flicker of apprehension in his eyes. "Allowing a mind-crafter to interrogate our soldiers could increase tensions."

"And this doesn't? This man tried to kill one of our top mind-crafters, General. The dhomvalen's son, no less." Aleren gestured to Kasiel as if there were any doubt about who they were discussing. "We will be involved."

"It will send the wrong message if we do not work together on this," Nevias added.

Itana nodded. "She is right. We will not solve these problems by dividing ourselves. Our methods may be different, but they are all valid and should be used in combination to demonstrate our commitment to this alliance."

Niskenya emerged from the trees and all the officers except Nevias retreated a step or two when she walked up behind Kasiel. He turned and reached back with his free hand to let her press her head against his palm. In that brief contact, he received a surge of protective affection.

Harel was staring at him when he faced them again, his weight on his rear foot as if prepared to retreat even farther from them. "How did you escape unharmed? This boy had impeccable aim."

Kasiel drew more deeply on the presence of his companions, not allowing himself to get irritated with the fact that the man had called a soldier who was probably a few years older than him a boy. "My eagle caught the arrow, General."

Harel glanced past them to where Nerith and Jhanik were tending the now sedated bird. He shook his head. "It's... uncanny."

Kasiel got the sense the man had almost said something less tactful, a feeling supported by Nevias's scowl and the slight narrowing of Aleren's eyes.

"We should address this now," Itana said. "We have some time here before we need to move on. Bring your Evokers, General Aleren." She met Kasiel's eyes, gesturing to Merrin and Jethan. "If we might borrow your soldiers for a few minutes to move the body to a more appropriate place, Ahninveth."

He glanced at his two companions, waiting until they each offered a nod of agreement. "Certainly."

"Thank you, Ahninveth Kasiel." Itana bowed her head, not waiting for his response or that of the others before she turned and started walking, gesturing for Merrin and Jethan to follow. Harel left with her, stepping quickly to keep up with Itana's long strides.

Nevias met Aleren's eyes. For a second, neither woman moved, then Aleren nodded and followed the other two officers away.

Nevias turned to Kasiel. "We need to work on your security, Ahninveth. It is obvious we are not the only ones who have noticed your value to us."

He had trouble believing that could come as much of a surprise at this point. "We can be more strategic in placing the tethdraks around my unit going forward."

"I was actually thinking of assigning a set of guards and moving you into one of the central tents," Nevias countered.

Niskenya growled, nudging his shoulder with her nose.

He patted the tethdrak's neck. "No. I stay with my unit. My beasts, positioned correctly, will detect danger long before any human guard."

Her lips pressed into a tight line. She glanced after the departing officers. "We will discuss this more later. For now, make certain your beasts are so arranged and do not wander."

"Yes, Dhomen."

When she struck out after the others, he returned to Nerith and Jhanik. Kince was back as well, talking with his tehnaak. He glanced at Kasiel and shook his head. He had found no other signs of danger. Niskenya lay down nearby, her head raised, her intense gaze sweeping the perimeter of the camp in her self-assigned guard duties.

Jhanik looked up at him, holding the raptor's head still while Nerith finished working on the damaged beak.

"I've never seen a wild creature bond with someone so fast. I've said it before, and I stand by it now. You're something else, Cavenos."

Cavenos. The Warden's Son. Crimson Claw of Vanris. He glanced toward the nearest Delaphinian campsite. In Vanris, he was a hero. In Delaphine, they feared him. To be fair, not much more than a year ago, he might have also feared someone like himself. What mind-crafters could do was disturbing to an individual raised in the absence of such things. With him, those abilities manifested in a way that was a lot more visible.

He crouched next to Nerith. "How does it look?"

"It's not that bad, but you might need to help him eat for several days to keep him from causing himself too much pain or damaging it more."

"Looks like you've got another permanent companion," Jhanik added.

He met the other Feral's eyes. "Mind if I take my tethdraks back?"

"All yours."

When he moved into the heads of the beasts, Jhanik immediately relinquished control. As Nerith finished, the other Feral stood, and Kasiel got up with him.

"I'll help set up a perimeter with my tethdraks."

"Thank you." Kasiel held his hand out. "I mean it."

"We're in this together," Jhanik responded with a tight smile and took his arm in a warrior's grip. "I may not love admitting that we need you as much as we do, but I can see the truth in it. You're the best Feral I've ever seen. You have the support of me and my unit any time you need it." He let go and walked away, his tehnaak and tethdrak flanking him.

"I'm impressed." Nerith stood once she had the raptor settled to recover from its sedation. "You two almost acted like adults."

He gave her a sideways glance, catching the reservation

in her slight smile. "Almost?"

"Why don't I hunt you down some mead? I imagine your nerves could use settling."

Glancing past her, he spotted Merrin and Jethan walking back. "I'd rather just have my unit around me right now." He began moving his tethdraks into position to guard their camp.

Nerith's smile warmed. "I think we can manage that."

That afternoon, they received the news that they would stay another night there. The investigation into the attempt on Kasiel's life uncovered a mess of conflict waiting to break out. The discovery wasn't particularly surprising, but they had to deal with it as best they could now that it was out in the open. Nevias advised them to be ready to march at dawn. No matter how far they did or didn't get with resolving current issues, they needed to move on. While she didn't explain why, Kasiel was confident it was at least partly to keep Sarket's gaze from turning toward Fallend and digging up the truth of their changed allegiances too quickly.

With both Kasiel and Jhanik cycling out tethdraks to keep watch, they opted to combine their camps, and the two units spent the evening getting to know each other better. Somewhat predictably, Etris and Jhanik's Speaker amused themselves for a few hours by holding a private side conversation that no one else was privy to. By the time they finished their evening meal, the two women had a clear friendship blossoming.

Since many of the rest of them had grown up in northern Vanris, in or around Doran, they fell into reminiscing with jovial stories about their childhoods there. Though it wasn't entirely intentional, Kasiel held himself somewhat apart from them all. He hadn't grown up in Vanris, let alone in the northern reaches. He sat watching the two units in silence when sudden tension from one of his tethdraks drew his attention. Jumping behind its eyes, he saw Emil and two other young Delaphinian soldiers, another man and a woman, approaching the edge of the camp. Their ebony skin and dark uniforms made it that much harder to pick them out of the shadows, but he could see that they had come unarmed.

He caught Jethan's attention, gesturing him over with a jerk of his head, and led his tehnaak out through the trees to intercept the new arrivals before they ventured too far into where the tethdraks were guarding. All three looked uneasy when he and Jethan emerged from the dark with Irith at Kasiel's side. Becoming more so when Niskenya joined them.

"I'm s-sorry. I told... I wanted to..." Emil couldn't seem to finish his thought, his gaze locked on the kanodrak.

Niskenya stopped beside Kasiel, and he placed a hand on her shoulder. "She won't hurt you."

"Amazing," the other boy breathed, looking like he was close to either peeing himself or sinking to his knees in worship. Maybe both.

Niskenya huffed, and all three jumped, but the startle apparently knocked Emil's words free.

"I wanted them to meet you. I told them about... running into you last night." A hint of pleading in his eyes begged them not to reveal the exact circumstances of that encounter. "After the attempt on your life, I thought it might be good if more of us could see that you're not so different." His gaze moved to Niskenya again, and he gave an awkward shrug.

"We're not." Jethan offered them a warm smile that Kasiel attempted to emulate. "I'm Jethan. The beast boy is Kasiel."

The other young man chuckled at that, then quickly cleared his throat, his gaze darting to Kasiel as if he feared angering him. "Leif," he introduced.

"Annora." The young woman swallowed hard when her gaze moved to a tethdrak lurking near Kasiel.

"You're welcome to have a drink with us, if you're feeling bold," Jethan said, a hint of friendly challenge in his grin. "We've got a few stoneglass bottles of Vanrian Black Mead we're sharing around."

Annora took a halting step forward. "Oh. I've heard that stuff is very good. Better than anything we make in Delaphine. We'd love to try it." She hesitated, glancing at the other two. "Wouldn't we?"

An opportunity to bridge the gap. They had to start somewhere. Not that Kasiel and Itana hadn't made headway in that area – an unexpected camaraderie if there ever was one – but it wasn't anywhere near enough.

"You would be welcome," Kasiel said, adding his encouragement to his tehnaak's offer.

Emil inclined his head slightly. "Thank you, ah... Ahninveth."

"We're off duty. Kasiel is fine."

Emil smiled. "Thank you, Kasiel."

Niskenya huffed and moved to one side, her posture tense, ready to leap into action, though she left them room to go past. Kasiel led the way with Irith next to him, listening as Jethan chatted behind him, his tehnaak trying to relax their visitors without using his ability. He had a knack for it either way.

The rest of Kasiel's unit welcomed the Delaphinians as he had known they would. Jhanik and a few of his companions were more hesitant, but they relaxed back into bantering and sharing stories again before long. Leif mostly asked questions, eager to hear tales of Vanris. Emil observed more than he spoke, but since Kasiel did the same, he wasn't about to judge the youth for it. Annora and Wedro fell into an odd competition revolving around war injuries, attempting to outdo each other. For as young as she looked, she had a surprising number of battle scars. By the time they split up to get some sleep, the Delaphinian trio was noticeably more relaxed.

Morning came early. Before they could get on the road, a messenger from Sarket arrived. With the assistance of a strategically positioned finch, Kasiel learned that the offer of negotiation with Sarket was being accepted. The allied force was invited to a proposed meeting between the Delaphinian and Vanrian commanding officers and some of Sarket's officers, including newly promoted General Kassian Danovan, at a lord's manor outside the town of Hellaris just over a day's ride to the west. As a gesture of good faith, Vanris and Delaphine allowed a third of General Thrasser's company to leave with the messenger. That they didn't include General Evanson, General Thrasser himself, or the alchemists in that group told Kasiel how limited that faith was.

Their army, though ready to depart, lingered for another couple of hours while they arranged and sent off the group being released, and the officers discussed the recent developments. A sense of unease spread through the camp. Kasiel couldn't feel it himself as clearly as his beasts and the many horses could, but the longer they lingered, ready to move, the stronger it grew, until he almost went to try prodding the officers out of their deliberations himself. Fortunately, that was about the time they came out on their own.

A smaller portion of the army split off to head further south. Based on his eavesdropping, he knew that the company was meeting up with another Delaphinian force to get into position to aid Fallend if Sarket found out about that alliance before they were ready. The rest would travel west to Hellaris. As the column pulled together, Nevias's Speaker called on Kasiel and Jhanik to bring their units up in front of the center, tethdraks and all, and form a buffer around Kasiel. The dhomen didn't want him near either end or the outer edges where he might provide an easier target. The arrangement reminded him uncomfortably of his first journey to Vanris, when Jethan and the others placed his life above theirs for the sake of the mission. This time, he wouldn't argue because he had a chance now to save their lives, but only if he survived long enough to see the war end.

Nevias resumed bringing members of his unit up individually while they rode, not forgetting the request they had made. Kasiel appreciated her even more for that.

He glanced at his tehnaak as they rode down a long road through open fields, the column spilling over the sides. "How's your back with all this riding?"

"It's holding up better than I thought it would. Still aches a lot, but I can handle that. Tath gave me some salve to soothe it. I can't wait until I'm old and all these injuries start haunting me. I can tell stories of our glory days to our kids between bouts of groaning." He twisted his face up in a dramatic grimace and faked an old man's voice. "Oh, my achin' back. Have I ever told you kids how that happened?"

Kasiel chuckled. "Our kids?"

"Well, not yours and mine, obviously, but I figured we'd each find a lady we could hold on to one of these days."

"One of these days?"

Jethan arched a brow at him. "Probably you first, given your riding skills and how good you are at taming beasts."

"I should push you off your horse," Nerith said, coming up on Jethan's other side.

"Present company excluded," he added with a wink.

Kasiel got a flash of growing hunger from the eagle soaring overhead. He reached out, quickly drawing in a small mouse from the field and bringing it all the way in and up one of Niskenya's legs. The kanodrak growled her irritation. With a twisting in his gut, he called down the raptor and put out his arm, then brought the mouse up on his opposite palm. The bird landed, his weight shocking, and snatched the rodent up without hesitation. It was small enough for him to swallow it whole before launching back into the air.

"You might avoid doing that on any first dates," Nerith commented.

Jethan laughed. "I don't know, it could depend on the woman."

Kasiel shook his head at them, though he found a smile curving his lips. If only he could imagine someone other than Velara being that woman. Or Nerith. He glanced over at her, catching her eyes for a moment. She looked away.

*

By the end of the day, they were traveling alongside a broad river. With the warm weather, the fresh, cool water was welcome. When they set up camp in the fields across the road from the river, units took turns wandering over to fill canteens, the officers keeping watch to ensure they didn't use it for cleaning until after everyone had topped off their drinking supplies.

In the morning, they were off with the sun, heading into more rolling hills and fields interspersed with thin forest groves. The road still followed the wide river closely as it raced along. As they continued farther west, the landscape became more rugged, with the river cutting deep into the rocky bank to form a gorge, making it so the water was no longer easily accessible. Mid-afternoon found them nearing a large manor that sat on an island in the center of the river. Their approach brought them up to the north side of the water, where a bridge stretched across the deep gouge the river made in the rock. To the south of the river, also separated from the manor by a bridge, Sarket's force had already set up camp. Farther west on the southern side of the river, the town of Hellaris spread out, the buildings, at least at a distance, appearing well-built and nicely maintained. A small but attractive settlement.

The island that the manor sat upon was too long and narrow to allow either side to bring a substantial number of troops across. Perhaps that was good, though something about it left Kasiel ill at ease. As soon as they got close, a group of four guards local to the town, judging by the unfamiliar livery, rode out to greet them. The army rippled to a stop.

Kasiel eased into the mind of Nevias's mount to watch and listen as the lead rider bent forward in a partial bow. "General Hackett and General Danovan welcome you to Hellaris. We have prepared rooms for Delaphinian Generals Kedran and Harel and Vanrian Dhomens Nevias and Aleren in the manor. Rooms have also been prepared for Generals Thrasser and Evanson should you wish to allow your guests to stay in the manor. We understand that Khevarin Seylin Markanis's nephew and the son of Dhomvalen Arhk Cavenos are in your company. There is room for us to accommodate them in the manor as well, should you wish it. Please let us know if anyone else will need space in the manor during your time here."

General Harel gave an abrupt nod in response. "We appreciate your hospitality. For now, we need only four rooms, along with accommodations for our guards. Once we have spoken with our Sarketi counterparts, we will let you know if more space is required. Thank you."

The man inclined his head, the perfect image of neutral poise. "Of course. We will have to ask that most of your troops set camp here, on the northern side of the river. There isn't enough room on the island for such numbers, and, for the time being, it seems prudent to keep the forces separated by the river. Access to the town must, unfortunately, also be restricted. The bridge to the west of the manor is undergoing repairs. If you need to enter the town for any reason, please inform us and we will arrange an escort."

"Naturally." Aleren spoke this time, the slightest edge in her tone telling Kasiel she disliked either this man or the situation. Likely both. "Might we have an hour to see to our troops and establish camp before we join the Sarketi contingent?"

"That is acceptable. We shall carry your message back and return in one hour to escort you to the manor." He leaned forward in another mounted bow, waiting a few seconds for a nod from one of the Delaphinian generals before leading his small group away.

Once they were out of earshot, Itana spoke, her gaze following their departure. "I do not trust them."

"Do any of us?" Aleren asked, glancing around at the other three officers.

"No," Harel answered. "Hence the reason our prisoners and your precious Feral will not be joining us in the manor."

The sneering way he said precious Feral put Kasiel's hackles up, apparently doing the same to Nevias, judging from the irritation in her tone. "Have a care, General. Ending this war benefits all of us, and the dhomvalen's son has played no small part in getting us this far."

"Apologies, Dhomen Nevias." Harel inclined his head to her. "I do prefer being allied to such a formidable power rather than at its mercy. Still, you can't deny that the boy's ability, like that of his father, is rather unsettling."

"And I have told you before, General Harel," Itana said, "that *young man* is someone I would trust with my life. If that is not enough for you, remember that he earned the favor of our king and queen. Our world is changing quickly. Try to keep up."

Harel cleared his throat. "Of course."

The group split up at that, signaling the army to move off the road and start setting up camp. Kasiel retreated from the horse's mind, grinning to himself.

"What is it?" Jethan asked.

"Itana just told off General Harel on my behalf."

"Do you find it odd that you and the woman who shattered your arm have developed this respectful... friendship, or whatever it is?" Nerith asked, her brow furrowed, as if the situation truly puzzled her.

"Immeasurably odd. Come on, let's get camp set. It sounds like we'll all be staying out here this time."

Jethan frowned. "Really? I was so looking forward to a soft bed."

"Maybe Niskenya will let you curl up with her." Kasiel chuckled when the kanodrak growled.

"I'd say that's a no." Jethan gave the kanodrak a mock pout as they moved off the road, keeping close to the rest of the unit.

"It sounded more like, 'try it and I'll eat you,' to me," Nerith added. "She's got good taste."

"Thanks," Jethan muttered.

Nerith grinned at him. "You know I'm kidding, right?"

He gave her an immediate scoundrel smile, wiggling his eyebrows at her. "Does that mean I can curl up with you?"

"Absolutely not."

That night, Niskenya paced on Kasiel's behalf. Nevias

told him she didn't want him in the manor or anywhere near it. In fact, she expected his unit and Jhanik's to remain as close to the center of the camp as possible with the tethdraks forming a buffer around them to keep threats away. He hated not being in the manor, and it had nothing to do with the food or sleeping arrangements. Out here, he had no idea what was going on inside. He had expected to find a few rodents or something he could at least use to spy. Sarket had the place cleaned out and sealed up better than a steel chest.

Nevias returned after dark to check in on them, and she wasn't alone. She arrived at their section of the camp in the company of General Kassian Danovan, whose eyes darted about, his hands clenched too tightly in front of him. He had two Sarketi soldiers with him, but with hundreds of Vanrian and Delaphinian troops surrounding them, that didn't amount to much protection. Nevias left him standing in the light drizzle at the edge of the buffer of tethdraks. Kasiel set two of the beasts to watching him as she approached.

"What's he doing here?" he growled.

Nevias arched a brow at him.

"Dhomen," he added, making his tone more respectful this time.

"He wants to talk to you. I told him that would only be possible if he came out here and that, even here, it would ultimately be your choice. I'll escort him back if you like."

Kasiel glanced toward the fire and spotted Jethan watching him. His tehnaak pointed to himself and then to Kasiel, his brows raised in question. Kasiel shook his head.

"It's fine. I'll talk to him if he's willing to meet me halfway." They started walking out into the midst of the tethdraks together, stopping partway to where Kassian waited. "How did the first meeting go?"

"Mostly formalities. Some arguing. The rare moment of agreement. Typical start to any negotiation."

"Do you feel like they're willing to compromise?"

Nevias gave him a long look. "This isn't your responsibility, Ahninveth."

"Helping to protect Vanris and her allies is. Sarket's intentions here are very relevant to my responsibilities," he countered as Irith came to sit beside him.

"You make a sound argument. Unfortunately, I don't have a good feeling one way or another yet. Are you ready to speak to him?"

"I suppose."

Nevias nodded, then continued to Kassian. After a few seconds of conversation, the Sarketi general walked out alone to meet him. He was out of his armor, dressed for negotiations. With his formal attire and his hair slightly mussed by the light rain, he looked even more like his brother.

"Ahninveth Kasiel." He bowed his head.

"General Danovan."

"I wished to ask you..." He trailed off, meeting Kasiel's eyes. After a few seconds, he clenched his teeth and shook his head. "Edmund really told you I was dead, didn't he?"

Kasiel nodded.

"I wish I could say that surprises me, but it rather fits him. When he left for Fernwallow, he told me he was going to raise a little boy he had found and work on some experiments. He wouldn't tell anyone what those experiments were. No one but that smith he spent so much time with."

"Garrick." Kasiel offered.

"That's right. Garrick Traven. I was in Andaro when they came there to head off the Vanrian group that had taken you. I helped give chase the night you came through. Edmund told me they had taken you against your will." He stopped there as if expecting Kasiel to fill in some blank for him.

The night Ahrin died. Knowing he was involved in that didn't endear him to Kasiel any. Could it have been his arrow that struck down the healer? "Mercenaries came hunting for me in Fernwallow. After they arrived, I overheard Garrick and Edmund saying they would kill me rather than let them take me, so I ran away. Nothing could have made me go back."

That wasn't entirely true. He had almost turned back for Danica and because he had felt so lost. Kassian didn't need those details. "Maybe he told you he found me, but Garrick and some others helped Edmund make a run into Vanris. They killed my mother and took me from my home. Then they pushed me down in the mud and cut my ears so he could hide what I was. I wasn't quite five years old. He spent the following twelve years experimenting on me. I can't say he didn't treat me well enough growing up, and he taught me some things, but my entire childhood was a lie. He was my only father figure for twelve years, and I don't know if he ever actually cared about me.

"Does that answer your burning questions, or is there something else you wanted to know?" Irith stood, responding to his irritation with a low growl. Kasiel placed a hand on the cat's head.

Kassian's gaze sank to the cat. "Everyone's afraid of you. Did you know that?"

"Unless they plan to harm the people I care about, they don't need to be. I'd rather not hurt anyone."

Kassian's jaw tightened. "What you helped do to our soldiers and their horses—"

"Will haunt me for the rest of my life."

Kassian continued to stare at the cat. "For what it is worth, I am sorry. Regardless of what you are, no child should have to go through what my brother did to you."

"Is that why you wanted to talk to me?"

He finally met Kasiel's eyes again. "As strange as this might sound, I think I was looking for something to make me feel better about the fact that I never liked my brother, and I can't bring myself to mourn him. We may be on opposite sides, but I think we can agree that Edmund was a selfish bastard and leave it at that."

"I think we can."

Kassian ran a hand through his damp hair. "Thank you for your time, Ahninveth."

"You're welcome, General."

Kassian started to turn away, then gestured to the nearest tethdrak. "Is it safe?"

Kasiel inclined his head. "This time."

He could feel the general's spike of anxiety through his close connection to Irith and the tethdraks. When the man turned and hurried to his waiting soldiers, Kasiel smiled and wandered back to join his unit.

The next day found all the beasts restless. Kasiel wasn't sure how much of that was his own disquiet reflecting in them. Or perhaps their unease was influencing him. He genuinely couldn't tell the difference. Nevias and Itana had come out to converse with a few of the other officers first thing in the morning before returning to negotiations with Sarket's generals. Kasiel watched the Sarketi camp across the river. Had it changed since the previous day? Something about the opposing army struck him as in a state of readiness or anticipation. Niskenya prowled the buffer where the tethdraks were, occasionally snapping at the other beasts. The energy he got from her was wary and protective.

It was almost noon when a few Vanrian guards came out to collect half of the Sarketi soldiers they were still holding hostage, including a few of the alchemists and General Thrasser. A large group escorted them across the northern bridge, then stood watch until they had gone around the manor and crossed the southern bridge to Sarket's camp.

"That's a good sign, right?" he asked when Darro came up beside him.

The extra Vanrian soldiers stayed at the manor, positioning themselves along the bridge and the walk to the entrance.

"Possibly. I would guess it means negotiations are going well. Though there is always the chance that Sarket gained the upper hand, and we were strong-armed into giving them up."

"Comforting as always." Jethan walked up beside Irith. The big cat licked his hand, and he breathed a soft laugh. "I like you too, beast."

Ahninveth.

Kasiel turned, spotting Etris walking up. "What is it?"

"Nevias's Speaker says you're wanted at the manor."

"You're sure?" Jethan asked.

"Yes. Just Kasiel."

"Why?" Kasiel asked, not at all surprised when she shrugged.

"I don't know what she wants, but apparently the Sarketi generals are going to their camp to question General Thrasser. While they're away from the manor, Dhomen Aleren would like to speak with you."

"Maybe she's trading you for a peace treaty." Darro shaded his eyes from the bright morning sun with one hand as he peered toward the manor.

Kasiel frowned at him. "You're a bundle of soothing thoughts today, aren't you?"

"It was a joke."

Considering the khevarin wanted him dead, it didn't sound all that far-fetched. That edge of unease that plagued him and his beasts intensified with the thought.

"I'll come with you." Jethan took a step closer, almost as if he meant to be Kasiel's guard.

"No." Defiance lit Jethan's eyes and Kasiel clenched his jaw for a second. His tehnaak was going to argue with him, but there was one way to end the fight before it started. "You will all stay on this side of that bridge, and that *is* an order."

Niskenya, perfectly tuned to his need, came up behind him, and he turned from them, climbing up on her back before they could make him feel any more guilty for pulling rank than he already did. He couldn't shake the sense that something was off this morning, and he didn't want his unit near the heart of things until he figured it out or the feeling went away. He forced Irith to stay with them.

The soldiers who had positioned themselves along the bridge appeared to expect him, offering respectful nods as they stepped aside to let Niskenya lope across, her weight making the sturdy wooden structure tremble. The drop to the river was a good thirty feet. Enough to make looking down from the kanodrak's back a touch unnerving.

When he dismounted and took a step toward the door, Niskenya growled her distress behind him. He turned back, leaning in until she touched her forehead to his. "In and out, my friend. I won't stay a minute longer than necessary. In the meantime, I wouldn't mind if you waited for me on the other side of the bridge."

The kanodrak huffed at him.

"Please."

He stood his ground until she reluctantly turned and strode across the bridge. As soon as she was on the other side, she spun around and sat at the edge, her claws almost touching the wood of the structure. He hoped no one would need to cross before he got back, because she appeared to plan on waiting there. With a fond smile, he turned and strode to the manor. One of the Vanrian guards near the door opened it for him.

"Ahninveth."

"Thank you."

Inside, it wasn't as bright. While his eyes took a second to adjust, Nevias walked up to him. Itana was talking to someone down a hallway to their left.

"What's going on?"

Nevias pressed her lips into a fine line and moved closer to him, speaking in a low voice. "General Harel and Dhomen Aleren feel like we're on the verge of a positive breakthrough. They thought agreeing to the release of some prisoners might nudge things in the right direction."

"You disagree?"

"I can't shake the idea that something is not quite right today. Forgive me if I sound paranoid."

Somehow, having her say that made him feel both better and worse about the situation. "You too?"

She gave him a scrutinizing look. "I do not find it comforting to know you share my anxiety, Ahninveth. You have good instincts."

"My beasts have good instincts." Which reminded him he hadn't fed the eagle in a while. Splitting his attention, he located the raptor and quickly brought it together with a small mouse that was attempting to get into the food stores in one of the supply wagons. He resisted the urge to use the bird to check on his companions.

"I would not give them all the credit." Nevias glanced around the room. "Come, Aleren wanted to speak with you, and she could probably use someone to interrupt whatever argument she and General Harel are having in the next room."

"Do you know why she wanted me here?" he asked, moving to fall into step with her.

"It's something to do with General Danovan, I believe."

One second, Kasiel was listening to Nevias. The next fell deep into Niskenya's mind. Rage and fear sent him reeling. He could taste acrid smoke, feel pain. Strangely muffled shouts rang out around him. Through the kanodrak's eyes, he saw mostly smoke as well. Something jabbed her leg, and she spun, sending a Sarketi soldier flying toward the gorge with the swipe of one paw. An arrow dug into her shoulder, and she roared their fury, charging through the thick smoke at a trio of archers who ran scrambling. She lunged, taking two down under her and tearing at them in a furious frenzy.

Her limbs grew heavy as she turned and leapt at another soldier, an undeniable weariness fogging her mind. Kasiel felt their connection slipping as she staggered. A bold soldier charged in at her with his sword raised. Even fading as she was, she ripped out his chest with a slash of her claws. Then she stumbled, falling to her side. He thought he heard the snarling of another beast as his awareness broke away from her, depositing him back into himself.

Breathing hurt. His throat felt as if some creature had raked claws down the inside of it. Kasiel could hear voices becoming clearer as the ringing in his ears subsided. Cracking open his eyes, he spotted two soldiers moving through the destruction of the hazy room. Thick cloth covered their mouths and noses, and they squinted against the acrid smoke. They weren't allies.

He closed his eyes, trying to stay still and listen. Desperately fighting the urge to cough.

"This one's alive. Looks like a servant," one man said.

"Kill her."

"She's Sarketi."

"General Hackett explicitly stated that no one survived the explosions unless they have value as a prisoner," the other soldier answered, "regardless of where they're from."

"Fine. Let's hurry this up. My fucking eyes are burning, and I don't want to be in here if those bastards find a way across."

He could hear them moving. Trying not to cough was becoming one of the hardest battles he had ever fought. Footsteps approached. How closely were they checking for life? If they were being at all thorough, there were things they were bound to notice when they got to him.

He held his breath.

"Havaad's light, this is the Warden's son."

Rough fingers pressed against his neck. A mind-crafting ability overflow he was less familiar with rolled over him, slightly reducing the sensation of that pressure on his neck. A Dampener trying to hide his pulse. But would it be enough? He had no way of knowing how strongly their ability affected the man checking him for signs of life. If it didn't work, was he still armed?

"Well, is he alive?"

Kasiel thought he could feel his sword hilt against his hip. Bracing, he got ready to grab the weapon.

"No. He's gone."

"Leave him then. We haven't got time to collect bodies."

Kasiel didn't move. His lungs burned with more than the need for air. The soldier took his hand away and stood as someone else entered the room.

"Any more survivors?" the newcomer asked.

"It doesn't look like it, sir. Did we get the kanodrak?"

"It's wounded and down, but they have too many archers and another Feral forcing us out. It's hard to say if we did enough to kill it. A few tethdraks have jumped the gap. We secured the khevarin's tehnaak and one of the Delaphinian generals. That will have to be enough."

"The Warden's son is dead." The man kicked his leg, and he barely held back a grunt.

"Good. That's no insignificant victory. The kano-drak matters less with him out of the picture." A loud crash sounded nearby. "Let's go, before our side blows the other bridge and traps us here."

Three sets of footsteps hurried from the room. Kasiel rolled over and got to his hands and knees, pleased to find that everything worked. Then he threw up, an extremely painful experience with his raw throat. A fit of violent coughing followed.

"Ahninveth."

The faint voice drew his attention to a figure sitting against the wall. As he crawled closer, he noticed the large spike of splintered wood pinning her in place through her abdomen. He sat back on his heels, eyes streaming from the burn of the smoke. Someone groaned nearby.

"You're the Dampener?" Talking hurt. His voice was rasping and raw.

She nodded, her eyes glazed with pain. "Nevias is alive, and two others in the side hall." She paused, grimacing as she pressed her hands around the spike of wood. "Cover... your mouth. This smoke has something in it that... will keep burning your lungs."

He could hear someone else moving in the room. He turned to the side to avoid coughing in her face. When the fit passed, he said, "You saved my life. I'm getting you out of here."

She shook her head. "I'm done." The tears running down her cheeks were from more than just the smoke.

A hand came to rest on his shoulder. "Come, Ahninveth Kasiel." Itana's voice also sounded slightly hoarse. "She is right. You can do nothing for her. Put this over your mouth and nose and come help me free your dhomen."

He glanced up at her. What looked like the sleeve of a shirt covered the lower part of her face. The cloth she was holding out to him had someone's blood on it, but he supposed now wasn't the time to be squeamish. He took it and tied it around his nose and mouth, wishing he had something to protect his eyes as well. When he turned back to the Dampener, she was no longer breathing.

After brushing her eyes shut, he followed Itana to where Nevias lay. She was prone near the door to the next room, fortunate to be a little out of the heavier smoke, but a large beam had collapsed, pinning her ankle and foot beneath it. Judging from her grimace and the sweat beading on her forehead, she was in no small amount of pain.

Kasiel crouched next to her. "We're going to get you out of here, but it might hurt."

Her eyes snapped open, and she grabbed his arm. "Kasiel! Are you all right?"

"I seem to be in one piece," he rasped.

"Come," Itana pressed.

Kasiel joined her and together they shifted the beam off, eliciting an anguished cry from Nevias. Itana didn't waste time. She gestured for him to help her. The dho-men couldn't set weight on the ankle, so they had her put her arms around their shoulders to half carry her out. An explosion shook the building.

"What was that?" Nevias rasped, her voice tight with pain, though not as raw as theirs were.

"They just blew up the southern bridge, I expect." Kasiel leaned slightly forward, catching Itana's eye on Nevias's other side as they made slow progress toward what they hoped was still a viable exit. "The Dampener said there was someone else alive in that hall you were in."

"Only a Sarketi serving woman," Itana answered.

"An innocent woman," Kasiel countered.

"Light of the Seven," she snapped. "You are too soft to be a soldier, Ahninveth. After we get Nevias out, I will go back for her."

"Thank you."

She rolled eyes that were streaming as badly as his from the sting of the smoke. When they emerged, a light breeze was blowing away the haze from the bombs. Niskenya lay amidst a collection of dead Sarketi men. The Vanrian soldiers who had been stationed outside were also dead. The northern bridge, or what remained of it, still burned. Several tethdraks that had managed to leap across were prowling the area outside the manor. They had also destroyed the southern bridge, and Sarket's army was already on the march out of there.

"Kas!" Jethan shouted from the northern side, a sharp note of panic in his voice.

Irith was with him, sprinting back and forth along the edge of the drop. The cliff cat stopped and bunched periodically, as if he meant to try the jump. Kasiel sent him a flash of discouragement while he helped Itana sit Nevias down. The Delaphinian general shook her head at him, turning to stalk back into the building. He was at Niskenya's side before Itana crossed the threshold. The massive beast was breathing but lay unconscious and bleeding from numerous wounds. No visible injuries were severe enough to explain her current state. Had they poisoned her? Sedated her?

He tore away the bloody cloth over his nose and mouth and went to the edge of the gorge. "We need..." A coughing fit doubled him over, his raw throat screaming in protest. Blood spattered the hand he used to cover his mouth. "We need a healer," he finally managed to shout, the effort triggering yet more hacking.

"We've got people working on a rough bridge already, but it's going to take a little time," a Delaphinian captain shouted back.

Kasiel glanced to the south side, half tempted to take control of some tethdraks and send them after the retreating force, but he would be sending them to their deaths. His gaze drifted to Niskenya. How much time did they have? And Nevias was suffering, her ankle literally crushed by the beam that had fallen on it. At the very least, she needed something for pain and to manage the swelling until they could deal with it. Itana staggered out the door, the Sarketi serving woman's arm around her shoulders. Blood ran from a wound on the woman's head, streaking her tousled gray hair.

"Move!"

He spun back around to see Jhanik on Arkos racing toward the gap, Nerith clinging desperately to him with a satchel over her shoulder. Kasiel tried to shout for them to stop, but the first croak he got out set him coughing once more. By the time he had control of it, they were across, and Nerith was scrambling down from the kanodrak's back.

She hurried to him and handed him a flask. "It's just water. Tath is putting together something that should help more. How do you feel?"

"I'll manage," he said, trying to ignore the pounding headache that was rapidly escalating and the returning nausea. Smoke wafted past, making him cough again. He turned away and covered his mouth, wiping the blood on his pants so Nerith wouldn't see it. For the moment, he wanted her to focus on other patients. "I can send the eagle to help carry supplies across if needed."

Nerith winced in response to the rasp in his voice, sympathy bringing a softness to her eyes. "What's our most urgent need?"

"Nevias's ankle was crushed, and Niskenya..." It wasn't the raw throat that made his voice crack this time.

Jhanik moved closer on Arkos. "I'll bring Tath across."

Kasiel shook his head. "You shouldn't risk it."

"Arkos can manage the jump a few more times. You need more than one healer, and we need to search for other survivors. We can't wait for them to get that gorge bridged."

Kasiel nodded. Jhanik was right. They needed any help they could get. The blowing up of the bridges had trapped them. He watched Jhanik and Arkos take another run and leap across the gap. Then he turned to see Nerith examining an arrow she had pulled from Niskenya.

Seeing Nevias still suffering where she sat against a log left him feeling both grateful and conflicted. He walked to Nerith. "Shouldn't..." he doubled over with another coughing fit.

She pointed to a bench off to one side. "Sit."

The serving woman sitting with her knees pulled to her chest alongside the manor was in a similar state, unable to control the violent cough. He sank to the ground where he was standing. Nevias was coughing periodically as well, though she didn't seem as afflicted as he was.

Nerith crouched in front of him, wiping a finger across his lip. She frowned at the smear of red on it. "I already gave Nevias something that should knock her out for a bit. I suspect we'll have to cut the boot to get it off. The sedative should kick in quickly. She insisted I focus my efforts on Niske until then. Not that I didn't want to. As for you, you need to stop talking, drink some more water, and rest for a few minutes while I try to figure out what they used on your kanodrak."

"I—"

She put a finger over his lips. "I didn't say that for my health. Now shut up."

Arkos landed on their side again with a grunt and Nerith stood, a hint of relief in her eyes when Tath slid off the beast's back carrying additional supplies. She looked up at Jhanik. "Can you make one more trip?"

He nodded. "It may have to be the last crossing. That's a big jump, even for a kanodrak."

"I need someone skilled with poisons—"

"Merrin," Kasiel croaked.

"Quiet." She scowled down at him. Turning back to Jhanik, she said, "Merrin, if you can."

Jhanik patted Arkos's shoulder, and they positioned themselves to get a run at the crossing again.

Tath hurried to Nerith. "Where do you need me?"

Nerith sighed, looking down at Kasiel. She rubbed a hand across her brow, leaving a streak of soot behind that she had probably gotten from touching him. "Everywhere. As soon as Nevias is out, we need to get that boot off her. While we wait, I could use help rinsing Niske's wounds. Until we know what they used to knock her out, we should assume it's dangerous."

Itana stepped out of the building, smoke still billowing out the doorway. Kasiel hadn't noticed her going back in. She braced one hand against the wall and stood coughing for a few seconds. When she straightened, he caught her eye and waved her over. Her eyes were redder now, watering again from fresh exposure to the alchemical smoke.

The serving woman walked tentatively up to Tath. "I could... help," she managed in broken Pandrean Common, her voice almost as raw as Kasiel's.

Tath looked up at the woman, her gaze lingering on the blood in her hair, then nodded.

The sedative had done its work on Nevias, so Tath instructed the serving woman on in how best to hold the dhomen in place while she figured out how best to go about cutting the boot off. Jhanik landed with Merrin, who jumped off and immediately started examining the weapons of the dead Sarketi soldiers around Niskenya. Nerith, her brow furrowed with intense focus, moved around Niskenya, removing a few arrows and rinsing the wounds she could get to.

Jhanik started toward the building. "Someone should look for Dhomen Aleren."

"She's gone." Their attention turned to Kasiel, waiting while he coughed a few more times. "They took her." He looked up at Itana. "And General Harel."

"That's going to complicate things." Merrin sniffed at the tip of a spear. Her gaze shifted to the kanodrak. "Rinse those wounds well. Let's hope they didn't get a lot of this into her. At her size, it would take a significant dose to kill her, but we shouldn't take chances. I'm going to need a few ingredients."

"Would they have what you need in the town?" Kasiel rasped.

"Possibly. The rest we might have in our healing supplies, but we can't get to the town right now. We seem to be short a couple of bridges." Merrin swept one arm out to point toward the still burning remains of the southern bridge.

"What if we sent a satchel and a note with..." He paused, taking a drink of water to try fending off more coughing. The headache flared, and he squeezed his eyes shut against the pain.

"Your eagle," Jhanik finished for him. "The nightstar eagle is revered, even worshipped in parts of this region. I think there's a good chance they would fill a request carried by such a creature. There should be something to write with and on in the building."

"Cover your mouth and nose before you go in there," Itana warned, breaking into a fit of coughing as she finished.

Kasiel closed his eyes and tried to reach out to Niskenya. Darkness dragged him in. A muted world of distant, muffled sounds, disorientation, and pain. He wrapped his mental presence around her, soothing and encouraging.

I don't want to do this without you, Niske. Stay with me.

"Is it safe to let him sleep?" he heard Itana asking.

"Let him be until Jhanik gets back," Nerith said softly. "I don't think he's asleep. I think he's with Niske. Her heartbeat just calmed. That might buy us some time."

ear. Pain. Protective rage. Hatred burned
through Kasiel – through Niskenya – driven
to greater heights by the overwhelming need
to keep him safe – to save her. The kanodrak
drew him in deeper, her anguish becoming his
– his pain becoming hers. Each wound from
arrow or spear, and the agony of the poison that sped
through her veins like a thousand tiny blades, cutting
them apart. His throat and lungs, raked raw by the alchemical smoke, making it harder for them to breathe.
The pounding in his skull discouraging them from
opening their eyes. Weakness plagued them, forcing
them to fight it with the last dregs of their strength.

Niskenya let out a deafening roar, surging to her
feet, ready to lash out at whoever had hurt them. She
moved over his body, confused by the people she found
around them. Her bonded's family, not their enemies,
and yet... She wavered on her feet, baring her teeth and
snarling at them, the unsteadiness making her vulnerable and more defensive.

"Kasiel!"

Nerith's desperate cry yanked him back into himself.
He rushed to his feet as Niskenya had done, but the
violent headache and a fresh wave of nausea knocked
him back to his knees. He bent over and threw up, his
raw throat protesting the abuse fiercely enough that it

was all he could focus on for several seconds. Niskenya snarled again, a distinct threat in her tone, his distress upsetting her more.

Kasiel reached out blindly, managing to place a hand on one of her legs. He sent calm across to her, a feat in itself given how calm he wasn't.

"I just want to help him, Niske. Please."

After a few more seconds, the kanodrak settled, moving a few steps to the side to let Nerith approach. She crouched down next to Kasiel, placing a steadying hand on his shoulder.

"We couldn't get you to wake up. Jhanik thought you might be trapped in Niske's suffering." Her voice shook.

He spat and wiped his mouth with the back of one hand. "Trapped in each other's suffering is more like it," he rasped. "How did you wake her?"

"Merrin made her list." Nerith helped him to a nearby bench, Niskenya practically breathing down their necks to stay close to him. "When we couldn't rouse you, Jhanik tried to take control of the eagle, but it attacked him for his efforts, so he and Arkos jumped across to the town."

Niskenya sank down near the bench, breathing hard as if she had been running for hours. Kasiel set a hand on her muzzle as he looked at the other Feral. He owed the man a great deal. "They were willing to work with you?"

Jhanik grimaced, casting a sour look toward Hellaris. "Willing might be the wrong word. We may have upset some locals."

"Arkos almost didn't make that last jump." Nerith glanced up at Jhanik with a look that swelled with gratitude.

"Thank you," Kasiel said, following her gaze.

Jhanik shrugged, gesturing toward the roof of the

manor. "You should name that eagle. It is clearly yours." Then his gaze moved to where the northern bridge had been. "It looks like our force will have a bridge in place shortly. I'm going to start searching the manor and grounds for anyone else in need of aid."

"Be careful," Nerith said, her attention returning to Kasiel now. "Don't move."

"I wouldn't dream of it," he whispered, finding that the irritation to his throat was less the softer he spoke.

As she wandered away to do whatever she intended to do, his gaze drifted up to the eagle. It cocked its head and looked back at him, a hint of impatience coming across the link. Not the most affectionate of creatures, but there was no doubt it had solidly bonded with him. He could send the raptor after Sarket's army, but there was nothing they could do about them right now. They had effectively trapped the allied force on the wrong side of the gorge, and the people who knew best what was going on were stuck in the center.

Sarket had Dhomen Aleren and General Harel now. They had also gotten General Thrasser and some of his force back, abandoning General Evanson and the rest of the Sarketi soldiers still being held by the Delaphinian and Vanrian alliance. That didn't bode well for their value as prisoners. It was going to take something more if they wanted to get Aleren and Harel back, assuming Sarket was even willing to negotiate. They had someone of great importance to Khevarin Seylin in their possession now. They wouldn't squander that advantage.

Nerith came and sat next to him, holding out a cup she had found somewhere. Likely inside the manor, now that the smoke was dissipating. "This should help with your throat and give your lungs a chance to start recovering."

Kasiel took it and sniffed it. The smell turned his currently fragile gut. Swallowing a rush of bile, he brought the cup up and slammed its contents. Rather than getting it over with quickly as he had hoped, the substance oozed down his throat like a slug, a sensation that further challenged his stomach.

"Don't throw up," Nerith commanded, as if it worked that way. "You may be my priority, but I have other patients and only so much of this to pass around."

He swallowed hard a few times, handing the cup back to her. When it finally descended, he swallowed once more and chuckled softly.

She arched a brow at him. "Is there something funny about all this?"

"I'm dead."

Her lips pressed together for a second. "That isn't even close to amusing."

"One of Sarket's soldiers declared me dead, thanks to the intervention of a Dampener who didn't make it out." Hatred flared in his chest, burning rapidly out to the tips of his fingers and toes. He grinned, baring his teeth like one of his beasts. "I can't wait to show them how wrong they are."

Nerith placed a hand against his cheek, her brow bunching in delicate ridges. "Don't let them ruin you, Kas. You're the one thing I can't bear to see them take away."

Her words yanked his rage out from under him. He closed his eyes as the headache seized control again, and bowed his head, seeing the Dampener there pinned to the wall, her last act saving his life. He clenched his teeth, sorrow sharpening the pain in his throat.

Nerith kissed his forehead. "I'm going to help Tath. The gorge should have a new, if much less attractive, bridge soon. Then, I suspect, you will have a part to play in whatever decisions come next. I suggest you take advantage of the moment to rest your lungs and body along with your kanodrak."

Nerith wasn't wrong. Once they laid the rough bridge across the gap, it was a matter of time before they had the survivors back on the northern side. Nevias was taken to the Vanrian command tent for further care. After changing out of his contaminated clothes and rinsing off the residue from the smoke, Kasiel went to the Delaphinian command tent where the rest of the army's ranking officers had gathered. Irith all but wrapped himself around his leg, anxiety pouring off the cat in the aftermath of their tense separation.

Tath and Nerith provided Kasiel and Itana with healing drinks they could sip at to make talking easier and help with the headache they both suffered from. Together, they brought the others up to speed on what had happened in the attack. After that, Itana gave them a brief rundown of how the apparently insincere negotiations had gone.

Since he wasn't involved in that part of things, Kasiel turned his attention to the eagle for a few minutes, slipping behind its eyes and flying high to the west to see if he could spot Sarket's army. It didn't take long. The raptor was fast and the army, while moving quickly, was still an army with all the civilian support and supply wagons needed to keep it functioning restricting its speed. If the allied force had an efficient way to get across the river, they might have some hope of catching up, but for now the gorge was a barrier. They could repair the bridge to Hellaris west of the manor or travel even further west in search of another crossing. Alternatively, they could go back east three or four hours to where the landscape was more level and cross there, but with Hackett's army heading west in a hurry, that would lose them significant ground. The delay could give the enemy time to select their battleground and put the new alliance at a disadvantage. At a distance, Kasiel couldn't spot Aleren or Harel, but a few enclosed wagons toward the middle offered promising options for transporting prisoners.

He absently touched the pouch with Sylaryth's claw and Katerin's ring in it. "What about Cabril?" He realized when he dropped back behind his own eyes to find them all staring at him that he had interrupted the current discussion.

"Cabril is not even a military target," Itana answered. "That keep has not been in use since Lord Myron was beheaded on charges of treason over a year ago." Her eyes narrowed, her gaze boring into him. "Why even bring up Cabril?"

How much could he say without breaking Lady Katerin's trust? Should that matter under the circumstances? "A member of the Fallend contingent," he paused, sipping from the drink to keep from coughing, "disclosed to me that King Lodmund moved his pregnant wife there for protection."

"How would this member know that, unless..." Itana nodded to herself as she took a swallow from her own drink. If she knew anything about Katerin De Clare's daughter's connection to the new Sarketi queen, then she might well have figured it out. Especially if she had noticed him speaking with her. "You are suggesting we turn the tables on General Hackett? Take Lodmund's queen and unborn child as our prisoners?"

"Would that work?" one of the higher ranked inveths asked.

"King Lodmund has struggled to secure an heir," a Delaphinian officer answered. "If the queen is there, she would be a valuable hostage, but how do we know if this information is reliable? Cabril's only a couple of days to the northeast, but that would be a couple of days we can't afford to lose if we gain nothing from it."

Kasiel shook his head. "We don't need to send the entire army there. In fact, it would probably be better if we kept the attempt as quiet as possible until we know if it's going to pay off. Let me lead a small company to Cabril while Hackett remains focused on our main force. He thinks I'm dead anyhow, so any scouts he sends out won't get suspicious if they don't see me with our army." Kasiel stopped there to take another drink, bothered by how winded that much talking made him. Over the edge of the cup, he noticed several looks of surprise. Had he forgotten to mention his being dead to them? "I can use my ability to confirm that she's there. If she is, we take the keep. If not, we fall back to a prearranged location to rejoin the army."

"That would deny us the advantage of the most powerful Feral in Vanris's army if there is a confrontation," a general countered.

Kasiel met Itana's eyes, ignoring the man. How quickly they had become accustomed to having his power available. "I would need to take a few other mindcrafters too, if I'm going to have a chance at taking this keep with a small group."

Itana clasped her hands. "Dhomen Nevias should be involved in this discussion."

The other dhomen and two third-rank inveths nodded their agreement.

Kasiel stood. "I'll check on her."

Itana took a step forward as if she meant to stop him or go with him, then she drew back and nodded. "Yes. That is probably wise, Ahninveth. If she is awake and able, we can always move everyone to the Vanrian command tent to accommodate her injury."

He offered a slight bow. "Thank you, General." Any attempt at a dignified exit quickly turned into an awkward stumble from the tent with the cliff cat pressing against his leg, unwilling to be separated from him even by a few inches.

Once outside, he scratched briefly behind Irith's ears on his way toward the Vanrian tent. He had to have gone mad. What other explanation was there for this sudden desire to prove Lady Katerin right? Although, that wasn't really his motivation. If they wanted to keep Aleren alive, given Sarket's determination to avoid peace, they needed some kind of leverage. Katerin De Clare's desire to protect her own daughter had offered them something that might be important enough to King Lodmund to work. Not only that, but it could be the key to forcing a decisive confrontation. He hoped his unit wouldn't hate him for volunteering them.

The guards outside the Vanrian tent saw him coming and one ducked her head inside. By the time he reached the entrance, she was holding open the flap for him to enter.

Tath and Nerith were both inside with Nevias, who was awake now. The two healers had her ankle and foot carefully braced using what materials they had available. Neither looked pleased. In fact, Nevias also appeared extremely unhappy, and sweat beaded on her forehead again, a clear indication of how much pain she was in.

"Ahninveth Kasiel, where are the other officers? We need to act quickly." She moved as if she meant to try standing.

"You can't put weight on it," Tath declared as she and Nerith both reached out, but Kasiel got there faster and knelt before the dhomen, effectively blocking her.

"I want to take a small company northeast to Cabril." He ignored the startled looks Nerith and Tath gave him. "Lady De Clare told me Lodmund has his queen hidden there for her protection. She's pregnant. If we can take her as our hostage, we might have a better chance at saving Dhomen Aleren." He got all of it out before his throat seized, forcing him to take a quick swig of the drink.

It was nearly empty. Nerith held a hand out, and he passed it to her. She went and started digging through one of their packs. Nevias was staring at him, her jaw tight with the pain she was attempting to deal with.

"Sorry, Dhomen Nevias, but I wanted to bring the idea to you before anyone else had a chance to try coloring your reaction to it."

"So that you could do so first, you mean?"

Kasiel's cheeks warmed. "I would need a few other mind-crafters to help pull it off. It's already too late to catch Hackett's army before they can pick their battlefield, and they clearly aren't interested in an alliance. Whatever..." He accepted a refilled cup from Nerith and took a quick drink. "Whatever it is they intend to use Dhomen Aleren for won't work in our best interests."

"They must be planning to ransom her for something from Khevarin Seylin. You are right, I don't see any way this can end well." Nevias wiped at the sheen of dampness on her forehead, her voice tight.

"Which is why we need to get our hands on Lodmund's pregnant queen."

"You need to take something more for the pain, Dhomen," Nerith said.

"Not until after I speak to the other officers." Her pain-glazed eyes turned to him. "You believe Lady De Clare?"

"I do. She said her daughter Hannah is with the queen. They were friends before the marriage. She asked me to get them away from Lodmund if the opportunity arose."

"Then she has a self-serving reason for telling you this. That makes me a little more inclined to believe her." Her fingers tightened on her thigh, and she sucked in a quick breath, clenching her teeth against the pain for a second. When she focused on him again, desperate hope shone in her eyes that reminded him of Lady De Clare. "Ahninveth Kasiel, you have an hour. Meet with your unit and anyone else you need to speak with. You might ask General Kedran if she knows of anyone in their army who is familiar with Cabril. Come up with a plan and a roster of troops you'll need. Convince me this is a good idea and that you are the best one to handle it." He stood as her attention moved to Tath and Nerith. "You two need to go with your Ahninveth. Send the other officers in to meet with me, along with one of the senior healers."

"Dhomen Nevias." Kasiel waited until her attention was on him again. "Sarket isn't concerned with Delaphine and Fallend. Vanris is their biggest threat. They would give General Harel back in a heartbeat if Delaphine agreed to turn on us and we both know it. We need to counter this quickly; in a way King Lodmund can't ignore. General Itana Kedran is our strongest ally in Delaphine's force. We need to leverage her support."

Her eyes narrowed as if she were trying to pick him apart. "Meet with your unit, Ahninveth. We'll talk more when you have a fully formed plan."

"Yes, Dhomen."

Tath and Nerith followed him out.

"I'll notify the other officers and ask General Kedran about Cabril," Tath said, her scrutinizing gaze on Kasiel. "Nerith, see if you can find Dhomen Aleren's healer. He's got a great deal of experience with these kinds of injuries."

Kasiel met Tath's eyes. What was she thinking? Was she angry with him for what he was trying to commit them to? Did she support it? Why was she so hard to read?

"I'll see you two at camp." He held Tath's gaze a moment longer before turning away.

As he went, the eagle launched itself from a nearby tree and swept along overhead. With a mental nudge, Kasiel got Irith to give him some space so he could walk. His throat started itching again, his lungs heavy, almost as if he had been running for hours. He sipped at the drink Nerith had given him, the liquid soothing away the irritation. If only it lasted longer.

Jethan hurried over when he got close to their campsite. Niskenya raised her head but didn't stand. He could feel the weakness, pain, and exhaustion she still suffered through their link.

"We need to talk," he said in a low voice, trying to save his throat. "All of us."

"Shouldn't you take a break from talking?" Jethan placed a hand on his shoulder as if needing to convince himself Kasiel was real.

"Soon."

The unit gathered in a close circle at his bidding. He didn't wait for Nerith and Tath. They knew what he was proposing. They would be back in time to voice their opinions on the idea.

He took a drink of the liquid and glanced around at them. "I know we're all tired, and I don't want to put any of you in danger, but we have a high value target we could go after—"

"We're with you," Wedro stated.

Kasiel chuckled. "I haven't told you what the mission is yet."

Darro shrugged. "The answer won't change but go ahead."

Kasiel hesitated. Would they really give him their support before even knowing the risks? After another sip, he continued. "I asked Dhomen Nevias to let us go to Cabril and try to take King Lodmund's pregnant bride hostage. I'm supposed to report to her in an hour with a plan and my troop requirements. Obviously, I have nothing without all of you, so that's where we start."

"Lady Katerin was right then." A smirk curled Kince's lips up.

Kasiel gave the other man a stern look, though it didn't stick. He had told them all what Lady Katerin De Clare confided in him, including her certainty that he would try to help given the opportunity.

"We're taking a small force?" Darro asked.

"And a selection of mind-crafters," Merrin added before Kasiel could respond.

"Yes. That's my plan. I could use your input on what the best arrangement would be. I want to take this stronghold our way."

"General Kedran is sending some assistance," Tath announced, walking in to join them. Nerith wasn't far behind her.

"Someone with knowledge of Cabril?" A spark of hope lit in his tortured chest.

Tath grinned, something in the expression conveying a fiercer side of her she rarely let show. "Better. Someone who helped take the stronghold when Lord Myron tried to make his stand there."

"Perfect. Tell us what you think would work, Ahninveth, and we can go from there," Wedro prompted as they all turned to Kasiel.

He stared back at them. They didn't doubt or question him. They weren't angry that he was trying to commit them to this insane effort. Instead, they rallied around him and started planning.

Avris met his eyes and laughed. "You still don't get it, do you? We're your unit, Kas, and your tehsheyn. Together, with you as our Ahninveth, we have gone farther and done more for Vanris than any of us could have expected to with anyone else. This could be crazy, or it could be genius. Either way, we're in it with you for the duration, however short or long that turns out to be. I don't think anyone in this circle would disagree."

Each of them backed up his words with a nod. Irith bumped Kasiel's hand with his head, earning a scratch behind the ears. To one side, Niskenya slowly blinked her milky white eyes and rested her head on her paws.

Jethan placed a hand on Kasiel's shoulder again. "Let's get planning."

Not long into their process, a Delaphinian soldier joined them, looking distinctly uneasy as she walked through the perimeter of tethdraks. Strands of unruly dark brown hair pulled free from a low braid, adding a hint of softness to her features. With the faint laugh lines etched into her light bronze skin, she looked to be around Darro and Kince's age or a few years older. She wore a mace at her hip, the grip as well-worn as her chain and leather armor. The sight of the weapon gave Kasiel a twinge of remembered pain in his right arm that radiated through him.

Unexpectedly, Emil, Annora, and Leif accompanied her.

"I'm Lucia," she introduced, her abrupt approach and the discomfort in her tone making it obvious she didn't want to be there. "I was told you need information regarding the stronghold at Cabril."

"You were told correctly. I'm Ahninveth Kasiel." He almost left off his rank to reflect her lack of formality, but it felt inappropriate to do so when she was being sent over to assist him on a military mission. If only there were a book to guide these cross-rank interactions. Maybe that would have saved him from sleeping with the khevarin's daughter. Though probably not.

Lucia glanced down at Irith. "I had a hunch you

were him."

Kasiel absently touched the cat's shoulder, trying to ignore the wary reverence in her tone. "You seem to have brought company."

She frowned at the three young soldiers who now stood beside her.

Emil stood painfully straight, as if he hoped to make himself look more formidable. "We wanted to offer our skills to support your mission."

"You don't have your own units to serve?"

"We do, sir, but out of regard for collaboration efforts with our new allies, we requested leave to offer you our service."

It wasn't a terrible idea. If they could make this more of a combined effort, especially if it was successful, it could help further strengthen the alliance with Delaphine. "We'll learn what we can from Lucia first. After that, we can discuss what value you might add to this mission. Is that acceptable?"

"Yes, sir," Emil answered without hesitation, his hopeful gaze drifting to Jethan.

Kasiel glanced at his tehnaak. Had Jethan's previous Charming unduly influenced the youth? For now, the possibility would have to be set aside before greater concerns. Later, he could ask him about it.

He turned his attention back to Lucia. "I hate to put more pressure on you, but I would like to use an Evoker while we talk. Not because I doubt you, but because it could help us get more detailed information."

The woman tensed, her hand drifting instinctively closer to her mace, a clear statement that his proposal made her feel threatened. Before he could try to assuage her concerns, Wedro spoke.

"Think of it as a way to improve upon your memory. Evokers can only see what we're actively thinking about, but they can catch details in those surface memories that we might not realize are important. We do use them for interrogations when someone is trying to hide critical information, but they're even more valuable in cases like this, when something our conscious mind dismissed as unimportant could save the lives of the people involved in a mission."

Lucia stared at Wedro. He looked like some kind of wild man, his hair uneven because of the firebomb, his shirt hanging off one shoulder to allow treatment of the burns on the other side. Kasiel was staring at Wedro too, though more because he wasn't used to him volunteering to speak that much, especially since Chander's death. Given the current state of his throat, however, he appreciated it. If only someone had reassured him about Evokers in such a way when he first came to Etrion.

Her gaze homed in on Wedro's burns, lingering there for an instant before it turned inward. Finally, she looked at Kasiel and nodded. "I'm not sure how I feel about the changes in Delaphine's alliances, but this is where we are now. The soldiers of Vanris have proven that they will fight with us and for us. I haven't been told why Cabril is important, but if it is, and it will help us stop Sarket, I will speak with your Evoker."

Kasiel inclined his head. "Thank you. I'm asking the members of my unit to risk their lives for this. That's not something I do lightly, and I will do anything in my power to keep them from having to pay that price."

A spark lit in Lucia's eyes. "Now that is a very compelling reason to do whatever I can to help you, Ahninveth Kasiel. You should have led with that."

With Nevias's permission, Kasiel summoned Aleren's Evoker over to sit in on their conversation with Lucia. It surprised him how vivid her memory of the attack on the stronghold to flush out Lord Myron was. Something had to have happened there to etch it in her mind. Something he would not ask her or the Evoker to reveal. All he needed was as much detail as possible regarding the layout and defenses of the stronghold. If no one was supposed to be aware it was being used as a sanctuary for the pregnant queen, then it might appear more lightly defended than it actually was. Lord Myron, knowing his life was on the line, would have done everything in his power to keep the attackers out. If the queen's protectors were trying to be discreet about her presence, there might be gaps in defense that could allow for a stealthier approach, but they needed to go in prepared for the worst.

By evening, after Nevias woke from an induced sleep during which the healers did more to stabilize her ankle, Kasiel, Jethan, Kince, and Darro were ready to propose their mission plan and troop needs to her. Kasiel let the others handle most of the discussion. Everything he did, even simple things like walking and talking, made him feel short of breath and irritated his throat. The smoke and whatever alchemical substances had been in it hadn't done him any favors. Itana was similarly afflicted, but at least she wasn't proposing to lead an ambitious side mission. If he let his companions carry most of the conversation with Nevias, he could hide the extent of his impairment and hopefully keep that from influencing her decision.

When they finished arguing in favor of the mission, Nevias sat silent for a few minutes, an occasional flinch speaking to the sharp pain from her injured ankle.

"Lucia and these three young Delaphinian soldiers you mentioned have offered to join your unit?"

"Yes, Dhomen. After speaking with them, they all have useful skills and Lucia's knowledge of the area could be invaluable," Kasiel answered, putting his voice back into the conversation after a sip from the flask he was carrying everywhere with him.

"I can only give you one Evoker."

Kasiel nodded. He hadn't expected to get two any-how. That she was considering letting him have every-thing else he asked for was more than he had dared to hope for. Before coming to her, they had agreed to pad their request on the assumption that it would give them a better chance of getting at least the most essential troops and supplies. He never thought she would go along with almost everything.

"Jethan, I'm promoting you to Ahninveth."

Jethan grinned, bumping Kasiel with his shoulder. "I knew I'd catch up to you, eventually."

A hint of a smirk touched Nevias's lips before pain twisted them into a grimace. "Kasiel, I'm promoting you to second-rank Ahninveth."

"Figures." Jethan rolled his eyes, though his proud smile belied the gesture.

"Thank you, Dhomen. Does this mean we have your authorization for the mission?"

She nodded. "Pull your unit together. If we're go-ing to keep Sarket from finding out that you're still alive, we need you out of here before sunrise. Also, if you still want to do it, the Bondmaker has been given my permission to make your tehsheyn official. It is up to you to decide if you would prefer to trade some of the little sleep you will get tonight for that."

"Thank you again, Dhomen Nevias," Darro said, the rest of them supporting the sentiment with solemn nods.

They got up and started filing out.

"Ahninveth Kasiel, another moment of your time."

Kasiel hung back, watching his companions depart, then turned to face Nevias.

"I have spoken with each of them. Your unit loves you, and it is obvious the sentiment goes both ways. Even your newest addition, Speaker Etris, has no desire to leave your service after your unit rescued her from the professor. You should know that Wedro and Kince had the strongest reservations, and for the same reason, though it took a little digging to get them to admit it. They both fear losing someone they care about to a powerful enough degree that this bonding makes them nervous. Surprisingly, neither Tath nor Nerith expressed similar concerns, despite their recent losses. In Tath's case, her level of fondness for you was unexpected. She hides it well. She regards you almost as a younger brother but tries to keep that protective affection in check to avoid smothering you with it.

"All of that said, I can see that you have something weighing on you. If you need to speak to them in private before proceeding, we have taken over the manor. I have ordered that one of the dining rooms be reserved for your unit and a good meal provided, given how important your next few days could end up being for all of us. That would also offer you a private opportunity to get things out in the open, should you need it."

He nodded. "The meal will be greatly appreciated, as will the privacy. Thank you."

"Whatever you have to say to them, you should also consider telling your commanding officer."

He met her eyes. "I'll take that under advisement, Dhomen. Will it cause problems for your company if I take these mind-crafters?"

"The mind-crafters I'm giving you are from Dhomen Aleren's company. I wasn't sure if they would join us in the first place or for how long, so my plans never required them. The mind-crafter I'm most concerned about losing is you, Kasiel, but we will manage. Our plan is to avoid confrontation while being just aggressive enough to keep their attention on us long enough for you to secure the queen if she is in Cabril." Nevias gestured to the exit. "Prepare yourself, Ahninveth. I hope this does not turn out to be a mistake."

"It won't. I will turn the tables on Sarket."

He left the tent, taking comfort from Irith at his side. Niskenya was asleep, still recovering from the poison. It felt cruel to ask her to get on the move again so soon, but among his requests had been an extra horse to take some of the burden off her until she was healthier. For once, he suspected she might tolerate him riding a lesser beast for a while.

The other three were back at camp where a flurry of activity was in process to prepare for departure. Kince had gone to inform the Delaphinian volunteers that their addition was cleared on Vanris's side. Since all were troops in Itana's company, the likelihood that they would receive approval from their commanding officer as well was good.

Jethan approached him while the others continued working. "We already discussed the Bondmaker. As soon as initial preparations are complete, the consensus is that creating the tehsheyn could improve our chances of success in Cabril, assuming the queen is there."

"She is, Ahninveth," Kasiel said, finding a smile for his tehnaak.

"You know, I doubt I would have gotten that promotion without you. Charmers don't often make rank."

"You've done more than enough to earn it." He drew a deep breath and blew it out. "I need to speak to all of you before we commit to the tehsheyn. There's something you should know. Something I should have told you before now."

Jethan's smile faded. "That's ominous."

Kasiel didn't bother trying to reassure him. "Nevias said we can use a room in the manor. She's having dinner provided. Let's finish up here and we'll go talk and eat."

The worry in Jethan's expression faded some. "I'm pretty confident that, if the food is good enough, we'll be fine with anything you have to say."

Kasiel chuckled as they set off to work.

The amount of preparation he couldn't do because of the injury to his throat and lungs left him stuck in a primarily supervisory role, which wasn't entirely inappropriate given his rank, but he hated it. It felt like a small strike against him, one he was about to compound with the revelations he had in store for them. Maybe it was a bad idea to tell them everything right before leaving on this mission, but he couldn't let them commit to the tehsheyn without knowing about his conflict with the khevarin and his father's motivations behind asking them to end the war.

When they broke to eat their evening meal, having an opportunity to enjoy food cooked in the manor's kitchens and eat in the comfort of one of the nicely appointed dining rooms helped everyone relax. The cozy environment brightened the moods of his companions, as did partaking of a few bottles from the local lord's wine selection. They kept their drinking to a minimum, given that they would depart before dawn, but a couple of glasses each was enough to ease the tension.

Kasiel swept out with his ability. With the manor no longer being secured by Sarketi forces, he had lured in some rodents. He used them now to check the areas around the private dining room and on the floor above it to ensure no one was eavesdropping.

"He must have known what they were planning when he came to talk to you, don't you think? Kas?"

Kasiel pulled back into himself, leaving a light connection to a few rodents as an early warning. Everyone was looking at him. "General Danovan?"

A few of them nodded.

"I imagine he must have. It seems deception is a talent that runs in their family." A flash of anger swept through him, driving Irith to his feet. Kasiel pushed it down. He didn't need volatile emotions making things more difficult. With a quick mental touch, he calmed the cliff cat and nudged him to sit beside his chair, placing a hand on the beast's shoulders. "Before we make our final decision and call in the Bondmaker, there are a couple of things I need to share with you."

"I thought we had decided," Tath said, an edge of disappointment in her tone.

"I won't ask you to enter this bond without knowing a few things."

Darro slid his hand into Tath's and brought it up to kiss the back of it. "Are you in such a hurry to tie yourself to another man?" He gave her a teasing wink.

"Don't be a calloch." She shook her head at him. "I'll be tying myself to you too."

Darro held her gaze, a smirk tugging at his lips. "This is getting more interesting. Maybe we can skip to the tying part then. I'm good with ropes."

A few of the others laughed.

"No, we can't, but you provide an inappropriate opening to discuss the first thing I wanted to bring up," Kasiel began. "You all know there's been something between Khesran Velara and I for a while that led to conflict with the khevarin." A few nods and several flat looks were enough of an answer. "We started, ah, sleeping together soon after we arrested Khesran Karith."

"Kas." Avris let out a soft groan that was echoed by a few others. "We knew you two were flirting and possibly engaging in some intimacy, the attraction was pretty obvious, but we kind of hoped you had enough sense not to plant anything in the royal garden."

Kince was staring hard at Kasiel. "So much for the secret I killed that assassin in Trenath to keep." He dropped that revelation like a small bomb in their midst.

"Shit," Merrin said into the ensuing silence.

Darro turned to his tehnaak. "Why didn't you ever

tell me about this?"

"To be fair, we hadn't taken it that far back then. Regardless, it gets better." Kasiel moved them on to take the pressure back off Kince. "Khevarin Seylin found out about our... gardening," he said, borrowing Avris's analogy, "and she was, well..."

"Vexed," Darro offered to a few chuckles.

"Really angry," Jethan muttered, shaking his head.

"Seething," Wedro suggested, looking a little too pleased to contribute.

"All of those things and more." Kasiel turned the fine silver goblet sitting next to his plate before looking around at each of them. "She decided it would be too unpopular to have me executed, so she sent a missive to Dhomen Aleren asking her to keep us on the front lines until I either died in battle or she secured an appropriate engagement for Velara."

"You almost did die this time." Nerith's pointed look suggested a level of annoyance with him that surpassed that of the others. He had earned it. When he met her eyes, she turned away, staring into the empty fireplace across the room from her.

"The point is, it's my fault that we're in this position."

"Even if you hadn't dipped your fingers in the khesran's honey, odds are good we would have ended up in the same spot just because of who you are and what you can do, Kas," Merrin suggested reasonably. "Maybe the khevarin will cool off in our absence."

"I think it was more than his fingers," Darro muttered, earning a smack on the arm from Tath.

"Do you love her at least?" Avris asked.

"I don't think that matters." He took a sip from a fresh batch of the mixture Tath and Nerith had made. He still had too much to say for his throat to cause him issues now. "Khevarin Seylin won't give me another chance to upset her plans." His chest tightened painfully as he said the words, and it wasn't because of his injury this time. Yes, he loved Velara, and that wouldn't change anything.

"I mean, maybe, if we ended the war," Etris suggested tentatively.

"Thank you, Etris. That brings me to the next subject." All eyes were on him again with renewed intensity. They wanted to know what could be worse than the khevarin trying to get them killed. Irith brought a paw up and placed it on his arm. Kasiel smiled at the cat. "I know. You're stuck with me regardless, my friend."

Then he turned his attention back to the others. Jethan in particular, where he sat on Kasiel's left. They had insisted on putting him at the head of the table as their ranking officer, which didn't make any of this easier. Before speaking, he touched briefly on the rodents around that part of the manor, ensuring their privacy.

"Out with it, tehnaak," Jethan pressed, unease in his sharp tone.

Kasiel drew a breath and let it out. "My father discovered, with the help of two Evokers, that Khevarin Seylin arranged the attack on my mother and I twelve – thirteen years ago in order to manipulate him into accepting the role of dhomvalen."

Kasiel didn't break eye contact with Jethan as his tehnaak pushed back from the table.

"No. My aunt can be ruthless and cold at times, but she wouldn't have done that. She was behind our pairing in the first place."

"And why was that?" Kasiel asked. "Why did she offer her nephew, a member of the royal family, as tehnaak to the son of parents who had no real influence at the time?"

Jethan shook his head, denying it.

"Because that man was the most powerful Frightener Vanris has ever known." Kince took a sip of his wine as if nothing interesting were going on, but there was a veiled intensity in the way he watched Jethan.

"And it didn't work," Kasiel continued. "Even after connecting Arhk to her family by pairing his son with her nephew, my father still refused her when she offered him the role of dhomvalen. He chose his family instead."

"He's right." Merrin's tone was gentle, as if she spoke to a scared child. "Who else in Vanris could have brought the power to the position of dhomvalen that Arhk did? With him by her side, no one dares to question the khevarin's authority. All she had to do was remove the one thing keeping him from accepting that role. Anyone familiar with our recent history knows he wouldn't have taken the position if he hadn't lost his wife and son."

"We were both supposed to die, Jeth. It was only by chance that the person who followed the lead she laid out happened to be looking for a mind-crafter child to raise as an experiment. I was supposed to have died with my mother."

Jethan closed his eyes and swallowed. "My aunt always got so upset with me when I insisted you were still alive."

Kasiel got up and walked over to him, placing a hand on his arm. The muscle tensed under his touch, but Jethan didn't pull away. A tear slipped free of one of his eyes. He stood suddenly and embraced Kasiel, who instantly wrapped his arms around his tehnaak, a flood of dizzying relief bursting through him.

"I can't believe... I'm so sorry." Jethan's voice cracked.

"*I'm* sorry, tehnaak. I knew this would be hard for you. I didn't want to tell you." He glanced around at the others over Jethan's shoulder, at the sympathetic sorrow in their eyes, and eased Jethan back from him. "I didn't want to tell any of you, but I had to, because my father wants revenge."

"That's why he wants you to end the war." Darro snapped his fingers. "He's trying to get into position to unseat her." His eyes narrowed at Kasiel then. "Or position you to."

"Trust me, I don't want the throne, and I don't want my father sitting on it, either. What I do want is to end this war, and I don't care why. But I'm not sure what will happen if we succeed." He met Jethan's eyes again.

"Only one way to find out," Wedro said.

"Exactly," Avris seconded.

"You two aren't really helping." Nerith stood and walked around the table to where he and Jethan were. "I know this is hard, Jeth, but we have a choice to make." Her gaze flickered to Kasiel for an instant before moving to the others. "We can formalize our tehsheyn and go on this mission. Along the way, maybe we can help Kas figure out what to do with all of this. Or we can turn our backs on our ahninveth and report this information to our commanding officer, hoping that whatever she does with it is the right thing."

Wedro stood fast enough that his chair scrapped the floor. His cheeks flushed slightly when all eyes turned to him, but he forged ahead. "The idea of making our tehsheyn real scares the shit out of me. Knowing we could create that bond, and I might lose one of you the way I lost Chander..." He paused, swallowing hard. Tears welled in his eyes. It was a few seconds before he could speak again, but they waited in respectful silence. "You are my family. I've made my choice."

"I feel the same," Tath added.

"As do I," Nerith said, meeting Kasiel's eyes.

Echoes moved around the table until Kasiel and Jethan were the only two left.

"What do you think, tehnaak?" Kasiel asked, a band

of fear squeezing his heart.

Jethan wiped away a tear. "I think there was a reason I always knew you were alive. We were meant to be tehnaak. Nothing can break what we have. Not even the khevarin of Vanris. This – you and everyone else in this room – this is my family."

They summoned the Bondmaker. When she joined them, it surprised Kasiel to see that she had milky white eyes eerily similar to Niskenya's. Jethan explained that Bondmakers weren't fully blind the way Heartsmiths were, but they did see the world differently. Kasiel couldn't help wondering if seeing through her eyes would be like looking out from Niskenya's.

She declined to give her name when Kasiel asked, insisting that her identity was irrelevant to what they were trying to accomplish. Then she led them to a smaller space in the manor. A cozy reading room where they moved the central table to one side and gathered comfortable chairs in the middle to create close, but separate, seating for all ten of them. She then had them each choose a spot to settle in and close their eyes. They were to think of the others sitting in that space with them and simply be aware of their presence.

While they sat like this, the Bondmaker moved around the room, snuffing out the sconces and candles, deepening the darkness behind their eyelids. Kasiel expanded his connection to Niskenya, drawing her into the experience.

The kanodrak moved her presence through him, taking comfort more than giving it this time. His heart ached to feel the anger and distress that overflowed in her at being vulnerable and in no state to protect him. He answered with a sense of comfort and security. They had others to protect them tonight. A family that would fight to the end with them. For them. Her temper calmed in response. She allowed him to guide her into the shared darkness. A sense of warmth and familiarity greeted them in that quiet room, accepting them into the fold.

Kasiel's awareness of his companions intensified, each of them becoming a clear, individual presence in the space. He could feel them almost as intensely as he could his beasts. Wedro's pain from his burns and from the loss that haunted him. A hint of bitterness that he knew was Kince. A familiar caring he would recognize anywhere as Nerith. Every one of them had a distinct presence, bridging the gaps to erase the isolation of physical separation. Each one drew closer until all of them touched, lazily spiraling together, their identities blurring. A brightness grew within Kasiel's mind. A light that was all of them, bound in a single presence. All their strengths and weaknesses merging. A vibrant, welcoming warmth that embraced them together.

Just when he was ready to let go of himself and surrender to that flawed, beautiful creation completely, the intensity eased away, settling gradually to a faint awareness in the back of his mind. One presence burned stronger than the others. Jethan, bound to him as both *tehnaak* and *tehsheyn* now.

A light flared beyond his eyelids, and Kasiel opened his eyes. The others were doing the same. The Bondmaker had lit a single sconce near the door. She came and perched on the arm of one couch they had shifted to the side.

"If I am to be honest, when Dhomen Nevias told me what you wanted, I doubted it would work. Groups this size rarely connect as easily as they think they will, but your tehsheyn was well on the way to forming many of these connections already. Your link to one another now will be stronger than ever before. Between the natural bond that was forming and the meddling of Ahninveth Kasiel's kanodrak, you might have completed this process without a Bondmaker in time."

Kince jumped on that last revelation. "What do you mean by the kanodrak's meddling?"

"Niskenya appears to have been drawing upon the threads of your lives for some time now, gradually weaving them closer together. Perhaps as an effort to provide more protection for her bonded companion. She could not have gotten it this far if you were not all so willing to support one another. I merely had to finish what she had already started. You are true tehsheyn now. Do not mistreat this bond."

"Wait." Darro leaned in. "Are you saying that kanodraks are Bondmakers?"

"Not exactly. Bondmaking is an ability they have long possessed, but only matriarchs, like Niskenya. You are quite fortunate to have her among you." An edge of warning entered her tone then, almost an admonishment. "She is irreplaceable. Watch over her as you do one another." She got to her feet. "Now, I understand you have preparations to complete."

They each thanked her before heading out. With so much to do, there wasn't time to dwell on what they had done or how this might change their relationships, if it did. They finished gathering everything together and took advantage of what time they had left to get some sleep.

When the time came to depart, Kasiel woke from his short slumber feeling strangely invigorated despite the hour and the injury to his throat and lungs. The others in their primary unit seemed more vibrant as well. Even Niskenya rose alert and eager to move on, though Kasiel could feel that her strength hadn't fully recovered yet. Their additions, including an Evoker, a second Charmer and Speaker, and two Dampeners, weren't as enthusiastic to get on the road. Emil and the other Delaphinians joining them had an energy about them, but it was more nervous than eager.

Jhanik approached when they were a few minutes from leaving. He had taken control of the tethdraks. Kasiel wouldn't have another Feral to act as backup if anything went wrong. Here, there were a few Ferals who, while not able to run the beasts in battle, could at least keep them from rampaging if Jhanik got badly injured or killed. That meant Kasiel's unit would have to go without tethdraks.

He nodded a greeting to the other Feral. "Are you all right with all of this?"

"If you mean, 'can I manage the tethdraks,' then yes. Though your leaving has gotten me moved off the front lines for a while. Perhaps I should thank you for that, but I dislike being idle. They're sending a rider to Vanris to bring in another Feral who can run tethdraks. Until they arrive, they're going to try keeping me out of the action."

A tension hung in the air between them that Jhanik seemed hesitant to bring up. "And?"

Jhanik glanced past Kasiel, his gaze focusing upon something or someone for an instant. "And I'm worried about Nerith. This is a risky endeavor, Cavenos. One that might not bear any fruit."

"It will bear fruit, but no matter what happens, you know I'll do everything in my power to keep her safe."

"I know you will." He lowered his gaze, the muscles in his jaw jumping when he clenched his teeth for a second, as if his next words needed to break past some wall. "You were foolish enough to let her go, but I know you still care about her. You care about all of them. Just...

watch out for yourself out there too. Vanris wouldn't be the same without you."

Kasiel breathed a small laugh. "Never thought I'd hear you say that." He held out his arm.

Jhanik took it, gripping it firmly. "Don't get yourself killed, you calloch."

"Same to you, my friend."

Kasiel walked back to his horse and began doing a last check on the saddlebags. When he glanced over his shoulder a couple of minutes later at where Jhanik had been, it shocked him to see Nerith standing with the other Feral. He watched Jhanik's fingers slide under her chin, tilting her head back in slow motion, their eyes meeting. He leaned in, hesitant at first, then with more confidence, until their lips touched. Kasiel turned away, crushing down a surge of possessive rage before his beasts could reflect or act on it. This wasn't his business. Nerith wasn't his partner.

The woman he had chosen instead would never be his again. That was the choice he had made. He had to live with it.

Telling himself that didn't stop jealousy from twisting its black blade in his chest, its poison seeping through him. His throat tightened, irritation setting off the first fit of coughing he'd had in a while. By the time it let up, Tath was at his side, grabbing the hand he had used to cover his mouth. She pulled it close enough to see the dark specks of blood on it and scowled.

"All this activity isn't good for you right now. I'll get you more of the drink. It will help your throat heal in time. Sip at it throughout the day today. Not just when your throat gets aggravated. Your lungs need to heal, and coughing will slow that process." She took a step closer to him, speaking in a low voice now. "She's moving on, Kas. It's a good thing, though I imagine it doesn't feel that way at the moment. If you need someone to talk to, I'm here. We all are." She gave his shoulder a quick squeeze and walked away.

They rode out an hour before sunrise with thirty soldiers, ten from his original unit, five extra mind-crafters, the four Delaphinian volunteers, and eleven more soldiers from both sides of the alliance individually selected by Itana and Nevias. Each one chosen for their willingness to be part of this mission and for the usefulness of the skills they could offer for the approach he had in mind.

Kasiel put his core unit in charge not only of helping manage their recent additions but also attempting to get to know them and integrate them into the group. By the time they reached Cabril, he wanted them all to be doing this for reasons beyond just the fact that they had orders to. He needed them personally invested in the success of their team.

Lucia rode near the front with Etris and Wedro, the latter of whom she appeared to be more comfortable with for whatever reason. Annora had also joined them. For his part, Wedro looked as if he enjoyed the distraction of talking with the two Delaphinian soldiers. That group rode behind Kince and Darro with Lucia offering periodic guidance forward based on her knowledge of the area to supplement the map Itana had provided them. Kasiel stayed behind them with Irith on one side and Niskenya on the other.

Jethan was unusually quiet with the members of the tehsheyn. He alternated between riding alongside Irith and working his way through the group to talk to some of their new recruits. Kasiel didn't need to ask to know that he was still trying to come to terms with the revelation about his aunt. Not only could he see Jethan's torment, he could also feel it to a certain degree. The added thread that bound them together on top of their tehnaak bond gave him an awareness of Jethan that bordered on the depth of connection he had with his companion beasts. Despite that underlying distress, Jethan was still a Charmer, and he could win people over with or without using his ability. For now, Kasiel would leave him to the process of getting to know their new members. The other things they could address in a more appropriate setting.

The absence of the tethdraks allowed Kasiel to manage an ever-changing network of birds, including his nightstar eagle, whom he had named Akyla, to watch for scouts and other threats or obstacles along the way. Outside of the eagle, he didn't keep any of them for more than an hour, trying to avoid dragging them too far from their territory or keeping them long enough for a bond to form. As intensely as Akyla had bonded to him, there was little chance of the raptor returning to his prior home, even if Kasiel tried to send him back.

It was nearing midday when Nerith rode up alongside Irith, taking Jethan's currently empty position. Kasiel absently encouraged the cliff cat around beside Niskenya to let her move in closer. It was strange to be on the same level as everyone else, riding a creature the other mounts weren't naturally frightened of.

"About that moment with Jhanik this morning—"

Jealousy flared and he crushed it quickly down again. "It's none of my business."

"Kas."

"It isn't."

"Maybe not, but it is impressive how much he's changed. Casting aside his pride and the family rivalry to learn to work with you has had an unexpectedly positive effect on him. That's your influence."

Kasiel thought Jhanik's pride was plenty intact, though he didn't say as much. He felt growing tension in Niskenya as she reacted to his barely contained emotions. "You're good at reading people, Nerith. Do you have any concerns about the new members of our unit?"

"You're changing the subject."

"I am."

Her lips tightened into a line for a second before an exasperated smile worked its way free. "All right. I'll let you get away with it this time. I think your Delaphinian soldiers are doing very well, both the volunteers and those assigned by General Kedran. They appear to be genuinely interested in learning to work with us. Your new mind-crafters are the ones who seem most uncomfortable. Particularly your new Charmer, Fenvar. It might be worth sitting down with them when we set up camp and helping them understand their roles in what lies ahead."

He glanced at her, trying not to focus on the image of Jhanik's lips pressed to hers that rose in his mind. "Would you help me with that? People are..." He hesitated, not sure how best to put it.

"Not afraid of me." She offered, her tone softening the unfortunate truth. "I'm happy to help them see you for the wonderful man and remarkable leader that you are."

"You don't need to exaggerate."

"By the Break, you're impossible," she snapped. "You are both of those things. People only fear you because your ability is extraordinary. Even other mind-crafters don't understand some of what you can do. You're untouchable to them. Show them that's not true. Show them you are just one of them at the end of the day."

He wanted to believe it was that easy, but he had never been one of them. When he first arrived in Vanris, he was an earless, southern-raised outsider. Somehow, he had gone from that to a figure they lauded as a hero and now feared only marginally less than they did his father. Was there a point in trying to explain that to her?

She was too smart not to see the problem.

"I'm sure you're right."

She gave him a long look, but he stared ahead, focusing part of his attention on jumping through his current arrangement of aerial scouts. After a deep sigh, she shook her head and lifted her reins. "I'm going to visit with our Dampeners for a few minutes, unless you want me to stay."

Something in her tone almost sounded hopeful, but he suspected he was projecting his longing for some kind of intimate connection onto her. Besides, this wasn't the right moment to get distracted by personal things. "No. Go ahead. We haven't got a lot of time to pull this unit together."

She nodded, her gaze and shoulders sinking as she slowed her mount and dropped away.

The land here was rugged. Stubborn trees eked out life in a harsh, old volcanic landscape. The black basalt that peeked through hardy brush, moss, and grasses had no smooth or forgiving surfaces. Footing was tricky for the horses with their inflexible hooves. It wasn't much better for Niskenya. As thick as the pads of her paws were, the rough rock scraped away at them. Darro and Kince tried to keep them to the smoothest paths, but it wasn't always possible, and travel here exacted its toll on their mounts.

They took a few quick breaks throughout the day, giving Kasiel and Niskenya a chance to rest. Their bodies had taken considerable abuse, and the unceasing travel didn't help with recovery. They stopped around mid-afternoon to set up camp. The plan was to make the final approach on the keep overlooking Cabril in the night, so altering their sleep schedule made sense, as did giving everyone an opportunity to get to know one another in the daylight. Traveling in the dark also lessened their chances of being spotted, though it made selecting the best path more difficult. He could use owls, with their excellent night vision, to aid that process.

Kasiel went a short distance away from the camp and lured in a mule deer, drawing the poor creature right into Niskenya's jaws. It felt cruel, but he needed to enable her recovery and hunting in this terrain after what she had been through was asking too much. He also urged several mice out into the open that Akyla enjoyed snatching up. They were small enough the raptor could swallow them whole, avoiding the stress on his injured beak of tearing apart his prey.

Kasiel breathed a weary laugh, placing a hand on Irith's shoulders. "You're the only one of us in decent shape, it seems."

The big cat purred, affection pouring off him.

"You are a sorry bunch," Merrin agreed, walking up on his other side.

Kasiel glanced at her. Her white-blond hair was almost the same color as his father's and the khevarin's. Something in the set of her jaw and her stance spoke to her strength and well-earned confidence as a warrior.

"I've been meaning to ask you something. How do you know so much about poisons?"

She met his eyes, a hint of a smile tugging at one side of her mouth. "Sometimes in war, and politics in general, there is a need for certain people to crop up dead. It requires a special skill set."

"You mean assassination?"

"Yes."

"You were an assassin? For whom?"

She smirked. "A woman never kills and tells. Suffice it to say, I found after a few years that I didn't love the work, but I try to keep my skills sharp in case my commanding officer ever needs someone to pass away discreetly. Like Jhanik, for instance." Her teasing wink reassured him she wasn't serious.

Kasiel chuckled. "We'll revisit that when we get back from this adventure." He considered her for a second, the way her pale gray eyes dispassionately watched Niskenya tear apart her meal. "On a more serious note, how would you feel about using those skills? There's a chance they could prove useful once we reach Cabril."

"I can think of no better reason to use them than to help my tehsheyn." Genuine warmth shone through in her smile, which was a rare thing for Merrin. "I didn't come over here for that, however. Several of your soldiers are curious about you and your beasts. I thought there might be an opportunity in that to build connection and help them become less anxious around you."

He glanced back toward the camp, noticing several individuals looking their way. "The Delaphinians?"

"All of them. Your beasts and your ability to work with them are a source of fear and curiosity to the Delaphinians, but Niskenya is a revered creature in Vanris, and your skills are uncommon enough that even your own people aren't sure what to think of you."

My own people.

When he looked toward the camp this time, he paid more attention, noticing that the ones casting curious glances his way weren't just the Delaphinians. "Let me see how Niskenya feels when she's done eating. I could introduce them to Irith and Akyla, but I suspect she's the one they most want to get close to. Thank you for your observations, Merrin."

"Ahninveth." She bent forward in a slight bow before walking away.

For the next hour, he gave Niskenya time to eat and digest while he helped set up camp and care for the horses as much as his damaged lungs and throat would allow. Those simple, mundane tasks seemed to help the others relax more in his presence. When he sensed calm from Niskenya, he approached her. She stood, catching on to the fact that he wanted something more than just to visit. She lowered her head, and he touched his forehead to hers, closing his eyes to focus on her presence in his mind. A deep rumble rose in her chest.

"I know you're tired, but will you speak to them with me?"

Affection answered him. Of course she would. There was no time at which she wouldn't do whatever she could for him. He brought his hand out and rested it on the side of her neck. She responded instantly, placing her massive paw against his forearm and curling her claws around it. Protective warmth embraced him. The surrounding smells and sounds changed, echoing in his head through two noses and two sets of ears. Fear and sorrow melted away. Irith, Akyla, and now Jethan were comforting presences on the edge of their connection. He might not have a romantic partner in his life, but with his companions and his tehsheyn, he would never be alone.

The eagle let out a cry then. Not moving, Kasiel slipped in to borrow its eyes. It had perched in a scraggly tree behind the kanodrak, gazing over them at a camp full of soldiers who were almost all staring in their direction now. Niskenya huffed, her claws slowly retracting. Kasiel opened his eyes and stepped back from her.

"I guess this is a good time to introduce you to everyone," he said, a slight smile winning its way across his lips.

CHAPTER SEVENTEEN

Introducing the rest of the unit to Niskenya proved to be the opening they all needed. The kanodrak had no interest in letting a bunch of strangers touch her, but she let them come relatively close, stretching out behind Kasiel while they all sat to eat and asked him about her and his ability. Irith was happy to make up for Niskenya's aloofness, particularly whenever it might earn him a bite of meat or a good scratch behind the ears. The cliff cat seemed more like a dog at times like this, though Kasiel would never tell him that.

When Kasiel's throat started protesting all the talking, Nerith and Tath intervened and helped redirect the group, encouraging the sharing of a few tales about the unit's exploits. As the afternoon wore on into evening, others chimed in with stories of their own experiences, and Kasiel watched with a sense of satisfaction as the distance between them dwindled.

When they got on the road again a few hours before dawn, though the uncertainty of the coming confrontation still lay ahead of them, he noticed an improvement in their willingness to interact with one another, himself excluded. Despite answering questions and introducing them to his companions, most of them continued to keep their distance. Niskenya's almost constant presence at his side likely didn't help with that, but he wasn't about to discourage her from sticking close, even if he thought she would listen.

It was around noon when Jethan returned to his place beside him. "I never realized how exhausting socializing could be."

Kasiel chuckled. "It does look trying."

Jethan sighed and rolled his shoulders as if he had somehow overused them chatting with people. "I miss Keyla."

Kasiel said nothing.

"Blast it. Sorry, Kas. I didn't mean to—"

"It's fine."

"Is it? You're supposed to be able to count on your tehnaak not to kick the sore spots when you're down."

Kasiel frowned, moving behind Akyla's eyes. "I made the wrong choices. Choices you warned me not to make. I don't think you have to pander to my broken heart."

"True." Jethan donned his best scoundrel grin. "I am pretty much a genius when it comes to making smart choices."

Kasiel snorted. "Oh, yes, like when you got thrown in the deeps for—"

"Hey, let's not get mean about it." His smile faded after a moment. "You know, I can feel your heartache now. Not as acutely as you do, I'm sure, but it's there."

"Sorry about that." Kasiel bounced between his avian scouts, releasing and replacing a few that were getting too far from where he had picked them up.

Jethan offered him a fond smile this time. "Don't be sorry. Sharing each other's burdens is part of why we made this tehsheyn real. Though, speaking of burdens, what happens if we actually pull this off?"

A ripple of tension moved through Kasiel. "You mean what's my father going to do? I honestly don't know. I..." He trailed off, focusing on the view from the eyes of a nearby raven.

The bird was flying along to the northwest of them, where a dirt track barely wide enough to support a single wagon had been painstakingly chipped out of the rugged basalt. A pair of riders in Sarket's colors were moving along at a fast pace, following the track south and slightly west. Not taking any chances, Kasiel quickly extended his ability, making the lead horse stumble and go down.

"I need a Dampener and two or three archers. Now." He turned his mount to move out of the group.

Kince veered off with him along with a Dampener named Rahlyf. Leif also turned to follow them. After a brief hesitation, one of the other Delaphinian soldiers broke off as well.

Kasiel glanced at Jethan. "You're in charge. Keep on this heading but slow the pace."

Jethan nodded and kicked his mount up alongside Darro, where Kince had been riding.

While he was gathering his group, it took little effort for Kasiel to convince the Sarketi soldier's horse that it couldn't walk on its front leg. The animal had taken a few minor scrapes in the fall, as most likely had its rider, but it was technically still sound. What mattered was that it didn't act like it was. He had the raven land on a nearby rock to keep watch and eavesdrop.

"Shit. We haven't got time for this." The Sarketi man now on the ground kicked a rock, then cursed again as he hopped away from the object that had apparently proven more durable than his foot.

The other man rested his reins on the pommel of his saddle. "This whole thing is pointless. You know that blasted farmer was probably drinking. Why would Vanris send a unit with one of their beast controllers out here?"

The man on the ground scowled up at him. "Let me

think. Maybe because the queen's out here."

The mounted man leaned forward, peering at the leg his companion's horse was still holding up. "But how would they even know that?"

"I don't know, and I don't care," the other man snarled, limping back to his mount. "We have orders to get word to King Lodmund, and I mean to do so. If you're willing to risk being wrong, you're welcome to stay behind. I'll take your horse."

The mounted man swung to the ground with a grunt and walked over to pick up the leg the other animal was favoring, inspecting it for injury.

Kasiel had his group dismount. In this terrain, they could move faster on foot and wouldn't have to risk injuring a mount. They also wouldn't draw attention as quickly without the horse's hooves clattering against the rocks. They still needed to be careful. This footing lent itself well to sprains and breaks. They got closer to the two soldiers than he expected to while crossing the lava field. Partially because they tried to make use of natural dips in the old broken ground, and because one soldier was examining the supposedly injured horse while the other was preoccupied with stringing curses together into creative, if somewhat nonsensical, sentences.

"The minute they spot us, someone needs to take down the man on the left." He glanced at Rahlyf. "I want the other for questioning."

The Dampener answered with a solemn nod.

They were still a good seventy yards away when one Sarketi soldier noticed them, shouting a warning as he drew his sword. Kince hit the predetermined target in the thigh, preventing him from running. Leif's arrow sank into the gap below his helmet, taking him down. The third archer dropped an arrow in the path of the other Sarketi soldier when he tried to make a run for the horse he believed to be in better condition. Rahlyf's focus turned inward, and the man stopped where he stood, flailing about with his sword in one hand.

"Havaad protect me! I can't see!"

Kasiel moved the horses out of the man's range to keep him from injuring them and continued toward him. By the time they reached him, he was on his knees, his sword held in a white-knuckled grip before him. He turned in their vague direction, responding to the sound of footsteps.

"Vanrian mind-fuckers," the man snarled, raising the weapon and swinging it wildly in front of him.

Kasiel glanced at Rahlyf and gestured to the sword.

"What? Where is it?" Deprived of sensation in his hands, the man dropped the weapon. "No!" He flailed about, cracking fingers that had no feeling against the unforgiving rock. "You Havaad-cursed, beast-born abominations!"

That was an insult Kasiel hadn't heard yet. He stepped forward, pinning the blade under one foot as an extra precaution. Trying to ignore the twisting of guilt at the terror in the man's unseeing eyes, he said, "Strip off his surcoat, tie his hands, and relieve him of any remaining weapons."

Kince stepped in immediately, Leif quickly joining him. Kasiel caught the attention of the third archer. "See if there's anything useful on the other one and grab his surcoat."

Tears tracked down the Sarketi soldier's face. He resumed cursing at them while Leif and Kince removed his surcoat, then disarmed and bound him. It took several minutes to get the dead soldier moved into a depression in the ground where he was unlikely to be noticed by travelers and strip him of his surcoat. The enemy garments were too potentially useful to pass up. Once they had the other soldier secured, Kasiel had Rahlyf return his senses of vision and touch to him. They led him and the two horses back toward where they had left their mounts.

By the time they caught up with the others, Kasiel wished he had taken Jethan with him. A Charmer might have gotten their prisoner to abandon his unending tirade of insults and curses. They found a relatively sheltered place amidst the sparse trees to stop and interrogate the man. Kasiel let his throat rest, leaving most of the work to their Evoker, Yserra, and Jethan. He asked them to keep the process as honorable as possible, given that they had Delaphinian allies watching. With a few strategic applications of the Dampener's skills, Irith happy to intimidate, and Niskenya looming, it didn't take long to pick apart the man's memories for information about the stronghold's current defenses. Then came the problem of deciding what to do with their prisoner.

It was Lucia who said what they were all thinking. "We haven't got the extra soldiers to watch over him if we bring him with us, and we can't let him go."

Kasiel's immediate reaction was to reject her words, but he remembered the night in Coranthis when Itana killed the woman they had used to guide them to Prince Elijah's stronghold. Itana had been right then, and Lucia was now. They couldn't set him free and risk him warning someone of their presence here, but they had too small a unit to spare someone to watch over him while they were trying to infiltrate the stronghold. Tying him up and leaving him somewhere was an option, but out here, wild predators would appreciate the easy meal.

Still, killing an enemy during combat was much different than ending the life of someone who was at your mercy, bound and unarmed. Watching a person die, seeing the terror and pain in their eyes before the end, wasn't something he cared to make a habit out of. But maybe he didn't have to.

He called the two Dampeners over to where his core

group was discussing the problem. "How much physical sensation can you stifle?"

The woman, Minera, paled. "You mean..."

Rahlyf's jaw tightened for a second before he gave a curt nod. "We can take away his pain, if that's what you want."

Minera swallowed and nodded. "A painless death is something we can give if we must."

Kasiel met each of their eyes in turn, holding the woman's longer. "I'm sorry. I know it's an awful way to use your ability and I hate to ask it of you, but if we must kill him, I see no point in making him suffer."

Minera nodded. "If we work together, he won't feel anything. We can't erase his fear, though."

"I can, at least to some degree," Jethan offered.

Kasiel met his tehnaak's eyes. He hated to ask this of him even more than the others, but he couldn't let favoritism show in front of them, at least not to this extent. "Thank you."

They walked back over to the man. He immediately started cursing at them, his hatred narrowing in on Jethan, who deliberately stopped in front of him.

"Go ahead and kill me, you Havaad-cursed bastards! I—"

"We're going to let you go," Jethan interrupted.

The man's mouth hung open for a second, his eyes locking with Jethan's. Then he leaned back slightly, wariness in his stance. "You're what?"

"We're going to let you go. We don't have enough people to put a guard on you, so we're going to let you go and you're going to leave this area."

While he was speaking, Kince started approaching from the side, but Merrin touched his arm. Their eyes met and Kince stepped back, letting her move around behind the man. She drew her dagger. Kasiel nodded to the Dampeners.

"I'm going to leave here," the soldier echoed, hope lighting his eyes as Jethan held his gaze.

"That's right. You get to go."

The man responded with a tremulous smile.

Merrin met Jethan's eyes over their prisoner's shoulder, and he took several steps back. In a smooth motion, she grabbed hold of the man's chin with one hand and lifted, drawing her dagger deep into his neck. Blood sprayed. The man looked confused, but it was clear he didn't feel the pain or even the fear that should have struck him in that moment. He tried to speak, but Merrin's blade had done too much damage.

Seconds moved past with agonizing slowness, the man's life surging from the gaping wound across his neck. Kince hurried over to help Merrin support him, the two easing him to the ground when he went unconscious. It would be a matter of minutes before his heart stopped completely.

It was done, and Kasiel, though he felt sick to his stomach, managed somehow not to throw up. He didn't feel especially pleased by that accomplishment. It struck him as a sign that he was getting used to the death.

"Let's get going. We want to be in position to move on the stronghold before tomorrow morning if we can." He turned away from the dead man, heading for his horse.

Lucia hurried after him, an approach that caught him somewhat by surprise. "I am increasingly impressed by you and your unit, Ahninveth. If ever we are enemies again, I hope my death, should it come, would come at the hands of someone like you, who would at least feel some sorrow for my loss."

He stopped beside his horse and faced her. "Do you expect us to be enemies again?"

She shrugged. "Delaphine and Fallend allied against Sarket for years before the Vanrian people provided them a new target. Sarket was always stronger and more aggressive. We lost more battles than we won. Then they decided you were the greater threat, so they set aside their efforts to subjugate us and proposed an alliance. If Delaphine thinks Sarket might win this, it wouldn't surprise me to see them pivot back to the former alliance. But having seen what Vanris can do when you put your soldiers and mind-crafters to work, I think the odds are in your favor."

Kasiel put a hand on the saddle, wishing it was Niskenya's he was about to swing up on. "Thank you for being the logical voice back there. I knew what needed to be done. I just hating taking a life, especially when they can't even defend themselves."

A sad smile curved her lips, sympathy softening her eyes. "I would like you a lot less if you didn't feel that way." With those words, she left him to go collect her horse.

Jethan rode up close as Kasiel was swinging into the saddle. "That sounded like progress. She didn't seem so scared of you."

"I'm not sure if we can judge progress based on Lucia. I get the feeling she's seen more than her share of awful things." He settled his restless horse with a thought and eyed Jethan for a moment. "How are you? I know you couldn't have enjoyed playing a part in that."

Jethan ducked his head, avoiding Kasiel's eyes. "We all need to pitch in to make this work. I did what was necessary."

"You forget I can feel your distress to some degree now, and it feels a little like a thundercloud just landed next to me."

"I'd like to take credit, but you could be feeling the real thing." He raised one hand, the reins draping over his thumb as he pointed north.

Kasiel looked ahead. The sky was darkening prematurely, turning a moody, charcoal gray. If a storm hit Cabril around the same time they did, it could help them. Then again, if it brought a lot of lightning, it could also make stealth more challenging. They would have to proceed as planned and see what nature had in store.

"We should get moving." He glanced around to find the others mounted and ready to go. Facing forward, he met Darro's eyes and nodded. "Lead on."

"Hey," Jethan began after they had been traveling for a few minutes, "do you think we'll be able to tell when each other is engaged in intimate activities?"

Kince barked a laugh.

*

As they progressed northward, the sky continued to darken with the approach of evening and the expansion of a massive storm. The horses grew more nervous, requiring Kasiel to invest additional effort in keeping them calm and tractable. A few fat raindrops fell upon his lead birds, through which he could now see the stronghold that sat outside Cabril, extending to the edge of basalt cliffs above a wide, slow-moving river. Their approach would take them up to the southwest corner of the keep. The river ran south along the eastern side of the town of Cabril, then it turned west, bordering the stronghold on the east and south sides.

The stronghold took up the entirety of a plateau set upon impressive, angular basalt columns at least fifteen feet tall on the north and west sides and twice that over the two sides the river ran along. Long stone ramps extended down on the landward sides with drawbridges built in at the top near the gates. There were a few sentries along the walls between distantly placed torches, though more of a token showing, supporting the idea that the structure was still unoccupied. The buildings that made up the keep inside the walls appeared mostly dark. A quick pass within using a small bird revealed that many of those windows had heavy black curtains covering them, thin seams of light showing at the edges of a few he investigated.

It appeared that King Lodmund was counting on the stronghold's reputation as currently without a resident lord to help him hide his queen. Kasiel was wholeheartedly in favor of his approach. He might be less so if he didn't have the ability to spy within using rodents to see how substantial the defenses really were, but the effort to limit visible occupants would likely work out in their favor.

Thunder rumbled, vibrating through the sill the bird perched on. Heavy raindrops started splattering down around it. Kasiel released all his avian scouts within the area of the storm to let them go seek shelter and drew Akyla and the few others keeping watch near their unit in closer. The hard part up front was going to be getting to the stronghold without being seen. In the process of scouting, he had picked out a natural u-shaped formation in a basalt cliff that would allow them to hide their horses. The animals would still be largely exposed to the weather, but at least no one was likely to stumble upon them in the storm. If they succeeded in taking the stronghold, he could bring the horses along after.

The rain had become a steady downpour by the time they reached the place where he meant to leave the horses. Their unit would split into two groups and approach from different sides. At least that was the initial plan. With the help of the Dampeners and the storm, they should be able to get to the gates without drawing attention. First, he needed to do additional reconnaissance within the keep to verify that the queen was there and scout out the resistance they would face.

He found a wet but relatively smooth chunk of

rock to sit upon. Niskenya came to stand protectively over him as he closed his eyes and reached out into the stronghold. He started within the outer wall, checking that there were no more troops moving about than he had spotted with the bird. There were actually less now, suggesting that some of the night sentries had stepped in out of the storm. If the queen had stayed here long without incident, he could imagine they might not be as diligent in their watches in this weather.

From there, he found more rodents to check in the barracks, the stables, and various other service buildings outside the keep. Then he moved within, cautiously wandering the halls in search of the stronghold's occupants. He counted a few more than forty soldiers in total and an array of serving staff, most of whom were in their beds. A couple of young, richly dressed women were surprisingly still awake, sitting on a large, canopied bed in a lavishly appointed bedchamber on the second floor of the central part of the keep. Incredibly young women, giggling nervously whenever the thunder crashed overhead to the apparent disgust of a well-dressed advisor or guardian sitting reading next to the fire. The man was careful to hide his sneers any time the women glanced his way.

One of the two was well into her pregnancy. Enough so that she appeared ready to burst at any moment. The other, a girl with features distinctly similar to Lady Katerin De Clare's, also looked as if she was with child, though Katerin had mentioned no such thing.

"Ah! Is that a mouse?"

The shriek startled Kasiel almost as much as it did De Clare's daughter and the man by the fire.

"Havaad have mercy," the man snapped. "It is indeed *just* a mouse. Calm down, Your Majesty, before your send yourself into labor."

As the man set his book aside and stood, Kasiel released

the rodent, letting it bolt for safety, and returned to himself. When he opened his eyes, a few of his companions were watching him curiously.

"Is everything all right?" Wedro asked. "You practically jumped off that rock a second ago."

"Yes. The queen apparently has no fondness for rodents and an excellent set of lungs on her. The important thing is that she is in there." He stood, placing a hand on Niskenya's shoulder. "We're good to move. They've got just over forty soldiers and some general staff. Most are asleep or trying to sleep. Even those on duty appear to be staying indoors out of the weather."

"We're the only idiots out here trying to get ourselves struck by lightning," Kince grumbled.

A few of the newer recruits nodded their agreement.

Kasiel pulled a bold grin, projecting more confidence than he felt with a boost from Niskenya. "If everything goes as planned, we'll have possession of the stronghold by morning and a warm, dry place to rest."

They made their way up toward the stronghold in the pouring rain with occasional rumbles of thunder and flashes of lightning overhead. There was little in the way of wind to move the storm along, so it hung above them, soaking through their clothes and the leather of their armor and threatening to do the same to their spirits. They used any cover they could find to avoid being seen in the periodic flares of light from overhead. The Dampeners watched the walls, ready to use their abilities if they spotted any soldiers looking their direction.

The weather was miserable enough that the sentries appeared to have all ducked into the shelters at the corner towers. When the unit was closer, they split up into two groups, each with a Speaker, a Charmer, a Dampener, and a healer. Jethan led the second team, taking Darro, Kince, Etris, and Tath along with Rahlyf and nine more soldiers. Kasiel took Merrin, Avris, Wedro, and Nerith, as well as the Evoker, Yserra, the other three mind-crafters, and the remaining five soldiers. Leif and Emil went with Jethan's group, but Annora and Lucia chose to go with Kasiel. His team also had Irith. Niskenya, much to her distress, would wait outside the walls until they had control of the keep unless something went wrong that required her intervention.

The two Speakers would allow the groups to maintain

contact and react quickly if either needed help. Kasiel was counting on the Charmers to be their first line of defense if they ran into solitary servants. Anything more substantial and they had the Dampeners to unbalance the odds in their favor. The goal was to take down any opposition as quickly and quietly as possible. The farther each group got without raising alarms, the better their chances of avoiding a large-scale fight. His aim wasn't just to gain a valuable hostage, it was to do so without losing any of his soldiers.

"Be careful, tehnaak. I'm not eager to find out what it feels like if one of us gets hurt." Jethan said, the worry in his eyes suggesting a worse possibility.

"You too. I plan on cracking a stone with you when this is over." Kasiel glanced around at them all. "In fact, I expect to share a drink with all of you before the sun rises. We know the healers won't allow you drink if you're seriously injured, so stay healthy."

They all responded in the affirmative, some with distinctly more enthusiasm and confidence than others. A few of the Delaphinians looked especially uneasy. That was understandable, though it made him wish he had pushed for an Enkindler or two. They were working as part of a dominantly Vanrian unit with numerous mind-crafters. Considering how young the alliance still was, this was a new experience for them. The success of the mission would mean a great deal for Vanris and Delaphine in more than just the acquisition of a valuable hostage.

"We all know the plan. Now let's make it happen."

Jethan met his eyes and nodded before they split. It was tempting to send Irith with that group just so he could try to protect his tehnaak, but he had to trust them. Besides, it would lessen his situational awareness if he split his attention that way. His team's goal was to reach the queen via the most direct route possible to avoid giving anyone a chance to sneak her out. Jethan's team would be focused more on handling guards and sentries in other areas to keep them from coming up behind Kasiel's group.

The first step required the Charmer – Fenvar on Kasiel's team – to approach the gate wearing a Sarketi surcoat under his cloak with the hood pulled up to hide his ears. Kasiel had scouted ahead with rodents to confirm that the gates into the stronghold had no more than two guards each. Minera crept up the ramp to hide behind an inset pillar meant to hold the lord's banner, getting as close as she could while remaining unseen to ensure anyone who stepped out on one of the watchtowers with a view of the gates would suffer an inexplicable night blindness.

They coordinated their approach with Jethan's team, using the Speakers to confirm timing. Watching Minera move into position while Fenvar made his way to the gate set Kasiel's nerves on edge. Not only because of how much rested on each step in their plan, but also because he knew his tehnaak would be doing the same thing at the other gate. He drew on the first two rodents he could find in the vicinity of the gatehouses and moved them into positions where he would be able to see and hear through them as needed. An instant after he slipped behind the eyes and ears of the mouse he had moved close to the northern gate, a soldier slammed his boot down on the poor creature. For a split second, Kasiel felt his bones and organs being crushed, then he snapped back into himself with a gasp.

Nerith placed a hand on his shoulder. "Are you all right, Kas?"

"I'm fine."

Other than a burning sense of guilt at the life he had carelessly ended and a chill that still moved through him from that flash of horrifying pain. Her hand slid down to his arm and stayed there as he refocused his attention on the rat at the closer gatehouse, using more caution this time when he moved into place to hear and see what was happening.

"We can't let you in here," the gate guard was saying.

"I've got an important missive from General Hackett for Captain Vollan." Kasiel nodded to himself, impressed by Fenvar's ability to hide his Vanrian accent and smoothly drop the name of the resident captain they had gotten from their prisoner. "I'll give it to you, but only after you let me in out of this Havaad-cursed weather. Look at me, I'm soaked through."

"That you are." The slightest change in the gate guard's voice told him the man had made the mistake of looking the Charmer in the eyes.

"The captain's going to want to see this right away," Fenvar pressed.

"He absolutely is. Let me get this gate open."

Kasiel prepared to move.

As soon as Fenvar was in, Minera hurried to follow so she could cut off all senses for the two gate guards. It fell on the shoulders of the two mind-crafters to kill these first soldiers, given that the rest of their team remained hidden near the bottom of the ramp. A few seconds after the two disappeared through the opened gate, Fenvar stepped into the light of a torch within the entrance arch and waved them up before ducking back out of sight.

The rest of them made their way quickly and carefully up the ramp. It was the Dampener's job to make sure no one spotted them, but that didn't mean they could be careless. Kasiel stayed close to his Speaker, Revik, waiting for word from the other gate. As they were reaching their entrance, and he was about to search for another rodent to go look for himself, the man caught his eye and nodded.

"The other team is inside, Ahninveth."

For a moment, Kasiel could breathe easier, but the hard part was just starting. Two of his Delaphinian soldiers donned the surcoats of the dead guards over their armor. Anything that could make their enemies hesitate at a critical moment and buy them a few seconds to act was worth trying. By doing so, they accepted that they might have to step into lead positions at some point going forward, but that discussion had happened before they left the horses to make their move on the stronghold.

A flash of lightning lit the courtyard as Kasiel and Merrin peered out through a narrow window in the gatehouse. Jethan's team was at the main entrance on the north side, closer to town. This ramp came into a service area with a stable, a smithy, and a pathway between two buildings that led to the lightly manned barracks. Directly across from them was a staircase that led to a second-level covered walkway passing over the path and around to an upper entrance into the keep itself. A route Kasiel had spotted when he came through with the bird earlier.

The only torches burning were those sufficiently sheltered from the downpour. Fat raindrops hit hard enough the splash made it almost look as if they were raining up from the ground. Standing water reflected the bright flash of lightning as jagged bolts ripped across a black sky. It would feel amazing to get out of that weather, and the rain would almost instantly obscure any footprints they left in the courtyard. Once inside, however, they would leave a trail of water anywhere they went. That significantly increased the risk of someone figuring out they were there and sneaking up behind them.

Wedro eyed the walkway. "Let me go first. If the door's locked, I can get us in."

Kasiel gave him a sideways glance. "You and Jethan?"

"Jeth can pick locks?" Wedro looked genuinely surprised.

"So can I." Merrin leaned in. "Send me, Wedro, and Fenvar over first. We'll handle getting in and take care of anyone lurking behind that door."

"Hold on."

Kasiel went in search of another mouse, trying not to think about the grotesque and untimely demise of the last one. It took him a few minutes to track one down and search out a way into the room beyond the door. It looked like a small war room that potentially doubled as a dining area for soldiers, judging from the arrangement of tables. Two men were in there now, one with stripes of rank on his armor that marked him as a captain. They appeared to be arguing about something. Despite the temptation, Kasiel didn't waste time eavesdropping.

"There are two soldiers in the room behind that door. They're arguing right now. One appears to be Captain Vollan."

Merrin nodded. "Avris and one more soldier will come with us. We should be able to get the door unlocked without alerting anyone in this storm. If they keep up their quarreling, even better."

"I'll go." Lucia stepped up next to them.

A hunger gleamed in her eyes that gave him a moment of pause, but Kasiel got the sense that whatever was behind it would work to their benefit. "All right. Rahlyf will make sure no one sees you, but don't be reckless. Get in and take them out. Quick and clean. I'll follow with the next group."

As they prepared to head out, he called Nerith and a few others forward to be the Dampener's extra sets of eyes, watching for guards. "You five will come last with Irith. He'll be a reliable early warning if someone spots you."

Nerith narrowed her eyes. "All the more reason he should go with you."

"He should go with our Dampener, who needs to be the first one aware of any threats." He met Rahlyf's eyes briefly, getting an appreciative nod from the man. "Revik will go with me so he can also give warning if we spot anyone while your group is crossing. End of discussion."

Her lips pressed to a tight line, but she didn't push the issue.

He turned and nodded to the first group, watching as they darted out, Rahlyf peering around the area through the doorway to search for any enemies who weren't inside hiding from the weather. After the first group started up the stairs on the opposite side of the yard, Kasiel ducked his awareness back to the mouse, checking on the two men in the war room. Only now there were three.

He turned to Revik. "Let them know there's now a third soldier behind that door."

The man nodded, his eyes losing focus for an instant. Across the way, lit by a flash of lightning, Wedro gave a quick gesture to confirm the information. Kasiel started his group moving as the first set went to work on the door. They were at the foot of the stairs when light spilled out of the doorway and the five up there rushed inside. He ordered his group to duck down on the walk and watch for danger for the last team. Then he hurried to the door that someone had closed again, perhaps to block off that beacon of light.

The coil of anxiety in his gut tightened, and he drew his blade, wasting no time ducking inside after his companions. As he went through, a wave of soothing rolled over him. Overflow from Fenvar, who was kneeling next to Captain Vollan. The captain had a hand clamped over a wound on his arm and was sitting on the floor a few feet away from one of his dead men, his gaze locked with the Charmer's. Wedro and Merrin were dragging the third soldier's body away from the opposite door.

The rest of their team filed in a few minutes later. Everyone moved softly, not saying anything. Kasiel met Revik's eyes, and he nodded. Jethan's group was still doing well. Any information beyond that would have to wait while Kasiel scouted out their nearest threats. Until then, they would assume danger behind the next door.

Kasiel turned his attention to the rodents in the keep, using a couple of mice to listen and check the nearby halls. When he confirmed the surrounding halls were empty, he turned to Fenvar. "Is there some reason the captain's still breathing?"

"I thought we should keep him alive," Rahlyf answered. "He is the captain here. He might have useful information."

Kasiel hesitated. He found himself looking at Lucia.

She flipped her palm up in a gesture of uncertainty. "It's a risk to leave someone alive behind us, but if we bind him securely and gag him, it ought to be safe enough. He should know if there are additional troops in the area or if they're expecting reinforcements here anytime soon."

"All right, but make sure he's secure." He eyed his team. "I need someone to stay with him and keep him from trying to draw attention."

One of the Delaphinian soldiers stepped forward. "I'll guard. My stealth skills aren't the greatest anyhow. I'd be more useful here."

Kasiel inclined his head to the man. "Thank you. You should be safe here, but if you get into trouble, leave him and come find us or hide if you need to. Don't take on anyone you're not confident you can defeat." He dipped his finger in a pool of blood on the floor and drew a rough map on one table. "Go left down this hall, turn right at the third hall down, and go straight to the end. That's the room the queen is in. That's where we're heading." He quickly wiped his finger clean, struggling to suppress a shudder as he realized what he had used for ink.

"Thank you, Ahninveth." The man offered a partial bow.

Wedro and Merrin took point as they moved out into the hall, with Kasiel and Irith behind them. Given the hour, most people would still be asleep, or at least trying to sleep through the storm, other than the unlucky guards and servants working the night shift. The cold stone hall was dimly lit by a few burning sconces. Long carpets on the floors kept a little of the chill at bay.

They were almost alongside the first door when a guard stepped out, holding his helmet under one arm, and staring into the room behind him with a broad grin. Wedro grabbed him, burying a dagger in his throat. Kasiel dashed into the room after Merrin in time to see her shaking her head at the woman on the bed, her finger to her lips to signal silence. The woman had her blanket pulled up to hide her nudity. Her hand went to her mouth and tears welled in her eyes when Wedro dragged the dying man into the room.

Fenvar wove past them and hunkered in her line of sight. "This is just a nightmare," he said, a powerful soothing rolling out from him. "You're going to lie down, close your eyes, and have a pleasant dream now. Doesn't that sound nice?"

She stared at him, a tear racing down one cheek, and nodded. Then she sank back on the bed and closed her eyes. The Charmer gestured toward the hall with a jerk of his head. They stepped over the dead soldier and moved back outside the room, shutting the door gently.

"That should hold her for at least a half hour. I

wouldn't count on much more than that."

Kasiel placed a hand on his shoulder. "That's good enough. We should be in a better place to deal with her by then."

Before they passed the next two intersecting halls, Kasiel peeked around them with a mouse he was bringing along. Irith almost made a snack of it once, so he kept a little extra attention on the cliff cat's intentions for now. Both halls were empty, but the next one down, the one the queen's room was in, had two guards toward the end in front of her door. He glanced around at his group.

"We've got two guards at the end of this hall," he whispered. "I don't think we'll be able to get close without them sounding an alarm."

"I can take one out with my crossbow." Merrin hefted the weapon for emphasis.

"I can handle the other," Nerith said, stepping forward.

He met Nerith's eyes. "Are you sure?"

Irritation darkened her expression, and he realized he had blundered. It seemed to be a habit he had with her.

Avris placed an arm around her shoulders and gave her a small squeeze. "She never misses."

"How do I not know this?"

Nerith shrugged and took the crossbow Wedro offered her. Kasiel leaned close to her as she started loading it. "Maybe if you carried one of those normally, I might have suspected."

She smirked as she carefully loaded the weapon. "No excuses for not paying attention, Ahninveth," she whispered back.

A smile crept across his lips as he took another look through the eyes of the mouse. "They have half helmets and partial plate armor. More palace formal than battlefield. If you can manage a throat or face shot that will drop them quickly, do it. Try to time it with the next crash of thunder. I'll have Irith ready to run in and finish them off if needed."

The two got their crossbows loaded. Kasiel held up a hand as he crept the mouse down along the wall, trying to avoid notice. The instant thunder started shaking the building, he ran the mouse out into the center of the hall, drawing the eyes of the two men down, and signaled Merrin and Nerith to go. They stepped out and fired in one fluid motion, moving as a near perfect unit. Their fingers had barely finished depressing the triggers when Irith bolted out, sprinting down to ensure no one survived. Looking out through the cliff cat's eyes, Kasiel saw the two men drop. The crash of thunder faded.

Wedro and Avris hurried down the hall with Kasiel and the others on their heels, wasting no time in case the room's occupants had heard anything. Given the region, it was all too likely that there would be another route out of the bedchamber meant for servants and emergencies. One of the two guards had reached for the door after he went down, but Irith interrupted him. The big cat glanced at Kasiel, blood on his mouth, pride spreading across their link.

Kasiel sent him praise as Wedro and Avris rushed into the room with their weapons ready. The two young women had lain down to sleep at some point. They snapped upright now, the queen's hand going to her swollen belly as fear flashed in her eyes. De Clare's daughter, Hannah, shifted closer to the queen, putting an arm out as if to shield her from them. The man who had been with them was gone, likely retired to an adjacent room.

"Who—"

Kasiel cut Hannah off with a sharp shake of his head and a finger to his lips.

As his team entered the room, he singled out Merrin,

Avris, Lucia, and the other five soldiers with silent gestures, quickly splitting them into two groups and sending them back out to search the adjacent rooms. He kept Wedro, Nerith, and the other four mind-crafters with him.

"Wh—"

Kasiel silenced her again, this time with a severe look of warning. The others returned a few minutes later, filing into the large bedchamber with the advisor and another serving woman in hand. Both were trembling and looked ready to pass out from terror. He couldn't hold that against them. In their shoes, with a team of fifteen armed enemies and two dead guards in the hall, he wouldn't be feeling overly confident either.

"Take the woman to another room and secure her. We'll deal with servants when we have full control of this place," he ordered, sending the second group, made up of two Delaphinian and two Vanrian soldiers, back out of the room.

As they departed, he met Revik's eyes.

The man's gaze unfocused for a few seconds, then he nodded. "Still good. They've run into some fighting, but nothing they couldn't handle."

Nerith moved back next to the door, watching down the hallway. Wedro positioned himself behind Kasiel, close enough to rush to his aid or Nerith's if necessary.

Kasiel faced the two women. "We're taking control of this place, Your Majesty."

The queen whimpered, closing her eyes. She didn't look older than fourteen or fifteen. Her skin was smooth and warm-toned, her eyes, when they opened again, a piercing deep blue within the curtain of her rich brown hair. She was a lovely child, but he couldn't see her as more than a child.

Hannah's blue eyes widened a fraction just as a phantom pain lanced through Kasiel's midsection. One hand went to his gut as if to cover a wound that wasn't really there, and he spun around, meeting Wedro's eyes. The other man's hands clamped around a wide blade protruding up through his abdomen below the ribs. Captain Vollan's eyes met Kasiel's over Wedro's shoulder, a savage grimace twisting his lips.

A scream of rage broke that frozen instant and Nerith leapt at the captain, driving her blade into the side of his neck. He yanked his sword free of Wedro's midsection, turning to face her. For a second, he wavered there, one hand letting go of his hilt to cover the gushing wound in the side of his neck. He looked surprised. Perhaps he hadn't expected a woman to attack him. If so, he was in for a bigger shock when Merrin's dagger sank deep into the back of his neck, and he went down, his blood-slicked blade hitting the floor with a clatter. A servant's door hidden in the wall behind him stood ajar.

Wedro reached out, his sliced hands dripping blood. Kasiel caught him, pulling the other man into his arms and easing him to the floor.

With a raw cry full of anguish, Nerith drove her blade into the dead captain's chest and left it there. Then she, Merrin, and Avris knelt on the floor around Wedro with Kasiel. The group that had taken the serving woman away came running back into the room. Wedro gripped Kasiel's arm tightly enough that his bracer felt like a vise. His other hand reached out for Merrin, who was trying to cover the bleeding hole in his gut. Blood already soaked the fancy rug he had gone down on from the entry wound in his back. When he finally got hold of one of Merrin's wrists, he pulled her hand away from the injury.

"No," Merrin choked out the word. "No, you can't go like this."

Kasiel felt as if his chest were collapsing. Nerith had worked her way to his side, where she could get a better look at the wound.

He met her eyes.

She shook her head, tears streaming down her cheeks.

Kasiel placed his free hand on Wedro's shoulder. The other man looked ghastly pale. "I'm sorry. This is my fault. I..."

Wedro's hand tightened even more on his arm, but some of the pain left his face and Kasiel realized their

Dampener, Minera, had moved in closer to help in the only way she could.

"It's all right, Kas," he managed, his voice strained. "I was never meant to be here... without Chander. But you helped me find... a family again." He paused, squeezing his eyes shut for a second. Then he opened them and met Kasiel's once more, his blue ones glazed with pain and struggling to focus. "That's good enough." He slid his bloody hand down from Merrin's wrist into her hand, taking hold of it. His eyes drifted closed. A few seconds later, both hands slackened and fell to his sides, the tension leaving his body.

Nerith felt for his pulse. "He's still alive, just unconscious." She brushed a tear from her cheek that was immediately replaced with more.

"Can you do anything?" Avris asked, pleading in her voice. "There must be something."

Nerith shook her head, her gaze going to the dark red soaking through the rug. "I can't. He's already lost too much blood, and a blade that size will have damaged internal organs. I..." her voice choked off with a sob then, and Kasiel put an arm around her shoulders, aware of the tears dampening his own cheeks.

He could feel Irith and Niskenya growing agitated with his distress. Someone was sobbing. It took a moment to place the sound as coming from the bed now behind him. His ears caught another sound as well.

Kasiel saw Hannah De Clare making her way around the end of the bed through Irith's eyes, a dagger tucked against her skirt where few of them were in position to see it, especially with their attention on Wedro. He gave the smallest shake of his head and a subtle hand gesture to direct the others to stay where they were. At the last second, he surged to his feet and spun, water from his hair spattering her face and dress as he caught her wrist in one hand and slammed her back into the bedpost, pinning her with his other forearm across her collarbones.

Fear lit her eyes, but she spat in his face. "Serves you right, you Vanrian monster!"

"You have a lot of nerve attacking me in front of my soldiers," he growled, Irith echoing the sound. "Are you trying to get yourself killed?"

"What if I am?" The tears and desperation in her eyes suggested she might be at that.

He held her arm over her head, squeezing her wrist until she dropped the dagger with a gasp. It clattered to the floor, and he kicked it away. "You're Lady De Clare's daughter, Hannah?"

The widening of her eyes was answer enough.

"She asked me to come save you. You're welcome." With a surge of rage, he shoved her to the side and back, landing her on the bed. He dug out the small ring Katerin had given him and tossed it on the bed next to her.

Still staring at him with wide eyes, she snatched up the ring and scooted back, wrapping her arms around the weeping queen.

"Ahninveth." Revik's tone was soft and tentative. "The other team wants to know who got hurt?"

Kasiel faced him and the man's brow furrowed.

"How do they know?"

"We're tehsheyn," he answered hoarsely, glancing down at Wedro.

The three women were still knelt around him with Minera near his head, focusing as she muted his pain sense. Not that it mattered as much now that he was unconscious, but Kasiel was grateful for her consideration. With the quantity of blood he had lost, it wouldn't be long before he was gone.

Looking at Revik again, he asked, "Is their team all right?"

The Speaker was silent a moment, then he nodded. "Only a few minor injuries so far."

A roiling hatred filled Kasiel. He stalked over and grabbed a pillow off the bed, earning a startled cry from the queen. Then he knelt next to Wedro and carefully lifted the man's head, sliding the pillow underneath it. When that was done, he stood and faced the Speaker again.

"Tell them we have the queen, and a group of us will make our way to the barracks next. It's time to wake up the rest of the soldiers. If—"

A sudden violent tug within him, like something being ripped away, cut him off with a gasp. Nerith stood and turned into Kasiel's ready arms, silent sobs shaking her shoulders. Merrin and Avris embraced where they sat on the floor and the Dampener stepped away. Kasiel sank more of himself into Niskenya, desperate for her strength, and invited her to do the same. Animal rage fed into him as the kanodrak pulled him behind her eyes.

She was standing in the rain, still as a statue, water pouring over her thick hide. Through her eyes, bringing visibility in the darkness, he saw a figure hurrying down the ramp on horseback. As they got closer, he recognized the Delaphinian soldier they had left with Captain Vollan. Whatever his reason, the man had abandoned his post. He had killed Wedro.

Lightning flashed. The horse balked and reared when the sudden brightness pulled Niskenya out of the dark. Panicking, the soldier tried to turn his mount around and the animal slipped on the wet stone. Then Niskenya was on them, claws and teeth ripping through flesh, powerful jaws snapping bones. It was over in an instant.

Kasiel sank back behind his own eyes, the taste of blood in his mouth. Merrin and Avris were standing now, hands on the hilts of their weapons.

"Merrin, Avris, you're with me and Irith, Lucia—"

Nerith pulled away from him. "I'm coming with you."

Kasiel met her eyes. "Good. Lucia, take Minera, Fenvar, and Annora to secure the remaining rooms up here. The rest of you stay and keep watch over our prisoners. Yserra, I'm leaving you in charge." He glanced around at his small group. "We'll go out the way we came in. We leave no soldiers alive."

"What about servants?" Lucia asked.

Kasiel glanced back at the women on the bed. The queen was still curled around her belly in Hannah's arms, crying. Hannah, her mother's ring on her pinky now, stared at him as though daring him to do anything she didn't approve of. "If they're combative enough to be a threat, kill them." The young woman flinched slightly at his words, glaring hatred at him. "Otherwise, tie them up until we can investigate the state of the dungeons in this place."

"What about me?" the queen's advisor asked. He stood trembling next to one of the other soldiers.

Kasiel bared his teeth in a savage grin, eager to draw blood with his claws – his blade. He could feel Niskenya coming up the ramp now, bloodlust burning through her – through them – like a fever. "Don't be combative."

Revik caught his arm. "The others still want an answer."

Kasiel looked down at Wedro, his features slack now, almost peaceful. "Tell them. They deserve to know who we lost." They deserved a chance to burn some of their sorrow in vengeance.

With part of his family around him, Kasiel strode from the room. They went out the same entrance they had come in through.

Avris paused on the way out. "What happened to—"

"Niskenya took care of him. He deserted his post. I don't know if he meant to betray us or just lost his nerve. Either way, it won't happen again."

Avris nodded, saying nothing more as they walked back out in the night and down the stairs into the pouring rain. Niskenya joined them, heading through the walkway to where the barracks were. Kasiel had the others position themselves around the courtyard and sent Niskenya to a dark alcove as he strode up to the door, waiting for a thunderclap to end before pounding his fist against it.

"We're under attack." He fell back easily enough into his former southern Fallend accent. "Get to the walls!"

A distant part of him admired how prepared they were. It was a matter of seconds before the door flew open and men came rushing out into the storm, ready to fight. A few were still fiddling with buckles on their armor or fastening on sword belts, but then they were expecting to get to the walls before they had to worry.

About fifteen had emerged when a crossbow bolt slammed into the face of a man who was putting on his helmet on the way out. That signaled their attack and Kasiel charged in with his group, Niskenya and Irith racing ahead into the fray. The bolt hadn't come from any of them, though. Kince emerged from the shadows up on the wall looking down on the yard, Darro and Tath with him. Jethan and Etris came in from another direction, bringing the rest of their telisheyn together, with that one crushing exception.

Kasiel fought like his beasts, raw anguish feeding his frenzy, his dark metal blade cutting through everything in his path. When he came back from that violent delirium, he was standing inside the barracks amidst numerous bodies, Irith, Jethan, and Nerith in there with him. Blood dripped from their weapons and spattered their armor. He met each of their eyes for an instant, then led them back out to the yard, into the cool, cleansing rain that poured over them, rinsing off some of the blood.

Lightning flashed, a little farther away this time, but still close enough to illuminate the others standing amidst more bodies. Etris stood at the center, her axe hanging in her hand, her head bowed so escaped strands of soaked blond hair obscured her face. Niskenya growled, still feeling the hurt and anger of their family around her. Kince, Darro, and Tath were down from the wall with the rest now. Kasiel leaned his head back and closed his eyes, letting the rain fall on his face and mix with his tears.

When he opened his eyes, they all moved in without a word shared between them and joined in a group embrace around Etris. Their tehsheyn, precious and new, had suffered a terrible loss, but those that remained would stand together to honor Wedro and support one another.

What they left behind was a mess. Kasiel lured the horses they had secured in the cliff alcove up into the stronghold to be put in the stables before they locked the gates. They removed any bodies from the main building, then sent the rest of Kasiel and Jethan's teams to do a sweep of the structure and grounds and secure it while the core group, now only nine strong, went to deal with the queen. They kept the Evoker, Yserra, with them to help with questioning if it became necessary. In the morning, after some rest, they could start working out a plan for getting their hostage and themselves safely away from this place.

When they returned to the main bedchamber, someone had already removed the Sarketi captain's body. Etris and Merrin pulled Wedro to another room using the rug he had bled out on. Tath, Nerith, and Avris went with them, deliberately robbing the two hostages of other women they might feel more comfortable turning to. Kince and Darro took the advisor to a separate room as well to act as guards while Yserra and Jethan questioned him. Kasiel and Irith stayed in the bedchamber with the queen and Hannah. The two women watched him and the cliff cat warily, but the queen had at least stopped crying.

"You're him, aren't you?" Hannah demanded. "The Warden's son."

"I am second-rank Ahninveth Kasiel Cavenos. This is my companion, Irith." The cliff cat sat next to him, tail lashing a few times as Kasiel's gaze drifted to that spot on the floor. He could still see Wedro lying there.

"If it pleases you, my lord," the young queen said, her voice soft and tentative, "we could speak in the library."

He looked at her then where she sat watching him with her frightened blue eyes, one hand on her bulging belly. "I would appreciate that, Majesty. You can call me Ahninveth, or Kasiel, if you prefer. I've never felt like much of a lord."

"Then you may call me Astrid, for I've never felt like much of a queen. Hannah, get me my dressing gown, please."

As Hannah hurried to the wardrobe, Irith following to ensure she didn't emerge with any weapons, Astrid struggled to get off the bed. Kasiel walked around, pulling off his gauntlet, and offered her his hand. She stared at it for a second as if it might bite before looking up to meet his eyes.

"Do you mean to kill us?"

"No. In fact, it's my goal to protect you, from whomever you need protecting from."

She held his eyes a moment longer, then took his hand and let him help her up. Hannah returned and moved around him, giving him a cold scowl as she draped the queen with a heavy green dressing gown trimmed in silver.

"Did my mother really ask you to help us?"

Kasiel stepped back, his gaze drifting to the memory of Wedro still lying on the floor. "Yes. She gave me that ring to tell you so. Your letters are how she knew where we could find Sarket's queen."

She winced, giving Astrid an apologetic look. "Does that mean Fallend has entered the alliance with Delaphine and Vanris?"

"Yes." His gaze drifted briefly down to Hannah's swollen belly. "She didn't tell me—"

"I didn't tell her. King Lodmund was concerned that Astrid's baby might die like all the rest, so he made a second one to improve his chances, I suppose." Though she lifted her chin defiantly, the slight quiver in her lip and the sympathy in the queen's eyes told him all he needed to know about how that had happened.

"But it wouldn't be the queen's child."

"Look at us." Hannah stepped closer to the other woman. "We could be sisters. He will keep us here as long as necessary. If her baby dies and mine does not, all he will have to do is claim that my baby is Astrid's. Even if she were to die in childbirth, he would merely have to keep that part quiet. No one would question him."

She was right. They looked alike enough to be siblings. A child from either of them with Lodmund as the father would be easy to pass off as the other's. "I'm sorry this happened to you. He will never touch you again." His gaze moved to Astrid. "Either of you."

"A bold declaration for such a young soldier," the queen stated.

"Older than you, Majesty."

"Hm." She lifted her skirts and walked around him as gracefully as she could, given that she looked ready to burst. "Come. Let's get out of this room."

Kasiel drew Irith back to his side and allowed Astrid and Hannah to precede him down the hall. He stopped them briefly, so he could let the others know where he was going and check on things.

"Sorry to bother you, Etris, but have you gotten any word from the others?"

There was a listlessness to the way she shook her head that he didn't like. She and Wedro hadn't been an official pairing, but she had acted as his unofficial counterpart within the unit, and they had worked together from the moment his team rescued her from Edmund's dungeons.

Her focus changed for a few seconds while Kasiel waited, then she met his eyes. "They've had to deal with a few more soldiers and found some additional servants, but no issues to report."

"Thank you."

Nerith caught his arm before he could walk away. "Do you want me to come with you? You probably shouldn't be alone with them."

"I've got Irith," he answered softly. "Take care of those who need you now."

Her jaw tightened. "And you don't need someone?"

Acting on impulse, he brought a hand up and ran his thumb lightly along her jaw, as if to smooth away the tension. "I'm not ready yet. I need to stay busy for a while."

She drew a breath and lowered her gaze, taking a step back from him. "I understand."

He wasn't sure she did, but that would have to wait. As would his apology for being so bold as to touch her that intimately when it wasn't his place to do so. Turning away, he nodded to Astrid and followed the two women to a modest-sized room lined with shelves full of books, many of them coated with dust outside of a single row on one shelf. He went to inspect that section as Hannah helped Astrid get comfortable in a chair and lit several candles around the room. The books on that shelf were mostly fanciful tales, the fingerprints in the dust on the edge of it made by small, slender fingers.

"Is one of you the reader?" he asked.

"I find the stories help me get through each day," Astrid answered. "My eyes don't like to follow the words as they are on the page, so I have Hannah read to me." Barely pausing for a breath, she changed the subject. "You are considerate of your soldiers."

He turned to see her eyeing him curiously. For one so young, she had a solemn maturity about her. Perhaps that was born of necessity, given her situation. "They're important to me. Many of them are like family. How long did King Lodmund plan to leave you here?"

She shrugged. "First, it was only for a month. Every time he sends word, it is a little longer. What will you do with me now that you have me?"

Hannah stood glancing between them, a frown tugging at the corners of her mouth.

Kasiel leaned against the bookshelf. "General Hackett got his hands on some valuable prisoners. The alliance wants to use you to negotiate for their freedom."

Astrid appeared to deflate before him, the spark in her visibly fading. "So you don't really mean to protect us?"

Hannah glared at him before turning to her friend. "It isn't as if anything has changed, Asti. We were Lodmund's hostages before. We're just someone else's now."

Lodmund's hostages? But wasn't she Sarket's queen?

He sent Irith over to Astrid, and she shrank back in the chair.

"He likes to be scratched behind the ears," Kasiel prompted.

Astrid warily extended a hand. The big cat sniffed

at it, then he pressed into it with his head. A child-like smile broke across her face and fresh sorrow shot through Kasiel at how young and innocent she looked. She started tentatively scratching behind Irith's ears, her smile brightening when he began purring. Then she gasped suddenly, putting a hand on her belly.

He took a step toward her, chest tightening with a burst of panic. "Are you all right?"

"Yes. This little monster kicks quite hard sometimes."

"You can feel the baby kick?" he asked. "Is that... normal?"

"Of course it is. It's inside me." Astrid laughed and his cheeks grew warm.

"It is late, Ahninveth." An edge of hostility sharpened Hannah's tone. "The queen should be resting. Is there anything you truly need to know that can't wait until morning?"

There wasn't really, he was just trying to stay occupied. "Yes. You're probably right. Just one last question for now. Do you know if there are any reinforcements or other troops expected here anytime soon?"

"Planning to stick around, are you?" Hannah snapped.

"Easy, Hannah." Astrid waved her friend off. "Captain Vollan insisted such conversations were not appropriate for ladies to concern themselves with. I am afraid I know little more than you. But you have my advisor. He usually knows what plans are being made."

Kasiel nodded. This was Sarket. They kept their women out of most things involving military or politics. "Would you like me to escort you to a different room? One where..." His throat tightened.

"Have you left us any suitable rooms without blood on their floors, Ahninveth Kasiel?" The queen raised her brows at him as if expecting an answer but didn't leave him the opportunity to give one. "No, I'll stay in my chambers. They cleaned up the floor as best they could and neither the blood of Captain Vollan nor that of your fallen companion will haunt me tonight. I am preoccupied enough by the child that will soon try to rip its way free of me."

The resentment in her tone caught his attention. "You don't want this child?"

"A child, someday, but not now, and not the child of a man with a string of dead wives and infants in his wake."

Was there anything reassuring he could say to that? He offered her his hand again. "Come, I'll escort you back to your room. I'm afraid I will need to assign guards."

She accepted his hand and let him pull her to her feet. "Thank you. I am not so agile right now. And I assumed you would keep us under guard. I had no illusions of this being a friendly takeover, even before you started killing people in my bedchamber."

Their company checked every part of the stronghold, pulled up the drawbridges, and secured the gates. The main keep's lower dungeon provided adequate space to lock up the servants. With such a small crew, they simply didn't have enough people to watch over everyone. Now that exhaustion and sorrow supplanted much of his rage, Kasiel had the presence of mind to ensure that they provided the prisoners food, water, and plenty of blankets and pillows. With twenty-eight of them in total after losing Wedro and the Delaphinian soldier who had tried to run, managing the stronghold was going to require a little creativity. They had Irith, Niskenya, and Akyla to help, though those three would also need rest at some point.

Kasiel and Jethan ended up breaking them into two teams, one with sixteen soldiers including Kince, Darro,

and Tath that would take the second shift of guard duties after a few hours of rest. The other group, made up
of Kasiel, his beasts, and the remainder of their unit,
would cover the first shift. Once everyone had some
sleep, they would figure out how to proceed. Having
spent time around Sarket's young queen, he had doubts
about her ability to travel in her current condition. But
that was a problem to discuss in the morning.

With the barracks a mess, they split several rooms in the keep amongst them, building fires in the fireplaces in each one to warm damp skin and dry wet clothes. They scrounged up dry garments by borrowing from the barracks and the servants' quarters. After their shift, the six members of their tehsheyn who weren't on watch climbed into two beds in a large room they split amongst them. Merrin, Avris, and Etris slept in one bed. Kasiel was in the other with Nerith between him and Jethan.

When he woke later, it was to the sound of Nerith softly crying next to him. Jethan had pulled her into his arms and was holding her while she wept, his own face damp with tears. Kasiel swallowed back a bitter pang of loneliness. He loved them both. It was good that they were supporting each other. They all needed to come together now.

He slid carefully off the bed. When he looked back, Jethan was watching him, his mouth starting to open. Kasiel held a hand up to stop him and shook his head, glancing meaningfully at Nerith. Jethan bobbed his head in a tiny nod and said nothing. They would need to gather and figure out the next steps soon, but he could give them a few minutes to let out some of their grief and compose themselves.

Encouraging Irith to stay, he grabbed a jacket off the back of a chair, not sure who it belonged to, and put it on. Then he eased the door open and slipped into the hall. From there, he left using the war room they had originally come in through and went out onto the covered walk. It was still raining, though more of a steady drizzle now than the downpour they'd made their attack in. The gray sky was brightening with dawn's arrival. Turning to his left this time, he climbed up a ladder to an open-sided watchtower.

Minera was at the top, leaning against one corner post, hugging her arms around herself in the chill morning and peering out over the rugged landscape beyond the stronghold. She straightened when he came up.

"Ahninveth."

"Relax, Min. I was just looking for a quiet spot to be alone."

She stared at him for a second, startling when Akyla landed on one of the half walls. "Oh, would you like me to leave?"

"Sorry. I didn't mean to be dismissive. I wanted to thank you for helping with..." He stopped speaking when his throat tightened, and tears welled in his eyes. Glancing away, he stared out over the river.

"I only wish I could have done something more."

He lowered his gaze, a horrible weight dragging him down. "What you did was more than most of us could. Why don't you go inside and warm up? We'll be gathering to discuss our departure soon."

She started toward the ladder, then paused. "Should you be alone right now?"

Niskenya's mental presence – loving and protective – wrapped around him. He glanced at Akyla. "I'm rarely alone, but thank you for asking."

"If you're sure..."

He nodded.

Still looking somewhat unconvinced, she left him.

A light mental nudge prompted Akyla to launch himself from the half-wall and soar out away from the tower. Kasiel sank behind his eyes. He spent a few minutes simply flying without purpose or direction. The land here appeared unexpectedly green and much less harsh from that vantage. Somehow, the moss and plants growing there, most of which looked half-dead up close, blended together to almost hide the angry volcanic rock from above. The nearby town of Cabril had a quaintness to it, but a sturdiness as well. Prepared for winters that brought heavy snow. The crops on the far side of it looked thin, not sufficient to support a sizeable population. There were flocks of sheep there, and he noticed a lot of goats too. Animals with smaller hooves that were better suited to the unforgiving terrain.

After a few minutes of idle observation, he took the raptor out on a wider sweep, searching for any signs of military approaching their location. When he found nothing of concern, he released the bird to fly where it wanted and returned to himself, staring out over the river. A few seconds before he started down the ladder, Akyla landed on one of the half-walls again, watching him with his head cocked to one side.

Kasiel paused his descent. "I'll lure some mice out of the barn for you, but your beak is healing. You're going to have to start hunting for yourself again soon."

The raptor let out a few short, sharp piping sounds before flying off again.

"Right. I'll reconsider my insolent ways."

He finished climbing down and went inside. Along the way back to the room, he ran into Lucia and Annora.

"Morning Ahninveth," Lucia greeted, a wary solemnity in her tone.

"I hope you both got a little sleep," he answered, unwilling to even offer a "morning" in case the unspoken "good" tried to make a mockery of his sorrow. One hand absently sank to the belt pouch where he had Sylaryth's claw.

"A little," Annora answered with a tired half-smile.

"I want to speak to everyone. Could you spread the word to meet in the lower dining room?"

"Of course, Ahninveth." They offered bows before striding away with a new purpose.

When he entered the bedroom, the others were awake and changing back into their own clothes. Modesty was something that typically got abandoned on missions. The need for expedience and efficiency outweighed that for privacy in situations where it was hard to come by, and everyone was supposed to be adult about it. Out in the field, it wasn't as hard to maintain the proper mindset, but it was a little different walking into a room with four half-dressed individuals, particularly when he had been intimate with two of them. It probably didn't help that, prior to coming to Vanris, he hadn't ever seen a woman naked.

He quickly shut the door behind him and lowered his gaze, warmth creeping up his neck into his face.

Someone on his left breathed a soft laugh. A moment later, Avris wrapped her arms around him and pulled him into a hug. She was naked from the waist up.

"Thank you for being you, Kas. I needed a smile this morning."

He let out a heavy exhale and hugged her back. "I hate you sometimes."

"I know." After a few seconds, she released him and placed a feather-light kiss on his cheek before walking away to finish dressing.

Trying to ignore them, he set about gathering his things and getting changed himself, grateful that the three women left the room before he had removed his pants. He suspected that wasn't entirely an accident, though it was unusual for them to take pity on him.

"We planning our departure this morning?" Jethan asked.

"Yes. I don't want to stay here, though I'm concerned about Ast... Queen Astrid's ability to travel." He glanced at his tehnaak. "How's Nerith?"

Jethan looked away. "As good as any of us."

Kasiel focused on dressing, clenching his teeth against the fresh stinging in his eyes. As he was putting on his belt, he looked into the dwindling fire. "Wedro. Who could have imagined back when I first met you all that I would ever miss him this much."

Jethan chuckled, the sound lacking his usual levity. "You know, that unit was mostly made up of people I hadn't worked with before. I only knew him and Chander a little longer than you did. Funny how fast someone can become an essential part of your life."

The door swung open abruptly and Yserra ducked her head in. "Our hostage is going into labor."

"Shit!"

Kasiel wasn't sure if he and Jethan said it at the same time or if the word just echoed that loudly in his head. Either way, they were both racing for the door.

"Get me Tath and Nerith," he ordered.

"Yes, Ahninveth." Yserra hurried off down the hall.

The door to the queen's bedchamber stood open, an almost animal noise somewhere between a scream and a growl rising from within. Kasiel made Irith wait outside as he and Jethan rushed in. Astrid was lying on the bed, her brow damp and eyes bright with pain and fear. Hannah sat on the edge of the bed next to her. Minera stood on the other side.

Kasiel hurried around toward where Hannah was, and she got up to intercept him. "You're sure it's coming."

"Yes!" Astrid shouted.

Hannah gave him a humorless look. "Probably set

off by the stress from your attack."

Nerith and Tath came running into the room then.

Kasiel cast a desperate look their way. "You two can help with this, right?"

"We're both battlefield trained, Kas," Tath answered. "This isn't a battlefield problem. We can probably assist, but this is not something we normally do."

"I have been present for animal births before," Nerith offered with an apologetic shrug. "I might be able to help some."

Astrid's gaze locked on Kasiel. "I wonder who it was that threw my physician and midwives in the dungeon!" Another animal cry escaped her then and her hands clenched into fists on the sheets.

"Tath, take a few others and collect her physician and midwives. We're going to need them. Nerith, anything you can do until they get here is appreciated."

Nerith looked at the girl on the bed, then at him. "I'll get water and rags. I'm sure they'll need those."

He watched her go, feeling desperately helpless. Hannah sat on the bed and Astrid clutched at her friend's hand. Tears began streaming down her cheeks.

"I don't want to die. Please," she sobbed, little more than a scared child.

Kasiel turned to Jethan.

Before he could put his thoughts into words, Jethan nodded and walked up beside Hannah. "Give me a second with her."

Hannah glanced at Kasiel, her hand tightening on her friend's. "No."

"Trust me." When she looked at Jethan, Kasiel felt a faint soothing move out from his tehnaak. "I can help."

Hannah hesitated a moment longer, then she put her other hand over Astrids. "This man is going to help you."

"Nononono. Don't leave me, please."

"It'll be fine. I'll be right here." Hannah forcefully extracted her hand to move out of the way.

Jethan sat where she had been, his unexpected, unwelcome presence earning him a glare from Astrid, which was exactly the intensity of attention that would put her right in his hands. "Queen Astrid," he murmured, "you don't need to be afraid."

"I am," she sobbed. "Roald's wives have never survived childbirth."

"None of them were you," Jethan answered, the sense of soothing growing stronger as he took her grasping hand. "You're going to deliver this baby and be just fine. You can do this."

Tears still streamed down her cheeks, but she started nodding. Then she tensed and cried out. Jethan's flinch attested to the power with which she suddenly squeezed his hand. When it passed again, she stared at him, desperation in her eyes. "It hurts. It hurts so much."

He placed his hand on her cheek, drawing all her attention to him. "It's going to hurt. You just need to be strong. It will be over soon, and you'll have a sweet little one that you brought into the world."

A smile brightened her sweat-dampened features. "Yes. Yes. You're right. I know you are."

"We need to clear out this room," the tall, dark-haired man entering the room stated, an air of authority in his voice. Three women followed him, all escorted by several of Kasiel's soldiers.

Kasiel walked up to him. "You're the physician?"

He raised his chin. "I am."

Lowering his voice, Kasiel said, "You will ensure that she makes it out of this, or you will pay the price for her life with your own."

The man narrowed his eyes, though a flicker of fear shone in them as they shifted away. "I will do everything I can."

"Do more."

The physician and midwives hurried to the bed when Astrid cried out again. Nerith returned with a pile of rags and a basin of water that two of the women came and collected from her, not looking her in the eyes as they did so.

One midwife stopped next to Hannah. "How long has she been having contractions?"

"They started a while ago. We thought they were just the false ones she's gotten before. We hoped they were. The timing..." She cast Kasiel an uneasy look. "She has had the others several times this week, but this time they kept getting worse and there was a rush of fluid from down there—"

The woman cut her off with a brusque gesture. "That's sufficient."

"All men aside from myself should leave the chamber now," the physician declared.

"I'm afraid you're not in charge here," Kasiel countered. He wasn't about to leave the queen alone in the hands of a man who might have been there when her predecessors died in childbirth. "Min, do what you can to help with her pain. Nerith and Tath, I want you here to provide assistance as needed and keep watch over things. Her physician and midwives will do nothing to prevent you from doing so." He said that part firmly. "Jethan." He met his tehnaak's eyes.

"I'll stay and help her."

"Thank you." He moved toward the door, spotting Yserra and Etris in the hall. Beckoning them over, he said in a low voice, "I want you two to stand guard inside the room. Yserra, keep Tath and Nerith apprised of any concerning thoughts you catch from the physician or the midwives."

The Evoker nodded.

"Etris, reach out to Revik if there are problems. I'll

make sure he knows where to find me."

"Yes, Ahninveth." Her answer was firm, though the faint glassiness of her eyes attested to her grief. Were his the same?

"Thank you." He stepped out of the way to let them inside.

Etris shut the door behind them. Farther down the hall, Irith was pacing restlessly.

Darro, leaning in the doorway of an adjacent room, glanced at the queen's bedchamber door. "I guess we're not leaving today."

Kasiel called Irith to him with a thought, placing a hand on the big cat's head. "It would seem that way."

"We should work out some rotating patrols and watches and consider getting rid of the bodies, or at least getting them farther away from the living areas."

Things to work on. To focus on. Kasiel nodded, his nerves sparking through him like last night's lightning had sparked across the sky. "Let's get everyone else to the dining room as planned and figure a few things out."

Kasiel had no clue what to expect beyond the birth of the baby, assuming that part didn't end poorly. How soon would mother and child be ready for travel? The longer they stayed, the greater the chances of discovery. Even with all their mind-crafters, he wasn't sure they had the manpower to hold this stronghold against a large force. Although, they had a significant advantage in the location's defensibility and the particular collection of mind-crafters they had on hand. The two Dampeners especially could prove extremely useful in the event of a siege, but that would only hold them for so long without help.

He could send someone with a message for Nevias and Itana, but he wasn't about to give up his mind-crafters and, under the circumstances, he didn't want to risk any of his core unit. That left the question of whom he trusted enough to deliver such an important message that he was willing to risk. They discussed options for a time in the dining hall without reaching a solution. It wasn't until he wandered out to visit Niskenya that his answer sought him out.

"Ahninveth Kasiel." Annora jogged out into the courtyard after him in the ongoing drizzle.

He stopped to face her, and she took several hasty steps back, nearly stumbling over her feet when Niskenya emerged from an open building next to him. The water rolled off the kanodrak's thick silver-gray hide, almost as though afraid to cling to her. He could feel her hunger and restlessness. It might be safe enough to let her go hunt today, but they would need to come up with a plan for feeding her if they got stuck here. Perhaps he could lure some of those local sheep into the corral near the stable. Stealing from the residents of Cabril wasn't ideal, but they only had so many options.

Kasiel placed a hand on the kanodrak's neck and faced Annora. "What is it?"

"I... ah..." She let out a nervous laugh. "It's probably blasphemous somehow, but I feel like I should kneel before her." She touched the hollow of her throat and then her lips. "Havaad forgive me."

"Kanodraks are revered creatures in Vanris. Your instincts wouldn't be so out of place there."

Annora nodded, her dark eyes still locked on the massive predator. "I remember you saying that when you introduced us to her."

"Did you need something?"

"Oh." She dragged her gaze to him. "Apologies, Ahninveth. I wanted to offer to be your messenger. I'm an experienced rider, and I have an excellent sense of direction. I know I can do it. It would be my honor to serve the alliance in this way."

He eyed her thoughtfully. Like her two companions, she was very young. Northern Delaphinian judging from the darkness of her skin. She had a lot of potential, not only as a soldier, but as a person. He didn't want to be the one to bring about the premature snuffing of the light she carried within her. And yet, he needed what she was offering. The hope in her eyes told him she wanted to do this.

"All right. But promise me you'll be careful. Go find Kince and Darro. They'll get the right supplies together for you, and Kince is an excellent judge of horses. Tell him I said to pick you out the best animal in the stable, regardless of who it belongs to."

She clasped her hands, bowing to him. "Thank you! I won't let you down."

"Don't let yourself down and I'm sure we'll both come out of this happy."

"Yes, Ahninveth!" She sprinted back toward the building.

Kasiel shook his head after her. "I hope I don't regret this."

Niskenya bumped his shoulder with her head, a soft rumble in her chest.

He stayed out with the kanodrak for a while, though Irith objected to the weather and eventually went in search of shelter. Kasiel watched through the cat's eyes until he settled in with Merrin and Avris, who were playing a subdued game of dice in the southwest gatehouse. He then did a brief search of the keep with the aid of various rodents. Most of those who weren't on watch, helping with the childbirth, or moving bodies were catching up on sleep, except for Revik who stood in a corner of the war room staring out into the rain, his focus turned inward, perhaps communicating with Etris.

Sending part of his awareness up with Akyla to do

another search of the surrounding area, Kasiel placed a hand on Niskenya's shoulder and began walking the yards and pathways between the buildings outside the inner keep with her. It wouldn't be for long, but this stronghold was theirs right now. His. Such a strange thought. He had won this place with his unit, killing or taking prisoner its occupants. There was a sense of power in that, but not one that made him feel good about himself, especially considering the price they had paid. He would give up this victory to have Wedro back. How odd that the man's death had, in a way, been rather similar to Chander's. Sudden, senseless, and unexpected.

This war had to end. Kasiel wasn't sure how much more loss he could take. He couldn't be the only one who felt that way.

Once they finished a circuit of the inner areas, Kasiel went up to the gatehouse where two of his other Vanrian soldiers were on duty. They opened the gate and put down the drawbridge at his request. Kasiel climbed up on the wall and watched Niskenya pace down the ramp while he drew a small deer in from the nearby area. The moment she spotted it, he released control, giving her a chance to hunt and stretch her legs without wandering too far. She was feeling strong enough now to appreciate the chase. Aware of his unease, after she caught it, she carried it up near the foot of the ramp to eat.

He stood watching from the wall in the rain until she finished and returned. Once the bridge was up and the gate secured, he walked her back to the smithy where she was taking shelter in the open building the forge was in. With her belly full, she was ready for rest, but she stood with him, pressing her head to his chest, her concern and affection washing over him. Kasiel leaned in, putting his cheek to the bone plating that protected her skull for a quiet moment, letting the water dripping from his hair mask his tears. Not that anyone was there to see them.

Irith sprinted over to join him when he walked into the building through the officer's mess. Revik nodded to him as he entered.

"Any news?"

"Not much. She's still in labor. Etris said the midwives think it may be a normal birth. One of King Lodmund's wives died from a breech, so it's good to know that won't be an issue at least. It's still too soon to be sure how it will end up, though."

Kasiel nodded, rubbing at his tired eyes. "Shouldn't it be over soon?"

"Not necessarily." He offered a kind smile. "You should get some rest, Ahninveth. You'll be needed again later. This might be your best opportunity. We know where to find you if anything happens, although I might recommend a room farther away from the queen's bed-chamber."

He was exhausted. The idea of lying down sounded wonderful, though he wasn't confident he could fall asleep. "Maybe just a quick rest. If you could make sure someone relieves the current shift soon, I'd appreciate it. And don't leave me out for more than an hour."

"As you say, Ahninveth." Revik inclined his head respectfully.

When Kasiel got out of his wet clothes and lay down on a bed in a room well away from Astrid's, Irith climbed up and stretched out next to him, his furry body a powerful source of heat. With Niskenya a drowsy presence in his head, it was only a few seconds before he was sound asleep.

CHAPTER TWENTY ONE

Kas."

Something brushed lightly across his cheek, and he opened his eyes to see Nerith sitting on the edge of the bed, a tired smile resting on her lips.

He blinked a few times, trying to orient himself. "Astrid?"

She nodded. "She's all right. There was some tearing, but I helped Tath take care of it. Their stitching techniques could use a little refinement, and their salves aren't nearly as effective as what we make in Vanris. She lost a lot of blood, but we've taken over her care. This is the part Tath and I excel at."

He shuddered at the thought of what might have torn. "The baby?"

"A handsome young heir. He seems strong, but a lot can happen when they're this small. He's resting with his mother now. We kept the one midwife who seemed most amenable to working with us up here to help. The other two and her physician are back in the dungeons. You should have heard that man railing at the injustice of locking him up and our barbaric cruelty."

Kasiel breathed a sigh and started to roll onto his back, but he bumped up against something solid. "Irith's behind me, isn't he?"

"Yes." Her soft smile warmed. "You two look rather

sweet sleeping together like this, though he appears to have damaged the covers in a few places."

"Not surprising." Kasiel moved to sit up against the headboard.

Nerith's gaze flickered to some of his scars and the chain of his ke'hanoath around his neck. It was next to impossible not to be reminded how it felt when she touched him in those places, and elsewhere.

"How long are we stuck here?" he asked, trying to divert those thoughts to things that were important.

"The queen won't be able to sit in a saddle for some time. A couple of weeks at best. Merrin and Avris helped Kince and Darro finish an inventory of the stronghold. There is no carriage, unfortunately. We might get our hands on a wagon in town, but even then, we shouldn't consider moving her for a few days, at the very least."

"They finished..." Irritation provided a welcome distraction from less appropriate thoughts. "How long have I been asleep? I told Revik not more than an hour."

"It's been about five hours. He was going to wake you, but Avris told him she would cut his feet off if he came anywhere near this room. She can be very convincing."

"Everyone needs rest. I should be with my unit."

She got up and stepped away when he grabbed the covers, turning her back to him to give him some privacy. "You're our leader. We need you rested. What would we do if you were too tired to make the tough decisions?"

"Horse shit. You're all plenty capable of making those decisions. You don't need me for that." He threw off the covers, earning a soft, annoyed growl from Irith. At least Nerith wasn't watching to see the effect her gaze and his memories had on him. He prioritized getting his pants on. "I need to talk to the others. I don't know what the stores are like, but we should probably stock them up in case we end up trapped here for a while."

Nerith turned as he was fastening the pants, her gaze slipping to the scar over his heart where Edmund had tried to end him. He remembered the feel of her hands moving around him as she bandaged the wound, the smell of her, the taste of her lips.

He blew out a frustrated breath, sending a lock of long red hair flipping to the side.

"Sorry." She turned to stare into the fire. "I miss the way we were before, sometimes."

"So do I. I just..." He trailed off as he pulled on his shirt.

"You love her." She faced him again. "I know."

"You deserve someone who can give you all of their heart, Nerith."

His pulse quickened when she came closer, her eyes locked with his. "That would be nice, but if you're ever willing to let me borrow a portion of yours, just for a little while..."

"You will always have a piece of my heart," he whispered, unsure whether she had closed that last bit of distance, or he had.

Their lips touched, tentatively at first, then rational thought disappeared, and he moved his hands to her waist and pulled her close, deepening the kiss. She melted against him, her hands sliding around his back, a hint of desperation in the way she clung to him. Yearning burned like fire in his veins.

Nerith broke the kiss, though she didn't let go of him. "I'm sorry," she murmured, her eyes downcast.

"I don't think you can take all the blame for this." As much as he didn't want to, he let go of her waist and stepped back. She returned her hands to her sides, making no effort to hold on to him. "I didn't turn to Velara because I had stopped loving you."

"That doesn't make this easier, Kas."

Fighting the urge to kiss her again, he retreated a

few more steps until the backs of his legs bumped up against the immovable wall of Irith, who had come up behind him at some point. "You're right. I don't know why I said that. I—" A knock on the door interrupted him, bringing a puzzling mix of relief and regret with it. He saw the same conflict in Nerith's features before she turned away. "Come in."

Jethan opened the door, his gaze falling on Nerith. "I see you got to him first. Do you..." He glanced between them. "Should I come back later?"

"Definitely not," Nerith answered too quickly. "I mean." She cleared her throat. "We have a lot to do."

Kasiel tugged on his boots. "You look tired. You both do. The two of you just helped deliver Sarket's heir. I think you've more than earned some rest." He picked up his sword belt. "Thank you both for that, by the way, it was a lot to ask."

"It was an experience." A wry smirk twisted Jethan's lips. "But we'll rest after we talk about some things. Come on, we called in the core group and everyone else who's not on active watch or guard duty together. At your orders, of course."

"Of course. Who's with Astrid?"

Nerith arched a brow at him. "Is it just Astrid now?"

"They have a special connection," Jethan teased.

He shook his head at them, though the moment of humor was like a balm to his aching heart, as he imagined it was to theirs. "If you two are through being pests, can you answer the question?"

"The midwife is watching her, along with one of the Delaphinians and Revik, so he can reach out to Etris if they have any urgent needs," Nerith answered, handing him his jacket.

A few minutes later, they sat in the dining room downstairs. A massive chandelier made of antlers hung overhead. Several stuffed creatures, including a bear and a werdyn cat, decorated the room. Kasiel itched to remove them all. He didn't think it would have bothered him this much before his ability awakened, but now, especially with Irith pressed against his leg, he found it nauseating. Still, it was the easiest room in which to accommodate them all.

Everyone was there except ten members of the extended unit, who were either on watch, on guard duty with the queen, or in the dungeons. Leif and Emil were there, eyeing him as if they wanted to ask something but were too nervous to speak up. He had a feeling it involved Annora. The two boys were still nervous around him, though Emil cast hopeful glances at Jethan a few times.

"It's become apparent that our hard-earned hostage and her son won't be ready to travel safely for a while. Given that," Darro paused, waiting on a nod from Kasiel before continuing, "we need to plan to stay in our new lodgings for a little longer."

"Which means we need to not only ensure we have adequate supplies and look for a better solution for handling the dead..." Kasiel stumbled for an instant on that word, and everyone in their tehsheyn glanced down at the table as if sharing the same pang of loss. He drew a breath and continued. "We also need to check fortifications and prepare for the possibility that our enemies could catch us here before we can move Lodmund's queen and heir to a more secure location."

"What are we going to do about the people in the dungeon?" Lucia asked.

"I had hoped to release them when we left here, but given the challenges we're facing, I'm open to ideas."

"Some of them might be willing to work with us, like the midwife," Nerith suggested.

"Maybe." Kince paused to take a drink of the wine they had brought up from the cellar. "But how do we know who we can trust? We can't put guards on all of them like we have her."

Nerith's face fell. "No, I suppose not."

Jethan leaned on the table. "We could bring a few of them out at a time to help with some tasks. Cooking. Cleaning. Give them a chance to get out of the dungeon. In small numbers, they could work under guard and go back to the cells at night. If we feed them well and give them what comforts we safely can, they should still come out of this in decent shape."

"We could also send one or two to town with a few of us wearing Sarketi armor to buy more supplies in case we do end up here for a while," Darro suggested. "If the fortifications are all in good repair, we can defend this place even with a company this small."

Kasiel nodded, his gaze going to the head of a boar hung above the main doorway. Would it be wrong to put their prisoners to work getting rid of the dead-beast decor? "I'll draw in some local sheep to keep in a corral by the stables. If we do get stuck here, we need something to feed Niskenya other than the horses. If I'm careful, no one will know where they went."

"Ahninveth?"

The tentative voice drew his attention to Emil. "Yes."

"Did Annora go out there by herself?"

He nodded. "Is she a capable rider?"

Emil frowned. "Absolutely."

"And does she have a strong sense of direction?"

"The best, but–"

"Good, because our lives could very well depend on her ability to do this. We are all in this together. When your group volunteered for this mission, you had to know there were risks. Annora assured me she could get the message to our army, and I chose to believe her. You should too, because we need to believe in each other."

He caught a faint sense of approval from Jethan. It was going to take some time to get used to feeling things from a source other than his beasts. Especially knowing his tehnaak could do the same with him.

They talked and shared wine for a few hours, planning their next steps. The following two days they spent checking fortifications, arranging food stores and supplies, and sending pairs of servants into town in the company of soldiers dressed as Sarketi guards to stock up on some things using the reasonably loaded coffers they found. If they didn't end up needing those stores, the servants would be well-stocked once they finally set them free. Kasiel stole several sheep from the local flocks, luring those who wandered from the herd to the corrals within the walls.

The river flowed alongside the village and curved around two sides of the stronghold, so they gradually stripped the bodies and tossed them over the wall into the water at night, hoping they would get dragged out by animals downstream and eaten before anyone discovered them. The stronghold wasn't large enough to facilitate keeping that many dead far enough away from the living areas for it to be safe.

Wedro was a separate problem. They had no effective way of preserving his body long enough to take it home with them, but it was just a body now. Still, dropping him into the river with their enemies was too much of an insult to stomach. Instead, they used the remains of two trebuchets destroyed in the prior siege of the stronghold to build a pyre in the main courtyard on the third day there – a bright, sunlit day – and burned him. The tehsheyn sat out watching the fire together into the night.

Most of them were still sitting there when a voice spoke into Kasiel's head.

Ahninveth.

Kasiel glanced back toward the keep and spotted Revik by the door.

Queen Astrid would like to see you.

Kasiel stood up from the wooden bench he was sitting on with Jethan, Nerith, and Etris. "The queen is asking for me. I'll be back."

Jethan removed his arm from around Nerith's shoulders where she had seated herself on the opposite side from Kasiel. A visual cue, perhaps, that there would be no more intimacy between them.

"Should I come, tehnaak?"

"No. Stay. I don't imagine I'll be long."

As he walked toward the keep, Irith bolted to his side. The big cat had been sprinting around the complex, burning off some of his energy. Kasiel would need to feed him if they became trapped behind these walls too. Niskenya raised her head, her silver-gray hide reflecting the light of the shrinking fire. She huffed once, and he got a sense of frustration from her that he understood. For now, he was still letting her and Irith out to hunt, but they had to remain within the walls the rest of the time. It was already getting to the kanodrak. He sent affection and a plea for patience back to her.

Revik walked to the queen's chambers with him and knocked on the door.

"Come in." There was a hint of a tremble in Astrid's voice.

Revik opened the door for him and followed him and Irith in, closing it again behind them. The Speaker positioned himself to one side of the entrance. The chamber was dark, lit only by two candles. It took Kasiel's eyes a moment to adjust after staring at the bright pyre. He hadn't spoken with the queen since the baby was born. She sat leaning against the headboard, the infant sleeping in her arms, supported by a collection of strategically stacked pillows. A faint, tired smile curved her lips as she gazed down at the child. She looked paler than before, and there were circles under her eyes. She appeared so young and vulnerable in that large bed that he couldn't quite get his head around the reality that this baby was hers.

Hannah sat in a chair next to the bed with a book in her lap, watching him while she twisted her mother's ring around her finger. The midwife frowned at him from one corner where was knitting with excessive vigor.

"Kasiel, come meet Jaysen, heir to the throne of Sarket."

Kasiel walked closer tentatively, afraid of waking the infant. He had heard its cries within the keep. The tiny human had the lungs of a monster. "Jaysen?"

A rude snort came from the midwife, but Astrid ignored it. "Sounds a little like Jethan, don't you think?" she asked, looking up at him.

Kasiel couldn't stop a light laugh. "You didn't name him for my tehnaak."

"I did. Your tehnaak and the others you left with me are a large part of the reason I'm alive. I firmly believe that, and I thank you for it."

"Does Jethan know?"

"Not yet." She adjusted the baby's blanket, a hint of a blush rising in her cheeks.

Perhaps Jethan had Charmed her through her birth a little too well. "Maybe you shouldn't tell him. It might go to his head."

"It should. Whatever comes, I owe you all my life, but I am afraid..." she paused, a tear shimmering, trapped in her lower lashes. "I am afraid I will cost you yours by forcing you to remain here."

Kasiel sat on the edge of the bed, getting a warning look from Hannah, though she refrained from sharing her thoughts. "Why?"

"The child came a little early, but not much before

its expected time. Roald will return soon to see if he finally has an heir. You can't stay here." The tear trapped on her lashes spilled free.

"We can't leave without you. You and little Jaysen here may be the key to ending this war. If we leave without you, Wedro will have died for nothing. Besides, I told you I wouldn't let Lodmund touch either of you again. I meant that."

She searched his eyes. "Will you hold me hostage forever, then?"

"I'm still working that part out." A dark twisting in his gut accompanied the thought that he could end up doing to this child what Edmund had done to him. But no, he had no intention of lying to Astrid and her son, and he meant to give them every choice he could in living their lives. The baby stirred, and he stood, worried that his nearness might have disturbed it. "How many men does King Lodmund travel with?"

"He prefers to travel with a smaller force. Around the size of yours, I would say, with a few servants. He tries to keep his movements discreet enough not to draw unwanted attention, but he's too arrogant to put effort into hiding his presence."

A smaller force wouldn't be able to take the stronghold from them, not if they kept the drawbridges up and the walls patrolled. He believed in his unit. The one weak link, the man whose actions led to Wedro's loss, was dead, torn to pieces by Niskenya. Those who remained seemed willing to stand together. He would need to make sure that didn't change.

He glanced at Hannah, her untrusting eyes staring back at him, as blue as the queen's. "How are you holding up?"

"What do you care?" she snapped back.

"Hannah." An edge of reprimand sharpened the queen's tone. "We have an opportunity to be something other than enemies here. Given all Kasiel has done for me, I would expect you to show him a more civil tongue."

Hannah pressed her lips into a thin line and folded her arms over her chest above her swollen belly, staring across the room at nothing.

"It's all right," Kasiel said. "You've both been through a great deal. I'll leave you to rest."

"Thank you." Astrid softened her tone for him. "And I'm sorry about the one you lost. I can see he was very important to you."

Kasiel met her eyes for a moment. She played this game skillfully, assuming she was playing. Earn the goodwill of your captors to ensure your own well-being and, in this case, the well-being of your child. How much of her apparent positive attitude toward him was false? All of it? None? He could always ask Yserra to accompany him the next time he spoke with her, but for now, he just wanted to sleep.

"Goodnight, Astrid." He glanced at the other young woman, who refused to look at him. "Lady De Clare."

"Lady De Clare is my mother," she hissed. "I'm just a king's whore."

He flinched inwardly, then turned and left the room, hearing Astrid whispering words of support to her friend as he shut the door. The queen was strong for such a young girl. Stronger than she should have to be.

He wandered through the halls, searching for the room he had used last. The idea of walking back out to the dwindling fire to watch the last remnants of Wedro become a pile of ash held no appeal. Turning down what he thought was the correct hall, he opened the door and froze. Merrin and Yserra were there, partially undressed, locked in a passionate embrace, Merrin's lips kissing a trail down the other woman's neck. Yserra let her head fall back, her eyes closed. Merrin's pale gray eyes opened, her gaze homing in on him.

Kasiel inclined his head and eased the door shut.

He walked to the next room down, the proper one this time, and knocked. When no one answered, he went inside and began stripping his clothes off, trying to get the image of Merrin and Yserra out of his head. He never thought of either woman intimately but seeing them half-naked together like that stirred him in places he wished it hadn't.

Irith hopped up on the bed as he pulled off his shirt and tossed it on the chair. The cat's attention turned toward the door a second before it opened with no warning knock, and Nerith walked in. She eased it shut it behind her and strode over to him, resting her fingertips lightly on one collarbone and sliding them along the path of his ke'hanoath to the symbol on his breastbone. Her gaze followed that touch, then she looked into his eyes.

"I know I can only have a piece of your heart, but tonight, I want all of your body to take me away from this. Can I have that?"

'No' was the answer that rested on his lips. It was the one he needed to give her if he didn't want to hurt her again. And he genuinely didn't want to.

"Please, Kas."

But he wanted to forget this sorrow too, if only for a little while. The instant their lips touched, the new tehsheyn bond balancing their passion and heartache between them, he started to.

CHAPTER TWENTY TWO

When morning came, Kasiel carefully extracted himself from the bed, managing not to wake Nerith. He dressed and backed out of the room, easing the door shut and closing the cliff cat in with her. Irith would somehow manage to climb onto the bed without disturbing her. He was certain of that. The cat had a knack for moving like a creature a third of his size when he wanted to.

Kasiel nearly jumped out of his skin when he turned around to find Merrin standing behind him. She arched one brow.

"None of my business," he stated, trying to block out the memory of her and Yserra. What the members of his unit did with their intimate moments didn't involve him in most cases, and he wanted to keep it that way.

Merrin nodded, glancing at the door behind him. "Mine either."

With that out of the way, he started down the hall, and she fell into step beside him, asking, "What did the queen want last night?"

"She's worried that Lodmund will be on his way here soon, if he isn't already."

"That's not ideal."

Kasiel snorted. "Very little of this is ideal."

"Although," her expression brightened, capturing

his curiosity, "I would rather like an opportunity to drive a spear through that man's chest."

Kasiel thought of Astrid and Hannah. "As would I."

"Where are we going?"

He didn't object to her self-assigned accompaniment. Often, when he thought he most wanted to be alone, he found that company was the thing his heart truly craved. Though, last night, that need had led him astray. "Up to the tower over the walk. I think it's time to send Akyla on another scouting run."

Merrin answered with a soft, affirmative grunt.

When they climbed up into the open-sided tower, it surprised Kasiel to find Jethan there, leaning against a corner post whittling at a small piece of wood. Merrin met his eyes and went back down without a word. The sky outside the open tower was speckled with wispy white clouds painted against a brilliant blue backdrop. It would be a beautiful day again.

"You knew I would come up here."

Jethan set the piece of wood on the floor. "Of course. You're my tehnaak and the only one among us who can fly." He cast a glance at the nightstar eagle as it swept in to land on the half-wall.

"I'm sorry I left you last night."

Jethan shrugged. "You weren't the only one to find solace in someone else's arms at the end of an emotional day. Merrin... vanished, and Darro disappeared with Tath, so Avris, Kince, and I drank a lot and threw daggers at some of the dining room decor."

Kasiel chuckled. "Did that improve it any?"

"Not really."

Kasiel slipped behind Akyla's eyes and sent the raptor out in expanding circles around the stronghold, searching for danger in close before pushing him out in sweeping arcs further to the southwest.

"Are you and Nerith an item again?"

"Last night shouldn't have happened," he answered, trying to focus on what he was seeing through his borrowed eyes.

"Maybe it should have."

"Please don't, Jeth. I can't stop loving Velara just because everyone says I should. It doesn't work that way."

"I know. I'd just like to see you happy, and I don't see how that can happen with Vel."

"It would make me happy to see you live to get out of this fucking stronghold." Kasiel growled under his breath, spotting a small force moving their way at a decent clip. Fear swept through him, bringing a prickle of sweat to his skin. He couldn't let it take control, though. He had people to protect.

"We have company coming?" Anxiety tightened Jethan's voice as he moved up beside him.

Kasiel swept a wide circle, watching the riders. They weren't rushing, which meant they likely didn't know there was any reason for concern yet, nor were they wasting time. "Unfortunately. At the pace they're coming, I'd guess they're expecting to spend tonight in the stronghold."

"That's going to be so disappointing for them," Jethan said, a flippant lift in his tone. Then he put a finger to the corner of his mouth, looking thoughtful. "Although, I believe there might still be open beds in the dungeon."

Kasiel shook his head and breathed a laugh. "I will always love you for your inappropriate sense of humor, tehnaak."

"I know." He touched Kasiel's arm. "Come on, we've got to get everyone together. We need to get this place locked down and make sure we all know our responsibilities."

Kasiel turned Akyla back toward the stronghold. "Right. We've got company coming. It's time to prepare our welcome."

Throughout the rest of the day, Kasiel used a selection of birds to watch Lodmund's approach. As they got closer, Sarket's colors and the members of their company became more apparent. Based on the extra embellishment and on his richly made surcoat alone, Kasiel picked King Roald Lodmund from the group. He was older, his surprisingly long hair run through with enough gray that the original color had become mostly lost. A precisely trimmed beard and mustache that exaggerated the hard lines of his face, an apparently popular style in Sarket, were the same steely gray. The strong features and lack of any excess flesh on his cheeks suggested his hefty build beneath the armor he wore was mostly muscle. Exposure to the sun had turned his skin a warm tan and gave a deeper etching to the lines of age on his face. Lines that spoke to scowls and anger rather than laughter and smiles.

Kasiel didn't fancy the idea of having a chat with him, and after what happened with Edmund at his castle, he had no intention of letting this man get anywhere near him or anyone else in his unit. They could shout at each other from a distance if Lodmund was willing to talk at all.

The first thing they did was make a final run into the town to pick up a few last items and collect an order of arrows they had placed with the local fletcher, buying out most of his ready supplies to make more if needed. While a group handled that errand, Kasiel let Niskenya and Irith out to hunt one last time, drawing prey into the area to keep them from wandering too far. They made one more round to check all the fortifications and confirmed watch schedules and responsibilities in case Lodmund tried to attack. With the small force the king had with him, he had little chance of taking the stronghold from them, but he might try something to test their defenses before he sent for reinforcements, which he would undoubtedly do right away.

Kasiel sent Akyla as far south as he could without losing contact to see if there was any sign of their own army sending aid. He found nothing, but that didn't mean they weren't coming. Under the circumstances, he had to trust that Annora had reached them. Believing otherwise wouldn't help him stay strong for the people relying on him.

By the time Lodmund's force rode into view from the walls, they had everything locked down. They had also, with the help of some of the more amenable servants, cleaned their clothing and armor and bathed so that the king would find them looking composed and comfortable in their new lodgings.

Lodmund halted his troops as soon as he saw the drawbridges were up. The king held back, staying well out of bow range. Through Akyla's eyes, Kasiel could see the suspicion in the man's expression. He slipped into the mind of one of their horses to listen. His nerves were humming with tension, but Niskenya and Akyla fueled him with their predatory confidence. Irith paced restlessly inside the gatehouse tower behind him and Jethan, growling occasionally. The poor cliff cat seemed to have become the primary repository for Kasiel's anxiety. Perhaps he simply lost out because Niskenya's presence was so dominant and Akyla's so aloof.

"Shall I approach and ask why they've raised the bridges, sir?" a soldier next to the king was asking.

"Not yet." Lodmund had a deep, rough voice. An unfriendly voice that immediately grated on Kasiel. "Something's wrong. See that bird." He pointed out the nightstar eagle perched on top of the gatehouse tower. "Several reports from the front said that the Bane's little bastard had been using one of those to scout."

I'm not a bastard.

Irith's snarl punctuated Kasiel's thought.

"Wasn't he reported dead at Hellaris, sir?"

"Did you see the body?" the king barked at him. "With their mind-fuckers running about, can we trust anything we don't see with our own eyes?

The soldier flinched, then turned his glare up toward the eagle, perhaps to prevent that look from falling on his king. "Blasphemous," he snapped.

"Not for him. He's using a creature his enemies won't want to shoot down." The king's eyes narrowed as he gazed at the raptor. His horse tossed its head. "No. This one's clever. We're not taking any chances." He held one arm up and made a circling motion. Their company turned back to the road and continued toward the town.

"Where's he going?" Jethan asked, standing next to Kasiel inside the tower and peering out through a narrow window.

Kasiel shook his head, pulling back to Akyla and launching out to track them from above.

"The others want to know what's going on?" Etris asked from where she stood in the doorway.

Kasiel held a hand up, watching through the eagle's eyes as the king's company approached a sheep farm on the edge of town. One soldier went to the house. It took a few minutes before he realized what they were doing. A flash of irritation moved through him, and he heard a snarl from Niskenya this time from where she had stationed herself in the yard nearest the gatehouse.

"They're getting rid of their horses." He hated Lodmund for being smart enough to remove one of his most reliable weapons from the equation.

"How did he figure that out so fast?" Jethan asked, similar irritation and a hint of unease in his voice.

"Apparently, Akyla's reputation spread quickly."

"But they thought you were dead," Jethan countered.

"It seems this man doesn't believe anything he hasn't seen with his own eyes." That was going to complicate things. He drew a deep breath, pushing back against a threatening edge of panic. "This changes nothing. It just means we lose some of our element of surprise. Lodmund obviously isn't an idiot, and we would be fools to assume he was. We'll have to talk to him. If we're stuck here anyway, we might as well try negotiating to see if we can draw some pressure off the rest of our army. It wasn't the plan, but we have our hostage. Maybe we can still turn this in our favor." He dared to humor a spark of hope. "Watch over things here. It will take them a little time to walk back, and I imagine our visitors will be in a fouler mood for the hassle."

"Great." Jethan turned to watch him as he headed toward the door. "Where are you going?"

"I need to talk to our hostages."

Outside, he gestured for Tath and Nerith to join him as he strode toward the main keep.

"You look good." Nerith glanced at him. "I mean, intimidating."

He caught himself bringing a hand up to check if his ears were covered. Of course they weren't. He had his hair braided back on the sides, and the symbolic ear cuffs in place. He was a Vanrian officer at war. He needed to look the part. "Thank you," he said, not looking at her.

When they entered the queen's bedchamber, Astrid was up on her feet, walking gingerly around the room. She met his eyes as they entered, her gaze taking in the armor, hairstyle, and ear cuffs. Her face paled and her hand went to her chest. "He's here?"

Kasiel gestured for Tath and Nerith to stop at the door and strode up to her, intentionally coming close enough that he had to look down to meet her eyes. He spoke in a quiet voice so only she could hear. "I need to know right now. Do you have any desire to return to your husband?"

Her lower lip trembled. She cast a glance at the baby being cradled by the midwife, who was scowling at Kasiel again. "No. Never."

He beckoned the healers, speaking in a normal voice now. "I need you to play along with me. I trust Nerith and Tath to be only as rough with you as necessary to make it believable without bringing you any harm. They know what you've been through and what healing you still need to do, but I need you to act afraid."

"I am afraid, Ahninveth. I am almost as afraid of you as I am of him."

Though he understood she had reason to be, her admission still felt like a dagger sliding into his chest. He drew on Niskenya and stepped back from Astrid, his gaze moving to Hannah, who had gotten up from her chair. "You'll wait here."

"I will not!"

"Let her come with me. Please."

He looked down at the queen, the kanodrak's wild power moving through him. "No." He turned to Fenvar, standing in one corner. "Keep her here. I'll send someone else in to help in case she or the midwife cause problems." He cast a glance over his shoulder at Nerith, who was staring at him as if she had never seen him before. "Get the baby. Tath, you escort the queen."

"Havaad curse you," Hannah spat, throwing the book she held at him.

With Niskenya fully engaged, he caught it easily and tossed it on the bed. Then he led them from the room as soon as Nerith had the baby. Fenvar stepped in behind them, ready to keep Hannah and the midwife from trying to follow with his ability or his blade. Kasiel sent the next member of his unit they passed, one of the Delaphinians, to join Fenvar in the room.

"Kas," Nerith spoke in a low voice, "is this..." She trailed off at his warning glance.

The raptor flew overhead through a sky that was growing dim with the coming of evening. Kasiel led them to the top of the wall, taking them all into the gatehouse tower. Jethan stood up from a chair, immediately offering it to Astrid. She eyed the hard wooden object with a look of distaste and Kasiel grabbed a surcoat that was hanging on the wall, folding it to give her something softer to sit on.

"Thank you." Her curt tone lessened the sentiment. Once she sat, she held her arms out for her son, who was starting to make small noises of distress that were sure to grow.

Kasiel nodded to Nerith, and she passed the child to his mother.

While they waited, Kasiel turned to Etris. "Have Revik tell Minera and Rahlyf to stay out of sight and be ready to blind any archers or bomb-throwers who come close enough to be a threat."

Etris nodded, her gaze on Astrid and the infant.

Before long, Lodmund and his company came into view. He left most of his men near the bottom of the ramp, bringing a group of seven up with him. One man let his hand stray too close to his bow and stopped walking immediately, reaching out frantically in front of him.

"Shit! I can't see! I can't see!"

Lodmund lifted a hand, signaling his group to stop. "Shut up!" he barked at the soldier. Then his gaze moved to the wall. "I know you're there, Warden's Son, and you know I'm here. Let's not waste each other's time."

His harsh voice carried up to them and Astrid hugged her child closer. A flash of hatred moved through Kasiel, accompanied by a hunger for blood that he was reasonably certain wasn't his own. Akyla let out a loud shriek from the top of the tower. Steeling himself, Kasiel stepped out onto the wall with Jethan and Irith by his side.

"You look good for a dead man." Lodmund chuckled. "I'd bet my soul that you don't have the men to hold this place."

"I can see that you don't have the men to take it from me," Kasiel called back.

"Where is my wife?" Lodmund demanded.

Kasiel glanced into the gatehouse. Nerith and Tath helped Astrid to her feet. As she walked out, Tath now holding a bared blade to her back, the infant started crying and Lodmund went stone faced.

Kasiel forced a cruel smile. "It's a boy, if you were wondering. A nice strong heir to your kingdom."

Loathing twisted the king's features. "I finally find a woman who isn't too weak to carry my seed, and you take her from me? I don't see how this is going to end well for you, boy."

Ironic that he called Astrid a woman and him a boy. This man would go out of his way to frame the world in a way that suited him. "I see it as a start to negotiations. Your army has taken Dhomen Aleren and General Harel. Perhaps we can make a trade."

"Perhaps, if you opened your eyes, you would notice that I don't have them here."

Kasiel turned and reached for the baby. Astrid pulled Jaysen closer to her, shaking her head. Tath met his eyes over the queen's shoulder, then grabbed the back of her neck and pushed the point of the blade against her spine hard enough that Astrid's eyes popped wide. Tears started falling from them as he took the infant from her.

He cradled the innocent life in his arms a moment before looking down at Lodmund, whose face had gone so red he appeared ready to burst into flames. "I guess you had better let me know when you do. It's difficult to keep an infant alive at this age without proper care."

"If anything happens to that child—"

"You'll do what?" Kasiel stepped closer to the edge of the wall. He kept the baby secure in his arms, unwilling to risk something going wrong, but leaned out slightly to give the illusion that he might consider dropping it. It took all his will to tune out Astrid's panicked scream and the baby's responding wail. When the noise died down for a second, he shouted, "Bring me what I want, and we'll talk."

Without giving the king a chance to respond, he led them all down the stairs to the inner courtyard. The moment they reached the bottom, he passed the wailing infant back to its crying mother. Akyla launched in the air, soaring up high to watch over the group outside the wall.

Lodmund hadn't wasted time yelling at the empty space. He was already down the ramp, snapping orders at his men. Kasiel would watch for riders to head out soon, hopefully to summon the portion of his army holding Aleren and Harel. They would have to retrieve their horses first, though.

He stepped into the lower part of the tower where Revik and the Dampeners were. "Keep watching them. We don't want anyone coming in close to the cliffs or the walls. I don't know if their bombs can damage the basalt here, but let's not give them a chance to test it. We need to have at least one Dampener and one Speaker out here at all times. Once they've settled, whoever isn't on active shift can go get some rest."

The three of them nodded and said, "Yes, Ahninveth."

By the time they were back in the keep, Astrid was walking as if each step caused her increasing pain. He glanced at Nerith and Tath. "Help her to her room. One of you should probably carry Jaysen for her."

Astrid turned on him, tears drying on her cheeks. "I will never let you near my son after this," she snapped. "You said you wouldn't let Roald touch me again. Was that just a lie to secure my cooperation?"

Nerith and Tath looked at him, unable to hold in the surprise that drew up their brows and widened their eyes. Astrid wavered on her feet, and Nerith put a bracing hand on the queen's shoulder.

He hadn't discussed his thoughts about this with the others. There had been too much else to deal with. He wasn't sure how they were going to feel about the things he had promised Hannah and the queen, since trying to follow through with them would put any plans to get Aleren and Harel back at risk.

Kasiel moved closer, lowering his voice. "Calm down, Astrid. I have no intention of letting him take you or your son, but I need time to figure this out. Putting out my demand for something it will take him a while to get buys me that."

She stared at him over the crying child in her arms. "He'll bring his army here."

Kasiel kept his gaze steady. She didn't need to know he had doubts about the truth in his next words. "We're going to do the same."

CHAPTER TWENTY THREE

A short time later, Kasiel was back in the dining room, its myriad stuffed dead things now full of dagger holes from Avris, Kince, and Jethan's activities the prior night. His core unit was with him, sitting around the table sharing a meal. Tath and Nerith were just finishing telling them all what they had heard him promise Astrid. While they did that, Kasiel flew with a small owl, watching their enemies.

"What are they doing?" Jethan asked.

"Lodmund sent out two riders. His company is setting up camp where they can watch our gates. Closer to the southwestern ramp. He also sent some men into town, probably to stock up on supplies, not that we left much for them." Most of the others were watching him when he slipped back fully behind his own eyes.

"You told the queen we weren't giving her and Hannah back to King Lodmund?" Darro asked, a sharp edge of disapproval in his tone.

Jethan gave him a pitying look that clearly said he was on his own.

"Yes. I did." Kasiel pointed in the vague direction of the queen's bedchamber. "Do any of you want to give those two girls, those children, back to him?"

Darro's expression hardened. "No, but we need them to bargain with. If they'll get Dhomen Aleren back for us, we'll do what we have to with them. You can't save everyone, Kas."

He shoved back from the table and stood. "I've noticed." His glare lingered on Darro. "You sound like my father." He glanced toward the side door, not sure if he meant to leave or merely stood to burn off a flare of frustrated energy.

Nerith also got up. "Kas, none of us wants to see those girls in Lodmund's hands again, but we need to prioritize the khevarin's tehnaak. No matter your history with her, Khevarin Seylin is still our leader and Dhomen Aleren is one of our people."

"If we make a deal with King Lodmund, do you think he'll honor it and let us leave here?" He pointed forcefully toward where Lodmund's company had set up camp, then dropped his hand self-consciously as he realized how much pointing he was doing. This was his tehsheyn. It was also his unit. Where was the line between family and commanding officer drawn? He softened his tone. "Do you really believe that he'll stand back and let us walk away?"

"He has a point." Kince looked up from where he had been carving something into the table with his dagger. "Even if he were to let some of us go, he will never let the Crimson Claw of Vanris walk away from here with his life."

"Please don't call me that." Kasiel wearily reached up to rub at the ache between his eyes.

"Why not? It has a nice ring to it. Do you prefer the Warden's Son?"

He scowled at Kince. "No."

"Let's not get sidetracked," Merrin said. "Kince and Kas are both right. Lodmund won't even consider letting Kas leave here alive, and he won't be enthusiastic about letting any of us go. Our only chance of getting out of this is if we get better support from our army than he does from his. If that happens, we might as well try to get those girls out of here too."

Avris picked at a slice of lamb shank. "We should have sent a messenger north to Vanris at the same time we sent Annora out."

"It's too late to change that now," Jethan said, watching Kasiel. "Annora should have reached our allied army by now, assuming they stayed on their intended course. That will have to be sufficient. They can always send a messenger north, though it's debatable if help could get here in time all the way from Vanris. We're in the place we're in. We need to do the best we can with it. Our Dampeners and archers can keep Lodmund's soldiers from firing on or trying to bomb the walls, so we're currently as safe as we can be. Once they get a larger force, we'll have a harder time keeping them off us. For now, not a minute should go by that we don't have archers and a Dampener ready to run to the defense of any position along the walls."

"Fortunately, they won't be digging their way through the basalt this place is built on, so we don't need to worry about that," Etris added. "I doubt even their bombs could damage it enough to be worth the effort. We can focus on the threats we can see. This place is very defensible."

"Which sounds like a good enough reason to enjoy this food and the wine Sarket's troops so kindly left in their cellars," Jethan said, raising his glass.

The others gradually did the same. Nerith sat and Kasiel followed suit, lifting his glass as well.

He glanced around at them. "To the only people I ever want to be trapped in an enemy stronghold with."

A few wry chuckles answered him as they drank and turned to their meals, slipping into the more relaxed conversation that familiarity allowed them despite the poor circumstances.

They left the dining room together a short time later, walking out into the large entry hall. Emil, Leif, and two other Delaphinians were coming in through the front doors.

"We're going to die here, aren't we?" Leif's voice rose with an edge of panic.

Emil spotted Kasiel and his tehsheyn and gave a slight nod and tentative smile before answering his friend. "No. We're not. And you know why not? Because we're here with the Warden's Son. The Crimson Claw of Vanris." Kince smirked at Kasiel as the young soldier tossed out the names with a touch of pride in his voice. "We're part of his unit, and they don't lose."

Leif cast a wary glance their way. "Maybe they don't, but one of his core group is already dead."

Avris took two fast steps toward them, her hand sinking to a dagger. "Yes! He's dead because one of you Delaphinian cowards—"

"Avris!" Irith punctuated Kasiel's shout with a snarl. Everyone fell silent, their eyes on him and the now bristling cliff cat at his side. Irith's hackles were up, and his teeth bared, the deadly beast that he actually was showing through. "Yes, the man who ran was Delaphinian. Yes, his actions led directly to Wedro's death. That does not reflect on anyone still here with us. If anything, it demonstrates just how important it is that we stand by each other. Our enemy is outside these walls. In here, you will all work together, or you will die together at his hands. We are in this as a unit, and we need to act like it. Anyone who has an issue with that or anything else can bring it directly to me."

Leif lowered his gaze. "Yes, Ahninveth."

Kasiel softened his voice a fraction. "I don't need your fear or abject obedience. What I need is your loyalty to me and everyone else in this unit." He cast a glance around at them. "I need that from all of you.

Every single one of us is critical to the success of this mission."

"Yes, sir. You're right." Emil said, his companions straightening beside him as he faced Kasiel. "Toward that end, I'd like to offer my sincere regrets that one of our countrymen caused you to lose someone dear to all of you."

The other three tentatively echoed his sentiments. Kasiel glanced at Avris. Her chest rose and fell, a tremble in the hand that moved away from her dagger.

She offered a nod to their allies. "I apologize for my harsh words. I spoke from a place of heartache and anger."

When the four Delaphinians accepted her apology, Irith relaxed next to Kasiel, and he gave a slight nod of approval. "That's a good start. Anyone not on duty should probably take advantage of the opportunity to get some rest. We're all tired and under a lot of stress."

As the Delaphinians left the hall, Darro placed a hand on Kasiel's shoulder. "Well done, Kas. You're getting good at this. You almost don't need us anymore."

Kasiel's hand snapped out and caught Darro's wrist as he spun to meet the other man's eyes. His gaze moved over them from there. His tehsheyn, but for an instant, they were something else. Humans as seen through the eyes of a beast like Niskenya. A strange, but accepted array of pack mates. Then they became his unit again, his family. "I will always need you. All of you. What do you think gives me the courage to face these things?"

Darro grinned, and Kasiel noticed a few smiles and approving nods from the others. "Get some rest, Ahninveth. You need it as much as we do."

*

By morning, Lodmund's army had grown to around

seventy men, most of whom, judging by their attire, were guards or citizens from nearby towns. The quick growth was unexpected, but, as of yet, they didn't have the means to get inside the stronghold. However, they were collecting the numbers to keep Kasiel and his unit under siege for some time if help didn't arrive. With the two Dampeners, they might sneak out in the night, but Astrid, Jaysen, and Hannah complicated things. A girl recovering from a difficult birth, a newborn baby, and a girl nearing her due date did not contribute to stealth, speed, or ease of travel.

They either had to abandon their hostages and make a run for it or hope help arrived.

Kasiel had spent the night in a room with his teh-naak. Nerith hadn't approached him for more comfort, and he was grateful for that. He wasn't sure he had it in him to turn her away if she did. Maybe, someday, he would figure out how to get Velara out of his head and heart, but that day hadn't come yet. It wasn't fair to Nerith to offer something he wasn't sure he could truly give her.

He spent the day keeping watch over their enemies, checking on his soldiers, and helping prepare more arrows with the extra supplies from the fletcher. They adjusted food allowances to siege rations for everyone except Hannah and Astrid, both of whom were providing for a life other than their own. He figured out a route through the complex that allowed Niskenya to stretch her legs some and went for a short gallop on her back, burning off a little of their excess energy together and letting his unit see him in the position of uncommon power the kanodrak provided him.

Lodmund, though he often glared at the walls, made no attempt to approach again. He was waiting. He kept his soldiers under orders to stay on alert for any wildlife, from mice in the ground to birds above, and to kill any such creatures on sight if they got close to his camp. It prevented Kasiel from continuing his eavesdropping and led him to drive most animals from that area to avoid their needless slaughter.

By nightfall, Lodmund had gathered another twenty-three men from somewhere. Kasiel had no additional troops, and no sign yet of their coming. He stood on the wall for a time, watching the deepening dark blanket the growing enemy camp, a sense of fear moving through him. Jethan stood with him, quiet and pensive. None of his usual humor rising to the occasion.

"Ahninveth Kasiel." Etris called to him, hurrying up the steps, a flicker of excitement in her eyes. The first emotion he had seen in them other than sorrow since Wedro's death.

"What is it?"

"I just received a message from the dhomvalen's Speaker. He's approaching with a small unit. He has his Dampener with him, but requests that our Dampeners help them get past Lodmund's camp."

Hope sparked in Kasiel, burning away his weariness from the day. He immediately sent the owl he had been using for nocturnal scouting south to seek out his father. It only took a few seconds to spot the group of twelve riders tucked into the alcove in the cliffs where Kasiel had hidden the horses the night they took the stronghold.

"Tell him to head to the northern ramp and stay close to the side of the plateau. I'll be tracking their progress with an owl. We'll have to get his group past Lodmund's entire camp, but they're less likely to notice us lowering that drawbridge, especially if the Dampeners help. We need Rahlyf and Minera both out here to blind and deafen our enemies as needed."

She gave a dismissive nod. "I sent word to Revik to wake Rahlyf. Min's already in the northern gatehouse tower."

The camp was far enough back to be out of range of Kasiel's archers. That gave them a reasonable chunk of land to move his father through at the base of the plateau. If they went carefully under the southwest ramp in the gap where the drawbridge came down, they might get past without drawing attention. They would have to go to the end of the northern ramp to ascend, however, and the lowering of that drawbridge was sure to be noticed by someone on watch without intervention from the Dampeners. They needed to be precise in their timing.

"Maybe they should leave the horses there," Jethan suggested. "Although, if they had to make a run for it..."

"They've already pulled the shoes off them. That should help with the noise," Etris added.

Jethan faced him. "I'll take care of all this, Kas. You get in position at the other gatehouse and get out there with that owl to keep an eye on things. It'll spot threats faster than anyone else is going to."

"Thank you, tehnaak. Etris, I need you with me so I can pass any threats I see to the dhomvalen's party and Revik."

Kasiel went down the stairs with Etris on his heels and ran through the complex to the other gatehouse. It would have been faster to run along the wall, but it might have tipped their enemy off to the fact that something was up. Once they reached the north tower and climbed up through to the second level, he put himself fully within the owl.

Taking the bird in close, he let Arhk and the others see it before climbing up a little higher where he could watch a broader area. The first part of their approach, coming up around the cliff to ascend the hillside, left them exposed. Kasiel found the owl a perch on a pile of basalt that looked like it might have been part of a fence at some point and kept a close watch on Lodmund's sentries on that side.

Arhk rode near the front, his Speaker on his right between him and the cliff. On his left rode a man Kasiel wasn't familiar with, but he wore the armor of Arhk's personal guards and the way he peered toward Lodmund's campsite suggested he was the dhomvalen's new Dampener.

"There's a sentry near the southwest corner of Lodmund's camp, about to turn their way." He trusted Etris to convey the information.

The group moved into the deeper darkness alongside the cliff and slowed their pace. The Dampener focused west. If he reduced the guard's night vision a little, the man's eyes would be unable to pick them out of the shadows without him realizing his ability to see was being tampered with. Kasiel forced himself not to hold his breath and turned the owl's attention to the next stretch.

"Rahlyf's already handling the next two sentries," Etris reported, presumably also sharing that information with his father's Speaker.

"Good. There's another soldier sitting awake beside an almost expired fire near the third sentry on the east side," Kasiel told her.

They kept careful communication between them all. Kasiel watched every step of their horses' hooves, and every breath the soldiers guarding Lodmund's camp took, trying to remember to take his own. Until that moment, he hadn't realized that he cared if his father lived or died, but he did. Far more than he probably should, and after Wedro's death, the thought of losing the insufferable man terrified him.

Kasiel waited until the last possible minute to order the lowering of the drawbridge. Niskenya paced below, not voicing the stress his tension was causing her only because his need required her not to. Irith was growling, though he did so quietly. The chains of the drawbridge rattled, the wood creaking, as loud as a thunderclap in the night as far as Kasiel was concerned. To his surprise, it didn't seem to draw the attention of the camp as he had expected it to.

His father's group increased their speed as the bridge descended, heading for the base of the ramp as fast as they dared in the dark. Kasiel kept the owl close, watching for ground hazards now, more than enemy threats. The odds of no one noticing at this point were slim. Now the Dampeners were fully in charge of keeping Sarket's soldiers from engaging.

"Tell them to follow the owl. I'll help them avoid hazards in the path. Have the Dampeners to do whatever they must to keep us hidden."

"Done." Etris replied.

The line of riders thinned out, falling in behind the owl as Kasiel sent it to the front, watching intently for anything that might trip the animals up. An eternity of seconds later, they turned up the ramp. Kasiel released the owl, moving his awareness into the horses to keep their strides steady and even on that last critical stretch. He heard the drawbridge thump down through his own ears seconds before the horses' hooves started pounding across it.

"How are we?" he asked, not taking his attention off the animals.

"Lodmund's camp is waking up, but the Dampeners have them restricted."

"Good." He stayed with the horses until they were safely within the walls, then released them, turning his attention to calming Niskenya and Irith. Akyla seemed less ruffled by his tension. Kitrix had rarely been as bothered by his emotional state as the other creatures either. Perhaps it was a bird thing. The sound of the drawbridge rising helped to make soothing his nerves and theirs easier.

A few minutes later, Arhk joined him on top of the wall, Jethan and the dhomvalen's three personal guards rushing to keep up with him.

"You work well with your team," Arhk said, removing his helmet.

"I have an excellent team," Kasiel answered, kicking aside the brief inclination to hug the man.

Arhk glanced out at Lodmund's camp where soldiers were rushing about in something of a panic, shouts sounding across the area as they tried to figure out what had happened. "I assume you have possession of the queen?"

"And the heir to the throne. Come, we should get down off the wall."

"She has given birth to a boy?" An edge of increased interest sharpened Arhk's tone as he accompanied Kasiel back down the stairs.

"Yes. Mother and child are alive and doing well, but in no shape to travel yet."

"Unfortunate timing, but help should arrive by the day after tomorrow." Relief swelled up in Kasiel so powerfully that he felt like he might float away. It took effort to pay attention to the fact that his father was still speaking. "I came ahead with a small group to investigate the situation as soon as I found out where you had gone." Arhk gave him a scrutinizing look. "You made a daring move that appears to have paid off."

"I'd argue that it's too soon to be sure of that," Kasiel said, rebuffing his father's confidence.

"Kas!"

The familiar voice caught him by surprise as he stepped to the ground. Turning, he saw Velara standing there dressed in a soldier's armor, a helmet tucked under her arm. The moment their eyes met, she started toward him and one of Arhk's guards moved into her path. The instant of delight that filled him at seeing her burst before a wild surge of anger.

He turned on his father. "Are you mad, bringing the heir to the Vanrian throne here? I know Khevarin Seylin did not approve of this."

Arhk glanced at Velara, signaling for two of his soldiers. "Escort her inside."

Kasiel turned to Jethan who was staring at his cousin with his mouth hanging open a fraction as if he couldn't believe what he was seeing. "Go with her, tehnaak. I'll join you soon." He avoided Velara's eyes, trying not to see the hurt, confused look she gave him.

"We will discuss this in private." Arhk's tone reminded Kasiel he was dealing with a man who significantly outranked him and everyone else there.

Right then, he wasn't sure he cared. "We most definitely will."

CHAPTER TWENTY FOUR

Kasiel gave the group escorting Velara a chance to get ahead of them before starting toward the keep. A vague, directionless sense of panic rose in him.

"Why is she here?" He growled the question under his breath and a much larger growl echoed him as Niskenya emerged from the darkness on his left when they rounded a corner. Her milky white eyes focused on Arhk, the one she accurately blamed for the distress her bonded companion was experiencing.

Arhk took a quick step away, turning toward her, a flicker of fear in his eyes that Kasiel found inappropriately gratifying. The dhomvalen's ability, like most mindcrafter abilities, only worked on humans, which meant he couldn't touch Niskenya with it, and he wasn't going to stop her if she chose to put him in his place. He didn't have enough men with him for that. For once, Kasiel's ability was enough to turn the tables, if only because the kanodrak would do anything to protect him.

He placed a hand on Niskenya neck, reluctantly sending soothing and patience through to her. She lowered her head some, huffing out a blast of warm breath into the cool air. "It's all right, Niske. I don't need help dealing with my father. He's my burden."

Arhk narrowed his eyes at Kasiel and gestured toward the inner keep. "Shall we?"

Kasiel led the way to a small study he had discovered in one corner of the second floor. Along the way, the Delaphinian members of his unit they crossed paths with shied away from Arhk the same way they did from Niskenya. They were almost to the study when he spotted Emil and Leif and stopped, calling them over. The wide-eyed looks of fear the two youths approached them with made him feel a bit guilty, but he turned to his father.

"The messenger I sent, Annora, did she reach the army?"

Arhk glanced at the two young men, understanding registering in his eyes. "She did. It was her information that explained why you had not returned to our army and what I might expect to find when I got here. She did well."

Relief overpowered some of the fear in their faces. Leif lowered his head in a slight bow to Arhk.

Emil inclined his head to each of them. "Thank you, Ahninveth. And you, Ward... ah, Dhom... Dhomvalen." The youth's face was bright red by the time he got the correct word out.

Arhk answered with the slightest nod.

"You're free to go," Kasiel said, watching as they raced off. From there, he took Arhk into the privacy of the study, and immediately turned on his father, ready to let loose his anger, but Arhk was faster.

"Velara insisted on coming. Seylin has selected a match for her, one she says she will not agree to. She asked to hide among my soldiers when I left Etrion." He walked to a shelf of books and started looking over them as if his explanation made everything fine.

"That's no reason to bring her into a war zone, let alone drag her into a stronghold that's under siege. You should have told her no. You're the Break-blasted dhomvalen of Vanris!"

Arhk faced him, his expression frustratingly calm. "If Sarket were to offer Khevarin Seylin a deal in exchange for her tehnaak, she might have been tempted to accept it and abandon your unit here. She will be far more motivated to see you succeed in this now that you have her daughter."

Horror formed a cold coil in Kasiel's gut. "I am not making Velara my hostage to manipulate my country."

"Your country indeed." Arhk smirked. "I am afraid you have already done so. You may call her your guest or even a member of your unit if it makes you feel better about the situation." He glanced back at the shelf, picking up an unmarked tome and flipping it open. "My guards and I will depart before sunrise. I expect you and your Dampeners to assist with that again. The other eight, including a Frightener, some excellent archers, and, of course, Khesran Velara, will remain here with you."

What was he supposed to do? He couldn't send Velara back out there, but she wasn't safe here either. Kasiel felt more trapped by what his father had done than by the position he had put himself in before Arhk arrived. "Where are you going?"

"I am going to intercept the army heading this way so we can plan our approach. With you here, Ahninveth Jhanik can bring the tethdraks in, and—"

"No. The army can't move in until they bring Aleren and Harel here. Otherwise, we won't get them back alive."

Arhk arched a brow at him. "He is bringing Seylin's tehnaak and the Delaphinian general here?"

Kasiel met his gaze, making himself stand tall and confident before it. "Those were my demands in exchange for his queen and heir."

"It will get considerably messier here if we allow them to arrive first. We could have our army take down

King Lodmund and—"

"If you helped, I could defeat King Lodmund now," Kasiel snapped. "With three Dampeners and two Frighteners, we could disable the force he has out there and our soldiers, along with Niskenya, could massacre them. Then General Hackett would kill Dhomen Aleren and General Harel the minute he found out. You want me to be a hero? That's not how I get there. I need them to live through this."

Arhk closed the book and set it down, his eyes never leaving Kasiel. "You are right, Ahninveth Kasiel. You will need to hold the stronghold after General Hackett's troops reach this place. I will bring our army in as quickly as possible once we confirm their arrival. Is there somewhere my guards and I might rest before we depart?"

Kasiel hesitated. In a way, he felt like he had won something, but by bringing Velara here, his father had also won, chipping away at any sense of victory he might have gained from the exchange. "Yes. I'll have one of my soldiers show you to some rooms."

When he stepped out of the study, Etris was waiting there. He met her eyes. "Could you show my father and his guards to rooms where they can rest?"

"Yes, Ahninveth."

"And do you know where..." Should he be looking for Velara? Etris knew the truth about his relationship with her. All his tehsheyn did now.

"Khesran Velara is in the queen's bedchamber, Ahninveth."

Why did that cause a dreadful sinking sensation in his chest? "Thank you, Etris." He turned to his father and bowed his head. "Speaker Etris will see to you and your guards, Dhomvalen. If we're done for now, I would like to speak with the Khesran."

Arhk nodded. "We will speak again before I depart,

Ahninveth."

Kasiel spun on the ball of his foot and strode away. When he reached the queen's bedchamber, he barely paused long enough to knock. The first thing he saw upon walking in was Velara holding Jaysen in her arms, smiling the most beautiful smile at the child that he thought he had ever seen. Two of Arhk's soldiers stood guard by the door, though whether they were protecting Velara from the queen and Hannah or merely ensuring that she didn't wander off, he wasn't sure, but the notion that he had gained another hostage sent a shudder of disgust through him.

Jethan stood at the foot of the bed, observing the three women, his brows pinched together. Astrid sat in the bed with a tempered smile as she watched Velara standing next to it with the baby, and Hannah hovered close to them. A grimace twisted the midwife's features, and she bared her teeth as though she wanted to bite him, but Kasiel was getting used to her hateful looks. Astrid and Hannah also appeared less than thrilled to see him. Velara, however, upon seeing who had joined them, passed the child to Hannah, then turned and rushed to him, throwing her arms around him in an almost desperate embrace.

"Kas!"

Before he could react, her lips were on his, soft and familiar. Lips he thought he would never kiss again. Nor should he be doing so now, and yet, he responded automatically, returning the kiss. The ache of longing and the heartache of loss – of believing he had lost her and of losing Wedro – swelled within him. The wonder of having her pressed against him lasted a second before the reality of where they were and who was watching crashed in. He took hold of her shoulders and forced her back.

"Jethan, please escort Khesran Velara out of here.

I'll join you momentarily."

"Kas?" Velara's query was soft, barely more than a confused whisper.

He gave a small shake of his head and looked away as Jethan took her arm and led her from the room. Arhk's two soldiers followed.

Astrid looked up at him. "The khevarin's daughter? You are more ambitious than I realized, Ahninveth Kasiel."

"Astrid—"

"Queen Astrid," she corrected abruptly.

He cringed inwardly. Her ongoing anger didn't come as a surprise. Whether out of necessity or otherwise, he had earned it. "I'm sorry about what happened on the wall. Lodmund had to believe I would hurt you and the child but trust me when I say I would never harm either of you. With Khesran Velara here, we will have all of Vanris behind us. I can get you away from him, but I still need to try getting Dhomen Aleren and General Harel back from Sarket too. That hasn't changed. This is a complicated situation. Bear with me."

"Khesran Velara seems to be a good person." Hannah regarded him with a curiously distraught expression. "I did not expect..."

"Her scars?"

Hannah nodded, twisting her mother's ring on her finger again as she spoke. "Before you came in here, she was telling us how you saved her life more than once. Listening to her, it's clear that she loves you. And my mother thought highly enough of you to tell you where her daughter was. Enough to believe you might help us. Given these things, I think it is only fair that we give you the chance you ask for, Ahninveth. Don't you agree, Astrid?"

Astrid nodded, though the tight line of her lips told him she hadn't forgiven him.

For the moment, he would take what he could get. "Thank you. I need to go deal with a few things, but please call on me if you need me."

"Wait." He stopped, watching as Astrid accepted Jaysen back from Hannah before looking up at him. "How did you get her past Roald's camp?"

"Mind-crafters, Queen Astrid. This place is overrun with them."

He left the room, sending the current guard on duty back in to watch over things. He didn't have to go far before catching up with Velara and Jethan in the next hall. Arhk's two soldiers were gone. Velara's back was to him as she spoke to Jethan.

"Thank you for sending them away, cousin. I almost felt like a prisoner."

Kasiel swallowed back a wave of guilt, placing a hand on Irith's head. The cliff cat pressed against his leg. "Are you hungry?"

Velara spun, absently pulling some of her hair forward to hide part of the scars on her face. "Kas, I..." She searched his eyes for a second, though he couldn't tell if she had found what she was looking for. "I am a little, but I had hoped for a moment with you first. Alone."

Nerith walked around a corner toward the end of the hall. She stopped when she saw them. Velara glanced in her direction, tipped off by some change in his expression, and Nerith ducked back the way she had come.

Kasiel drew a breath, his fingers sinking a little deeper into Irith's fur. "Jeth..."

"I'll go arrange some food options. You two can talk in our room. It's just a little farther down the hall." He started walking away, then turned back. "Oh, Vel, how's Keyla?"

Velara smiled. "Insufferable. She spends far too much time talking about you, as if I haven't had enough of you already."

Jethan grinned and gave her a wink. "You're welcome."

When he was gone, Kasiel gestured vaguely down the hall. "This way." As he started walking, she took his hand, slipping her fingers between his.

He used opening the door a few moments later as an excuse to free himself. His heart felt like it was vibrating with excitement, but this wasn't the time to let emotions take over. He shut the door behind them and quickly put a hand up to discourage her approach. She drew back, looking hurt again.

"Vel, what are you doing here? It isn't safe."

"Mother found a suitor she likes. I couldn't stay there and let her marry me off when you are all I can think about." She pushed his hand aside and walked up to him, her silver eyes cutting through his defenses. "I'm marrying you, Kasiel Cavenos. I don't care what my mother says."

He retreated a step, bumping into the door. "Vel, we need to talk."

She drew back. One hand went to her lips, a hint of panic sparking in her eyes. "Oh, by the Break. You don't want to marry me, do you? Is it Nerith? It is, isn't it?"

"No. Yes." He shook his head. "It's not Nerith." Although, they did need to talk about that.

Her voice tightened with the threat of tears. "Is it my scars?"

"No. Never." He stepped up and caught her hands in his. "Vel, there's nothing in the world I would love more than marrying you. I really would, but it's not that simple."

"I don't care. I'm heir to the throne. There must be some benefit that comes with that. I will not marry someone else."

She stomped a foot in frustrated anger, and Kasiel's resolve fractured. He pulled her to him, wrapping his arms tightly around her. "I missed you so much." His voice cracked with the threat of tears.

Velara embraced him for a few seconds, then she eased away, watching as he roughly brushed a few tears from his cheeks. "Kas, what happened?"

They sat on the edge of the bed, and he started to tell her. First, about his confrontation with her mother. He continued with the awful ways he had used his ability, the assassination attempt, nearly losing Niskenya, and losing Wedro. Then he told her what he was most afraid to tell her. He shared the awful truth about what his father had discovered regarding the khevarin's involvement in his abduction and his mother's death. When he finished, Velara got up from the bed and walked to the fireplace, staring into it in silence.

"Vel?"

She said something so softly he couldn't make it out.

Nerves dancing with uncertainty, he stood and walked up behind her. "What was that?"

She turned and looked into his eyes, hers shimmering with unshed tears. "I knew."

His chest tightened as though bracing for an impact, making it harder to breathe. "Knew what?"

"I've known for some time what my mother did to your family to get Arhk to serve as dhomvalen."

His gut twisted. Secrets. Why did everyone keep such secrets? "How?"

She turned away enough that he couldn't see the worst of the scars on her face. "My mother came to Doran for my fifteenth birthday. One of her rare visits. I was naïve enough to think she was actually there for me at first, but she was there to speak to Father. Nakhul and I loved to eavesdrop on Father during his private meetings, but he didn't want to do so with her there. He resented how rarely she came to visit us. So I hid in a wardrobe in Father's chambers and spied on them by myself.

"Mother was upset. I remember that because she was always so cool and collected, but at the time she seemed anxious. Jethan had recently approached her after getting word of the rumors that there was a Vanrian youth living somewhere in the southern reaches of the Pandrean Alliance kingdoms. She said he was sure it was you and he begged her to investigate. Anyhow, Father apparently already knew the part she had played in your disappearance because he got angry, telling her he had warned her at the time that she was going too far. That if Arhk ever found out, he would destroy them. He even encouraged her to have your father killed, but she refused. She said she still needed him and believed she could keep him from finding out the truth. I didn't understand everything they were talking about, but I got enough to recognize that what she had done to your family was awful."

A rising heat sparked through him, and desire had nothing to do with it this time. "And you never told anyone? You never thought to tell me?"

"I was young and scared, Kas. I remember crying, curled up in that wardrobe for some time after they left the room. With how upset my father was, I knew I should pretend I had never heard them. But I was also heartbroken for Arhk. It may come as a shock, but I've always thought of him as something of an uncle. A cold, arrogant, but reluctantly affectionate uncle. Whenever he came to Doran, he would bring me a gift or take me to the market to select one of my own. He never did that with my brothers. I believe it was because interacting with them reminded him of what he had lost. *Who* he had lost.

"I tried to forget what I had heard, and it worked to a point. I put it from my mind and stopped thinking about it in time, at least until I ran into you in the hall at the palace. As stupid as I know it's going to sound,

I think my heart stopped being mine the moment I looked into your eyes." She faced him now, searching the eyes she claimed to have lost herself so quickly in. "I kind of hated you for that. I never wanted anyone to have such power over me, but I couldn't stop thinking about you, especially after our talk in the garden when you told me you and Jethan would help me and keep me safe. I promised myself then that, even if I never got any closer to you than I was in that moment, I wouldn't let my mother hurt you again. But she tried to, and this time it was because of me."

The anger that was rising in him at the thought that she would keep something this important from him hit a wall in that moment. The love in her eyes, the determination when she spoke of wanting to protect him, and the raw pain when she said those last words, it all left him teetering on an edge with rage on one side, and something entirely the opposite on the other. He had a choice. Similar to the one he had made once with Nerith, when he learned she had been spying on him for the khevarin. He regretted his actions then because it hurt someone he cared deeply for. How he reacted right now to what Velara told him would determine the rest of their relationship, if they even had one. Despite knowing they had no future, he didn't want whatever they did have to end tonight. She was here, real and warm, and he loved her.

Tears slipped down her cheeks. "I know Arhk has every reason to hate my mother — you both do — but he won't kill her, will he?"

Forcing the anger back, he brushed away a tear that had escaped down her cheek, feeling the texture of her scars under his thumb. "I won't let him." He kissed her then, tasting the salt of tears on her lips.

When he drew away, she looked up at him. "I know it was stupid to come here. I do. But I would rather die here with you than stay in Etrion and marry someone else.”

He smiled. “Me too.”

A soft laugh escaped her. “Calloch.” She kissed him then and started sliding his jacket off his shoulders.

He escaped her lips for a second. “I thought you were hungry?”

“I am.” She grinned, her silver eyes sparking with an inner fire. “I’m ravenous.”

Irith was curled in front of the door, a solid barricade, when someone knocked a while later. Kasiel woke lying on his side with Velara's back against his chest, his arm draped over her naked waist. So many things were wrong with her being there, but when her eyes opened and she rolled onto her back to gaze up at him, one hand sliding into his hair, he focused on what was right and captured her lips in a deep kiss.

The knock came again, and Jethan's voice reached through the door. "Kas? The dhomvalen's group is getting ready to head out."

"I'll be right there."

With a groan of protest, he pulled away from her and climbed out of the bed to collect his clothes, which had ended up all over the floor. Velara got up with him and started dressing.

"You should stay and sleep."

She slipped on her shirt. "I want to come. Besides, I technically outrank you, so you'll just have to let me."

"Yes." He walked over to her, sliding his hands around her waist and pulling her close. "But you are under my protection now." She met his kiss too eagerly, waking up parts of him he thought sated.

"Mm-hmm. I look forward to being under your protection a great deal."

There was another knock and the sound of Jethan clearing his throat.

Kasiel pulled away from her. "Come on then. Jeth's right, we need to get them out of here while the dark makes it easier for our Dampeners to work."

They were about to leave the room when the image of Nerith seeing them in the hallway jumped into his mind. He paused with one hand on the door handle, a cold dread settling in the pit of his stomach. "Vel, Nerith and I..." He trailed off when she brought a finger to his lips.

"I like Nerith. Don't ruin that. Besides, whatever happened between you happened when you were still foolish enough to believe I wouldn't fight my mother for you." She moved her finger away.

"Yes. Your mother who is going to have me executed for certain now."

She gave him a tight smile. "You keep your father from killing her and I'll figure out how to keep her from killing you, deal?"

He gazed into those bright silver eyes for a moment. "I'm honestly not sure who has the worse side of that deal."

Velara grinned. "You've met your father, right?"

"Good point."

He pulled open the door.

Jethan stood outside, his gaze jumping to Velara. With a slight shake of his head as though he still couldn't believe his cousin was there, or that his tehnaak was sleeping with her, he gestured down the hall. "The Dampeners, Speakers, and several of our archers are already in place."

"Thank you." Kasiel added depth to his tone, hoping to convey gratitude not only for getting things ready, but for giving him the time with Velara.

"Don't mention it," Jethan returned, the crooked

grin that tugged at his lips making it apparent he caught the entire meaning.

As they walked, Kasiel engaged the owl again. It was lingering closer to the stronghold, forming a bond with him through the continued interactions. He swept it out high over the enemy encampment. Despite it still being a few hours before dawn, the camp was far more active than it had been the last time he checked. Their earlier antics had drawn considerable attention. A good third of Lodmund's soldiers were up and patrolling the area, their eyes on the stronghold gates. Every one of them appeared armed with a bow, and they had brought some horses down from the village. Seven of them stood in a line on the south edge of the camp, saddled and ready to give chase. Kasiel smiled at that. Let them try to ride the animals. That was one thing he was confident wouldn't be a problem.

Arhk and his personal guards were waiting in the courtyard. All three wore black and dark metal armor, their black horses equipped with matching gear. They were well-prepared for a nocturnal run.

"You're sure you want to do this?" Kasiel asked as he strode up.

Arhk met his eyes, exuding an almost unnatural calm. His gaze shifted to Velara at Kasiel's side, the barest threat of a smile tugging at the corners of his mouth. "I need to let our army know your plan, to ensure that they do not move in too soon, assuming you still wish to stay your planned course."

"I do." He let his focus turn more to the owl for a second, sweeping over the camp. "They're waiting for us to do something. Our Dampeners will have to hit them hard from the start this time, though they might avoid striking off alarms too quickly if they gradually reduce the dark vision and hearing of those closest to the ramp." He gestured to Arhk's speaker. "Tell Revik and

Etris to have the Dampeners start that now. Spread the change out over a few minutes." Realizing that he was giving his father's soldier orders, he faced Arhk, inclining his head a fraction. "Apologies. I overstep my place."

"Do as he says." Arhk's tone offered no insight into whether Kasiel's boldness had vexed him.

"They have some horses, but you don't need to worry about mounted pursuit. If anyone's foolish enough to get on one, I'll handle it. Anything on the ground will be your problem once you're out of range of my Dampeners. Which..." He trailed off, following a sudden hunch out past the edge of the cliff. The suspicion proved correct. A group of fifteen riders waited tucked up against the bottom of the lower cliffs near where they had left their horses that first night. That natural alcove provided too perfect a hiding spot.

"What is it?" Arhk asked.

"They have fifteen men hidden in that alcove you waited in before your approach last night. Looks like seven archers and eight fighters on horseback." They obviously didn't realize how far he could reach with his ability. "My Dampeners won't be able to do much about them from here, but I can deal with the horses."

"You need not concern yourself. I have a Dampener of my own. Besides, I could take this entire force down with my ability if you allowed it, Ahninveth. Fifteen men will not be a problem."

Kasiel drew back into himself, keeping his link to the owl. "If I allowed it?"

Arhk offered a faint smile. "I may outrank you, but this is your mission. Help get us past their primary force, and we will manage things from there."

"Don't use your ability." Arhk's eyes narrowed, and Kasiel rushed ahead. "Everyone knows how powerful a Frightener you are. It's why they have so many names for you. Let me and your Dampener handle them. I think it's best if they don't suspect you were here. Lodmund is arrogant and bloodthirsty, but he's not stupid. He already knows his position right now isn't great. I'd rather not risk him deciding to retreat."

Arhk gave a slow nod after a second. "We will do this your way."

Respect. There was respect in his father's eyes. Kasiel's throat tightened. He hated that part of him still wanted this man's love so badly. Arhk wasn't the type to hand out affection, though enough people had suggested that he wasn't always this way, back before he lost his family. Their eyes locked for several seconds, and he got the uneasy feeling Arhk knew where his thoughts had gone.

Kasiel broke eye contact. "We should get into position."

A hand on his shoulder surprised him. He met Arhk's eyes again, eyes just a few shades paler than his own.

"Stay focused, Kasiel. You can change the course of this conflict here. Consider how you want to proceed when the armies arrive." Arhk's hand tightened, giving his shoulder a brief squeeze before he turned and led his mount and his guards toward the gate.

Kasiel watched them go. "Don't get yourself killed, you calloch," he said under his breath.

Velara moved closer and silently slipped her hand into his.

"Come on, tehnaak. Let's get them out of here." Jethan led the way to the gatehouse where Etris and Minera were waiting.

Revik and Rahlyf were at the other gate, covering that part of the wall and surrounding landscape. This time, they were sending the group out through the southwest entrance. Enough sentries watched the northern gate now that it made sense to prioritize getting Arhk's team clear of the camp as quickly as possible. One of the Delaphinian soldiers had discovered a barrel of grease tucked back in a storage room that they used on the chains to lower the drawbridge. It wouldn't eliminate the noise, but it would hopefully make it a little quieter and a lot smoother going down.

Kasiel's Dampeners were already at work, reducing the vision and hearing of the enemy sentries, of which there were three times as many now, by miniscule increments. The dark of night and a slight cloud cover that had moved in took some of the burden off them. With their selection of unshod black horses and the hoods pulled up on their black cloaks, Arhk and his three guards were as invisible as they could be. The trick was that, this time, the drawbridge had to be lowered first, which meant the enemy camp was going to spring to life before the riders had time to start their descent down the ramp. Three Dampeners should be enough to sew chaos and prevent anyone from intercepting them, and Kasiel had his newly arrived Frightener up in the gatehouse as well, ready to add to the confusion if necessary.

Kasiel drew the owl down and perched it above the gate. He glanced at Minera. "Ready?" After the Dampener nodded, he turned his attention to Etris. "And the other team?"

"They're ready."

Jethan turned to the group operating the windlass. "Put it down. Smooth and steady, but as fast as possible."

With the portcullis already raised, Arhk's group could bolt the moment the drawbridge was down. Kasiel took the owl up as it started descending, scanning the camp. It wasn't halfway before a horn blared out a warning from somewhere within the enemy force. Kasiel cursed under his breath. He hadn't expected to get away with it as easily as last time, but that didn't mean he hadn't hoped for it.

"Blind anyone who poses a threat to the southwest ramp. Don't worry about deafening them. They already know we're up to something. Keep an eye out for archers and bomb-throwers."

"Yes, Ahninveth," Minera answered.

"Passed along, sir," Etris added after a brief pause.

Shouts rang out through the enemy camp and soldiers scrambled, grabbing equipment as they made a run for the southwest ramp, only to be cast into blackness the moment they got in range of the Dampeners.

An instant before the bridge thumped into place, Kasiel heard the horses running across it and down the ramp. He took the owl out ahead of them, picking the best route to get them away from the enemy force as quickly as possible. Some of Lodmund's soldiers were attempting to keep going despite their inability to see, a few with the leather satchels he knew held alchemical bombs.

"A little Frightening might be in order. Just enough to discourage them," he said, counting on the new mind-crafter to step in.

Some shouts from those the Dampeners had blinded changed to screams of terror.

"Try to avoid any permanent damage if you can," he added, "but prioritize the safety of the dhomvalen's group."

"Understood, Ahninveth," the woman answered, a distance in her voice that said she was fully invested in her task.

Arhk's group wasted no time. They sprinted off the end of the ramp and cut left, following the owl. In seconds, they were clear of the camp, and Kasiel cut them across to the roadway before breaking off to handle the next task.

"Drawbridge."

Jethan didn't hesitate. "They're clear of the camp. Get that drawbridge up!"

Sarket's hidden group was on the move, heading

out at speed to intercept Arhk and his guards. Kasiel dove his ability into their horses, not letting them get far enough that Arhk's Dampener would need to take his attention off the road ahead to deal with them. He threw the animals into a frenzy; biting, kicking, rearing – anything to get rid of their riders and keep them from posing a threat to his father. Through it all, he tried to avoid killing anyone. There would be injuries, plenty of them, but pointless slaughter wasn't his goal, merely the successful escape of his father and the three guards with him. There would be lives lost here, but it didn't have to happen tonight.

When Arhk's group was well on their way, Kasiel released the horses and drew back into himself. He heard and felt the drawbridge settle in place against the wall. Letting out a heavy sigh of relief, he glanced over at Etris. "We did it."

The chaos below gradually brought itself back to order. Kasiel was trembling, exhausted from living on the edge of panic while pretending he was calm and confident. He tuned out the now angry shouts and orders from the camp and sank into Niskenya, letting the kanodrak's fierce presence shred his fears. His longing to run with her was as strong as her desire to run. Turning the tables, he invited her in, drawing them both behind the eyes of the owl as he sent it out after Arhk's party, speeding over the landscape. For a few seconds, that exhilarating flight gave them both a taste of freedom, but it wasn't nearly enough.

"Kas."

He pulled back into himself, encouraging Niskenya to do the same, and opened his eyes. Jethan was peering out through the window of the gatehouse.

"What is it?"

His tehnaak grimaced apologetically. "I think Lodmund wants to talk."

Kasiel glanced at Velara. "Go down to the courtyard." To his surprise, she nodded and left them. He turned his attention to the others. "The usual rules apply. If anyone poses a threat, take away their sight. We don't attack his group."

Jethan and Irith accompanied him out onto the wall. Lodmund and a small party of his men were coming up the ramp that Arhk's group had escaped down. The king looked livid, his face visibly red even in the dark.

"You had company, Warden's Son," he shouted up. "I'm hurt you didn't invite us to your gathering."

Kasiel forced a smile. "Oh, I wanted to invite you, but I noticed your men seem to have a problem with losing their way in the dark."

A look of pure disgust twisted Lodmund's features. "Are my wife and son still in there?"

"Of course they are. Newborns don't travel well. If they did, we wouldn't be having this conversation now."

"Show them to me."

Kasiel wavered for a split second, almost sending for them, but he needed to stay in control. Lodmund would take advantage of the smallest show of submission. Niskenya wrapped him in her strength. "No. They're sleeping. I'll bring them out later."

"Havaad curse you, if you don't bring them out now, I will—"

"What? What will you do? Lay siege to my stronghold? I think we're past that point. Until you have Dhomen Aleren and General Harel here, I have no interest in your demands or your threats."

"Kas." Jethan's voice was soft, but it held an edge of warning.

"Your stronghold!" Lodmund roared. "You will not leave this place, Warden's Son. Not with your life." With that declaration, the king turned and stalked back down the ramp.

Kasiel watched him go, grateful to Niskenya for giving him the courage required to mask his fear.

Jethan shifted closer to him. "Why provoke him?"

He exhaled, not afraid to let Jethan hear the slight shake in his breath. "I've learned enough about hatred in the last couple of years to know it leads to bad decision making. The more he hates me, the less likely he is to leave here when he should, and the more likely he is to make mistakes in his strategy. Focusing him on me also means that, if this all goes wrong, I might be able to bargain for your lives with mine." He turned and started down the stairs.

Jethan trotted up beside him. "You know we won't let that happen, right?"

He cocked a brow at his tehnaak. "Part of me was hoping you would say that, but if you mean to prevent it, you might want to come up with a plan just in case, because Roald Lodmund detests me."

"All else aside, tehnaak, I love the hint of pride that comes into in your voice when you say that." Jethan finished with a soft laugh and a shake of his head.

A grin found its way across Kasiel's lips. "Honestly, being worthy of that man's hatred makes me feel like a slightly better person."

When they got to the bottom where Velara was waiting, she reached for his hand. He let her have it for a moment before it occurred to him that they should be more careful. Of course, many people here had already seen them holding hands. It might be too late for discretion. Still, out of an abundance of caution, he gave her hand a quick squeeze before taking his away.

"I need to talk to a few people." He met Velara's eyes. "I should check in with Nerith, in particular. I need to make sure my unit is in good working order."

A strangled noise escaped Jethan, followed by a

snort as he tried desperately not to laugh.

Velara smirked. "I can assure you that your unit works—"

Kasiel stopped her with a finger to her lips and shook his head. "Please don't finish that thought. You are both terrible people."

Velara clasped her hands before her and shrugged her shoulders, giving him her impression of a demure smile. Then she kissed the finger he had on her lips.

Warily, he drew his hand away. "Are you all right with my talking to Nerith alone?"

"I trust you, Kas." She took a step closer, her expression turning serious. "Although, before you talk to her, maybe someone should ask you if this is what you want? Am *I* what you want? You could be with Nerith. It would be less complicated, even with the conflict between your parents." A hint of moisture welled in her eyes, but she didn't look away. She was genuinely offering him a way out.

Jethan took several steps back, letting himself fade into the nighttime shadows as he watched them. Irith moved up next to Kasiel, but he didn't reach down to the cat. Nor did he seek comfort from Niskenya.

"I come with a country and an exceedingly angry mother attached," Velara added when he said nothing.

A country. He hadn't wanted to be a soldier, and she was laying the role of khemron at his feet, assuming they ever married, which was still highly unlikely. Then again, wasn't that what his father wanted? For him to win the heart of Vanris. Maybe there was a way this could work. It wouldn't be easy. But if he stopped the war and returned a hero with the dhomvalen's backing, maybe they could take control of the country through less violent means. A political marriage, if properly presented, could gain the support of enough of the populace that it might allow them to nudge Seylin out of power. But his life would always be difficult. There would be no finding a quiet home somewhere to live out his days working with beasts in peaceful ways, even if the war did end.

He met Velara's eyes, their silver reflecting the flickering light of a nearby torch. She would fight to be with him. How far was he willing to go to be with her?

Kasiel made his choice and stepped closer, no longer caring who might see. He placed his hand against her cheek. "I love you, Velara. I will face whatever challenges lie ahead if it means I can keep doing exactly that."

A few tears slipped free as a relieved smile broke across her features. She stepped in and kissed him, a kiss that would make it obvious to anyone watching that their relationship went well beyond friendship.

Since morning wasn't far off, Kasiel opted to approach Nerith after a little more sleep. He thanked everyone who had helped get the dhomvalen's group away safely, made sure those who needed to rest went off to do so, then returned to the room with Velara and Jethan. His tehnaak offered to find a different place to sleep, but they both insisted on figuring that out in the morning as well. Instead, he stayed, but opted to stretch out on a pile of blankets on the floor, giving them the bed.

When Kasiel woke in the morning, it was to the soft click of Jethan shutting the door behind him as he slipped out. For a few seconds, he considered waking Velara, if for no other reason than to steal a kiss, but she was deep asleep. Exhausted after a night of too much excitement. It was enough to appreciate the fact that she was with him for a moment before he carefully climbed out of bed, dressed, and snuck out, leaving his contentedly snoozing cliff cat to watch over the khesran.

When he stepped into the hall, he spotted Nerith coming his way and offered her a nod of greeting.

She cast a quick glance at the door to the room, then looked at him, or more through him. "Jethan said you wanted to speak to me." As she spoke, she held a handful of peeled orange slices out. "I also thought you might like a little something to eat."

He accepted some of the fruit. The first bite was sweet, juicy, and bursting with guilt. "Walk with me?"

Nerith nodded and gestured for him to lead, placing a slice of orange in her mouth. They didn't speak as he led the way out to the walk and up to the lookout tower above it. One of the other Vanrian soldiers from his unit was up there. Kasiel politely dismissed him when they arrived. Once they were alone, he brought Akyla in and inspected the raptor's healing beak before sending the bird out again to scout. Finally, he drew a deep breath and turned to Nerith.

The morning was cool and gray, with a light misting of rain falling. It felt appropriate somehow. She looked tired, though he imagined he did as well. The night hadn't left much time for a proper rest.

"You don't have to act so guilty, Kas. You've done nothing wrong."

He pushed his hair out of his face, lowering his gaze. "I wish it felt that way."

"You were honest about the fact that she held your heart still. I asked you for a night, and you gave me that. Whether I hoped it would lead to something more is irrelevant. You never offered me more."

He hesitated, letting himself feel the wind under Akyla's wings and wishing for a moment that he could share that escape with her. "It isn't irrelevant to me. I never wanted our relationship to cause you pain."

"We've brought each other pain more than once, Kas. Maybe that's just a sign that we should stay what we are. Friends. Family. And stop trying to confuse things with something else."

"Is that how you really feel?" He got a flicker of disquiet through his connection to Akyla and glanced out of the raptor's eyes to see a sizeable army approaching from the southwest carrying Sarket's banners. Not a surprise, though the sight still sent a chill through him. He refocused on Nerith to find her watching him patiently.

"Yes. Or perhaps I should say that it is what I think. My heart is not so easily turned from its course, but it will adjust." Her gaze drifted to the southwest, the direction they all knew the army was likely to come from. "We're expecting more company?"

"We are," he answered, "but that can wait. I'm not done here."

A subdued fondness warmed her smile. "I find it amusing that the boy I met when you arrived in Vanris has become the man in front of me now, dismissing the approach of an enemy army, so he can make sure his former girlfriend isn't too brokenhearted. If I had to lose you to someone, at least it was to someone who could stand beside you without becoming lost in your shadow as you prove to the world how extraordinary you are."

His throat tightened with a sudden pain and one hand sank absently to touch the pouch that held Sylaryth's claw. "I don't want to be extraordinary. I just want to be good enough to protect the ones I love."

Nerith stepped up close and slid her arms around him, drawing him into her embrace. As he returned the hug, she kissed him on the cheek and whispered in his ear, "That's why we support you, even if it means defying our own khevarin. It's why we love you, Kas."

He pulled her in tighter, and for once there was no yearning for more from her, just a deep, comforting love for someone dear to him. "Thank you," he whispered back.

They stayed that way for a minute or more, then, as if an hourglass had run out, they drew away from each other. Kasiel slipped back behind Akyla's eyes, scanning the approaching army. The next part of the plan was almost in place. It was time to gather with his unit and discuss what was coming. His strategy hinged on one last piece, the allied army of Vanris and Delaphine showing up at the right time. It seemed reasonable to talk about how they would proceed if that didn't happen too.

As he pulled back from the raptor, Nerith brushed a touch of moisture from his cheek and straightened his shirt. Then she started down the ladder. "I'll call the unit together. You can decide if anyone outside of our tehsheyn should join us."

By which he knew she primarily meant Velara. First, he had a restless kanodrak to appease. He could feel Niskenya's tail lashing as she prowled the various pathways and yards within the outer wall. An irritable kanodrak wandering the grounds couldn't be helping to put anyone at ease. As he climbed down, he reached out for her with his mind and received a mental growl in response. By the time he made it to the courtyard below, she was there, tail still lashing, claws digging runnels in the dirt.

Kasiel approached her, aware of her power and her wild sentience. She growled loud enough that one of the soldiers Arhk had left him glanced down from the wall, fidgeting with his sword belt. When he saw Kasiel walking toward her, he offered a respectful nod, looking relieved. Kasiel returned the gesture before settling his attention on Niskenya.

"Soon, Niske," he murmured, stepping closer to reach out and touch her neck.

She pulled back with another growl. Sending patience across, he approached again and reached out, not quite touching her this time. Niskenya turned and stalked a few strides away, then she looked back, watching him through her milky eyes. He closed his eyes and opened himself to her, inviting her in, trying to construct images of his plan in his mind so that she might see what the near future held. A few heartbeats later, the side of her face and then her neck brushed against his outstretched hand. She stopped before him, her warm breath mingling with his in the cool drizzle. Her restless energy settled a little.

Kasiel smiled, relaxing into the strength and confidence she brought to their bond. He could feel her muscles twitching with the urge to run. Not the controlled pace the stronghold grounds restricted her to, but a full, free run.

"Me too, Niske, me too," he murmured. "Just a little longer."

She pressed her armored head to his forehead, the contact careful, and passed affection to him. Then a flash of mischief provided inadequate warning before she thumped him with that rock-hard armor.

"Ah!" He winced as she jumped away with impressive agility for such a massive beast. Kasiel rubbed his head. "You're a menace."

A surge of amusement answered him. He laughed as it infected him and took a run at her. Niskenya leapt to the side, sweeping his feet out from under him with one broad paw, the claws fully retracted. He slammed down on his back, and she stepped over him, putting her nose in his face.

"You're a bad kanodrak," he said with a chuckle, aware that several people had come out into the drizzle to see if their commanding officer was about to be eaten by his mount.

Niskenya nosed his cheek gently before stepping back to let him up. Kasiel stood and walked closer to her. Leaning against her, he placed his ear at the join of her neck and shoulder to listen to the powerful beat of her heart for a moment. When he moved back, their audience was hesitantly dispersing to return to whatever duties had brought them out here to begin with.

Kasiel patted her neck once before backing away. "Soon," he promised again.

She answered with a surge of hunger.

After setting a sheep loose to feed the kanodrak, Kasiel returned to the keep. Velara was waiting outside the dining room, looking distinctly uneasy.

He walked up and took one of her hands. "What's wrong?"

"Jeth said maybe I should join you all, but..." Her hand tightened on his.

"You know everyone, Vel. You've spent time with them."

She met his eyes. "That was before they knew for certain that we were sleeping together, and before my mother sent you all to the front lines, hoping to get you killed because of it. Oh, and before they knew the part my mother played in your rather unfortunate history."

Kasiel leaned in and kissed her, a long, soft kiss full of promise and hope. As he drew back, a loud clang from one corner of the entry grabbed their attention. They both turned to see Leif and Emil standing there, Emil holding the neck of the tall candelabra he had apparently walked into. The two boys were staring at them.

"Uh, sorry. We were just leaving." Leif hastily helped his friend rebalance the candelabra before grabbing his wrist and hurrying out through the front doors.

Kasiel smiled and turned back to Velara. "I promise you they won't hold those things against you, but you don't have to come if you aren't comfortable."

"Maybe I shouldn't. I'm still khesran and the heir to the throne. With things as they are, I don't think it would be helpful if they felt the khevarin's daughter was exerting her influence over you or them."

"You're sure? It would be an honor to have you at my side." Even as he said the words, he knew she was right.

"Not this time. Not yet. I'll go visit Queen Astrid and the baby. Let me know how it goes."

"Take a guard with you, please."

Her brow furrowed. "You're worried the queen will attack me?"

"Not Astrid, no, but Hannah has teeth, though you seem to have calmed her."

Velara stepped close, brushing back a strand of hair that had worked free of one of his braids. "Does that surprise you? She's angry help didn't arrive until after the king raped her. She resents your group helping Astrid through the birth of her child as well, and she feels guilty for feeling that way."

"I not sure I understand."

"Because you're a man, and you live in Vanris. Hannah has lost value as a bride because of what the king did to her, but now that Astrid and her child are doing well, she has no value to him, either. She's afraid of what will happen to her, even if you don't give them back to Lodmund." Her eyes met his, the silver of a fine blade. "Which you won't do."

"Not if I can help it."

"Good." She placed a light kiss on his lips. "Lead well, my love."

"I'll do the best I can." He watched as she walked away. If this worked, there would be plenty of time for her to become more engaged with his tehsheyn. Right now, all their futures hinged on them figuring out how to make it work.

*

By evening, the rocky fields to the west of the stronghold had grown a healthy crop of soldiers. Lodmund's army stretched across the landscape. General Hackett and General Danovan were both there. Several light trebuchets were being assembled, designed to hurl larger versions of their hand-thrown alchemical bombs over the walls. Mechanisms that could operate from beyond the range of Kasiel's Frightener and Dampeners.

As dark began to fall, Lodmund brought Aleren and Harel to the front, both bound and gagged, and made them kneel within sight of the stronghold's defenders. Then he ascended the ramp with Hackett, Danovan, and a few others by his side. Kasiel climbed to the top of the wall, flying south with the owl as he did so to look for the friendly army he hoped to see soon. Jethan accompanied him as usual.

"I've brought what you asked for," Lodmund shouted up. "Now here's what's going to happen. I will give you Dhomen Aleren in exchange for the queen, my son, and the queen's attending lady. When the trade is complete, I will grant your unit safe passage from here provided I keep you, Warden's Son, as my prisoner."

Nothing in the offer surprised Kasiel, beyond perhaps the choice of words. They both knew Lodmund wouldn't keep him alive as a prisoner any longer than it took to run a sword through him. He couldn't help wondering how many people within these walls would consider giving him to the king in trade for their lives. "And General Harel?"

"Delaphine must be punished for this betrayal. I'm afraid Harel stays with me."

Kasiel met Kassian Danovan's eyes, watching with a sense of satisfaction as the man shifted his feet and looked away. He was a coward. A figure who would go along with whatever the person currently holding power wanted. In Hellaris, that had been General Hackett. Here, it was King Lodmund... for now.

"No," he answered, pleased with how well his voice carried. He sounded strong and sure of himself. Maybe someday his confidence would match that voice.

"Dhomen Aleren *and* General Harel in exchange for Queen Astrid, Lady De Clare, and your son." A trade that would never happen if he could do anything to stop it, but it was safe enough to offer, knowing it wouldn't satisfy Lodmund. "We'll discuss additional terms after that's settled."

"I'll consider your proposal." He wouldn't. His tone told Kasiel that he had already dismissed the counteroffer. "You have until dawn to make your decision. If you refuse to be reasonable, my army will attack. It is a generous offer considering you don't have the power, even with your collection of mind-fuckers, to keep my army out now."

Dawn. He only offered that because they needed time to finish assembling trebuchets.

Lodmund was right. Sarket had a big enough force there to capture the stronghold, but not without a costly fight, and the king would prefer not to risk his heir if he didn't have to. He would give them a little time for the sake of finishing preparations, but he was impatient and tired of dealing with them. Kasiel in particular. The reprieve wouldn't last long.

"We'll sleep on it," Kasiel called back, letting his partial absence help him present a lack of concern in his tone. He was busy soaring with the owl, searching.

Lodmund raised his voice, shouting louder this time, to make certain others on and around the stronghold walls would hear. "I extend my offer to anyone within who will accept it. You may leave this place unharmed if you deliver me Ahninveth Kasiel Cavenos."

Kasiel turned his back on the king's cruel smirk and walked away, descending into the courtyard. Jethan and Irith stayed close at his side.

"I don't suppose you've got good news?" Jethan asked, keeping his voice low.

"No. Not yet, but I will soon." A chill of unease

coiled around him. What if their army didn't come in time? Who would be the first to try lowering the drawbridge to offer Lodmund Kasiel's life? He kicked his doubts aside with all the conviction he could draw upon, which was more than he would have expected thanks to Akyla's potent arrogance. "My father may be a calloch, but he has a personal interest in seeing us pull this off. Right now, we are the pawns of his extended vengeance."

"Do you think he'll go along with your plan?"

The chill returned. Niskenya lurked in his mind. She had no patience for nonsense. His or his father's. "He'd better."

For a heartbeat, he was so thrown off by the snake of motion the owl spotted coming along the narrow roadway in the darkness that he didn't realize what it was. The allied Vanrian and Delaphinian troops stretched out in a long, thin column to fit within the less hazardous confines of the carved path, traveling along at a decent pace for such a large force. More unexpectedly, they were making their way without torches or any other means of light beyond the moon and stars peeking through the dispersing cloud cover, trying to avoid detection by scouts in the area for as long as possible.

Kasiel swept down the length, quickly coming upon the tethdraks and Jhanik. Kenna was there with Raxxa, acting as Jhanik's backup for the tethdraks, he supposed. Had she traveled south with his father? There hadn't been enough time for the messenger from the army to reach Etrion and return, so Arhk must have brought her for his own reasons. Her tehnaak, Therin, was with her, which was good. It meant Kasiel would have at least one Speaker in the army for Etris to reach out to whom he fully trusted, but they were still too far out for either Speaker to make that connection yet. They were at the edge of his limits with the owl, but they would close in quickly.

Jhanik spotted the owl and pointed at it. "Looks like they know we're coming," he said, glancing at Kenna.

She smiled up at the bird and waved.

Kasiel grinned and turned the owl, sinking lower to fly next to them for a couple of flaps of its wings, then flew up again to search for scouts in the area. "Our army is coming. They should be in range of our Speakers before too long. Get Etris and meet me outside the queen's bedchamber. I have a few questions for Astrid."

When he reached the room and stepped inside, Velara and Hannah were sitting on either side of Astrid on the bed, the infant between them, the subject of all their attention for a few seconds after he entered. Then Velara looked up and motioned him over, taking his hand when he stopped beside her.

"Isn't he the cutest thing?"

Kasiel looked at the child and Jaysen stared back at him with his bright blue eyes, faint wrinkles forming in his brow. His tiny mouth opened into an O while he considered the only other male currently in the room. "I suppose he's all right for a round-eared southerner."

Velara elbowed him in the leg. "Kas!"

He breathed a laugh, surprised that, for the briefest instant, the world outside that room had vanished.

Velara got up and wrapped her arms around him, resting her head on his chest. He returned the embrace, holding her close. Hannah made a point of not looking at them, but Astrid watched them thoughtfully.

"You are quite fortunate to have found love."

At the queen's words, Hannah left the bed and returned to her usual chair, snatching up the book on the nightstand and glaring daggers into it.

Kasiel felt a twinge of pity for the girl. Either way, she faced a hard road ahead, assuming she didn't suffer the fate of Lodmund's wives before Astrid. "I had questions about the laws of succession in Sarket. If something happened to the king, would Jaysen still have a claim to the throne?"

Astrid's eyes narrowed a fraction and Hannah looked up, her interest suddenly piqued. "You intend for something to happen to Roald?"

Kasiel shrugged as Velara drew back to look up at him. "It's war. People die. I want to know what happens to the leadership in Sarket if he should die."

"According to the law, the king's firstborn son would inherit," Astrid explained. "In Jaysen's case, he is too young to be crowned, so a regent would take his place. I imagine that would be one of Lodmund's cousins. His line has always had a problem with childbirth, so he only has one sibling, and her gender excludes her."

"Not you either, then?"

Velara moved beside him, her hand slipping into his.

"No." Astrid adjusted Jaysen in her arms. The infant continued to watch Kasiel, his eyes bright and curious. "As queen, I would be a figurehead until my son could ascend, but I wouldn't have any actual power." She smiled at the child. "I think he likes your ears."

Kasiel carefully removed one of the decorative ear cuffs, then held it out to the baby. Jaysen's eyes went wide, and he reached for it, arms wobbling, too uncoordinated yet to grab it. Astrid took it and held it for him, letting him feel it.

"Kas?" Velara questioned softly.

"It's not like he's going to hurt it." Turning back to Astrid, he asked, "Who are Lodmund's cousins?"

"General Hackett and General Thrasser," Velara answered for her.

Astrid nodded. "Hackett's as awful as Roald, but Thrasser's—"

"Cautious," Kasiel interrupted, "and he cares about his men. Someone who might work with us."

"You know him?" Velara looked as surprised as Astrid.

"I've intimidated him out of fighting twice now, so I wouldn't exactly call us friends, but I know who he is. Last I saw him, he was still a hostage in our army, unless they've released him since."

"If something happens to Roald, the king's advisors will try to put Hackett in place as regent," Astrid stated with certainty.

Kasiel nodded. "Thank you, Astrid." He held a hand out, and she gave him back the ear cuff, which appeared to have a spot of drool on it now.

"What are you planning?" the queen asked.

Hannah was still watching him, the faintest spark of hope in her wary gaze.

A timely knock on the door gave him an easy escape. "Get some rest. The next twelve hours could get interesting." With that, he led Velara from the room.

CHAPTER TWENTY SEVEN

Kasiel had Etris trying at regular intervals to reach out to Therin and his father's Speaker. Therin would give him a direct line to the Ferals, which he needed for this. Jhanik in particular. He preferred not to involve Kenna beyond keeping her as a backup, primarily because she didn't have the added advantage of a kanodrak like he and Jhanik did.

While they waited, he encouraged others to rest if they could. He sat in the partial shelter of the forge with Niskenya and Jethan, observing the enemy camp through various animals he had brought back into the area and the progress of their own army with the owl. A quick scouting run with a few mice helped him verify where Lodmund was keeping Aleren and Harel within the selection of tents they had put up near the center.

Work on the light trebuchets was progressing faster than he liked, but it gave him another use for the mice once he had them inside the camp. The tiny creatures were hard to spot in the dark, so as soon as Lodmund's soldiers finished work on a trebuchet, Kasiel sent a couple of mice over to chew stealthily partway through some of the ropes that would be under strain. With Jethan offering guidance on which ropes to damage, the sabotaged devices would hopefully break upon use, doing more harm at the source than anywhere else.

"Have either of you slept or eaten?"

Nerith's voice pulled part of Kasiel's attention back, though he stayed behind the eyes of a mouse currently chewing a nice chunk out of a sling rope.

"No. Not yet tonight," Jethan answered.

"I'll bring some food out."

"Did Merrin make it?" Jethan asked the question Kasiel would have if more of him were present.

"Yes, she got down the wall and across the river. She seemed to struggle with the current some but got across fast enough not to end up where Lodmund's scouts might see her." The unmistakable admiration that filled her voice resonated through Kasiel. He was lucky to have Merrin. He was lucky to have all of them. "Is Kas watching the armies?"

"Yes, and sabotaging Lodmund's trebuchets." Jethan's delight at that rippled through their bond, perhaps more strongly because of how open Kasiel was to outside influence at that moment considering all the creatures he was connecting with.

"That's a worthy endeavor." Kasiel found it odd that he could hear the faint smile in Nerith's voice. "Make sure he doesn't overdo it, though. You remember what happened in the Break. If he gets another headache like that, he's going to find it hard to follow through with the rest of this, and we can't do it without him."

She had a point. Kasiel sent the mice into hiding and pulled back from them. That would have to be enough mischief for now. He opened his eyes, a faint throb behind them warning him to heed Nerith's words. Before he could say anything, Etris came jogging up.

"I've reached the Speakers in our army," she reported. "Merrin is with them now and has been riding with the dhomvalen, explaining our plan. They're ready to follow your guidance coming in."

"I'll go grab something for you two to eat," Nerith

said, dismissing herself.

Kasiel got up from where he sat reclined against Niskenya. "You don't need—"

"You both need to eat. Don't make me force it down your throat, Kas." Nerith stalked away before he could say more.

Jethan's grin said he agreed with her, so Kasiel let it go, turning his attention to Etris. "Can you select who hears you?"

"Yes. Everyone has a different mental presence, though it's harder to differentiate at this distance."

"That's fine." Kasiel focused on the owl he had monitoring their army. Niskenya got up and stood behind him, her warm breath on the back of his neck reminding him of the man whose head she had bitten off on their mission to rescue Jethan. Not the most comforting memory.

Before he could register much, a shout came from the nearby tower. "Ahninveth! Rider coming in fast from the south."

One of Lodmund's scouts, undoubtedly carrying word of the opposing army's arrival. It took less than a second to connect with the horse and bring it skidding to a stop from a full gallop, a slight twist of its body at the last instant sending the rider flying over the animal's head. Bile rushed to the back of his throat as he watched the man's neck snap on impact through the horse's eyes. Lodmund needed scouts away from the camp, and there was only one efficient way to move them around. Up to now, Kasiel had allowed them to do so without interfering with their mounts, but this, the moment the king needed them most, was the perfect time to exercise his ability. A waste of life that Kasiel hated being part of, but it would give Lodmund one more reason to despise him.

He slipped back behind his eyes. "Etris, can you

focus on the dhomvalen and Nevias's Speakers, and Therin?"

She nodded.

"Good. We want them in position and ready to move when needed. I don't expect negotiations with Lodmund to improve, but we might intimidate him into surrendering or retreating once the army is in place. If not, I need them prepared to hit his force with every Dampener and Frightener we've got between us. I need chaos around the edges and as deep in as they can reach. Minera can influence the area around the command tent, but her ability will be significantly weaker at that range. My father and his Dampener are both stronger. I would rather keep Minera's attention on protecting this place and have them focus on giving Jhanik and I a chance to reach the tent they're keeping Harel and Aleren in."

Etris's focus changed as she passed that along. "They have questions."

"Not until I'm done." When she nodded, he continued running through details of the plan they had made, most of which Merrin would have already shared, but he wanted to be certain she covered everything. He glanced at Jethan when he finished, looking for confirmation that he hadn't missed something.

"That's the gist of the madness." The tension in his jaw added an unspoken note to how uneasy he was with the idea of letting Kasiel go out there.

"They have more questions, and apparently Nevias thinks you've lost your mind," Etris relayed flatly.

Kasiel heaved a sigh. "All right, what questions?"

"Ahninveth!" The shout came from the gatehouse tower again. "The king—"

"Warden's Son!" Lodmund's roar traveled over the wall.

Kasiel cringed. Perhaps he had pushed it too far this

time. "Shit! Etris, head to the upper part of the gate-house. Tell Revik to wake the others and have someone bring Astrid and her son out. Then tell the dhomvalen we may have to move up our timeline."

"By how much?"

"Sometime in the next few minutes would be fantastic." With that, he sprinted up the steps, slowing to a walk as he reached the top of the wall to avoid appearing as concerned as he was. Irith and Jethan hurried after him.

"Kas, what did you do?" Jethan asked as they strode to the parapet.

"I took down the scout that was riding in. I think I may have found the limits of his patience."

Lodmund was standing below on the ramp, a few of his men at his side bearing torches.

"I honestly thought you would have learned my name by now," Kasiel called down.

"You don't deserve a name, boy," Lodmund shouted up at him. "You killed one of my scouts."

Kasiel leaned on his hands on the wall between two merlons and peered down. "With the stress we've all been under, Sarket's King, I was worried the noise of your scout galloping into camp like that might interrupt your beauty sleep."

Lodmund's face reddened in the torchlight. "It's close enough to morning. If you surrender yourself to me right now, I will let the rest of your people leave this place unharmed. You have three minutes."

That wasn't enough time. In the camp, under the faint light of early dawn now peeking over the horizon, they were making final adjustments to the trebuchets. Several were sure to fail, but he hadn't damaged all of them. Lodmund's troops were up and moving now as well, getting ready for a full-on assault.

Kasiel turned to Jethan, his gut shrinking into a

quivering ball of dread. "We need Astrid and the baby out here now." To his relief, the wail of the infant reached his ears at that moment. Judging by Lodmund's deepening scowl, it reached his as well. Kasiel took a breath and leaned out again, careful not to let his voice shake. "If I only had myself to worry about, I might consider your offer. But we do have a little one in here."

"My son had best be at my side in the next few minutes, or I will tear this place down and kill every Vanrian and Delaphinian soul behind those walls. I've had enough of dealing with you."

The man wanted his son. He didn't have the decency to pretend he cared about the child's mother this time. Kasiel thought of the two young girls he had under his protection. Of Astrid's terror as she labored in the bed, certain she would die. Of Hannah's fear that she would have no place after this, if she even survived the birth of her own child, and her bitterness because of what Lodmund had done to her.

"The feeling's mutual," he growled under his breath.

Darkness moved through Kasiel. A sensation that combined animal bloodlust with a more sentient loathing. He could feel the cold stone of the bottom step leading up to the wall under Niskenya's massive paw where she now stood, blocking Astrid and the two healers with her from ascending. The kanodrak understood their plan and her part in it. What she didn't understand was the need to wait. The source of her bonded companion's hatred was in front of them and vulnerable. Like Lodmund, she had run out of patience, and she had grown restless trapped behind these walls. Kasiel felt the last strands of his self-control unraveling before her overwhelming authority.

"We're going now."

Jethan grabbed his arm. "It's too soon, Kas."

Not bothering with the steps, Niskenya leapt to the

top of the wall, coming up beside them. She snarled at the men below, and Lodmund and the others with him took several steps back. Perhaps, because they hadn't seen her, they assumed Kasiel didn't have the kanodrak with him. They might have believed that she died from the poison in Hellaris. Whatever the truth, Kasiel relished the sudden fear in their eyes, sharing Niskenya's thrill of excitement in response. Her blood pounded hot and fierce through their veins.

Akyla cried out as he launched from the tower. Irith growled, his hackles rising.

"Kas." The frantic edge to Jethan's voice caught his attention, but it was the genuine fear he felt from his tehnaak that made him hesitate.

Niskenya moved closer, lowering her torso to make it easier for him to mount.

Kasiel met Jethan's eyes, struggling to recognize him as something other than an obstacle in their way.

"Kas, none of this matters to me if I have to leave here without you."

Niskenya enfolded him in her brutal strength, her protective fury. Kasiel climbed up on her. She didn't have the saddle on, but being on her back was as familiar as walking now. They were one creature. Every move she made would be his as well.

"Kas!"

Somewhere in his mind, he recognized that feminine voice, but it wasn't important, not right now. Their claws flexed, digging into the stone. A low growl rose in their throat as Jethan stepped closer.

"Wait!" Jethan insisted, his voice rising with alarm. "Just a few more minutes and we'll have help."

Kasiel looked down at his tehnaak, feeling strangely disoriented when he flexed his very human hands. For a moment, he was sitting upon Niskenya rather than merely an extension of her being.

"Jeth?"

A horn rang out then. When it stopped, Kasiel heard the rumble of horses moving across the landscape faster than they should, given the terrain and the darkness. He reached out and touched horses and tethdraks.

"It's their Havaad-cursed army," one of Lodmund's companions shouted.

Niskenya flexed her claws again. Kasiel tightened his grip with his legs and leaned into her movement as she leapt from the wall.

Behind them, he heard Jethan calling out, though not to Kasiel this time. "I need our Frightener and our Dampeners protecting Kas now! Get some archers watching the northern gate! Raise the portcullis and start lowering the drawbridge on this one! I need a horse and at least six mounted volunteers for what could well be a suicide mission! And take the hostages back inside!"

His words faded into the background as Niskenya landed on the ramp beyond the gap where the drawbridge would rest. The king and his men were sprinting toward the bottom. As the kanodrak came galloping down after them, they started jumping off the sides, taking their chances with the remaining small drop. One wasn't fast enough. Niskenya's jaws caught the back of his neck and head, lifting him in the air and sending him flying in a spray of blood. Kasiel didn't see which one it was. It didn't matter.

He felt her intention shift a second before she prepared to go off in the direction Lodmund had gone. Kasiel struggled back to himself, fighting the influence of her intoxicating wildness and power.

No.

They were supposed to be out here for a reason. It was too early. Their army wasn't in position yet, though they were very close. Already, he could feel the overflow from his two Dampeners and the Frightener rolling out around him. The other thing he felt was new – Jethan's fear and determination moving through him. He could still try to accomplish his goal.

A vibration went through him as Niskenya growled, but she let him choose their course. They continued down off the end of the ramp into the rising chaos. His mind-crafters were going to work on the troops that had been running for the ramp to protect the king, dropping them into blindness as the kanodrak plunged into their midst. Three of the trebuchets launched, one successfully, the other two failing as ropes snapped, slamming alchemical firebombs into the Sarketi army.

Kasiel reached out to the approaching tethdraks. The moment he touched their minds, Jhanik backed out, relinquishing control while maintaining enough connection to reclaim them if necessary. The other Feral wasn't far away now, and the speed with which his kanodrak's presence gained strength told Kasiel he and Arkos had raced out ahead of the rest of the army with the tethdraks.

Behind him, he heard horses galloping down the ramp. A quick touch on the animals told him enough to know that Jethan had gotten the volunteers he called for, and they were heading out to protect his route back. A part of their original plan, but far riskier now without their army in place to provide support. He and Niskenya had messed that up.

Staying low on the kanodrak's back, he focused them on the central tents, reaching ahead with a small fragment of his ability through a mouse to confirm that the prisoners were still where he expected them to be. He felt another wave of power, much stronger this time. The brightening dawn sky darkened from Arhk's unmistakable overflow and soldiers around them started screaming, some swinging blindly at the air while others dropped their blades and tried to run.

A sharp pain swept up his right arm, making him suck in a breath. It took a second to realize that the wound was Niskenya's, a cut on that foreleg from one of those chaotically swinging blades. As best he could tell, the soldier hadn't been trying to hit her, merely to defend himself from the horrors manifesting in his own mind with the dhomvalen's influence. The kanodrak barely missed a stride, her focus now fully aligned with Kasiel's.

With Dampeners hitting them from the walls of the stronghold and from the south within the arriving army, the southern and southwestern edges of Lodmund's force were crumbling. After a third failed trebuchet launch, they abandoned all but the first successful one, rather than risk losing more men to their own bombs falling upon their ranks. Unfortunately, they used that one to launch a second bomb over the wall. Kasiel couldn't chance splitting his attention again to see what was happening in there. He could do nothing to help them right now.

The chaos around the edges provided a perfect opportunity to move the tethdraks in. The reptilian predators plunged into the enemy soldiers, slashing and biting as they went, taking down anything in their paths. He focused a few through the mess, drawing them in to help support the rescue effort. Arkos was close, sprinting out ahead of the tethdraks now. Jhanik was keeping two with him as well to help eliminate threats. Kasiel kept a couple more on the other Feral's trail to make sure he had enough to secure his path back out, assuming they made it that far.

A soldier ran into Niskenya's path, and she leapt over him, a sting along their belly telling Kasiel the man either had enough sight still to attack them intentionally or had merely gotten lucky while flailing about. They were nearing the central tents, so it was possible they were moving beyond the reach of their mind-crafters now. Reason enough to be more wary of the enemies that surrounded them.

Jhanik's almost there. Lodmund's launched an attack against the northern gate, so we had to send Rahlyf over. The army's Dampeners are trying to get close enough to provide more support.

He hoped Etris could feel his gratitude for her update. The attack on the north gate was unfortunate, though not entirely unexpected.

Pain shot through Kasiel's side. Glancing down, he saw an arrow wedged in his armor toward the back of that side below the ribs. The armor had done its job and kept it from sinking in too deep, but it still hurt a lot, particularly with their movement shifting it around in the muscle. Gritting his teeth, he grabbed the shaft and pulled, trying to yank it out. It snapped instead, just outside the armor, doing nothing to relieve the problem.

Niskenya twisted, slamming her shoulder into a soldier in their path and sending the man flying back. Then Kasiel ducked as she plunged through the entrance of the target tent. Fresh agony seared through him, stealing his breath away. It took a few seconds to realize the wound wasn't in his flesh, but in Niskenya's, or mostly in Niskenya's. The spear that came up through the muscle over her shoulder and the side of her neck sank almost an inch into the inside of his thigh, penetrating the armor.

A spearman stood holding the shaft of the weapon, looking almost more surprised than they were by his success. Niskenya's jaws closed over his head, satisfaction sweeping through him with the sensation of cracking bone between their teeth as she crushed his skull.

CHAPTER TWENTY EIGHT

Kasiel slid back off the point of the weapon and leapt down, pain shooting through his wounds as he landed. Other than the now headless man lying discarded in a puddle of blood and two battered prisoners, the tent was relatively empty. A soldier came running in the back entrance, axe raised to attack. Kasiel drew his blade in one swift, instinctive motion and met the charge with a lunging thrust. The dark metal sword sank through the man's chest armor and out the back. As he yanked it free and turned to Niskenya, Jhanik came running in through the front entrance, having rationally left his kanodrak outside.

The other Feral took in the scene quickly. "Take care of Niske. I'll get these two untied. The tethdraks and Arkos can handle any soldiers that try to get in here for a few minutes."

Kasiel answered with a quick nod and turned to the kanodrak. Her pain pulsed through him, disorienting and debilitating. The only option was to pull the weapon out. She couldn't move with it hanging from the wound that way.

"I'm sorry, I should have checked in here again," he murmured.

A surge of affection rose through her pain in response. Perhaps she realized she hadn't given him much of an opportunity to scout ahead. That didn't make him feel any less awful about the injury she suffered.

He took hold of the haft, cringing inwardly, and opened himself to take on as much of her pain as he could bear before pulling it out. The agony of it knocked him to his knees, the air once more sucked from his lungs.

"Cavenos." Jhanik was at his side, genuine concern in his voice.

Kasiel accepted the hand he offered, letting the other man help him back to his feet. He could feel the warmth of blood running down his leg inside his armor and the arrow in his side shifted again, adding to the pain. Someone held a threadbare blanket up in his line of sight. He turned to see Aleren standing there, her cheekbones more pronounced than he remembered, and her eyes deeply shadowed. A few bruises and other injuries suggested their treatment of her hadn't been gentle. She looked better than Harel, who Jhanik was helping to his feet now.

"For Niskenya." Aleren nodded to the blanket.

He took it and used his dagger to split it in two so he could put pressure on the entry and exit wounds. "We need to get out of here quickly."

Jhanik winced as shouts and snarls came from outside the tent. One of his tethdraks or Arkos must have taken a wound. "Can Niskenya still carry anyone?"

"We haven't got a choice. I'll take Aleren. She's lighter. I'll soak as much of Niskenya's pain as I can."

Jhanik nodded. "I'll run the tethdraks around us and do my best to keep threats off you. The beasts farther out are still on you, I'm afraid."

Kasiel nodded. Then an ominous pressure and deepening darkness moved in around them. "You may not need to do much. It appears the dhomvalen is exerting a little more control over the situation."

"For once, I'm glad he's here. Though please never tell my parents I said that." He moved over beside Niskenya. "I'll help you mount."

"I can manage."

"You have a fucking arrow sticking out of you and blood running down your leg, Ahninveth," Aleren snapped. "Let him help."

Those were facts he couldn't argue with. He let Jhanik give him a leg up on Niskenya, wincing from the pain it caused them both. When he settled, Jhanik gave Aleren a leg up behind him. Her arm bumped the remains of the arrow shaft on the way up, and Kasiel sucked in a sharp breath.

"The arrow. Sorry." Aleren shifted her weight carefully behind him. "Where's your saddle?"

"Long story, but if I'm going to be soaking her pain and managing the other tethdraks, I need you to keep yourself on. Grab on to me and don't lose your balance or we're both going down."

"Understood."

They followed Jhanik and Harel out to where darkness, most of it unnatural now, and pandemonium ruled. With Arhk's increased influence, the Sarketi soldiers around them were running from or directly combating nightmares, many of them falling to the group of tethdraks or the flailing blades of fellow soldiers in their distraction. One beast lay dead, trapped under a net and riddled with spears. The others were still fighting, though several had sustained injuries.

The tethdraks on the periphery were taking people down as needed, but Kasiel had been holding them back, trying to avoid unnecessary slaughter. Dampeners and a few Frighteners mostly controlled the perimeter. He reached out to find Akyla while Jhanik struggled to help Harel up on Arkos. The raptor didn't have the level of night vision the owl had, but they were called nightstar eagles for a reason. Their vision in the dark was adequate for most tasks. The eagle also didn't suffer the overflow effect of the Dampener and Frightener abilities that the humans did, so the world was moving fully into dawn from its perspective.

From above, he could see three black scarred areas full of bodies in Lodmund's army where the sabotaged trebuchets had prematurely deposited their deliveries. Given that they intended those projectiles for the stronghold, Kasiel didn't feel guilty. The allied force had swung in around the southeastern and southern sides of Lodmund's army, Dampeners and Frighteners exerting influence over everyone who got within their range. The enemy had put forth an impressive effort to haul around the base of a light trebuchet just enough to aim the sling so that it was now throwing its deadly ammunition in a more southerly direction. It had struck the allied army twice, doing considerable damage with the larger firebombs. Now it sat idle. Arhk's ability had reached far enough to disable its operators.

Kasiel effortlessly took over one of the tethdraks Jhanik was controlling and sent the beast in along the line of his father's destruction. In a few seconds, it reached the trebuchet and tore into it, turning part of the wooden construction into kindling.

"We need to move," Jhanik shouted, now mounted with Harel behind him. "The southeast corner near the road will get us to safety the fastest."

Kasiel nodded, drawing the tethdrak back and releasing Akyla, so he could focus on taking more of Niskenya's pain while she moved. The kanodrak ran, but her stride was uneven and slower than normal. Her intense agony, along with pain from the wound in his leg and the arrow in his side being shifted about, sucked up nearly all of Kasiel's ability to focus.

"I need you to take the rest of the tethdraks as soon

as you can," he called, the strain in his voice apparent even to his own ears.

"Hang in there, Cavenos," Jhanik shouted back. "Just a little farther."

Kasiel was barely aware of the enemy soldiers around them, flailing blindly in false darkness or at war with their fears. At some point, he couldn't have said when, he realized the surrounding people were allies, not foes. Someone was helping Aleren down from Niskenya, who stood trembling beneath him, and Jhanik was taking control of the tethdraks.

Kasiel reached out to Akyla again, checking the way back into the stronghold. Jethan, along with Leif, Emil, and several others, was fighting at the base of the ramp, keeping the path clear for him and Niskenya. With only Minera helping on that side, they had a decent battle on their hands. At the northern gate, Lodmund had a force on the attack, holding position near the base of the ramp despite the efforts of Rahlyf and several archers on the wall. They appeared stuck for the moment, unable to gain ground, but not giving any either.

"Ahninveth Kasiel, you—"

Niskenya responded instantly to his intent, despite her pain and the blood she was losing. Without looking to see who was speaking, he put his energy into supporting the kanodrak as she made a run for the ramp. The moment he was clear of their army, he felt the overflow of a Dampener focusing around him, helping ease his passage through those fighting Jethan and the others. Kasiel watched Sarket's soldiers start flailing blindly, their vision suppressed, and took control of his companion's horses, sending the animals back up the ramp with no concern for the wishes of their riders. Niskenya followed them, her strength flagging and her limp growing worse. Kasiel struggled to take enough of her pain away to keep her going.

The drawbridge started rising the moment the horses were across. It was a couple of feet in the air before Niskenya reached it. She made the leap, barely keeping her legs under her when she landed. Then they were inside, Nerith and Tath rushing out of the gatehouse as he dropped off the kanodrak. He almost fell when his feet met the ground, but somehow Jethan was there fast enough to catch hold of him.

Kasiel sagged back against his tehnaak, giving himself a heartbeat to rest. His head was throbbing. Irith ran over to him, but stopped short of making physical contact, seeming aware of his injuries.

"You did it, Kas. You took away his hostages."

Scanning the group that had been protecting the southwest ramp, he spotted a few injuries, but nothing dire. Niskenya, however...

"Tath. Nerith. Help her, please." He placed a hand on the kanodrak's neck, her agony pulsing through him. "I need you to let them treat you. I'll be back as fast as I can." He glanced at Etris. "Tell our army to retreat. No more attacking. Just defend now. Tell them to use their Dampeners and Frighteners to keep Lodmund's troops off them. Then let the northern gate know I'm on my way over."

He started walking, but someone stopped him with a hand on his shoulder and yanked the rest of the arrow out of his side. Kasiel gasped in surprise more than pain. Compared to what he was still soaking up from Niskenya's injury, this was a mere pinch, but it caught him off guard.

He turned on Kince. "Break-blasted calloch!"

Nerith scowled at Kince.

The other man shrugged. "What? It needed to be done. It was just going to do more damage stuck through the armor like that."

"He's right," Nerith conceded. "And you need to

be checked out, Kas. We should see what damage that arrow did." She looked down. "Is all the blood on your leg from Niske?"

"Let's pretend it is. I'll be back. Take care of Niske." He strode away from her, ignoring her frustrated huff.

Jethan, Kince, and Darro joined him and the cliff cat. Along the way, Avris, and to his surprise, Merrin, who must have made it back inside during the confrontation, fell in with them as well. Tath and Nerith stayed to tend to Niskenya and Etris remained behind as a point of contact, since Revik was at the northern gate.

The damage from the firebombs that had made it over the wall was substantial. Several buildings were burning, with one completely collapsed at the point of impact, and several of his soldiers worked at putting out the fires. At least he saw no evidence that anyone was caught in those strikes. With as few people as they had inside the walls, they had everyone assigned to one station or another, none of which were in that area, fortunately. A collapsed portion of the stable burned, but he refrained from reaching in to investigate the state of the horses. If the hit had injured any animals, they were in the hands of his unit for now, and Niskenya got priority there.

They're going to have to knock Niske out.

Kasiel passed comfort and calm in waves to Niskenya, stealing the positive emotion for it from Irith's pleasure at being by his side again.

"Kas!"

He didn't slow as Velara came hurrying out to fall into step alongside Jethan, since Irith showed no interest in moving out of the way. Under different circumstances, Kasiel might have made space for her, but he needed the cliff cat happy. He required that unconditional affection and devotion the animal had developed for him to keep him strong enough to support Niskenya.

"Is everything all right inside?"

"Yes. I told Hannah and Astrid you had things under control."

He glanced over at her, managing a chuckle despite the growing headache. "I appreciate the confidence."

"She knows you have us to help," Jethan said, smirking at his cousin.

Velara arched a brow at him. "I knew there was a reason I was worried."

Kasiel stopped at the stairs up to the wall by the northern gate and faced Velara. "You can't go up there. Under no circumstances is Lodmund to know we also have Vanris's heir behind these walls."

Her eyes narrowed, anger tightening her jaw. "That's why Arhk didn't stop me from coming. He wanted to give his son another hostage. Someone you could use as leverage against my mother. What an idiot I've been!" She threw her hands up and started turning away.

Ignoring the slightly alarmed looks on the other's faces, he stepped in and caught her hands. "You're not wrong, Vel, not about his intentions, but you will never be a hostage. I won't allow it. We'll handle my father and the khevarin and all the rest of it our way, but we need to finish this first."

She met his eyes, a spark of anger still flashing in hers. "I trust you, Kas, but you have to know how dangerous your father could be if he doesn't agree with the way you intend to do things."

"We can do this." He punctuated the statement with a kiss, a brief one given the situation. Then dizziness and nausea hit him, and he stabilized himself with a hand on her shoulder.

"Are you all right?"

Rage swelled, but it wasn't his. He forcefully pushed more affection and calm to Niskenya, glancing back toward the other gate. The dizziness got stronger, then she slowly faded from his mind. It was a sensation he found deeply disturbing, even knowing she was in expert hands. Her absence was like losing a vast part of himself.

"Niske's out. I need to get up there. Check on Astrid for me?"

Velara nodded and struck out for the keep. The other four cleared the path for him and Jethan to head up.

At the top, Kasiel looked out over the ramp. Lodmund had around forty men making their way up it now, armed and ready for combat. They had to have bombs among them, though they were being careful to keep them hidden if they did. Their progress came in fits and starts, some of their number halting periodically with that directionless gaze that said they had lost their vision, but it didn't last. Beyond the base of the ramp were more men, knelt in ranks and staring blankly at the ground as if waiting for something. Rahlyf was in the gatehouse, leaning against the wall and peering through the narrow window, deep lines of stress etched in his forehead, his jaw clenched.

Kasiel turned to Revik. "He's struggling?"

Revik nodded and spoke into Kasiel's head, possibly to avoid disturbing the Dampener. *He's been trying to keep them from getting up the ramp and stop the ones below from joining them, but he's never done this much at once. He said his head feels like it's splitting in two. His influence at the base is holding, but they seem prepared to wait him out. Up closer, he's faltering.*

Kasiel walked over and placed a hand on Rahlyf's shoulder. "Just a little longer. I'm going to try putting an end to this. Let Lodmund and his immediate group approach."

Rahlyf answered with a curt nod, beads of sweat glistening around the edges of his hairline.

Kasiel stepped out onto the wall and shouted down.

"Sarket's King!" He waited for Lodmund to look up at him. "We've taken your hostages. Our army is backing off. Surrender now, and you and the rest of your men will survive this."

Another soldier ran up next to the king at that moment. There was a quick exchange, and Lodmund snapped something at him. The man turned and started down the ramp, bringing a horn to his lips and blasting out the call to pull back.

Lodmund looked up at Kasiel again, his lip curled in a disgusted sneer. "You killed my cousin, Warden's Son," he shouted up. "I will never surrender to you or your mind-fucker queen. I may not win this day, but I mean to take as many of you bastards as I can out with me."

Kasiel glanced discreetly at his tehnaak.

Jethan nodded. "When you went down the ramp, the man Niskenya took down was General Hackett."

"Mostly a happy accident," Kasiel commented under his breath, "though it might complicate things now."

He slipped behind Akyla's eyes, flying out over the camp. Some of Lodmund's soldiers were busy checking the trebuchets and making repairs to those that needed them. They had three that he hadn't gotten to with the mice and, at the speed they were working, they would have a few more of them functional again soon. The rest of Lodmund's army was pulling back and regrouping, now that the Vanrian and Delaphinian alliance wasn't actively attacking. Satchels were being passed between some soldiers that likely held alchemical bombs.

"Your people don't have to die here," Kasiel called down.

"If I surrender, will you give me my wife and son and let me walk away provided I swear to grovel at the feet of that Vanrian bitch who leads you?"

Kasiel hesitated. If Lodmund surrendered and swore

fealty to Vanris or Delaphine, Astrid and Jaysen, and possibly Hannah as well, might end up back in his hands. They would certainly be bargaining chips in the negotiations. Yet, no matter what deal they struck, Vanris and her allies could never trust this man. He was proud, smart, and seething with hatred.

Lodmund barked a laugh. "Your silence tells me you know it won't end between us as long as we're both alive. You're a clever little bastard. Come out here, Warden's Son, and settle this the Sarketi way. Face me in single combat. If you win, my army will surrender to Vanris. If I win, your army agrees to leave here and pull troops out of Sarket."

Kasiel glanced at Jethan. "Would he honor that?"

"Not that it's a good idea, but yes. Beating the life out of each other in single combat is how they solve most of their disagreements in Sarket."

Kasiel gave him a flat look. "You're being facetious."

"Actually, no. That really is how they do it." Jethan glanced uneasily at the man glaring up at them from the ramp. "Don't you remember studying that for the political section of your assessment tests?"

"Honestly? No. All I remember from that week is a lot of stress, self-doubt, and spending time with the juvenile tethdraks." *Sylaryth.* He reflexively touched the pouch at his belt. The tethdrak's memory was always with him. He suspected that would be true forever. Of course, the way this was going, forever might not be that long for him. He leaned forward and shouted down, "You'll enter the stronghold with no more than ten soldiers, and we'll settle it in here. If I win, Sarket's army surrenders to me *and* swears fealty to Vanris."

"Your commanders will honor this agreement?" Lodmund shouted.

"They will," Kasiel shouted back, infusing his voice with Akyla's confidence and arrogance.

"Kas," Jethan hissed. "You can't. You're injured and Niskenya is out. Lodmund is an exalted warrior in the southern kingdoms. He's too strong for you. We'll get someone from the army to negotiate a proper deal with him. He'll bend to the right pressures."

"He won't, and even if he does, what happens to Astrid and Hannah?"

After a few minutes of conversation with General Danovan and another man, Lodmund shouted back his answer. "Twelve soldiers, and I leave with my wife and son if I win. Single combat, or more slaughter on both sides? It's your choice now, Warden's Son."

Kince stepped up beside him. "I can hit him from here," he whispered.

Kasiel glanced out through Akyla's eyes again – at the trebuchets, the bombs being moved around, and the sheer sea of soldiers waiting to throw themselves against the allied Vanrian and Delaphinian army. They would fight until they died or Vanris's mind-crafters wore down enough that the allied force lost their advantage. Letting Kince kill Lodmund might end it, or it might not. Either way, it would be a dishonorable finish that wouldn't provide Kasiel with the political sway he needed.

"You have fifteen minutes to gather your twelve soldiers and prepare." Kasiel called back. "If a single soldier more tries to ascend that ramp or if you try to bring any bombs up, my Dampeners and archers have permission to attack at will."

"Understood. And Ahninveth—" the king's smile was cruel when he gestured to a soldier carrying a bag up the ramp "—I brought a little present for you."

Kasiel tensed, ready to signal his archers and Rahlyf. The soldier upended the bag and dumped out a mass of dead rodents and birds.

CHAPTER TWENTY NINE

Jethan, Kince, and Darro helped Kasiel prepare in a room in the stronghold. With Tath and Nerith working on Niskenya's injuries, they didn't have a free healer, so they put a snug wrap around the wound in his inner thigh and another around the one below his ribs. Both were flesh wounds, though deep enough that stitches would have been the preferred treatment. For now, this would have to be sufficient.

"This is madness," Darro was saying as he secured the bandage around Kasiel's torso. "You're in no shape to fight, and you don't have Niskenya to help you."

"Lodmund has to die. This is the only way I can kill him now without appearing dishonorable." Kasiel finished reattaching the ear cuffs he had removed to fix his braids.

"And why does Lodmund have to die again?" Kince asked from where he leaned against the wall flipping a dagger in one hand. Only so many people could help bandage Kasiel and get him back into his armor at once, after all.

"Because he'll never respect an oath of fealty to Vanris," Kasiel answered.

"Oh." A crooked smile tugged at one side of Kince's mouth. "Not because we don't want to give him his child bride back?"

Kasiel frowned at him. "Does it matter if I don't want to let the bastard touch her again when what I said is also true?"

Kince shrugged and tossed his head, throwing his long blond hair back out of his face. "Remind me why we have to be honorable about this, then."

Kasiel blew out a heavy breath. Was he being a fool, simply playing into his father's hands? "Because I need Vanris behind me when I get back to Etrion. Remember how the khevarin wants me dead?"

"And you still want her daughter."

A knock at the door saved Kasiel from having to respond to Kince's comment.

Etris poked her head into the room. "The dhomvalen and Dhomen Nevias are both demanding to know what's going on."

"Tell them I'm negotiating with King Lodmund. I'll let them know how it goes."

There was a momentary pause, then Etris focused on him again. "Dhomvalen Arhk is concerned that you don't know what you're getting into and would like us to lower the southwest drawbridge so he can join us."

Had his father guessed what kind of "negotiations" they were engaging in? "Tell him..." Tell him what? That he had this under control. Did he? "Tell him... no."

Etris's brows pinched together. "If it's all the same to you, I'm going to tell him specifically that you said no."

"That's fine." Etris inclined her head before ducking out. When she was gone, Kasiel glanced at Darro and Kince. "If you two could excuse us, I'd like a moment with my tehnaak."

"We'll meet you in the courtyard, danro," Darro said as he and Kince walked toward the door.

"Wait. Tell Velara to stay inside with Astrid and Hannah. And maybe don't mention that I'm planning to fight Lodmund. Also, I'd like Fenvar and Yserra to make themselves available. If I somehow do win this, an Evoker and a few Charmers might come in handy."

"Consider it done."

Jethan continued helping him into his armor for a few minutes in silence after the others were gone. He seemed willing to let Kasiel linger in his own thoughts until he was ready to speak. A quick foray out over the fields with Akyla revealed that Lodmund's army was still holding back, but no less busy preparing. Their allied force was much the same. Tending wounds, recovering, and getting ready to move in again if necessary. Lodmund himself was heading toward the northern ramp with the agreed upon twelve soldiers accompanying him. Interestingly, that included General Danovan and General Thrasser, the latter of whom Kasiel hadn't known was even there, at least not with Lodmund's army.

He retreated into himself. "Jeth, did you ever use your ability on me to help me get through when I first came to Vanris, or on the way there?"

Jethan met his eyes, his gaze steady. "No, Kas. It may come as a surprise, but you got through all of that on your own. I only ever tried to use my ability on you once, and that was today, when I was afraid you were going to die if Niskenya took you out on the field too soon, but she wouldn't let me in."

Kasiel was silent for a moment. His bond with the kanodrak was something special, but today it had shown a darker side. Not her fault. At the end of the day, she was a wild creature. The ways of men made little sense to her. Her building frustration with her confinement and her confidence in them had put them both in danger and resulted in serious injury to her. When she recovered, if he was still alive to do so, he would have to figure out how to balance her influence better. What was important at this moment, however, wasn't his bond with Niskenya.

"You're wrong, tehnaak. I didn't do it on my own. Every step I've taken since you rescued me from those mercenaries, I've had you at my side or driving me in some way. I didn't do any of this on my own."

Jethan pulled him into a hug. "Calloch. Just know that if it looks like you're going to lose against Lodmund, I'm going to do something dishonorable."

Kasiel returned his embrace, letting himself stay there for a moment in that place of comfort and safety. "You have no idea how glad I am to hear that."

After a few seconds, Jethan pulled away from him. "Do you have a plan?"

Kasiel adjusted his armor over the bandages. Both wounds still hurt something fierce, but he couldn't do much about that. At least he didn't have to soak up any of Niskenya's pain now, nor did he have her to support him in combat, which scared him more than he wanted to admit. "Try not to die?"

"Good plan. I'm honestly not sure what else to tell you. Lodmund's a burly man, but don't let his mass deceive you. It's all muscle. He's strong and fast. He won't give you a chance to catch your breath once the fighting starts."

"Have you seen him in combat?"

"No, but I've heard stories and read enough about him."

The nausea from Kasiel's headache, which he had yet to mention to anyone else, intensified. Probably from nerves, given the situation. And when had he last slept or eaten? Darro was right, this was madness.

"Are you ready?" Jethan asked.

"Yes," he lied, placing one hand on the hilt of his dark metal sword.

When they walked out into the courtyard, he

could see the portcullis on the north gate being raised. Lodmund had arrived, a fact that gave Kasiel the powerful urge to throw up. Irith pressed closer to his leg, giving him affection and feline confidence. Akyla perched on a watchtower, his aloof arrogance helping Kasiel hide his fear.

All the members of Kasiel's core unit met them in the courtyard, except Tath and Nerith, who were undoubtedly still stitching up Niskenya as quickly as they could before she woke. Fenvar and Yserra took the healers' places, and Lucia joined them to represent the Delaphinians and fill the empty spot left by Wedro. Most of the others were in the towers ready to defend either side of the wall, waiting by the gate to escort Lodmund and his men to the courtyard, or inside the central keep watching over hostages.

"You better not get yourself killed, country boy," Avris said as he joined them.

"Oh, I really hope not to."

Merrin stepped up close to him. "The biggest mistake I see people make in a duel is panicking if they lose their weapon. The minute you panic, you've lost. Lodmund is strong, and he favors a large axe. He's going to try disarming you. If he succeeds, worry less about getting your sword back and more about doing damage however you can. He's fast, but you're faster. Your dagger is an excellent alternative for doing quick damage, but you need to get in close to use it. If I remember correctly, he wears a broadsword too. His weapons can serve you just as well as your own, and you're likely to catch him by surprise if you go for them. Lastly, don't let Niskenya's absence shake you. I've fought you with and without her helping you. You've learned a lot from letting her instincts guide you. Trust that experience."

"Thank you, Merrin. You almost make me believe I can do this."

She met his eyes, the steadiness in her gaze boosting his confidence. "You can, Kas. If your doubts creep in, remember your tehsheyn is watching, and we believe in you."

The others nodded or added words of support when he glanced around at them. Then he spotted Lodmund's group entering through the gate under heavy guard from his soldiers. The king strode toward them, proud and confident, looking as if he owned the place, which, technically, he did. His gaze as he got closer flickered to the fire-damaged buildings, then took an inventory of Kasiel and his companions. Niskenya was, fortunately, out of sight. Not knowing where the kanodrak was would hopefully make the king and his men a little more wary of stepping out of line.

"Warden's Son." He came to a stop a few yards back. "I find myself pleased you survived long enough for me to snuff out the light in your eyes from up close."

Irith growled, his hackles rising. General Danovan shifted his feet, looking desperately uncomfortable. General Thrasser regarded Kasiel thoughtfully, his expression lacking either shame or anger despite the fact that Kasiel had taken the upper hand in two encounters with him now. Had he made peace with those humiliating defeats?

"We have our agreement," Kasiel stated, refusing to humor the king's taunt. "If you win, your wife and son will return to you, and our army will pull out of Sarket. If I win—" the king interrupted him with a derisive snort that Kasiel forced himself to ignore, "—Sarket surrenders to me and swears fealty to Vanris."

Lodmund gave a curt nod and gestured to Thrasser, who stepped forward.

"The rules of single combat in Sarket are simple," the general stated. "You enter the circle with only the weapons you carry. If you get disarmed and your weapon falls within the circle, either combatant is permitted to make use of it. If it lands outside the circle, it is gone. No one outside the circle can intervene in any way until the dispute is resolved. The dispute is considered resolved when one combatant is dead. Any questions?"

"You're sure you want to do this?" Jethan asked in a low voice.

"I'd have to be crazy," Kasiel whispered back, eyeing the haft of the axe poking above Lodmund's shoulder and the sword at his belt. The man wore some decent plate armor too, without many vulnerabilities, particularly in the front. What it lacked in terms of agility, it made up for in pure defense.

Jethan managed a soft laugh, though worry shone in his eyes. "Don't force me to be dishonorable."

"No questions," Lodmund stated.

Kasiel echoed the king's reply.

A couple of Lodmund's soldiers counted out the size of the ring in paces, and everyone stepped out to form a boundary around that space. The observers stood in a single row, planning for the potential need to move back quickly if the fight came too close. When that was done, Thrasser stepped inside the circle and gestured to Kasiel and Lodmund.

"If our challengers would enter the circle."

Kasiel felt cold, his gut roiling with a barely contained sense of panic. Irith growled, the tone of it higher than normal in his distress. Realizing the potential problem there, Kasiel dominated the cliff cat and sent him to one of the nearby buildings, a solidly built storeroom. Darro jogged over and opened the door, waiting until Kasiel forced Irith inside to shut it and hurry back to the circle.

Lodmund stepped in across from Kasiel, looking too much at ease. Maybe this was a mistake. Did he truly think he could win against a seasoned warrior like Sarket's king?

Kasiel absorbed some of Akyla's aloofness, trying to ignore Irith's growing distress. He hated locking the cliff cat away, but if he got injured badly enough, or killed, he wouldn't be able to control the animal. They had made an agreement and, more importantly, he didn't want his own companions injured if the cat broke the circle and started a full-on melee in the courtyard. Niske was another problem. If he died here, what would they do with her? Prevent her from waking up?

Lodmund sneered as he adjusted his gleaming partial helm, then drew his axe.

Setting his thoughts aside, Kasiel reached farther outside the walls, drawing on some of the cold lethality of the tethdraks, and managed a Feral grin. He drew his dark metal sword.

Thrasser backed out of the circle. "Begin."

Lodmund wasted no time. He charged in with a heavy swing, perhaps hoping to end the combat before it started. His men letting out a roar of support. Kasiel dodged to the side, not wanting to take the power of the strike into his arms with a block. A few with that much force behind them would fatigue him too quickly. He spun and swung, hoping to catch the other man with a blow to the side, but Lodmund had already moved into his next swing, back around at Kasiel. The dark metal blade bit through one of the bands of steel that protected the axe's haft as the two weapons collided.

Lodmund's eyes narrowed. He knew now that the dark metal blade was stronger than his steel, a revelation Kasiel had hoped to share in a far more devastating manner.

Kasiel dodged the next swing and parried the one after, getting too good a feel for the bone-jarring power behind Lodmund's attacks. That the man could put so much strength into a swing and still be that fast was concerning. The axe blade swept close enough to his face as he made another desperate dodge that he felt the tickle of a breeze against his cheek amidst ongoing shouts of alternating encouragement and intimidation from the Sarketi side. His head throbbed, the surge of panic making his headache flare.

Lodmund came in with another powerful swing at a lower angle before Kasiel fully had his bearings, his hands sliding toward the end of the haft for more leverage. Realizing that he didn't have time to move out of range, Kasiel jumped forward, trying for a stab while he was in close. The force of Lodmund's swing gave the big man the counterbalance to twist clear, and the metal-banded haft of the axe caught Kasiel in the side. Pain blasted through him as ribs cracked beneath the impact. He stumbled, losing his focus for a critical moment. His eyes met Jethan's at the edge of the circle as they widened in alarm. Then he twisted around, struggling to get his blade up fast enough.

Lodmund's axe came down hard, but Kasiel's sword met the haft and cut almost completely through, catching in the steel banding on the other side. The king roared and threw the ruined weapon aside, ripping Kasiel's hilt out of his hands as he did so. People around that edge dodged out of the way when the entangled axe and sword flew clear of the circle.

With pain fogging his thoughts, Kasiel clung to Merrin's words warning him not to panic, but Lodmund was drawing his broadsword now, removing that as an option. Kasiel grabbed a dagger from his belt, barely getting it free before Lodmund's blade hit the back of that hand. A piece of dark metal plating on his gauntlet protected him from the cutting edge, but the impact was enough to send a burst of pain through the hand that made him drop the dagger. The king's fist struck Kasiel in the face, his steel covered knuckles splitting his lip. He staggered back, weaponless and reeling, clutching his hand at his waist. Lodmund's men pounded weapons against shields and armor, calling for the king to strike the final blow.

Pain clouded Kasiel's thoughts. He was going to die and let everyone down. His unit, Niskenya and Irith, Velara, Astrid and Hannah, his father, all Vanris, really. He could hear Irith attacking the door of the building, slamming against it in a frenzy of desperation and rage. He wondered again what would happen when Niskenya woke to find him gone, the way he had once woken to find Sylaryth dying?

Sylaryth.

A strange thing happened as he darted clear of another attack. He still clutched his hand at his waist as if protecting an injury, but only to hide the fact that he was digging into the pouch he kept on his belt. The pain that fogged his thoughts started dispersing, being soaked up not by Niskenya or any other beasts, but by the familiar presence of the members of his tehsheyn. The people who loved him and believed in him. Strength, encouragement, and faith flooded in, sweeping through him, propping him up.

Kasiel's hand closed on Sylaryth's claw. *I need your protection once more, my friend.*

Lodmund grinned. "Goodbye, Warden's Son."

The king charged, a hint of surprise sparking in his eyes when Kasiel lunged toward his attack. He shifted to the side at the last second and dropped to one knee, twisting to rake the deadly claw into the back of Lodmund's leg, slicing muscle and tendon as it passed through. The king staggered, his damaged leg buckling beneath him. Kasiel was on his feet already, turning to grab the front of the other man's helmet from behind. He reached under Lodmund's neck with the claw and dug it deep into his throat, ripping it around the side below his jaw and up toward his ear. Blood sprayed hot over his hand and the men from Sarket fell abruptly silent.

Kasiel let go and staggered back, staying upright through the strength given to him by his tehsheyn. The bystanders Lodmund was facing retreated out of range of the arterial spray of blood. Kasiel's eyes met Merrin's, and she gave a slight nod. The king wavered on one knee, wet choking noises coming from his throat. His head turned as if he were trying to look at the three women, one holding an infant, who had emerged from the keep. Then he fell, landing face first in the dirt.

A moment of stunned silence followed before Thrasser entered the circle and put a finger to the undamaged side of his king's throat. After a few seconds, he stepped back, his gaze going to the bloody claw in Kasiel's hand.

"A beast's weapon," he murmured. Then he looked around at the bystanders. "I, General Wilkin Thrasser, as mediator and as cousin to the late King Roald Lodmund, declare this single combat fairly won. As agreed in advance by the two parties, Sarket surrenders to you, Ahninveth Kasiel Cavenos of Vanris."

One soldier with Lodmund's party raised a horn to his lips and blasted out a mournful sounding wail that Kasiel suspected was the announcement of the king's death. Another call followed it, this one the declaration of surrender.

Akyla swept in, flashing a quick sense of expectation to Kasiel. With his family still soaking up part of his pain, he brought his arm up to receive the nightstar eagle. When the raptor landed, Thrasser looked at it. Then he met Kasiel's eyes and sank to one knee. The other eleven Sarketi men followed suit.

Outside the walls, Kasiel could hear the clanging as hundreds upon hundreds of Sarketi soldiers dropping their weapons. Then another sound broke the stillness.

That of a baby crying. Thrasser and the others rose, turning to face the queen. The general started toward her. Then he stopped and glanced at Kasiel, who looked at Astrid, letting it be her choice.

The queen nodded and Thrasser approached. A soft look of wonder lit his face as he stared down at the bundle in her arms. He met her eyes then. "Have you named the child?"

"Jaysen, General Thrasser, his name is Jaysen."

"King Jaysen Lodmund," Thrasser announced, gesturing to the baby as he faced his comrades. "Welcome your new king."

The men rose and turned, so they might now kneel to the infant. "Hail, King Jaysen Lodmund!"

The shout made the child cry louder. Akyla launched back into the air.

Astrid met Kasiel's eyes then, and he gestured to Avris and Merrin. "Escort the queen and her lady back to her rooms."

The two women did as he ordered, and Kasiel felt more of his pain returning as they departed. His head started throbbing again. Velara didn't go with them. She came to him instead at the same time Jethan did, worry nearly upstaging the anger in her eyes.

"If you ever do something like this again without talking to me first," she hissed under her breath, "I'll have you thrown in the deeps for a month."

Thrasser stood staring at Velara, his forehead pinched as though he thought he might know her from somewhere. Then his brows went up, and he sank in a partial bow. "Khesran Velara Markanis, we were not aware of your presence here."

"I certainly hope not, General Thrasser," she answered curtly, "or it would have been quite the poorly kept secret. You are the king's surviving closest kin now, are you not?"

"I will be made regent with the king and General Hackett both gone, if that is what you are asking, Khesran."

"It is. There are details of surrender and the swearing of fealty yet to be negotiated, but first, we must tend to Ahninveth Kasiel's injuries. General Danovan may take half of your men and, if needed, a cart from our stables to transport the late king's body back to your army. The rest shall stay here with you under guard until we are ready to begin negotiations. Our soldiers will escort you, General Thrasser, and five of your men to our dining hall for now, where you will be provided food and drink to refresh yourselves while you wait. Is there anyone else from your army who should attend these proceedings?"

"Not anymore, Khesran. If you would allow General Danovan to return, it might be helpful to have a second ranking officer in attendance."

"I understand that General Evanson went with you when our army released you."

Thrasser lowered his eyes. "I am afraid his mind has not returned to him, Khesran."

"I am sorry to hear that." She cast a scrutinizing gaze at Danovan, then turned to Kasiel. "Ahninveth, is General Danovan's continued presence as witness to these proceedings acceptable to you?"

"It is," Kasiel answered shortly, afraid to say more lest his growing pain become apparent.

"We appreciate your tolerance, Ahninveth." Thrasser bent in another bow.

As some of the allied soldiers gathered around Lodmund's remaining men with Darro and Kince stepping in to oversee that part, Velara led Kasiel away from the circle with Jethan supporting him, guiding him toward where they had left the healers with Niskenya. Etris let Irith loose from the storeroom and the big cat sprinted over, giving Kasiel a chastising growl as he fell in beside them.

Kasiel rubbed his thumb along the bloodied tethdrak claw still clutched in his hand.

Thank you, Syl. I owe you my life again.

Nerith stayed out to finish tending Niskenya while Tath accompanied them inside to deal with Kasiel's injuries. She was finishing a few stitches in the arrow wound when he heard footsteps approaching and voices in the hall.

"I will speak with him first, Dhomen Aleren." Arhk's hard tone permitted no arguments. "We shall join you in the main hall shortly, assuming he can still walk."

"As you wish, Dhomvalen."

A set of footsteps retreated, and Velara stood as Arhk entered. He scanned the room, his eyes settling on Tath first. "Are you finished?"

"I am, Dhomvalen." Tath secured the wrap to hold the bandage in place. As she straightened, she offered Kasiel a sympathetic look. "If you'll excuse me, Ahninveth."

"Thank you, Tath." He watched her go, then started carefully pulling on his shirt to cover the wound along with the black bruises across his ribs.

"Ahninveth Jethan, if you would escort Khesran Velara to another room, I would like to speak with my son alone."

Neither of them moved, looking to Kasiel for direction instead. Their choice to prioritize his decision over that of the dhomvalen brought a scowl to Arhk's lips.

"It's fine," Kasiel said.

Velara leaned in and placed a light kiss on his cheek before leaving with Jethan.

"You inspire an almost disturbing amount of loyalty in those who follow you," Arhk commented.

"Perhaps because I'm not a calloch."

Arhk's jaw tightened, but, surprisingly, he let the insult go. "That devotion may explain how I find you still alive after some of the questionable decisions you have made today. Based on her continued affection for you, I assume Velara remains unaware of our conflict with her mother."

"You would be wrong about that." Kasiel grimaced as he got up from the bed. Too much of his body hurt. "She and I discussed it and came to a place of understanding. There are a few things I need to clear up with you before we go into negotiations with Sarket."

"You assume you will be part of those negotiations?" Arhk's tone neither agreed nor disagreed with the notion.

Kasiel met his eyes. "That's the first thing. I *will* take part. You see, Sarket surrendered to me, not to Vanris or to her allies. Therefore, I need to be present for the negotiations. Velara will also take part. General Thrasser – King Regent Thrasser, I suppose – is already aware of her presence here. In fact, she spoke with him briefly."

Darkness edged in around Arhk's eyes, the pressure in the room increasing, then it vanished, and he shook his head, a faint smile curving his lips. "I should not encourage you, but I must admit that I am impressed. You recovered the hostages and defeated one of the most renowned fighters in Sarket in single combat, without your kanodrak's assistance, as I understand it. And you kept the rest of us out until you could guarantee yourself and Velara a place at the table for the negotiations. I doubt I could have manipulated the situation any more effectively. Though I might not have risked as much as you did to see it through."

Kasiel frowned at him. "You know, I don't believe most sons have to change the course of their country's future to get their father's approval."

Arhk walked closer, holding his gaze. "You are right, Kasiel, nor do most fathers have to mourn their son's death for twelve years before getting the chance to know them. This situation has not been an easy one, especially with Seylin manipulating things. I have been neither kind nor loving toward you. I am not certain I know how to be. Regardless, you should know that I am proud of you. I am exceedingly proud, and you mother would be as well."

Kasiel nearly choked when Arhk hesitantly embraced him. His chest tightened, not a great sensation given his injuries. "Took you long enough," he murmured, gingerly returning the hug.

"Try not to push your luck." Arhk let go and stepped back from him.

The faintest shimmer of what might be the start of tears shone in Arhk's eyes, but Kasiel chose not to hope for too much, especially given the challenges that still lay ahead. "We should get Velara and head down to start negotiations, but before we go, I should also tell you I mean to marry her after we return to Vanris."

"She agrees, even knowing that we intend to see her mother punished for what she did to our family?"

We and *our family*. He liked that Arhk addressed this as if it were something they were undertaking together, father and son fixing the wrongs of the khevarin. Unfortunately, Kasiel's plans had branched away from his father's. Still, he didn't want to destroy the connection that they had found in this moment just yet. "We can talk about all of that more after we handle things here."

Arhk started turning away, then he faced Kasiel again, his fine brows pulling together. "How did you defeat Lodmund?"

Kasiel managed a tired smile. "I'll tell you about it on the way to join the others."

*

Negotiations carried on for several days. They sent out messengers on the first day to inform the leadership of Vanris, Delaphine, and Fallend of Sarket's surrender. The one heading to Vanris also carried a note from Velara letting Khevarin Seylin know she had followed Arhk of her own free will to avoid an unwanted engagement and would be returning with their army soon, hoping to have a more rational discussion about the subject.

Despite initial resistance from Sarket's side, Astrid attended the negotiations as much as she could, given the recent birth of her son. The hardest part was convincing Aleren and Arhk to go along with having Sarket swear fealty to Velara as future khevarin and representative of Vanris. The two had very different reasons for objecting to the idea – Arhk because he had his hidden agenda to overthrow Seylin, and Aleren out of a desire to protect Seylin's rule. Velara's presence at the negotiations, however, along with Astrid's support of the proposal, won Thrasser over. He appreciated dealing with someone he had met in the flesh and seemed to respect that the khesran left the safety of Vanris to witness events for herself. No one saw a need to tell him that wasn't why she had come.

Delaphine's representatives didn't object to Sarket's swearing of fealty to Vanris as much as Kasiel expected them to. Perhaps something in their existing alliance agreement with Vanris made the arrangement appropriate, or maybe it had more to do with who had defeated King Lodmund in the end. Either way, they provided the kingdoms of Delaphine and Fallend with substantial protection from Sarket's aggression in the agreements that were made.

More complicated negotiations followed. Vanris and Delaphine wanted to install advisors and a military presence in Sarket, an idea that met considerable resistance, but Thrasser ultimately caved to a lesser number than initially proposed, as Kasiel had suspected he would. They also demanded that Jaysen be sent to Vanris upon his eighth birthday to be fostered there until his fifteenth, at which time he would return to Sarket to begin taking over his role as king. That had been Velara's idea, one she discussed at length with Astrid, who, while not fond of it, eventually admitted to the potential value of the future ruler learning Vanris's ways. Kasiel couldn't help wondering if Velara employed her Charmer ability to nurture her growing bond with the Sarketi queen, but he had no intention of asking. Some things it was better not to know.

The night before they were to depart, General Thrasser sought Kasiel out, finding him on the wall with Jethan and Etris. Darro and Kince were in the nearby tower playing dice, close enough to offer support if needed. Given that Kasiel's unit had taken the stronghold in the first place, no one argued against them continuing to occupy it, though a few of Vanris's ranking officers, Arhk included, had moved into the keep with them for the short term. With the conflict ended, they released the castle serving staff from the dungeon and gave them the choice to stay and work or collect their belongings and leave.

Thrasser brought a few guards with him when he came up on the wall. Neither of them was foolish enough to believe the cessation of active conflict made them friends. He also wore the former king's broadsword at his waist.

"Ahninveth Kasiel, might I have a moment of your time?" His gaze flickered to Irith, who currently stood between them.

With a thought, Kasiel moved the cliff cat to his other side next to Jethan. "You may, Majesty."

"General is fine if you must use a title. I have yet to be coronated, and the whole idea still puts me ill-at-ease." He walked up next to Kasiel. "Lord Jethan," he greeted with a nod before turning to face out over the fields lit by campfires.

Jethan responded in kind, watching the future king regent intently.

"You don't wish to rule?" Kasiel asked.

"It was never something I aspired to, but I will serve my country in whatever capacity is required." He shifted the sword belt as if uncomfortable with the weight of the heavy blade.

Given his military experience, Kasiel suspected it was that weapon specifically that bothered him. Perhaps they had more in common than they realized, though, for now, he saw no sense in revealing his aspiration to marry Vanris's future khevarin to this man.

They stood in silence for a moment, Kasiel choosing to let Thrasser decide when he would say whatever he had come up there to say.

Thrasser's gaze wandered to the Vanrian and Delaphinian army that still partly blocked Sarket's departure. "I warned Roald that fighting you was a bad idea," he finally said.

"Why?" Jethan asked. "Most available information pointed at him being the more likely victor."

"A few reasons," Thrasser began. "I believe the time has come for things to change, as it will come again someday in the future. There is also something about you, Ahninveth Kasiel. A determination not born of cruelty or greed that I believe makes you stronger than those motivated by such things. When I faced you in the Break, you made it quite clear your goal wasn't the slaughter of all your Sarketi enemies. If anything, it seemed to me to be quite the opposite. I almost wish you were Vanris's ruler. I think you would make a good one."

Jethan subtly bumped Kasiel's arm with his elbow and Kasiel gave his tehnaak a look of mock warning, then he turned toward Thrasser. "I admire that you didn't needlessly risk your men in the Break or at our encounter on the Delaphinian border. Knowing their lives matter to you tells me you could be an excellent king. I must ask, though. It doesn't seem like you approved of King Lodmund's ways. Did you want him to lose?"

"I did not want my cousin to die, no." A catch of sorrow in his voice lent sincerity to his words. "I can honestly say I wasn't eager to see him win, either. He would have resumed fighting, and I suspect it would have resulted in a significant loss of life on both sides. I also suspect Sarket would have ultimately lost. Your mind-crafters are more... formidable than I think any of us realized."

"Vanris never desired anything more than to be left in peace. Throwing the full force of our mind-crafters at the Pandrean Alliance in the beginning would have made that impossible. With only Sarket still against us and showing no sign of backing down, it made sense to our leadership to get more aggressive."

Thrasser nodded. "Then you understand that knowing more of what your mind-crafters are capable of will only make it harder for the southern kingdoms to trust you?"

Kasiel breathed a laugh. Even that caused pain in his injured ribs. "You might recall that, thanks to General Danovan's brother, I grew up in the south. Until a couple of years ago, I didn't know mind-crafters existed. So, yes, I understand better than most."

"You seem to have adjusted remarkably well." His gaze shifted meaningfully to Irith for a moment.

Kasiel glanced at Jethan, reaching out with his mind at the same time to touch Niskenya, Irith, Akyla, and the tethdraks out in the camp. His hand moved to rest on the pouch holding Sylaryth's claw. He smiled, though the bitterness of loss tempered the expression. "I've had a lot of help."

Thrasser pushed away from the wall. "Thank you for your time, Ahninveth. It may be unlikely, but I would welcome you at my coronation, and it would please me to see you involved in ongoing discussions between our countries."

Kasiel inclined his head. "Thank you, General Thrasser. You honor me with your words. Your sentiments might be less unreasonable than you think. For now, I hope your journey home is a peaceful one."

Thrasser gave a slight nod. "Yours as well." His gaze jumped to Jethan. "Both of you."

Kasiel watched him start down the stairs with his guards before turning to look back out over the campfires of two vast armies, spread out like fallen constellations. Sarket's force would depart first thing in the morning with their newborn heir and soon-to-be crowned king regent. A well-appointed carriage brought in from the closest large town would accommodate Astrid and her child. Hannah would ride with them, though she seemed reluctant to trust them with her life as her own labor crept closer.

Kasiel had offered her a place with them, so their healers and mind-crafters might assist with her childbirth the way they had with the queen's. She had not turned him down yet. Nor had she accepted. He had cleared the offer with the dhomvalen, who seemed to find it curiously amusing, on the off chance that she made a last-minute decision to join them. The possibility that he might still fail to save her from Lodmund didn't sit well with him.

"You almost sounded like an adult there," Jethan teased.

Kasiel chuckled, wincing at the accompanying pain in his ribs. "You're an ass."

"After everything you've accomplished, you still look like the world weighs heavy on your shoulders." Jethan's expression became serious as he turned and leaned against the parapet to face him. "You stopped the war, Kas. You did more to protect the people you care about than anyone else in all Vanris."

"We stopped the war, Jeth," he corrected, hearing that weight Jethan spoke of in his own voice.

"Is it Hannah?"

Kasiel sighed. "All this, and I still have to step back and admit that my father is right. I can't save everyone."

"You've come closer than most."

Kasiel stepped away from the wall. He yearned to see Velara outside of negotiations, but the stronghold had gotten much too crowded, and their relationship was still technically a secret. "Are you eager to see Keyla?"

Jethan grinned. "I am. I could happily fall into her warm arms and stay there for weeks after spending so much time staring at these cold, stone walls."

They started walking toward the stairs together, gingerly in Kasiel's case, and he put a hand on Jethan's shoulder. "Well, for your sake, I hope Khevarin Seylin is in a forgiving mood if my father tries to dethrone her."

"Maybe we could throw the two of them in a cell in the deeps and let them fight it out."

Kasiel smiled. "That might be the best idea I've heard yet."

*

In the morning, after a surprisingly tearful goodbye from Astrid, Sarket's army departed. Hannah made the unexpected choice at the last minute to go with Kasiel's unit to Vanris. She promised the queen she would join her in Andaro after her child was born, and she could travel that far. Astrid had asked Kasiel to promise her he would provide Hannah as much care as if she were the queen when her time came to give birth, to which he responded, "I didn't give you that care because you are a queen, Majesty." An answer that appeared to reassure both young women and earned him approving smiles from his tehsheyn.

When the time came for the allied force to depart, Velara summoned Kasiel and his extended unit that had taken the stronghold up on a low cliff overlooking the army. Jethan and Irith were beside him, with Niskenya on the far side of Jethan, still too injured for Kasiel to ride. His core unit stood in close behind them, including Evoker Yserra, who had requested to join them in Wedro's vacant position. With the approval of the dhomvalen and the rest of his tehsheyn, she became part of the unit. The war might be at its end, but there would still be battles to fight and many a military escort to provide as the political aspect of arranging alliances and treaties became the new focus. The rest of the extended unit fanned out behind the front group.

It was a cool morning. Sunshine fought a light cloud cover for ownership of the sky. As more of the soldiers below noticed their gathering on the cliff and stopped what they were doing, Velara signaled a man waiting off to one side, and he brought a horn to his lips, blasting out the call for attention.

Velara raised her head, peering boldly out over the allied force as she gestured for Kasiel to move his horse closer. "I am Khesran Velara Markanis, heir to the throne of Vanris." The declaration received a surge of cheers, at first primarily from the Vanrian side, most of whom had remained unaware of her presence there until that moment, but the Delaphinians, excited by the victory and the prospect of going home, were quick to join in. When they quieted, she continued. "I have with me Ahninveth Kasiel Cavenos and the combined Vanrian and Delaphinian force that rode out here under his command and captured this stronghold. These brave soldiers took the Sarketi queen and heir hostage in a bold move that forced a confrontation with King Roald Lodmund himself. With the help of this remarkable alliance, Ahninveth Kasiel and Ahninveth Jhanik rescued Dhomen Aleren and General Harel, robbing the Sarketi king of his hostages. When the king still refused to surrender, Ahninveth Kasiel boldly faced him in Sarket's tradition of single combat, defeating him honorably and securing Sarket's surrender."

Another surge of cheering, louder this time, forced her to pause. The smile she gave Kasiel was enough to make him shift his mount closer still. As the noise died down again, he spotted his father with the Vanrian dhomens, all of whom were watching them with an intensity that carried a warning. Aleren looked as if she wanted to come drag them off the cliff by their ears, a feat that would be notably easier in Velara's case, since part of *his* ears would simply come off. Regardless, it was a warning neither of them were going to pay heed to. They hadn't cleared this speech with their commanding officers or the dhomvalen in advance for a reason.

"The actions of this allied force," Velara went on, "under Ahninveth Kasiel's leadership, have brought us to a place where peace is, for the first time in our lives, finally possible. Negotiations between the four kingdoms will go on for some time, but unlike me, the majority of you will be spared that tedium." A smattering of laughter met that remark. "This group of Vanrian and Delaphinian soldiers has changed the course of our futures. Without hesitation, I recognize them all as heroes. Given," she shouted the last word as a cheer started going up. She took Kasiel's hand, and the noise faded, a sense of anticipation spreading through the army. "Given the celebratory nature of this moment, I cannot bring myself to wait any longer to announce that the extraordinary hero at my side, Ahninveth Kasiel Cavenos, and I are engaged to be married."

The Vanrian troops exploded with excitement, dragging Delaphine's force into the celebratory chaos with their enthusiasm. Velara leaned over and Kasiel moved to meet her in a warm kiss, ignoring the daggers of ice being glared at them from where the Vanrian officers waited. It was done. Not just in front of Vanris's army, but Delaphine's as well. When they parted, Velara's gaze went to the officers, her smile unfaltering, a gleam of challenge lighting her eyes. Arhk ignored her, staring at Kasiel, a slight shake of his head promising that they would have words later.

"Let us all return to our homes victorious!" Kasiel shouted, raising his hand up with Velara's still clasped in it.

His words, punctuated by a ground-shaking roar from Niskenya, intensified the cheers of the allied forces. Irith shifted closer to Kasiel's horse. The general dislike of the racket by some of his beasts, including the tethdraks that had survived the fighting, left him itching to move on. Another part of him recognized that what they were doing was necessary for the plan they had put together with his unit. Knowing Velara loved him enough to tie herself to him for the rest of her life also made it easier for him to find a smile that would please their audience.

When they left Cabril, Velara reluctantly yielded to the wishes of their officers and Kasiel himself and joined Hannah and Dhomen Nevias – who had difficulty riding with her injured ankle – in another carriage they had tracked down for the purpose. Once she was safely within, Kasiel took his unit, including the tethdraks, and created a protective barrier around it. Dhomen Aleren and General Harel had the option of joining the three, but they opted to ride with their soldiers, having gotten a chance to rest and recover from Sarket's harsh treatment during the days of negotiation.

They were on the road less than an hour before Arhk's Speaker spoke into Kasiel's mind to let him know the dhomvalen requested his presence. An inevitable summons, but one he had hoped might not come so soon.

Kasiel blew out a breath and glanced at his tehnaak.

"Your father?" Jethan guessed before he could say anything.

A weary grin escaped him. "Yes. Keep an eye on Irith."

The cliff cat growled.

Kasiel frowned at him. "What? You're annoyed with me too?"

Jethan gave him a hard look that he wasn't sure he had earned. "You locked him in a storage room when you fought Lodmund. Of course he's upset with you. And, come to think of it, you never really let him do anything. Nearly anytime something significant happens, you leave him behind. He's probably getting a little sick of that."

"Maybe, but at least he's still alive."

Jethan scowled, his hands tightening on his reins, and Irith growled again. "Alive and perpetually confused by the fact that you bonded him, but don't want him around. He is your companion, Kas. He deserves better, and he hasn't got the deeper understanding to realize he has to demand it like Niske and the rest of us do. I thought you learned that you only hurt the ones you love when you keep them at a distance."

"I have, it's just..." Kasiel's hand shifted toward Sylaryth's claw.

"Don't!" Jethan's look held a warning. "Syl is gone, and it's time to let him rest. He was there when you needed him. Right now, you *don't* need him. You need the flesh and blood companion at your side."

He drew his hand back and reached out to Irith with his ability. If he stayed at the surface of the cliff cat's mind, he met up with affection and devotion. Most of the time, he didn't go any deeper. Today, he did, finding a web of confusion, frustration, and a hurt that had no physical source. A dark twisting sensation moved through his gut. Twining his mental presence more thoroughly into the cliff cat's, he sent a surge of affection laced with a sense of remorse and shame.

Irith looked up and made a soft chirruping sound, countering him with devotion and the equivalent of a mental purr.

"Come on, Irith, maybe you can eat my father if he steps out of line."

With the cliff cat beside him, he urged his mount up to where Arhk was currently riding in front of the barrier of soldiers and tethdraks Kasiel had set up around the carriage. Arhk's guards fanned out, forcing a wider buffer of space around him as Kasiel moved his mount up next to him.

His father glanced over at him, his gaze sinking to the horse for a second. "I am not used to being able to look you in the eyes when you are mounted."

"Niske's still healing. She isn't ready for a rider yet."

Arhk's jaw tightened a fraction. "Yes. Your impatience left her with a serious injury."

Kasiel said nothing. Admitting that the kanodrak had taken over for that brief period didn't seem like the wisest idea, even if it would remove some of the blame for her injury from him. It might be something he could discuss with Adnar when they got back to Etrion. But not with his father, and not here.

"It was a cunning move, announcing your engagement with an army of Vanrian and Delaphinian soldiers standing witness. I wondered why you seemed so confident of that outcome." A grudging admiration took the edge off the irritation in his voice. "Seylin will have a difficult time turning that tide now. But we did have plans for dealing with the khevarin. Plans your future bride might not approve of."

Kasiel cast a look around. No one other than Arhk's guards rode especially close, but that didn't guarantee no one could hear them, unless... He glanced at Arhk's Dampener who answered his questioning look with the barest of nods, confirming that he was influencing the hearing of those few riding close enough to be a risk. Given that no one seemed to notice, the effort had to be masterfully subtle. A handy use for a skilled Dampener.

"*You* had plans, Father. Plans you gave me only the slightest glimpse of. What you did give me was a list of things to accomplish. You encouraged me to become a hero and win the heart of Vanris. You told me to end this war. Haven't I done those things, regardless of how great the challenge?" He kept his gaze ahead, calling on Akyla's aloofness to help him hold on to his confident tone and posture.

"You have, and I have doubted you every step of the way. For that, I am sorry."

Encouraged by the genuine tone of remorse in his voice, Kasiel faced his father. "I believe it's my turn now to ask something of you."

*

Most of Delaphine's army split off not long after leaving Cabril to return to their capitol, but a smaller company, led by General Itana Kedran, accompanied Vanris's force to the edge of the Break. Lucia, Annora, Emil, and Leif were among them, volunteering to continue serving as part of Kasiel's extended unit as long as proximity gave them the opportunity to do so. It was both flattering and, in some ways, a bit confusing, since Leif and Emil still startled like nervous deer if Kasiel spoke to them.

Annora didn't seem to share their unease, at least not openly. She appeared determined to continue putting on a good showing after her successful effort to reach their army as his messenger. Lucia had taken the younger woman under her wing, teaching her combat and scouting skills that would always have a use somewhere, even if the peace they were negotiating lasted. Kasiel wanted to believe it would, but unless the other kingdoms learned to trust their mind-crafters, the threat of more fighting would continue to hang over them all. Those were things to worry about later, however.

When they prepared to part ways at a Delaphinian watchtower on the border, Lucia and the three young soldiers said their farewells to the rest of his unit. Kasiel was happy to see the tentative smile that tugged at Emil's lips when his tehsheyn praised the youth's performance as a soldier and his acceptance of their differences during their time together. That, along with the friendship that had grown between him and Leif, gave Kasiel hope that he would be able to move on from the loss of his friend.

Itana took Kasiel aside before they parted ways. "You have done well for yourself, young Feral, though I suspect more challenges lay ahead for you." A knowing smirk toward the carriage made him wonder how much she had guessed about the circumstances around his and Velara's engagement. "I wish you luck and look forward to hearing tales of your adventures on the lips of travelers until our paths cross again."

Kasiel inclined his head respectfully. "Our relationship may have had a rough start, but it has been an honor serving in this army with you, General Kedran."

She chuckled. "You will fight these next battles. Then, one day, you will come to me and call me by only my first name, and we will share a drink to the victories and the losses we have both seen."

"I look forward to it, General Kedran." He grinned when she shook her head at him, then turned to join up with his unit as they merged back into the Vanrian army entering the Break.

They arrived in Etrion at dusk a couple of days later. Kasiel's tehsheyn, along with Arhk and his guards, escorted the carriage to the palace amidst enthusiastic crowds. Reports of their victory were sent the day after Sarket surrendered. Word of the announced engagement, however, would arrive with them. As dhomvalen, Arhk used his authority to deny Dhomen Aleren's request to ride up the hidden side passage so she might give Khevarin Seylin forewarning of such things. Aleren was a potential complication, but also a known quantity that they could deal with if it became necessary. She had been quiet for the return trip, perhaps struggling to come to terms with her ordeal as one of Sarket's captives. Kasiel knew little about that time beyond the battered condition he had found her in. As far as he was aware, she hadn't spoken of it to anyone. But when Arhk told her he wanted her to stay with the group riding to the palace, she looked at Kasiel and bowed her head without arguing. He didn't know what to read into that.

Jhanik took the tethdraks outside the city gates, leaving Kasiel only Niskenya and Irith to accompany him. Akyla, he encouraged to go hunt while it was still light enough to require less effort. Niskenya would wait in the courtyard for now. This encounter needed to be handled expediently, before Seylin heard about their announced engagement from anyone else. The khevarin would be expecting them. Scouts in the Break and guards on the walls would have given her plenty of warning of the army's approach. Kasiel was counting on her being eager enough to see her rescued tehnaak and her missing daughter, that she wouldn't suspect anything out of the ordinary from their return. The note Velara had sent ahead with the messenger after Lodmund's defeat hopefully helped lay the groundwork for that.

When they entered the palace, Kasiel sent Nerith and Tath along with two guards to find Hannah a room to rest in. The journey hadn't been easy on her considering how close she was to giving birth. Two more guards fell in alongside them, escorting them to an audience chamber near the palace's private quarters. If the two were at all confused by Kasiel's full unit and Arhk's guards going with them, they didn't question it. They wouldn't, not with the dhomvalen of Vanris and the khevarin's tehnaak present.

Darro and Kince stopped outside the door along

with Etris, who would let Arhk's Speaker know if any problems arose while they were within. Jethan, Yserra, Merrin, and Avris continued inside with Kasiel and the others.

Seylin met them wearing an elegant, draping gown of silver and ivory. As ever, the perfect image of grace and poise, though her composure faltered when they all entered. Her gaze flickered uneasily around at them, eyes narrowing slightly when she spotted her daughter standing close to Kasiel. Then Aleren stepped forward, and the khevarin drew a deep breath, sudden beads of moisture sparkling at the edge of her lower lashes like gemstones.

"You are all right," she breathed, as if she had been unwilling to believe it until she saw with her own eyes.

Aleren walked up to her and Seylin pulled her into an embrace, her eyes closing as she held her tehnaak to her. They stood for a moment, frozen in time, a look of the purest relief on the khevarin's face. It was comforting, in a way, to see such a powerful display of affection from her. It helped Kasiel believe they were going about this in the proper way.

When the two parted, Aleren stepped to one side and Seylin's expression soured. Her gaze focused on Velara's face for a second, then drifted down to the hand holding Kasiel's, their fingers twined, before moving back up to settle on him.

"Ahninveth Kasiel, you return to us as the man who defeated Sarket and brought an end to this war. An accomplishment we wish we could praise without hesitation. Yet somehow, despite our warnings, you still seem to feel you have a right to our daughter. Perhaps a few days in the deeps while we plan the festivities to celebrate your victory would help drive the point home." She gestured to her guards. "Arrest Ahninveth Kasiel."

The guards started toward him.

"Do not arrest him." Arhk's deceptively soft voice stopped the guards in their tracks.

Seylin glanced around at them, taking a small step closer to Aleren, a hint of uncertainty in the sudden clasping of her hands. "What is this?"

Arhk's lip twitched into a faint sneer, a hint of darkness moving in at the edges of his eyes. "I have had twelve long years to bring your army completely under my control, Seylin. I did not realize how useful that was going to be until I found out that you took my wife and son from me. Against all odds, my son has returned to me, and I am giving him your country."

Seylin moved another step closer to her tehnaak, her composure faltering as her gaze darted around at all of them. Aleren's hand drifted toward her sword, then she met Kasiel's eyes and hesitated.

"No," Kasiel declared. Noting the hint of guilt and uncertainty furrowing Velara's brow, he gave her hand a gentle squeeze. "No, you're not, Father. We talked about this. You're giving Vanris to my fiancé, Khesran Velara."

Velara drew a quick breath and straightened, raising her chin as she rallied and faced down her mother. "No matter your opinion on the subject, Kasiel and I will be married. After you make appearances at the coming celebrations supporting that match, Mother, you will announce that you are stepping down now that peace is on the horizon and will transition your leadership to me. Then you will go to Doran with Dhomen Aleren. You have spent far too little time with your tehnaak and your husband over these many years. You might use this opportunity to learn who Nakhul is, so he does not become as much of a stranger to you as Karith had. Who knows, perhaps a mother's affection and guidance would have sent your former heir along a better path. Meanwhile, Ahninveth Kasiel and I, with Dhomvalen

Arhk's support, will handle the resolution of this war and the challenges that follow. You and father may continue to manage affairs in the north under the supervision of advisors and guards appointed by me."

"This is madness," Seylin declared. "You cannot possibly believe that you can just force me from my position as khevarin." She glanced around the room, finding no one there to stand beside her. Her pleading gaze fell upon Aleren. "You must know this is wrong?"

Aleren gave her tehnaak a gentle, sad smile. "What I know is that being khevarin changed you, Seylin. I know that what you did to Arhk and his family all those years ago was very wrong. I miss the loving, happy woman you were before all of this. Maybe that woman is still in there somewhere."

Aleren glanced at Kasiel and Velara's clasped hands. "As for this match and their future, Ahninveth Kasiel has done so much for Vanris, often with as little bloodshed as possible, considering the nature of war. Not only does he care about our people, he cares about the people we face as well. He also saved your tehnaak's life. I believe that your stubborn refusal to see that he is, in fact, an excellent match for your daughter comes from a place of guilt and fear. These two could do wonderful things for Vanris together. Arhk and Kasiel have every reason to bring this to a much less pleasant end, but they are offering you something better. Give yourself permission to let this all go, Seylin. Step down and you might find that you can enjoy life again."

Seylin glanced around at them, her hands drawn close to her chest, looking much like a cornered animal for a few seconds. Then something changed in her eyes, and she straightened, her hands returning to her sides as she took a confident step forward.

"I am khevarin of Vanris. Any wrongs I may have committed in the past I believed were necessary to protect this country. I am needed here."

A powerful sense of confidence and truth filled Kasiel as she spoke, but it lasted only a second before Niskenya rejected it from his mind with a flare of rage. His lip lifted in a silent snarl, and he closed his hand on the hilt of his dark metal sword. Tension rippled through the rest of his unit, a few of them reaching for their own weapons.

"Your ability doesn't work on me, Khevarin," he warned. "I advise you to stop trying to manipulate the situation. You're only going to make it worse for yourself."

His words seemed to break the brief hold she had gained over some others in the room. Fury twisted Arhk's features, darkness moving further into his eyes as he drew his sword. Kasiel tensed, his grip on his own weapon tightening. He didn't want to have to fight his father here, but he promised Velara he wouldn't let the man kill her mother. It was a promise he meant to keep.

Seylin shrank back from the sword, shying closer to Aleren again. "You swore an oath to serve me, Dhomvalen Arhk. I demand that you stand down."

"You had my wife killed! They cut my son's ears and took him to be raised in another country!" Arhk leveled his blade at Seylin and Velara grabbed Kasiel's arm, but he waited, gesturing for his companions to hold back while he watched his father, giving him a chance to express the intense anger born of the loss Seylin had inflicted on him. "For twelve years, I gave you loyalty you had no right to. If not for the love of your daughter and the remarkable compassion of my son, neither of which you deserve, you would be pleading for your life right now, not just your throne. I suggest you accept the terms they have offered you while I am still willing to do this their way, because you will not like the alternative."

Aleren touched her tehnaak's arm. "Seylin."

Seylin looked at Velara. "Turning against your own mother. I do not know what kind of ruler you will be, Velara, but you are clearly ruthless enough to make difficult choices."

Irith growled, and Kasiel stepped forward. "You won't try to put this on her. What you did will never be forgiven. You live by her grace and her grace alone. Perhaps it was good that you were absent most of her life. She learned to be a much better person without you."

Velara touched his arm, drawing him back beside her. "Guards, take her to her rooms and see that she doesn't leave them. Dhomen Aleren may visit her if she wishes. We trust you will keep her secure and unharmed, Dhomvalen Arhk."

For several seconds, Arhk held his blade out, its steadiness attesting to the strength hidden in his lean frame. Kasiel kept his hand on his sword hilt. Then Arhk sheathed the weapon.

He bowed to Velara. "I will do as you ask, Khesran." When he rose from the bow, his eyes weren't on Velara. He was looking directly at Kasiel. "Until a worthy ruler sits this throne again, I swear my service to this country through the khevarin's heir, Khesran Velara."

Velara inclined her head to him. "And we are most honored to accept it, Dhomvalen."

Kasiel stepped closer to Velara, watching as his father and a selection of guards moved around Seylin and escorted her from the room. Aleren followed them, pausing next to Kasiel and Velara as the others continued out.

"Thank you for letting her live. Had she done to me the things she did to you and your family, I'm not certain I could have been so forgiving."

He took Velara's hand, feeling the tremble of emotion in it that she was hiding from her expression. "I think sentencing my fiancé's mother to death would make for a poor wedding gift." He managed a tense smile, silently urging the dhomen to leave.

"Thank you, all the same," she turned and followed the group escorting Seylin from the room.

As soon as they were gone, Kasiel met Jethan's eyes. His tehnaak nodded and gestured toward the door, leading the others from the room. The moment they were out, Velara turned to him, burying her face against his chest. He wrapped his arms around her and placed a kiss on her head, holding her close while she wept.

That week held many celebrations, not the least of which was Velara's ascension to the throne. Great enthusiasm met the official announcement of her engagement to Kasiel. There were still some who held his southern upbringing against him, but they were drowned out by voices of those who reveled at seeing the man who brought down Professor Danovan and ended the war – a kanodrak rider no less – raised up alongside the new khevarin.

They held off on the wedding for almost two months so Kasiel's unit could help quell ongoing battles that erupted in the Break as some forces tried to protest Sarket's surrender and swearing of fealty. With so many eyes on him now, putting forth that effort only strengthened support for the coming marriage. As future khemron, Arhk insisted that he have additional protection on the battlefield. They added Yserra's tehnaak, the Dampener Minera, and another soldier, a friend of Darro and Kince's who had lost his tehnaak in the fighting, to his unit, bringing the total to twelve. Jhanik's full unit also got assigned to Kasiel, so that he always had someone with him who could take command of the tethdraks if needed.

The arrangement gave Nerith and Jhanik more time together. Kasiel watched as a relationship began growing between them with an ever-present twinge of remorse. Velara was the one he chose, but his heart never had stopped loving Nerith. She was part of his tehsheyn and the first woman he had a genuine relationship with. Jhanik, however, had proven to be more worthy than he initially appeared. Kasiel contented himself with making it apparent that he had a protective eye on her, the way an older brother might, so the other Feral would hopefully think twice if he ever considered treating her poorly.

During that time, Hannah had her baby. A healthy young girl born under the careful supervision of Vanrian healers. Once they deemed the Crimson Break safe to cross for dignitaries from other kingdoms, Katerin De Clare came in the company of a group of diplomats from Fallend to discuss new alliance terms now that Sarket was defeated, and to see her daughter and new granddaughter.

Kasiel joined Velara in Etrion for talks with their allies and the ongoing discussion of the terms of Sarket's allegiance to Vanris. Now that Sarket had bent a knee to them, Fallend and Delaphine wanted assurances from Vanris promising that the two greatest military powers on Pandrea would not join force and turn against them. Kasiel suspected they might never be completely comfortable with the arrangement, no matter how many guarantees Vanris offered. He was also confident that Fallend or Delaphine, had Thrasser sworn fealty to them instead, would not be able to hold Sarket in check for long the way Vanris could. Since they ultimately agreed to the arrangement, he suspected they felt the same.

While they were out dealing with various conflicts, Kasiel asked Jethan and the others about Vanrian weddings. They teased him mercilessly, making up tales of bloodletting and vows of subservience. When the day finally came, however, his tehsheyn stood behind him with all the affection and support that had brought him to love them.

Weddings in Vanris, it turned out, started as private affairs. The morning of, Jethan escorted Kasiel to the Heartsmith. Velara and Keyla met them in the main chamber where Heartsmith Ganok's assistant showed them to a second, more intimate side room. Two tables, covered with a soft, purple fabric trimmed in silver, stood arranged alongside each other with space for the Heartsmith to work between them. Velara lay with her right arm to the center and Kasiel with his left, given that his right already had the former khevarin's tattoos of recognition and a few too many scars.

They rested the selected arm on a movable table placed between them, their hands clasped at the center. The blind Heartsmith sat in the middle, preparing his tools and three bowls of ink. One with Kasiel's red, the other two with Velara's pale off-white and the silver for the fine line that would border it.

"It is an honor to get to write part of your story, Khevarin Velara," Ganok said as he passed a small cup to her.

She took a sip and handed it back. "Your work is legendary, Heartsmith. It is I who am honored."

"And you, Ahninveth Kasiel," Ganok said as he handed him the cup, "your story has gone places no one could have ever imagined. I am privileged to be the one who gets to tell it."

Kasiel sipped from the cup and handed it back. "I would have it no other way."

The Heartsmith went to work, creating a beautiful piece of art that started above what would have been Kasiel's ring finger if they were getting married in the southern kingdoms, and the same finger on the right hand for Velara. The elegant symbols extended in a serpentine pattern up almost to the elbow using an intricate interweaving of the colors. It included the symbols of both families and those of their tehnaaks. Kasiel couldn't help smiling to himself as he considered how similar Jethan and Keyla's tattoos would be if they were to marry at some point.

He was distantly aware of their tehnaaks standing nearby, hands clasped much the way his and Velara's were. One thing stood out more intensely than anything, even the sting of the ink application, and that was Velara's hand, warm and real in his own.

When the tattoo was complete, Jethan and Keyla helped each of them up. More of a formal gesture than a necessity. Before they departed, Ganok approached them.

"Your stories shall influence each other from this moment forth. Respect one another as you would your tehnaaks and honor the tale that your hearts tell together." He offered them a deep bow.

"Thank you, Heartsmith Ganok." Velara said.

Kasiel echoed the sentiment, inclining his head to the blind man. Perhaps he couldn't see the gesture, but somehow, he always seemed aware of such things.

As they stepped out into the hallway, Kasiel leaned in, intending to kiss Velara, but Jethan caught his shoulders and pulled him back.

"Ah! None of that. You'll see *plenty* of each other later." He grinned at Keyla.

Velara smiled as their tehnaaks led them off in different directions, giving him a small wave. He shrugged helplessly and let Jethan guide him away.

As they walked, Kasiel turned his arm this way and that, examining Ganok's fine work. "What would happen if one of us died? We'll always have this tattoo tying us together."

Jethan barked a laugh. "I love how you always ask these kinds of questions *after* you've done something you can't undo." Kasiel arched a brow at him and Jethan relented, his expression sobering a little. "The same thing that happens when someone loses their tehnaak. There are a few ritual symbols added to it to memorialize the loss."

"What if we parted intentionally?"

"Same thing. That bond was still lost and the memory of it is worth honoring." Jethan winked at him. "Planning your exit strategy already?"

"You know Ferals, we do get restless." He smirked when Jethan gave him a wary side-eye and his tehnaak bumped him solidly with his shoulder.

"You're a calloch."

Jethan led him to his rooms, the sitting area of which had been transformed into a staging area to get him ready for the next portion of the ceremony. From what everyone told him to expect, palace attendants would prepare him for this part of the process. Now, though his clothing and other accessories remained, his tehsheyn appeared to have driven out the palace staff. All the surviving members of their original group, Darro, Kince, Merrin, Avris, and Tath, stood as he entered. Nerith and Etris were also there, as part of the bonded tehsheyn. Though they weren't there in the flesh, he knew that Wedro, Chander, and Ahrin were there in their hearts and memories.

"We hope you don't mind, country boy," Avris said, gesturing to the others, "but we thought, for a day like this, you might prefer to have your family help you."

Kasiel smiled, swallowing against the tightening in his throat and the sting of emotion that brought moisture to his eyes. "I wouldn't have it any other way."

Kince gestured to an array of food on the table, the start of a faint grin twitching at the corners of his mouth. "Have something to eat then, because making you presentable could take a while."

"Only with amateurs like you on the job," Kasiel countered, setting off laughter in the room.

The next several hours were some of the best of his life. They ate, joked, and reminisced while Avris and Nerith worked two braids along either side of his head and arranged a new set of dark metal and silver symbolic ear cuffs in place. For once, no future battles hung over their heads, and none would hopefully for a very long time to come.

He slipped off to his bedroom briefly to change into the fitted black pants and snug black shirt he would wear under the rest of the ensemble. The sleeves on the shirt ended at the elbow to keep the new tattoo fully visible. He didn't love that it revealed the scars on his right arm from Edmund bleeding him and from the surgery after his encounter with Itana's mace, but those were as much a part of his story now as the tattoos.

Over that, he wore an elegant, ceremonial fitted vest in the black and purple of Vanris with an abundance of elaborate silver embroidery. The last layer was a full length fitted jacket of faintly metallic black material with more elaborate embroidery, in silver and purple this time, down the front. The sleeves split open at the elbow, hanging loose below that point to leave the new tattoo exposed. Gleaming dark metal created decorative spaulders at his shoulders and accented his black boots and the snug black belt that crossed in an X at his waist.

"I don't know, Kas." Darro eyed him thoughtfully, a half-eaten slice of bread in one hand. "We brought you to Vanris not expecting much. Look at all you've accomplished since then. For an unambitious country boy, you've done exceedingly well. You're about to marry and become khemron of Vanris."

"I have no interest in ruling. You know I'm just doing this so I can continue to enjoy the palace amenities. I'm counting on all of you to advise me and keep me out of trouble going forward like you've always done." He picked up a slice of the black evalis fruit and popped it in his mouth.

Merrin laughed. "Do those advisory duties extend to the marital bedchamber, because this could get really interesting?"

"Absolutely not. I'm figuring that part out just fine on my own."

Tath breathed a laugh. "Are you sure of that?"

Kince leaned close to Tath, giving Kas a teasing wink. "Maybe we should ask Velara."

"I'm certain he's doing fine," Nerith said, her cheeks coloring.

"I second that," Avris added.

A broad grin split Jethan's features. "If anyone would know..."

Kasiel felt his face growing hot. "You are all officially banned from the ceremony and festivities."

Their laughter almost drowned out the knock on the door, but Kasiel caught it. "Come in."

An attendant stepped in. "Dhomvalen Arhk Ca—"

The others fell silent as Arhk strode around her. "His father. You may leave." Arhk's attire wasn't notably different from his typical elegant black garb. If anything, it was more understated than usual, without as much embroidery or dark metal accenting. A visible effort to let his son have the foreground tonight. "It is time. You look..." Arhk gave him a quick once over and a pleased smile curved his lips. "You look fit to be Khevarin Velara's match."

"Thank you, Father." Kasiel glanced down at the new tattoo on his arm. "You have..." He trailed off when Arhk took off his jacket and handed it to Etris, who happened to be standing closest. Then he approached Kasiel, pulling up his sleeve as he did so. "Your mother's ke'hanoath was the blue of a storm-tossed sea. It suited her." He revealed a tattoo like in style to the one Kasiel now had on his arm, only done in silver and steely blue. Woven into it in a few places were some elegant symbols in thin lines of black. Arhk's fingers touched one of those marks. "Ellaris will live in my memory and in my story for the rest of my life."

"It's beautiful." Tears stung Kasiel's eyes for the second time that day.

Arhk pulled his sleeve down and reclaimed his jacket. "Shall we?"

Kasiel glanced at his tehsheyn. "Can one of you take Irith out the side door in case he needs to relieve himself before you meet us out front?"

Tath slipped her arm through Darro's. "We'll make a group outing of it. Don't let him get lost on the way there, you two," she added, glancing at Arhk and Jethan.

"We'll keep him in line." Jethan smiled at Kasiel, the glow of pride in his eyes making Kasiel's chest tighten.

Because the marriage bonding of the new khevarin was an event that affected all of Vanris, and because Etrion was not a city that previously saw many such ceremonies within its walls, they would have the second part of the ceremony in the outdoor auditorium. The same location Seylin recognized Velara as heir and gifted Kasiel the saddle Niskenya wore in recognition of his accomplishments.

The kanodrak waited in front of the palace with Arhk's black stallion and enough additional horses to accommodate Kasiel's tehsheyn. Several palace guards in formal regalia would accompany them as well. When the rest of the group joined them with Irith, they mounted. Sparks of anxiety shot through Kasiel like lightning, as if a violent storm had settled at his core. Niskenya sent comfort to him, a deep rumbling purr rising from her.

As they started moving, he peered out through Akyla's eyes where the raptor perched on a rooftop in view of the stage. It was late-afternoon and sunny, though not exceptionally hot this time of year. They had repurposed decor from military celebrations, adding flowers and plants from the vast greenhouse to give it a warmer ambiance. Seylin sat off to one side of the main platform, looking less than pleased, along with former khemron Genyith and Velara's younger brother Nakhul. Dhomen Aleren sat with them, as did Velara's tehnaak, Keyla. The Bondmaker who had made Kasiel's tehsheyn official stood at the center of the stage.

When they reached the aisle, everyone except Kasiel, Jethan, and Arhk dismounted. His tehsheyn strode up the center, each offering him words of encouragement as they passed. After they had taken their seats near the front, Velara emerged from the building behind the stage. She wore a long gown of the same metallic black he wore, with embroidery in silver worked along the split front that revealed a shimmering purple underskirt. Decorative dark metal tassets curved over the hips of the dress, attached by a thinner version of the belt he wore. A cape of transparent silver hung in folds from the backs of thin straps that went over her shoulders. The same material hung in open, off-shoulder sleeves, leaving her arms mostly bare. A delicate silver tiara rested upon her brow where the faint lines of her ke'hanoath created a second one. Shining purple stones were worked into the braids of blood-red hair along both sides of her head. To his surprise, the arrangement left the scars from the attack at Delaphine's summer palace visible. She was exquisite.

Suddenly, he wanted nothing more than to race up to the platform. Fortunately, Niskenya had more self-control this time.

The Bondmaker's soothing voice rolled out over the auditorium. "Khevarin Velara Markanis, Ahninveth Kasiel Cavenos approaches. Do you wish to welcome this man as your equal, to share not only your life from this point forward, but also the guardianship of your people?"

He could see her smile clearly through Akyla, her lips painted red, her silver eyes enhanced with a dark lining. "I offer this moment to my people. Do you accept Ahninveth Kasiel Cavenos as your khemron?"

His chest seized for an instant, then a roar of approval rose from the crowd. If anyone objected, their voices went unheard.

Velara waved them to silence. "Yes, Bondmaker, my people and I do."

"Come forth, Ahninveth Kasiel Cavenos."

With Jethan, Arhk, and Irith still beside him, he rode to the front and dismounted. Someone came to collect the horses. Niskenya ascended the platform of her own accord and went to lie at the back behind Velara and the Bondmaker. Realizing it would be pointless to argue with the kanodrak, Kasiel pretended it was part of the show and walked up with his father, Jethan, and the cliff cat. At the top, the three left him before Velara and went to sit with her family, Arhk offering a single smug smile to Seylin as he took his seat.

"Kneel and take each other's hands," the Bondmaker instructed. When they had knelt facing one another in front of her on two soft purple and silver pillows, she said, "Close your eyes."

It was remarkably difficult to close his eyes with that storm still flashing through him, but Kasiel made himself do so.

"Your ke'hanoath, the stories of your lives, are now joined. Today, you become part of each other. In the way of tehnaak, or tehsheyn, you join the threads of your lives as tehanyehn, a joined spirit." The Bondmaker spoke in a slow, almost singsong voice. "Feel the hands you hold. Know them as you know your own.

Move through them to feel the spirit of the one before you. Accept the bonds within each other that link you to your tehnaaks, your families, and, on this extraordinary occasion, the honored kanodrak that joins us here today."

Kasiel drifted, letting the sensation of Velara's hands in his become his world, catching the scent of her gentle perfume. He could feel Niskenya with them, helping the Bondmaker guide the threads of their lives together. For a second, he almost tried to move behind the kanodrak's eyes, but that wasn't appropriate here. This time, he needed to be within himself as the man who had agreed to be bound to the amazing woman in front of him.

After a few seconds, he could feel Velara in a new way, the beat of her heart, the thrill of excitement and hope racing through her like the lightning in his storm. Her warmth, her strength, her deep, true love for him. It took his breath away.

"Open your eyes."

He did so, meeting her silver ones that gazed deeply into him.

"Rise, Khevarin Velara Markanis and Khemron Kasiel Cavenos. From this day forward, you are tehanyehn. Cherish each other as you cherish your tehnaak."

Kasiel knew it wasn't part of Vanris's ceremony, but no one told him he *couldn't* kiss the bride the way they did at some southern weddings. He stood, drawing her up with him, and leaned in, cupping her cheek in one palm as he touched his lips softly to hers. Velara didn't object. Instead, she stepped closer, sliding her arms around his neck and deepening the kiss. Part of the ceremony or not, it earned another roar from the crowd.

The rest of the evening involved a few brief speeches, followed by celebration and dancing throughout the city. Keyla and a group of performers did a special dance to honor their bonding. At some point in the evening, Kasiel lost track of Jethan, noticing that Keyla vanished around that same time. He and Velara slipped away soon after, retiring to her rooms in the palace.

She wasted no time in going to work on the outer layers of his clothing. "You're mine now, Khemron," she said with a mischievous smile. That smile faltered a moment later, and her hands paused at his belt. "I could feel her, you know, during the bonding." She met his eyes. "Niskenya. You are hers. I felt as if my presence within you was something she could get rid of if she chose to."

Kasiel forced a smile. He hadn't told her what the Bondmaker shared with them about the kanodrak's abilities. If she wished it, he suspected that Niskenya really could break the bond between them. He didn't think she would ever do that to him, though. She cared for him too much. "Niske is a unique kind of companion. A revered creature who is part of both our lives now. The two of you hold very different places in my life." He slid two fingers under her chin and gently urged her to look up at him. "I love you, Velara. I just vowed the rest of my life to you."

Her smile returned, lighting up her features, and she moved closer, resting her arms on his shoulders. The spark of mischief and desire reignited in her eyes. "You know, when Jaysen comes to Etrion, he's going to need children his age to help him adjust to life here."

Kasiel arched a brow, sliding his hands around her waist. "Children? In Etrion?"

"Why not? We're not at war now. Maybe it's time we let the people in our military cities have families."

"So, this problem of Jaysen having someone around his age to spend time with is something you would like us to start solving ourselves?"

She shifted closer until her lips brushed against his.

"Mm-hmm."

Kasiel grinned and kissed her, the spark of their new connection filling him with a passion that was more than just his own.

The young boy lowered his practice sword and brushed his long, dark auburn hair back from his face on the side that wasn't braided. What would his family – his people – think if they saw him that way? In the past few years, he had moved beyond the initial homesickness that hung over him like a storm cloud and embraced more of Vanrian culture, finding ways to blend in with their society, though his round ears would always mark him as southern born.

The girl facing him looked disappointed when he lowered his weapon. She was only a few inches shorter, despite being just over a year younger, and wore two sets of braids in hair the same blood red as her mother's.

"We're not done," she complained.

"I know," Jaysen responded, though he left his sword lowered, letting the point settle in the sand of the small practice ring. "I was just wondering. Your mother's a Charmer. Your father's a Feral. What do you think you'll be?"

Veyl's gray-green eyes, the same color as Kasiel's, only paler like her grandfather's, flashed with impatience. "A khesran."

"Funny," he returned with no little sarcasm. "You were born a khesran."

"And you were born a king." She tapped the blunt

wooden blade against her hand.

He rolled his bright blue eyes at her. "You know that's not what I mean. What kind of mind-crafter do you think you'll be after your Trial? It's only a couple of years away now."

She lowered her gaze, kicking up a puff of dust with one boot. "I don't know. Mother said that being first-born doesn't guarantee I'll be one. She was the second child in her family, and she got the ability instead of her older brother. That's apparently part of why he hated her enough to try having her killed."

Jaysen drew back at that, alarm widening his eyes. "Really? Would you kill your little brother if he got an ability, and you didn't?"

"I guess we'll find out after my Trial." Veyl bared her teeth in a faintly predatory grin at the eagle perched on a nearby rooftop.

A smack on the arm pulled Kasiel partially back to himself.

"Stop spying on the kids! You're terrible."

He grinned at Velara, rubbing the slight sting out of his arm. "I was just checking on them. Veyl is definitely your daughter."

She settled crosswise on his lap where he sat on the padded bench at the foot of their bed. "Just checking on them would be looking quickly through Akyla's eyes and moving on. If you stop to listen too, you are spying."

"Don't tell me you wouldn't do the same if you could."

"That's not the point." She gave him a quick kiss before getting up to go finish dressing.

Merrin and Avris taking the children for afternoon weapons training gave them occasional opportunities like this to enjoy time alone together. Time where they could appreciate each other in ways that didn't seem to happen all that often while ruling a country, even in periods of peace. It was a rare moment that at least one or the other of them wasn't being called upon for something.

"Aunt Merrin, make him fight."

Kasiel slipped back behind the eagle's eyes to see Merrin strolling into the ring. Years hadn't changed her much. She was still fit and strong, with an air of casual threat about her that the newer age-lines in her face did nothing to diminish.

"Dhomen Merrin when you're training," she corrected. "I think you two have had enough for today. Jaysen is still recovering from that bash to the knee you gave him a couple of days ago."

"I'm fine," Jaysen protested, the tan skin of his face picking up a hint of pink.

"I'd still rather you not push it yet." Merrin held out her hands.

Veyl and Jaysen gave her their practice swords hilt first with a measure of respect that Kasiel appreciated. Merrin did as well, judging from the faint curve of her lips. The trace of relief apparent in the way Jaysen's shoulders relaxed told Kasiel his knee might not be as fine yet as he pretended it was. The injury wasn't serious, but he knew from far too much experience how distracting pain could be, and any lack of focus could lead to a worse injury.

Veyl turned a pensive look on Jaysen, her brow furrowing as if she considered the fate of all Vanris. The seriousness of her expression brought a fond smile to Kasiel's lips. "I have something to talk to my parents about. Go see if the others are done, and I'll meet you by the kitchens." She sprinted off before Jaysen could respond.

Kasiel retreated into himself and stood. He caught Velara when she started walking past and pulled her into his arms. "Our daughter wants to talk to us." He punctuated the sentence with a kiss.

"Does she? It looks as if that's your problem, my Feral darling. I promised Nerith and Tath that I would come with them to look at the new section of the healer's building." She gave him a lingering kiss before extracting herself from his embrace. "Good luck, and don't forget to meet us in half an hour by the garden entrance." With a devious smirk that made him wonder what exactly she had planned for this evening, she hurried out the door.

Irith padded up alongside him, and he placed a hand on the cliff cat's head. "I suppose that makes you my backup. Good thing Veyl adores you."

With the cliff cat following along, he struck off toward the side entrance he had seen Veyl heading to through Akyla. She burst in just as they turned down that hall. Her eyes lit up when she saw them, and she sprinted the last stretch. For a few seconds, Kasiel let himself imagine what it would be like if that smile and enthusiasm were for him, but he knew better. Irith braced his feet as she slammed into him with a full force hug.

"Easy, Veyl. He's not as young as he used to be."

"He likes it," she said, burying her face in his thick fur.

The cat's loud purring supported her argument.

"Don't I get a hug from my daughter?"

She pulled back from the cat and shrugged. "Maybe when I'm older."

Kasiel pressed his lips together, fighting to hold in the laughter that bubbled up at that. How maddeningly precocious she was. He hoped her brother didn't follow in her footsteps when he reached her age, but, so far, Tavin was all heart.

"I used to get hugs from you all the time."

"Yes, but I was little then." Before he could point out that she was only eleven now, she leveled a grave stare at him. "Can we talk, Father?"

Kasiel nodded, matching her intensity, and led her to the war room. Somehow it seemed an appropriate venue for a serious conversation with this wild creature they were raising. He gestured to the door with his chin.

She pranced over, forgetting her gravity for a moment, and opened it, offering an exaggerated bow as she waved him in. "Khemron."

Kasiel breathed a laugh and caught her by the shoulder, steering her ahead of him. The war room saw little use these days, though attendants kept it organized and free of dust. With his much longer strides, he passed her and went to pull out a chair. She sank into it, her slight frame filling less than half the seat, legs dangling above the floor.

Kasiel turned a chair to face her and sat, Irith stretching out alongside them. "What did you want to talk about?"

"You know how you and Mom have been encouraging me to consider a new tehnaak since Minya died?"

He nodded, feeling the all-to-familiar twisting ache in his chest in response to that name. It had been nearly three years since Jethan and Keyla's daughter died because of a defect in her lungs that she had likely been born with. They had a second child almost two years younger than Veyl, who seemed healthy still, though the incident had made both parents more protective of the girl. She was Tavin's tehnaak. Tath and Darro's twin boys were paired as well, so they couldn't be options for Veyl. There were other children in Etrion, but none he knew of who didn't already have someone. He couldn't imagine who she might have in mind, so he braced himself for the likelihood that he would have to disappoint her.

"I want Jaysen to be my tehnaak." She dropped the ludicrous notion like a heavy rock in his lap.

He let out a sharp exhale and answered without hesitation. "No."

Veyl's lips pressed together, a storm rising in her eyes. "Why not? Because he's not Vanrian?"

"That would be one reason, yes. Another being that he is going back to Sarket when he turns fifteen to become king. That would force you two apart in about three years. Do you really want a tehnaak you'll never see?"

"But you always say that living here will help him feel more connected to our people when he's king. Wouldn't having a Vanrian tehnaak make his ties to us even stronger?"

Kasiel sat back. When had she become such a devious little politician? Still, he shook his head. "You make a fine point, Veyl, but it would bring you both sorrow in the end, and it might make it harder for his people to accept him if he were that openly entrenched in our culture."

"Father, I—"

"No."

She jumped to her feet and stomped toward the door. "You wonder why you don't get hugs!"

Kasiel stood, drawing upon Niskenya for the power and reassurance of her presence as he waited until Veyl's hand reached for the handle. "Do you want to visit Niske with me before training tomorrow?"

"No!" She stilled, keeping her back to him. "Yes, but I'll still be mad at you. Can Jaysen come?"

Breathe in. Breathe out. Two more years and they would find out if she was a mind-crafter. Thankfully, they had his tehsheyn and his father to help with her either way. If not for them, he couldn't help wondering if she might end up being the opponent who finally defeated him, albeit through sheer emotional exhaustion.

"I suppose."

She stormed out. He sat back down and relaxed there for several minutes before going in search of her. He found her outside the main kitchen. She sat on the floor in the hallway sharing pilfered fruit and pastries with Jaysen and Ahrin, one of Tath and Darro's boys, named for Tath's former tehnaak. Arhk was also with them, sitting on the floor with the newest iteration of his elegant black and dark metal jacket flared out behind him as he demonstrated the proper way to peel one of the black evalis fruits. He glanced up when Kasiel approached and gestured to the floor next to him. Ahrin shifted over to make room.

It was unnerving how much Arhk still looked like he had that first time Kasiel saw him. Even sitting on the floor with the children, there was an unsettling air of danger and power about him. Kasiel suspected his father had aged less visibly in the last twelve years than he had.

"Khemron Kasiel," Jaysen greeted, bowing his head respectfully.

Kasiel returned a subtle nod. "Prince Jaysen." Despite four years living with them, the boy was still formal with him outside of private chambers, but his answering faint smile said it pleased him when Kasiel responded in kind, so he almost always did.

Veyl scowled at him as he sat with them, still apparently holding a grudge over his decision regarding her tehnaak request.

"Now you try." Arhk put them each to work with a fruit of their own. Then he leaned closer to Kasiel and asked in a low voice, "What did you do this time?"

"I told her she couldn't take Jaysen as her tehnaak," he whispered back.

"A wise decision. I thought she told Velara he was insufferable only two days ago."

Kasiel shrugged. "Now I'm the one who's insufferable."

"I suggest taking her to visit Niskenya," Arhk advised.

Kasiel breathed a laugh. "Already planned for to-morrow."

Arhk smiled, something he seemed to do a lot around Veyl, and nodded his approval. Speaking at a normal volume, he said, "Are you not supposed to be meeting Velara now?"

Kasiel looked around at the three children industriously peeling their fruit. The way they stole glances at each other's progress told him it had already turned into something of a competition. "You're certain you have this under control?"

"Completely."

"All right," Kasiel got up, earning a huff of annoyance from Irith, who had just started laying down.

"Can he stay, Father? Please." Veyl set her fruit aside and stood, putting a hand on the cat's shoulder.

Kasiel crouched in front of her. "You'll take good care of him?"

"Promise!"

"All right then."

"Thank you!" Veyl threw her arms around his neck in an abrupt and extremely brief hug before returning to her spot. "Come on, Irith. You can lie here, behind me."

Kasiel smiled and sent a wave of warmth and gratitude to the cliff cat as he encouraged him to stay. It took little effort. The cat was almost as fond of Veyl as she was of him.

When he reached the garden entrance, Velara was there with Keyla, Jethan, and Nerith standing near the door to the private west dining room. Her smile warmed every inch of him. That she could still be that pleased to see him after so many years struck him as nothing short of amazing. His tehnaak's smile was just as welcoming and equally cherished.

Velara met him with a kiss, then stepped back and took Nerith and Keyla each by the hand. "Enjoy your evening, you two," she said, as they started walking away.

"Wait." Jethan looked as mystified as Kasiel felt. "Where are you three going?"

Nerith gave the door a meaningful glance before they continued on their way, already falling into conversation amongst themselves.

Kasiel shrugged when Jethan looked at him and gestured to the door. "Shall we?"

"After you."

"You're only saying that so you'll have time to get away if it's a trap," Kasiel said, reaching for the handle.

"Naturally," Jethan answered with a chuckle.

The interior of the dining room was dimly lit by a series of muted wall sconces and a crackling fire. Ten seats were arranged around a circular table laden with food and drink, five of them currently empty. Darro, Kince, Tath, Merrin, and Avris stood up from the other five.

Kince grinned. "The guests of honor."

All five raised their mugs to Kasiel and Jethan and repeated the words in unison.

"Fourteen years ago today," Darro began, "a young royal upstart most of us barely knew led our unit in an attack on a group of mercenaries to rescue a scrawny danro we all thought wouldn't last the night. We had no way of knowing then how much that moment would mean to all of us and all of Vanris. All of the Pandrean continent, even. To honor that occasion, we invite you both to join us and celebrate the events that brought together this tehsheyn that changed all our lives forever."

Kasiel swallowed a lump in his throat as he and Jethan took places at the table. There were settings for three more, the plates empty, but the mugs filled with Vanrian Black Mead for Ahrin, Chander, and Wedro – those from the original group who they had lost along the way. Several stoneglass bottles sat upon the table with the generous array of food, waiting to be opened.

As soon as he sat, Kasiel raised his mug. "When I ran away from Fernwallow, I didn't think I would ever find a place to call home, let alone a whole new family. Thank you all for giving me the best home and tehsheyn anyone could ever wish for. Now, let's crack some stones!"

THE END

Kasiel's Glossary

Vanrian terms I've learned

Calloch	Rank ball of monkey shit. A favored insult in Vanris.
Company (military)	The units and unions under the command of a single dhomen or ahndhomen.
Crack a stone	Popular Vanrian phrase meaning to open and drink a stoneglass bottle of Vanrian Black Mead. Vanrians love that stuff.
Danro	Someone who is lost / out of place / doesn't fit in (me).
Evalis	Black fruit used to make Vanrian Black Mead. Imported from the original Vanrian homeland.
Ke'hanoath	Each Vanrian's individual story represented in symbols tattooed somewhere on their person.
Kenis Seed	Medicinal plant component used for sedation.
Melinar	Medicinal plant extract used for sedation. Considered too strong to use on humans.

Mindcraft	Unusual abilities possessed by some Vanrians to manipulate the minds of humans or animals.
Mind-crafter	Someone with a mindcraft ability.
...na sek	Appended to an officer rank when a promotion is temporarily granted for a specific mission.
Sheyvyosk	Stinky smegma.
Stoneglass	An light metal alloy that looks like stone and is extremely durable. Primarily used to make bottles for Vanrian Black Mead… naturally.
Tehanyehn	A romantic spirit pairing (considered a deeper form of the marriage vows practiced in the southern kingdoms).
Tehnaak	Spirit siblings, bound to each other through a ritual of some kind and raised together.
Tehsheyn	Spirit family.
The Deeps	Vanrian solitary confinement.
Union (military)	A grouping of three regular units combined under a third or fourth level ahninveth or inveth.

Unit, Regular (military)   A group of thirty-nine soldiers under a single inveth or ahninveth.

Unit, Feral (military)   A group of nine soldiers and up to twenty beasts under a single Feral ahninveth.

RANKS & TITLES:

Khevarin   Ruler of Vanris – the rough equivalent of a king or queen.

Khemron   Spouse of the ruler of Vanris, shares some of the leadership.

Khesran   Child of the khevarin and khemron – basically a prince or princess.

Dhomvalen   Protector or warden. A Vanrian military leader who answers only to the khevarin. (My father.)

Ahnvaris   Dedicated guard for important persons.

Dhomen   A Vanrian officer – the rough equivalent of a general in the southern kingdoms. There are four levels.

Ahndhomen   A Dhomen who is also a mind-crafter (slightly outranks a dhomen). There are four levels.

Inveth

A Vanrian officer – the rough equivalent of a captain in the southern kingdoms. There are four levels.

Ahninveth

An Inveth who is also a mind-crafter (slightly outranks an inveth). There are four levels.

Inren

A Vanrian common soldier. There are four levels.

Omren

A Vanrian mind-crafter common soldier. There are four levels.

Idrek

A Vanrian recruit – soldier in training.

Odrek

A Vanrian mind-crafter recruit – soldier in training.

Other things of interest

Anso nut butter

Made from tree nuts grown in Fallend. So creamy. I wish they had this in Vanris.

Havaad

A god worshipped in parts of the southern kingdoms, particularly in Sarket.

Pandrean Alliance

An alliance formed between the three southern kingdoms of Delaphine, Sarket, and Fallend to fight Vanris.

Mindcrafting disciplines

Charmer

A mind-crafter who can manipulate an individual or small number of individuals to go along with their suggestions.

Dampener

A mind-crafter who can interfere with the way people's minds perceive their senses, effectively taking away the sight, sound, smell, and/or touch of individuals or groups.

Enkindler

A mind-crafter who can inspire positive or negative emotions in individuals or groups.

Evoker

A mind-crafter who can see and sometimes alter a single individual's surface thoughts and memories.

Feral

A mind-crafter who can connect with, influence, and control the minds of animals or groups of animals.

Frightener

A mind-crafter who can access the fears of individuals or groups and cause them to see terrifying visions, sometimes permanently scarring their minds.

Heartsmith

A blind mind-crafter who can tap into people's deepest thoughts and emotions in an abstract way to read the story of who they are in order to tattoo it upon their skin.

Speaker

A mind-crafter who can speak into the minds of individuals or groups, limited somewhat by range and visibility (less so if their subject is also another Speaker).

New creatures I've encountered

Cliff Cat

Large wildcats native to the mountains in Vanris. Some Ferals use them in combat. They have a deep blue-gray coat with darker blue stripes down the spine along either side of a ridge of longer hair. Their eyes are sapphire blue, and their tails end in a puff of hair the same blue as its stripes. They tend to be around waist high to a man at the shoulder.

Kanodrak

Impressive Vanrian predators brought to Pandrea from the original Vanrian homeland. Taller than a horse and used as mounts by a few Ferals.

Vaguely feline with a silver-grey, scaled hide and milky white eyes. They have bone armor plating that starts at the nose and runs along the spine to the base of their long tail. Their massive front incisors extended below well below the lower jaw.

Sandhawk

Desert hawks commonly seen in southern Vanris and around the Crimson Break.

Sandhopper

Type of desert mouse that can hop on long hind legs found in and around the Crimson Break.

Tethdrak

Vanrian predators brought to Pandrea from the original Vanrian homeland. Some Ferals use them in combat. Built a little like a hound, but reptilian. Adults are mid-rib high to a man at the shoulder. The thickly muscled limbs and torso are covered in light shades of red and brown scaling with spiked plates along the length of the spine and thick tail. Two backswept horns extend from the head and their massive jaws bristle with sharp teeth.

Werdyn Cat

Large wildcats common in northern Sarket. Broad swaths of charcoal fur tipped in white puff out around its face with tufts of white at the top of its ears, giving it an owl-like appearance. They have scales beneath their fur and a coat that repels water. Tend to be more active in inclement weather.

Places

Andaro

Capital city of the kingdom of Sarket.

Cabril

Town in old volcanic region of Sarket.

Coranthis

One of the largest cities in Delaphine. (falling down the hill)

Crimson Break

War-devastated, desert region between Vanris and the southern kingdoms.

Crimsondale

Town where the incident that started the war happened. Now part of the Crimson Break.

Daco

Town south of the Crimson Break in Sarket. Some animal in this region probably found and ate the missing tops of

	my ears.
Dekingham	Main capital of Delaphine.
Delaphine	Western kingdom on Pandrea. Home to the Delaphinian people.
Doran	The northern capital of Vanris.
Etrion	My home. The southern capital of Vanris. (Do you really need two capitals?)
Fallend	Southern kingdom on Pandrea. Home to the Fallenese people.
Fellenvar	First town north of the black crags in Vanris.
Fernwallow	Small village in Fallend where I grew up.
Hellaris	Town in Sarket.
Katis	Vanrian military base slightly southeast of Etrion.
Katovan	Destroyed town in the Crimson Break. The Hall that survived there is in an agreed upon neutral zone sometimes used for negotiations.
Norvask	Northern capital of Delaphine – summer palace. (Maybe you do need two capitals.)

Pandrea	The continent.
Riftwater	Abandoned town in the Crimson Break southeast of Etrion.
Sarlsberg	City in Delaphine near border with Sarket.
Sarket	Western kingdom on Pandrea. Home to the Sarketi people.
Sharith	Vanrian town east of Etrion.
Vanris	Northernmost kingdom on Pandrea. New home to the Vanrian people after volcanic activity drove them from their original island home.
Vareyl's Warning	Black crags that create a natural border between northern and southern Vanris. Called Vareyl's Gift before the war.

People

Adnar	Vanrian ahndhomen (a Feral / Nevias's tehnaak)
Ahrin	Vanrian inren (Tath's former tehnaak – a healer)
Aleren	Vanrian dhomen (Seylin's tehnaak)
Andross Gaverin	Nerith's father

Annora	Delaphinian soldier
Arhk Cavenos	Dhomvalen of Vanris – My father (a Frightener)
Astrid Lodmund	Queen of Sarket
Avris	Vanrian inren (Merrin's teh-naak)
Barden	Leatherworker in Fernwallow
Brand Evanson	Sarketi General
Branith	Dhomen of the city guard in Etrion
Ceanna Durmond	Queen of Delaphine
Chander	Vanrian inren (Wedro's for-mer tehnaak)
Darro	Vanrian inveth (Kince's teh-naak)
Edmund Danovan	Man who raised me in Fern-wallow
Ellaris	My deceased mother – killed when I was taken
Emil	Delaphinian soldier
Erikson	Delaphinian watch captain
Etris	Vanrian omren (a Speaker)
Fenvar	Vanrian omren (a Charmer)

Farren	Vanrian dhomen and combat instructor
Ganok	Vanrian Heartsmith
Garrick Traven	Blacksmith in Fernwallow
Genyith	Vanrian khemron (Seylin's husband)
Hackett	Sarketi general
Hannah De Clare	Katerin De Clare's daughter
Harel	Delaphinian general
Harif	Vanrian inren (a healer)
Iatan	Vanrian inren (a healer)
Itana Kedran	Delaphinian general (former mercenary)
Ivette	Delaphinian insurgent
Jaysen Lodmund	Crown prince of Sarket
Jethan Markanis	Vanrian omren (my tehnaak – a Charmer)
Jhanik	Vanrian ahninveth (a Feral kanodrak rider)
Jorgan Birk	Delaphinian captain.
Jortan	Vanrian history instructor in Doran
Kaden Durmond	Second prince of Delaphine

Karith Markanis	Vanrian khesran (Seylin's eldest child and heir)
Kasiel Cavanos	Vanrian ahninveth (a Feral kanodrak rider – me)
Kassian Danovan	Sarket officer – Edmund's brother
Kastus	Vanrian ahndhomen (an Enkindler)
Katerin De Clare	Fallenese delegate
Kenna	Vanrian ahninveth (a Feral / Therin's tehnaak)
Keryk	Vanrian inren (Jhanik's tehnaak)
Keyla	Velara's tehnaak
Kince	Vanrian inveth (Darro's tehnaak)
Leif	Delaphinian soldier
Leysa	Vanrian inren (Nerith's former tehnaak)
Loak	Mercenary (bad person)
Lorin	Mercenary (also bad)
Lucia	Delaphinian soldier
Mahlik Durmond	King of Delaphine
Merrin	Vanrian inren (Avris's teh-

	naak)
Minera	Vanrian omren (a Dampener)
Myron	Prior lord of Cabril in Sarket
Nakhul Markanis	Vanrian khesran (Seylin's youngest child)
Nerith	Vanrian inren (a healer)
Nevias	Vanrian dhomen (Adnar's tehnaak)
Nix	Mercenary (she's bad too)
Nok	Barkeep at The Twisted Vine in Etrion
Piers	Delaphinian insurgent
Rahlyf	Vanrian omren (a Dampener)
Revik	Vanrian omren (a Speaker)
Rihane	Khevarin's healer
Roald Lodmund	King of Sarket
Safya	Khesran Karith's wife and tehnaak
Setera	Vanrian ahninveth (an Evoker)
Seylin Markanis	Khevarin of Vanris (an Enkindler)
Sorval	Vanrian dhomen

Tarik	Vanrian city guard inveth
Tath	Vanrian inren (a healer)
Therin	Vanrian soldier (a Speaker / Kenna's tehnaak)
Treya (Ilsa)	Vanrian omren (a Charmer)
Velara Markanis	Vanrian khesran (Seylin's middle child)
Veyl	Vanrian child
Vollan	Sarketi captain at Cabril
Wedro	Vanrian inren
Wilkin Thrasser	Sarketi general
Yserra	Vanrian omren (an Evoker)
Zafyr	Vanrian ahnvaris (an Evoker / one of Arhk's personal guards)

ACKNOWLEDGEMENTS

If you've been in my life while I was working on this series, you know how completely it pulled me in. Kasiel's story has been an extraordinary adventure for me as well as an escape from difficult things. I am grateful to him and his companions for the joy they brought me while I shared their story on these pages. There are also many people who deserve my appreciation, so I will try to capture them all here.

To Linda, who was my first reader as always and provided so much support and valuable feedback throughout the process. I can't imagine doing this without you.

To Kai, who took the brunt of dealing with my constant distraction and obsessive need to write at all hours of all days, and still allowed me to read the book to him out loud. Thank you for your patience.

As always, my best friends and beta readers, Rick and Ann, who somehow continue to stand by me regardless of where my crazy goes. You are now, and always will be, my tehsheyn.

To my additional beta readers, Todd and Jordan, your feedback was invaluable. You are greatly appreciated. And to all the ARC readers who have joined me on this journey, thank you!

As always, I want to acknowledge the fantastic team who helped me put together the finished book. Robert Crescenzio, my incredibly talented cover artist whose vision helps bring these books to life in his art. Melissa Nash, the fantastic map designer who helped realize Kasiel's vision of Pandrea. Alexander Lockwood, my fantastic editor, fellow author, and now friend. Brian Short, my amazing formatter, whom I would also like to thank for your excellent company on many coffeeshop writing days. I love working with you all.

To my other friends and family, know that I love you and value your place in my life even if I don't call you out specifically here.

Last, but certainly not least, to my readers. To me, books are a collaborative effort between the author and their readers. Without you, this world would only ever come to life in my head. I hope you enjoy experiencing it as much as I did and will continue along the journey with me through the rest of this series.

AUTHOR BIO

Outside of my career as an author, I am a professional technical and creative writer, spider wrangler, animal lover, and devoted cat mom. Writing fantasy and science fiction stories has been a lifelong passion for me. I love to include in my work the diversity I see around me and draw upon my myriad life experiences doing everything from wild cave exploration and horseback endurance riding to practicing iaido and archery.

•

Thank you for taking time to read this novel. Please leave a review if you enjoyed it.

•

For more about me and my work visit me at http://elysiumpalace.com.

OTHER NOVELS by NIKKI McCORMACK

CLOCKWORK ENTERPRISES
The Girl and the Clockwork Cat
The Girl and the Clockwork Conspiracy
The Girl and the Clockwork Crossfire

FORBIDDEN THINGS
Dissident
Exile
Apostate

ELYSIUM'S FALL
Dark Hope of the Dragons
Dark Savior of the Dragons

SILVERBLOOD RAVEN
A Path of Blood and Amber
A Path of Secrets and Dreams
A Path of Storms and Reckonings

STANDALONE WORK
Golden Eyes
The Keeper

www.ingramcontent.com/pod-product-compliance
Lightning Source LLC
Chambersburg PA
CBHW031334010826
48972CB00012B/141